PENGUIN BOOKS

STRANGERS TO OURSELVES

Shashi Deshpande is the author of nine novels, and several short stories, which have been included in various collections and anthologies. She has also written numerous essays, some of which have been included in anthologies such as *Writing from the Margin* and *Subversion*'. She has recently written her memoir *Listen to Me.*

Her novel *That Long Silence* received the Sahitya Akademi Award in 1990. Deshpande received the Padma Shri in 2009.

Praise for Shashi Deshpande

'Deshpande does not shirk from the big questions, grief, betrayal, death. [She] forces us to accept Indian life in all its stifling details and its magnificent unpredictability [...] She works with a lapidary skill, placing fragments of bone, skin, hair, voices, words, memories that she sets within a frame as exact as one of Ray's celebrated "scenes".' – Geeta Doctor

'She sets the reader free to explore the notion of being simply human rather than forever imprisoned behind the bars of caste, community and gender.' – Manjula Padmanabhan

'She weaves her tapestry with quiet coloured threads but the picture which emerges is vivid, beautifully detailed, entirely realistic.' – Lisa Lau

'Her special value lies in an uncompromising toughness, in her attempts to do what has never been attempted in English, her insistence on being read on her own terms...' – Meenakshi Mukherjee

Strangers to Ourselves

Shashi
Deshpande

PENGUIN BOOKS
An imprint of Penguin Random House

PENGUIN BOOKS

USA | Canada | UK | Ireland | Australia
New Zealand | India | South Africa | China | Singapore

Penguin Books is part of the Penguin Random House group of companies
whose addresses can be found at global.penguinrandomhouse.com

Published by Penguin Random House India Pvt. Ltd
4th Floor, Capital Tower 1, MG Road,
Gurugram 122 002, Haryana, India

Penguin
Random House
India

First published by Harper Collins 2015
This edition published in Penguin Books by Penguin Random House India 2024

10 9 8 7 6 5 4 3 2 1

ISBN 9780143463979

Typeset in Garamond Regular at SÜRYA

www.penguin.co.in

Why should a man's mind have been thrown into such close sad sensational inexplicable relations with such a precarious object as the body?

– Thomas Hardy

There are two passions that govern human life: one is the desire for progeny, the other for a place of one's own. We live our lives in pursuit of these goals, we measure our lives by our success in achieving them. All else is ephemeral, passing, of no significance – something it takes us an epiphanic moment to realize. Battling with the fearful truth of human mortality, with the transience of human life, we look for immortality through our children; to have children is to be part of the infinite chain of humanity. As for the desire for a place of one's own, it begins the moment we are rudely expelled from our first home, the womb. Since then, we are haunted by a sense of loss, though we don't know what it is we have lost, though we can't remember what it is we had. And yet we are forever held in thrall by a yearning for a place to belong to, a place we can call our own. The unbearable loneliness of a human being, and the growing knowledge that we are incomplete in ourselves, often makes the search end in a person rather than a place. And so love is born. The two desires, the desire for progeny and the desire for a place of one's own, become so intertwined that we never understand that they are two separate strands. And yet, all human stories come out of these two desires, all stories of love begin with them.

Falling in love has had no place in Aparna's plans for her life. That is over for her, she has done it once, she has been singed and burnt. Knowing that she had mistaken the counterfeit for the real, she had lost confidence in herself and the very idea of love. If I could be so deceived once, how do I know it won't happen again? How can I trust a man, or my own judgement of a man, ever again? And so she had opted out of the search for love which occupies so large a part of human life in adulthood. And then she meets Shree Hari Pandit.

It is only chance that takes Aparna to the music programme that day. She had almost not gone, she had, in fact, forgotten about it, when she saw the card on her table. She remembered it then, but decided it was too late. Besides, she was tired; it had been a long day, with two new patients starting on their chemotherapy and one of them not responding well. She was way behind schedule and the thought of going home, of having a bath and going to bed, was tempting. But she knew that when your boss invites you, you can't turn down the invitation, specially when he says, 'I haven't invited many people from the hospital, you must come.' And so she had a wash and changed into the set of clothes she had in her locker, clothes not good enough for a social occasion, but they will have to do, she told herself.

Here she is now, at the entrance of the shamiana put up on

the terrace of Dr Bhagat's apartment. The music has obviously begun some time back, the singer is well into his raaga. She stands hesitant, when people's heads turning warn her boss that someone has just come. He looks back, waves at her and mouths, *Take a seat.* She gets into an empty seat in the middle of a row, trying to create as little disturbance as possible, whispering 'sorry' as she goes past trousered knees, expensive saris and gauzy dupattas. A few moments after she settles down, the singer comes to the end of his raaga. There is the usual shifting of bodies, the whispers, the clearing of throats once the applause dies down. The singer turns to the taanpura player and begins, like all the singers she has seen, to tune it once again. Dr Bhagat waves to her, she goes to him and says, 'Sorry, sir, I got delayed.'

'No problem, Aparna. That's okay. But my wife wants to meet you. Don't go away without meeting her. And go and have a cup of tea or coffee or whatever you want.'

She quickly has a cup of tea and, feeling revived and refreshed, goes back to her seat. She hasn't seen anyone from the hospital among the audience and wonders once again why she has been invited. 'My wife wants to meet you', Dr Bhagat had said. Was it a polite nothing? Or was it the truth? But she has never met his wife, she knows nothing about her. So, why…? A young man, mike in hand, goes to the dais and she stops surmising. The man says, 'We will now resume our programme, please take your seats.' With the usual warning to 'please put off your mobiles', he moves away and the singer takes over. Drawing his mike to himself, the singer says, 'I will now sing the raaga Yaman.'

Some people consider Yaman an ordinary raaga. But it does extraordinary things to me. Her father's words suddenly come back to Aparna, it's almost as if she can hear him speaking. And the moment the singer begins, something happens to her. She sits up, her heart beating faster, two quick vigorous movements that, as a doctor, she knows are odd. Hearts are meant to work silently, they are not meant to be heard; when they are, it means something is wrong. But this is not a physical thing; in fact she does not understand what is happening to her, unable to connect the jolt to the man she is looking at, the man whose voice now fills the place. A voice that, without any accompaniment, seems to draw attention to its purity. The tabla and harmonium player are waiting to join him, the tabla player's fingers playing a silent accompaniment on his tabla, the harmonium player leaning forward a little on his instrument, his right hand idle on the keys, the left hand clasping the flap, waiting for the signal to start. The singer's voice begins on a low note. When it rises, it seems to her he is pouring its richness and purity into her emptiness. She makes a small sound, an exclamation of pleasure; a joyfulness pervades her. Her neighbour, an older man, smiles at what he thinks is her enthusiasm. She is unaware of him, unaware of everything but the singer and his voice. When the aalaap ends and the tabla and the harmonium join him, she begins to breathe normally. Now he is no longer alone, now the three of them are in it together, creating a harmony of sound. He smiles at his accompanists when they reach the sam, the dominant note, together, a smile that is fleeting, but which seems to linger before her eyes. When he moves to the *drut*, the quick movement, he waves to them both, palms up, as if saying, 'Come on, come on', and she smiles to herself.

He comes to an end and there is loud and enthusiastic applause. She does not join in. It seems impossible that polite applause can be the response to the extraordinary experience she has just had. She sits silent and still through the final piece of the performance, an abhang, 'which I learnt from my grandfather, my first guru,' the singer says, touching his ears, as musicians do when they speak of their gurus. He sings this with emotion, but her inner being, like a taut string, is still throbbing to the earlier piece.

Then it is over. The compere makes a little speech of thanks, the singer – she hears his name for the first time, it is Shree Hari Pandit – and his team are given flowers, envelopes discreetly concealed under the bouquets. Then the compere asks the guests to help themselves to the food set on the other side of the terrace. People get up, they move towards the tables. Aparna wants to leave but realizes she must meet Dr Bhagat and his wife. He is surrounded by a number of people and she waits patiently for her turn. When he sees her, he says, 'Did you enjoy it? I'm so glad you came, Aparna. Don't go without having something to eat. And say hello to my wife. Oh, there she is.'

He calls out to a woman talking to a group; she comes to them and he introduces Aparna to her.

'You are Gavi Dandekar's daughter, I hear?'

'Yes.'

'I was a great admirer of his.' She is speaking in Marathi. 'I've seen many of his plays.'

Aparna is always surprised when this happens. She thinks that since his death, her father has been forgotten, his plays rarely staged. And yet there are still times when suddenly someone speaks of him, the way this woman is speaking. Aparna remembers the man at the immigration counter when she returned to India. He had looked at her passport, then looked up and said, 'Gavi Dandekar's daughter?'

'Yes.'

He had nodded, gone back to his earlier inscrutable official self and pushed her passport back at her, but she had been pleased, as she is now. She feels as if the woman is giving her father back to her.

'I acted in a play of his when I was in college. I loved theatre, but when I got married I had to let everything go.' There is regret in her voice. 'When you marry a surgeon, it's like goodbye to everything you wanted to do.'

Aparna's smile is hesitant. She is eager to leave, to carry the precious experience she has just had, intact and unsullied.

Her hostess, perhaps sensing her eagerness to get away, says, 'I hope we'll meet again. I'd like to talk about your father. Let me know any time his play is being staged. And please don't go without having something to eat.'

Aparna realizes she's hungry, that there's nothing at home for her to eat. She goes to the table and, taking a plate moves away hoping no one will talk to her. But one of Dr Bhagat's assistants – how is he here? – comes to her and tries to engage her in conversation. He seems equally surprised to see her; the questions he asks make her realize that his sense of being singled out has been dented by her presence. When he begins to talk of hospital politics, she moves away before he can destroy her mood and clatters down the stairs. There is a small crowd waiting for the lift. She waits patiently for her turn and when she reaches the ground floor, wonders for the first time how she is to get home. She does not know this area, she has no idea of what buses ply here. She is waiting on the road, hoping for a taxi, when a man comes out of the building; she immediately recognizes him as the singer, Hari Pandit. He seems to be in a hurry. She is surprised, even a little startled, when he comes straight to her.

'You are Gavi Dandekar's daughter, Aparna Dandekar?' This is the second time she has had that question asked of her this evening. And he says her name so familiarly and easily that in her confusion she thinks she must have met him somewhere. But would she have forgotten him if she had?

Later he will tell her that he had inquired about her and gotten her name and the fact that she was the dramatist Dandekar's daughter from Dr Bhagat. 'It made it easy for me to approach you,' he will say.

That is much later. Right now she a little taken aback, but after her meeting with Dr Bhagat's wife, accepts the fact that her father, so completely forgotten as she had thought, is still remembered. He has come back to her twice this evening. No, thrice, because she had thought of him in connection with the raaga Yaman.

'Yes,' she says.

'I met him once. Long back. Many years back. And you were with him.'

'I?'

'Yes, you…'

There is a sudden burst of voices as his team emerges from the building, carrying their instruments with them. 'Shree…' one of them calls out.

'Don't go away, I'll be back,' he says to her and goes to them.

There is a short colloquy between them, at the end of which he comes back to her. 'Can I drop you home?' he asks.

'No, it's okay. I'll get a bus. Or a taxi.'

'Only rich people live here. There aren't many bus routes this part of the city.'

A car stops near them. The driver, his taanpura accompanist, gets out and says, 'Here, Shree. Take it.' He makes a polite namaste to her before going on to join the others.

'Come on, get in.'

She still holds back. 'And they?'

'They have a van, we need a bigger car for the instruments. Please come.'

She realizes that to refuse now is to make a fuss, something she hates. She gets in.

'Where to?'

She tells him. 'Okay,' he says, and starts the car.

'What,' she will ask him later, 'if I had said I live in Dahanu or Dahisar?'

'I'd have dropped you just the same.'

This is not his car, he explains, but his friend's. And then he goes back to what he was saying when he was interrupted.

'I met your father once.'

'So you said.'

'And you were there as well.'

'I don't remember.' She wonders whether he's making it up, a ploy to get to her.

'You were there,' he says emphatically. 'I was acting in the play, I was playing the lead role. They wanted someone who could sing, therefore, me. That evening the director told us Gavi sir was coming. He was very excited about it. Your father came backstage when the play was over. You were standing a little distance away. You had a friend with you.'

'I just don't remember.'

'I will never forget that evening because...' He hesitates and goes on. 'Gavi sir told me, "Don't act. Go on with your music. Music is where you belong." Gavi sir knew a lot about music. And you?'

'Doctors are ignorant of everything but their own world.'

'So are we all.'

He falls silent after that and speaks only when he has to ask for directions. They get off the main road now and enter a lane. The last building, she tells him. He gets out when she does and begins to lock the car.

'Please don't come. There's no need. And thank you for giving me a lift.'

'I'll come in with you.'

'No need,' she says firmly.

He has turned away, but suddenly comes back to ask, 'Can I have your mobile number, doctor?' At her look of surprise, he adds, 'Who knows, I might need a doctor.'

She laughs at his naivety. 'I hope you never need me. I'm an oncologist. Cancer specialist,' she adds in response to his look of inquiry.

'You're working with Dr Bhagat saab?'

'Not *with. Under.* He's there…' Her hand goes above her head. 'And I'm here…' she says, pointing to her knees.

'But I may want to invite you to my music programmes. Did you like it today?'

'Very much,' she says simply. His face glows with pleasure. She will soon come to know that he is transparent, he can never hide his feelings.

'So, please…'

'I'll give you the hospital number.'

He looks as if he might argue, but something in her face makes him silently feed the number in his mobile, turn around and walk back to the car. She wants to be alone, to think dispassionately of the flood of feeling that has been aroused in her. When she goes to bed, she sees his face, the gesture he makes when he wants his accompanists to do something, the way he lifts his palm when he wants the tablawala to move to a faster beat, she thinks of the intensity on his face when they are only a heart beat away from the moment when all three of them will reach the sam together, the smile, the absolute pleasure on his face when they do, she remembers the glow on his face when she admitted she had liked his performance… He is beautiful, she thinks. And then, immediately, I've been deprived of sex for too long, that's why I'm obsessing about a man I've just met.

And then suddenly it comes back to her, the meeting he had spoken of. She had been in her second year of Medicine then and her father had suddenly appeared at the hostel as he often did. 'When I miss my girl I get into the train and come to Mumbai,' he said once.

'Go on, Baba, enough of your lies. I know you come to see your drama people, your friends, your publishers.'

'All right then, I won't come. Save your mother the trouble of making laddoos and chivda for you.'

That time, however, he confessed that he came without

giving her mother any notice. 'She had no time to make anything for you. But don't worry, I'm taking you out to dinner – you choose the place.'

At the last minute, when they were already on their way, he sprang it on her that he had to go 'only for a few minutes' to see a drama before dinner. 'The director won't let me off. In fact, I came for that.'

The play was a musical. Her friend Emily, who was with them, could not understand the high-flown Marathi and kept asking Aparna, 'what are they saying?' Fortunately, most of the play consisted of songs. One particular song, the leitmotif of the play, it seemed, was sung by all the characters, making Aparna and Emily giggle each time they began. Aparna's father was enjoying the music, specially that of the lead actor, acting the role of a boy in search of a guru. Aparna was used to her father's constant 'wah wahs' but when, at the end of what she learnt was called a 'raagamala', he called out a loud 'shabaash', Aparna was embarrassed. The boy, however, instead of going on with his dialogue, turned to Gavi and made a deep bow, almost Japanese style, his hand on his heart. Emily had enjoyed the little byplay. Aparna knew that Emily, like many others, was in awe of her father without having read him, without even knowing what Gavi wrote, only because he was a real writer.

After the play they went backstage. Emily and she stood a distance away and watched. The director seemed overwhelmed, the entire cast came up to meet Gavi, most of them bending down to touch his feet. One of them was the boy who had played the lead, a boy who had sung with whole-hearted, whole-throated sincerity, a boy whose talent shone amidst the amateurishness of the play. That boy was Hari Pandit, who had now fulfilled the promise of glorious manhood her father had glimpsed in him then.

Why didn't I give him my mobile number, she thinks. Why

was I so disgustingly damnably coy? Why have I let one bad experience sour me? Maybe I was right, she thinks. If he wants to contact me, he will keep trying. But he does not, not the next day, nor the day after that. As the days pass, she thinks that perhaps he has learnt she's a divorced woman, she decides to forget him. In any case, she is preoccupied now, not only with her work, but with her search for a place to live in.

And then he turns up in the waiting room on her outpatients' day.

She comes out of her room and is walking blindly through the waiting room as usual, afraid that a patient, who hopes to see her inspite of not having an appointment, will catch her eye and ask for 'just a few minutes of your time, doctor'. The lights have been dimmed to indicate that consultation hours are over, but the impatience, the anxiety of patients, seems to linger in the air. Her peripheral vision catches a figure getting up from his seat. She turns, an involuntary movement, and sees him coming towards her. There is, in spite of the dim light, an instant recognition, a streak of joy within her.

'Dr Dandekar…'

She stands stock still. 'You? What are you doing here? Are you well?'

'Of course.'

'Then what are you doing here?'

'What do you think? I came to meet you.'

'But here?'

'You gave me your hospital number. I kept trying for days, but could never get you. Then I had to go to Sangli. I returned only today. Can I talk to you?'

'Here?'

'Anywhere you say.'

'What is it?'

'I want to give you an invitation.'

She laughs in sheer relief. 'Oh, is that all? You can give it to me now.'

He looks around. 'No, we can't talk of music here.'

She laughs again. 'All right, let's get out of here.'

Outside, she looks at him and says, 'Okay, give me the invitation. When is your programme?'

'Where is your car, doctor?' he asks abruptly.

'I don't have a car.'

'Then how do you go home?'

'I take a bus or a rickshaw.'

He instantly stops a rickshaw going past and gets in after her.

'Are you kidnapping me?'

'No.' He tells her to give the man her address and says, 'No, I thought I'll drop you home.'

'Making a habit of it?'

He nods. They don't speak, it's too noisy, they know conversation is impossible. When they get out, she quickly pays the rickshaw driver, ignoring his protests. She realizes she has to invite him home. Once inside her flat, she asks him to sit and goes inside. When she comes out after a wash, she finds him staring at the room, at the plethora of fat cushions, the billowing curtains, the divan on which you could only loll.

'I would never have imagined you living in a place like this.'

'It's not mine. It belongs to a friend. He's abroad. Can I get you some water?'

'Yes. Room temperature, not cold.'

He is still looking around when she comes with the water.

'You find this odd? My sister Madhu says it looks like one of those naachwali places in films.'

'Are they like this?'

'I don't know. I've never seen one.'

He speaks to her in 'pure shuddha Marathi' as her father used to say. She speaks her own brand of Marathi, with English words sprinkled in plenty. This is the groove they will settle into, each comfortable with her/his language, comfortable with the other's as well. There is an intimacy about his speaking in Marathi, but she can always move back, distance herself when she wants to, by speaking in English, a tactic which he takes note of, though she scarcely knows she is using it.

'In any case, I'm not going to be here for long. My friend is coming back for good. Soon. I have to vacate this place.'

'What will you do?'

'I've spread the word. I should find something. Even if I don't, my friend says I can stay on here until I find something.'

'What about her?'

'Him, not her. We'll share.'

A faint frown crosses his face. 'You can take my house,' he says. 'It's very simple, not like this.'

'And you?'

'Oh, I'll go somewhere, I can stay with one of my friends.'

It reminds her of her father's casual, 'I'll be with one of my friends. Or at the lodge,' when her mother asked him where he would be staying when he went to Mumbai.

'I don't think it will come to that. I'm sure I'll find a place,' she tells him. 'And I have two homes in Mumbai, anyway – my mavshi's place and her daughter Madhuri's house. So then, what about your invitation?'

He brings out a small, modest card. 'It's in Dombivli. In the evening at six. It's a Sunday. Please come.'

'I'll try.'

'Don't try, just come. I'll ring you on the day to remind you.'

'Okay, but I can come only if there is no emergency.'

'Pukka?'

'Ek dum pukka.'

He looks satisfied, rather than pleased. As if he has got his way. She gets up, making it clear the visit is over, but he lingers. 'Tell me if you need any help in finding a house. Or if you want my house.'

'Sure.'

'And your mobile number?' he suddenly asks.

She gives it to him. 'I'll give you a missed call,' he says, 'so you'll have mine.' Then he is gone. When she closes the door after him, she leans against it as if she can no longer keep up her pose of indifference. Even as she enters her bedroom, her mobile rings. She lets it ring, then switches it off, knowing she has his number with her now. He's going too fast, she thinks. He's too eager, too open about his eagerness. And what about me? What am I doing?

Bedside manners are not formally taught to medical students. There are no textbooks, no classes for this subject, no exams to test their knowledge. Students learn by observing the doctors they admire and by listening to their remarks which are, most often, what can be called obiter dicta, throwaway statements. Many times, without their knowledge, students begin to imitate their teachers, a habit that stays with them for a lifetime. Students can't help but notice how brisk, commanding and reassuring the doctors are with their patients in a free ward and how, with private patients, the reassurance comes first. But it's not easy for Aparna to give her patients, who have been told they have cancer, any kind of reassurance. How can glib words help when they've just gone through a major surgery and are facing what patients find even more terrifying – chemotherapy? They have heard stories of the remedy being worse than the disease, they know little of the drugs used, but they see the visible evidence of the havoc they create in the bald heads of patients who have gone through chemotherapy. She's had so many patients – mainly women – ask her the question, 'Will I lose all my hair, doctor?' as if this is their main concern.

'The good news,' her first oncology boss had told her, 'is that we don't have to give our patients the bad news; the surgeons, the pathologists, the radiologists have already done that. Our job is only the rest of it. But the bad news is that, even if some battles are won, the war most often ends in defeat. And we have to be with our patients until that end, we have to hold their hands until they let go.'

These are not the things to be spoken of to a patient. From the beginning, Aparna refused to take recourse to a false smile, faked optimism or synthetic cheer. Nor, she realized, does a lugubrious face and a solemn manner do anything but scare the patient. She has learnt to steer a middle course between the two. She does not take refuge in medical jargon, either. She has learnt to be brief, matter-of-fact, to speak only of the treatment protocol. To speak as normally as possible. Yet she can't leave patients without any hope whatsoever. The one hope she offers is real. 'Your enemy will have retreated at the end of the chemotherapy,' she tells those patients who, she knows, will understand and accept these words positively.

Aparna is looking into the new patient's file when the woman enters. It gives the patient a little time to compose herself, she has always thought. And gives her that little moment she needs before she faces a new patient.

'Can I sit down, doctor?' the woman asks, a hint of impatience in her voice. Aparna, still not looking at her, gestures to her to sit down and continues flipping through the file, wondering where to begin. What do you say to a patient like this one? The words *'Invasive ductal carcinoma, triple negative'* cannot possibly be translated into something even faintly positive or reassuring. Though, actually patients are easy to fool. They want the doctor to say, 'You'll be all right.' Or 'You're lucky, a new drug has just come out which works miracles'. And patients, eager to be reassured, to be given hope, will cry out Hallelujah! Patients *want* to hear good news, they will accept all the good news you give them. But Aparna scorns the easy way out. She also knows that there can be exceptions to every rule, that patients with dire diagnoses have rallied and lived for years, that there are always circumstances, situations, imponderables, incalculables which affect each prognosis. But this is also why it can work the other way as well: there can be a drastic and swift race to the end, instead of the slow measured movement that was predicted.

Aparna is readying herself to speak when the woman says, 'No good news, is there, doctor?'

Aparna puts the file away and sees her for the first time. She does not have the usual dazed look of patients who have had their lives suddenly overturned by the bad news of their disease. But she knows that, even if she does not show it, the woman will be struggling to come to terms with what has happened to her.

'There is a lot of good news here. The tumour is quite small, we caught it before it infiltrated, only one node is involved and the margins are clear.'

'It's still triple negative breast cancer, isn't it? It sounds thrice as dangerous.'

'Dr Bhagat must have told you all about TNBC.'

'TNBC sounds much more innocuous, doesn't it? Sorry. Yes, Dr Bhagat has told me about it. I know that it does not respond to hormonal treatment.'

'Nevertheless, I promise you will be treated to the best of our ability. The drugs are now much safer and the good news for you is that TNBC responds very well to CT, I mean chemotherapy.'

'Yes, Dr Bhagat told me that too.'

'I see here that he didn't want a mastectomy. He suggested you have a lumpectomy. Why was a mastectomy done then?'

'That was me. I didn't want to have some cells lurking somewhere and becoming – what do you call it? – *colonies*?'

A small smile appears on Aparna's face as she thinks of how apt a word it is. 'Clusters,' she says tersely. And adds, 'Your tumour had clear boundaries.'

'My mother, an enthusiastic gardener, used to say – spare one weed and it will take over the whole garden.'

'That's why I'm here. To do the weeding. To get rid of any weed that has been left behind. Anyway, let's examine you.'

Aparna rings the bell for the nurse and while she's helping the patient with her clothes, Aparna goes to the patient's file on the computer.

Jyoti Dave, 45-year-old female, two pregnancies, two children, no major illness, no earlier surgery…

'The patient is ready, doctor.'

Aparna washes her hands and goes to the table. As usual, Dr Bhagat's surgery is excellent. Clean, the wound healing well.

'Are you regular with your exercise? Good. Raise your arm please.' The patient makes a small grimace. 'Hurts? It'll improve. The lymphedema is subsiding. That's good news.'

Finally she goes to the breast. Aparna can no longer count the number of post-mastectomy patients she has seen, nevertheless, when she sees a women without a breast, or both, she always has a sense of shock and outrage. She remembers the young woman who was still breast-feeding her baby, the look of shock and grief in her eyes at what had happened to her body, at the loss of the breast which had given her such joy when she fed her baby.

Now she lightly passes her hand over the breast, feels the scar. It's healing well; there's no weeping.

'When did they remove the drainage tube?'

'Two days ago.'

'Dr Bhagat has done a splendid job. And he's right. You didn't need to have your breasts removed.'

'What use are they?'

'Sorry?'

'I said, what use are my breasts to me? No babies to suckle, no lover to caress.'

Aparna is startled. The woman has broken out of her patient's role, she has rocked Aparna's authoritative doctor's chair. But she ignores the comment, for some reason it makes her uncomfortable, and finishes the rest of her examination in silence. When the patient comes to her after she's dressed, Aparna is keying some entries into the computer.

'All right, Mrs…'

'Call me Jyoti.'

'Okay, Jyoti, you have to undergo these tests.'

She gives her the list. Jyoti takes it and silently puts it away. For the first time, Aparna realizes that the patient is alone. It almost never happens, it has never happened in Aparna's experience. 'You've come alone? Isn't there anyone…?'

'My problem is too many people. There's a long list of people wanting to be with me, they must have drawn up a roster.'

'Then…?'

'I wanted to meet you alone. I wanted you to talk to *me*, not to someone else. Doctors have a bad habit of ignoring the patient, as if being ill makes you an idiot.'

She has done it again, made a remark that does not belong in this room. Again Aparna ignores it. 'Please don't come alone for the chemotherapy.'

'Don't worry. And I'm not alone. My daughter is waiting outside. I let her come on condition she sits outside.'

Your business, Aparna thinks. And says aloud, 'Okay, so we start on the CT after we get the results of all these tests.'

She gives her the schedule: 'an interval of three weeks between sessions, longer if your blood count is not satisfactory'. She tells her about the drugs being used. We use three drugs, she says, and tells her what they are, what they will do to the cancer cells. It's given through an IV infusion, Aparna says and then speaks of the side effects she can expect. 'And you will lose your hair, I'm sure you know that.'

'Of course. First thought.'

'But it will grow back, it starts growing back by the time your chemo sessions are done.'

She tells her to pick up some material outside at the desk, giving more information about her diet and other things, asks if she needs to talk to a counsellor. The woman is brief and monosyllabic in her replies.

'And you have to trust your doctor. We are going to fight this together.'

There is a small smile on the woman's face as if she had expected this, as if she's saying, spare me the rest of your spiel. 'Don't worry, doctor, it's my body, my life. I value it highly.'

This woman, Aparna thinks, does not require any placebos. And so she says no more, and the woman gets up saying, 'Thank you, Dr Dandekar.'

'That's all right.'

She goes back to the files, is looking up her next patient, when she is startled by the woman's voice. 'Doctor…'

She is waiting, holding on to the back of her chair.

'Yes, anything you want to ask?'

'Are you Gavi Dandekar's daughter?'

This is the third person to ask her the question in a very short period of time. 'I'll be forgotten soon after my death,' her father had said. 'Once they've finished with the false praise, the forced homage, it's over. It's all bunkum that writers survive. Most don't. Almost none do. Only one man,' he had added, 'only one man still lives, he's still read, still staged – that inexhaustible man, Shakespeare.'

She – everyone who knew him, actually – was familiar with his great admiration for the Bard. 'It's because of him that I studied English literature. Such a mistake,' he said once.

'Yes,' she says now to her patient.

'My mother and aunt never missed any of Gavi's plays,' the woman says. 'My aunt thought that perhaps you were his daughter, she wanted me to ask you. Sorry about the intrusion.'

'That's okay.'

When she has gone, Aparna thinks, it's the first time she has been recognized as anything but a doctor in this room. The first time a patient has spoken of anything but the disease, the treatment. Their lives overturned by the chance, at times a serendipitous discovery of the disease, patients are not interested in anything but their struggle with it, they are single-mindedly absorbed in fighting it. Whereas this woman…

If Aparna, when she entered the world of oncology, had thought that the disease had been mapped out and charted, that she had only to follow the path traced by the surgeon, she soon realized she was wrong. She had thought that the disease, identified by the pathologist and radiologist and frontally attacked by the surgeon, would leave her with no more to do than the scrubbing and the mopping up, so that all traces of it were wiped out. But she soon realized the truth being drummed into them for the past few years: that each patient's story was different, each cancer came with its own individual traits, as individual as the person it had latched on to. Which meant she had to deal with each patient, each cancer, as an independent entity.

At first Aparna had thought that Jyoti would be one of those patients who go on the internet, look up all the facts, then argue with the doctor, something that Aparna, like many doctors, does not care for. But Jyoti had not done that. She had listened quietly to whatever Aparna had to say. Looking into her past medical history, listening to her, Aparna thought that Jyoti would be able to go through the chemotherapy fairly well. She's a strong woman, she thought, her desire to have a mastectomy showed that. And her comment on her breasts had shown her to be someone not cast in the usual mode. Age was on her side. When she comes for her first chemo session, she startles Aparna once again. She has shaved off her hair, leaving behind a very short fuzz.

'I thought that rather than wait for my hair to fall out – they say it falls off in clumps – I'd do it myself.'

Her daughter – whom she has introduced as Mira – is with her this time and Jyoti notices how the girl keeps her eyes away from her mother, as if the sight of her shaven head hurts her. It tells Aparna why Jyoti had come alone the first time. In spite of believing, like all doctors do, in not getting personally involved with a patient, Aparna always finds herself associating with a patient's battle. Yet her purpose remains limited – to help patients get through their chemo sessions with as few problems as possible, to set them on the path to recovery. But now the daughter's visible tension, her agitation, which is just under the surface, brings back her own struggle with her mother's cancer. The girl is too young, she thinks with pity. I was about this age when my mother was diagnosed with stromal sarcoma. I was a medical student, yet I was not prepared for what my mother had to go through. I was as stricken as this child is. She has a fleeting thought – where is the husband and father? Is she a widow, a divorcee, is her husband away (even then she would have expected him to come) or is he just plain irresponsible?

Mother and daughter seem very self-sufficient, as if they are used to being on their own, to managing on their own. When Aparna goes to see Jyoti just before she is hooked up to the IV, she notices that the girl seems calmer. She has put away the few things she has brought on the bedside table and is reading a book. Aparna explains the procedure to Jyoti and Mira – the anti-emetic first, then one drug, and when it's over, the next drug.

'I thought you have it all together. They call it a cocktail, don't they?'

'No, it's one after another.'

When the nurse starts the IV, Jyoti speaks to Mira. 'I have a staff meeting today. Sister will know where I am, you can ask her to inform me if necessary. And there's another doctor who'll be here – Dr Mishra. He'll be coming around soon.'

Aparna has one more patient starting his chemo today. She is always tense and anxious when she has a patient undergoing a first session. But this patient, an older man, looks very peaceful, listening to music. When he sees her, he takes off his ear plugs.

'Okay?'

'So far so good.'

'Enjoying the music?'

'Enjoying the change from politics,' he says. As she walks out of the ward, she wonders, as she often does, at the resilience and courage of human beings, at the way we accept what at first seems impossible. The man, a journalist, had been dazed and confused when he had learnt of his malignancy, angry at what he considered an interruption in his life. His wife and children had been unable to reach him, he had been morose and depressed. Now, here he was going through the chemo peacefully, his wife by his side, showing no sign of the fear which had made him so distraught, as if he has come to terms with it.

The meeting takes longer than she had thought. When it is over, she goes to the journalist. He makes a V sign to her, indicating that it has gone well.

'But I had a strange experience, doctor,' he says, suddenly garrulous, perhaps with relief, as patients are after the session is over. 'I kept thinking I was falling down – I had this sensation of falling, and then, just before I actually fell, I'd come out of it.'

'Will you be writing a book on your experience?"

He laughs, a little awkwardly. 'You know the thought is always in a journalist's mind, we think that one day we will write a book. But no, I'll try not to write about this. Too many books already, we don't need one more. Though you never know, I may find myself writing sometime.'

'Write if you feel like it. It will help you to shed the load.'

'Let's see.'

When she gets to Jyoti, she sees two nurses and Dr Mishra with her.

'What happened, Sudhir?'

Dr Mishra takes her aside. 'She was bad. She started getting rigors within minutes of starting the IV. Sister called me, but it settled down in a while. Then nausea and vomiting began.'

'Doctor,' Mira comes to her, her eyes large with fear. 'Doctor, she…she…'

'Relax, Mira, these reactions do happen, we can deal with them. You just relax and leave it to us. And keep moistening her mouth with ice.'

A little later she tells Mira, 'We may want your mother to stay the night.' The girl nods. 'You can ring up and ask someone to come. And I think you should go home.'

'I'm fine. And I rang up my aunt, she's a doctor.'

Jyoti is lying flattened in her bed. She smiles wanly at Aparna. 'What a commotion,' she whispers.

'We need to work for the money we earn, don't we?'

'Miru?'

'I've asked her to go home.'

When Aparna goes out, she realizes what Jyoti had meant when she spoke of a 'long list of volunteers'. There are about five or six people waiting to talk to her. The woman who first addresses her introduces herself as a doctor. 'I'm Dr Apte, a paediatrician. Dr Dandekar, how is Jyoti?'

'She's okay. I'm going home now, but the duty doctor will be here. The night nurse, Sister Reema, is very efficient. Don't worry. And will one of you be here?'

'Yes, my sister is staying. And Saguna will be here, she works for Jyoti. We're taking Mira home.'

'Good.'

Aparna rarely thinks of her patients when she goes home. But today the girl has brought back memories of herself when her mother was ill. I have walked the path this child will have to walk on, she thinks, I have gone through the anguish she has already begun to experience. She remembers her fear that her mother would die, her constant hope that a miracle would save her, her anxiety that her mother should not know her fears or thoughts. She read up on stromal sarcoma, she talked to a senior, hoping to know more. But all that he said was, 'Why do you want to know? The doctors in charge will do their best.' It was kindly meant, but, she'd thought angrily – what if it was your mother? Though, years later, when she knew more, when she knew better, she thought, maybe he was right. If I had known how terrible a cancer it was, I would have lost hope, I would have been paralysed by fear. How could I have helped my mother then?

Aparna's anxiety about finding a home now overtakes all her other concerns. She suddenly realizes that she does not have too much time left to find a place to move into. She is not as insouciant about it as she had made Hari Pandit believe. She has spread the word in the hospital, she looks up the ads in the newspapers daily, she surfs the internet, but so far she has drawn a blank. True, she can go to her cousin Madhu's house. Aparna knows that both Abbas and Madhu will welcome her for a while but, except for Abbas' room which is sacrosanct, their house has people walking in and out the whole day. Abbas's sisters and their children still think of themselves as living together, though they now have three apartments on different floors. Taimavshi's house is quieter, but Aparna is reluctant to trouble her. Since her daughter-in-law Anju's death and Sada's mourning, which seems never to end, she has aged perceptibly. If I go to her, she will begin looking after me and I don't want that. The easiest option is to continue to be where she is until she finds a place. Her friend has urged her not to think that she has to move out. 'We can share the apartment. Surely you're not worried that I'll force myself on you, Aparna?'

No, she is not worried about that. Though she knows that contiguity is a terrible facilitator and she could find herself in his bed, or he in hers, as a convenient arrangement. The truth is that Aparna needs her privacy, she does not want to share her space with anyone during the few hours she is at home. The ideal solution, one she did not mention to Hari, would be to move into her own apartment, next to Taimavshi's. However, she had ruled it out immediately. Taimavshi had accepted her explanation that she hated commuting, though she could not help saying, 'Your mother bought this place mainly for you.'

'Anandibai,' her father had said to Taimavshi, 'you haven't done me any favour by persuading my wife to buy a place next to yours. With Apu in Mumbai and you next door, why will Sulu want to be in Chandrapur? She'll abandon me.'

But it was he who visited Mumbai more often when Aparna entered medical college, suddenly appearing at Aparna's hostel, saying 'I missed my girl'. He never stayed in Sulu's apartment, though. He continued to stay with his friends, or at his favourite 'Konkan Lodge'. And ultimately, though none of them had had any premonitory shivers when he had spoken of Sulu abandoning him, Sulu did come and live in Mumbai and never went back to Chandrapur after that. For Aparna, the place is haunted by her mother's suffering, not only the anguish at what had happened to her marriage, but her physical suffering. By the time they diagnosed her problem as stromal sarcoma, it had already infiltrated into her abdomen. Though she was a medical student, Aparna's knowledge of the disease had been minimal, her fears enormous. She knew that there was not much hope; yet she wanted to believe that the massive doses of radiation and chemotherapy that her mother was given would save her. Now, knowing what these did to a patient, Aparna wonders at the stoicism with which her mother endured it all. She did it for my sake, she thinks, she knew how desperately I wanted her to live.

No, I can never live in that house, Aparna thinks. It seems to her that she will have to go to an agent, something she has resisted so far. And then, suddenly, her search for a house ends, the problem resolved in a most unexpected and satisfactory way.

Mira turns up with the results of Jyoti's blood tests one evening. The tests are okay, Aparna tells her, she can come for her next chemo session, and asks her to fix a date. Mira lingers, very hesitantly she speaks of Jyoti's non-existent appetite. 'She eats like a sparrow, I'm so frightened for her.'

I was like you, Aparna thinks, I was also frightened that if she didn't eat, my mother would die. But I can't share this with you because my mother's battle ended in death. You don't want to let that thought enter your mind.

'Mira, she can't go back to her earlier self in a day or two. You have to remember her body has taken a beating. First the surgery, then this. She is fighting a great battle, using all the resources of her mind and body. We're here to help her, but most of the fight has to be fought by her. Think of that.'

Though the girl seems less distraught after Aparna's pep talk, the worry lines remain on her young face. She realizes, however that she's taking Aparna's time and moves away. Then comes back as if she has remembered something.

'Doctor, one of the nurses told Saguna, the night she stayed with Ma, that you are looking for a house?'

'Yes.'

'We have an apartment we're thinking of renting out. Would you be interested?'

'Where is it?'

'Not far from here. It's in the same building as our place. It's minimum auto fare distance from here.'

'And how big?'

'Two bedrooms. Largish rooms. It's an old place. Would you like to see it, doctor?'

'Yes, yes, I would. If I can.'

'No problem. I'll take you. Whenever you have time.'

They decide on the next day. 'Just call me when you're free, I'll be here in fifteen minutes.'

'Walking or rickshaw?' she asks Aparna, when they meet.

'Whatever. Let's start walking, may be easier than waiting for a rickshaw.'

Mira has lived in Bombay all her young life, she walks through the crowds adroitly dodging people, almost unaware of them. They get off the main road and enter a side street – it's a dead end, Aparna notices – and enter a building. Not a very tall one, dwarfed, in fact, by the others on the road.

'My dad bought a place here first. Then, a little later, Ma's brother and mother bought one on the second floor. That's the one we're renting out.'

As soon as she enters, Aparna knows she wants this place. She feels instantly at home, she has a fanciful thought – rare with her – that the house is welcoming and accepting her. Perhaps it's because the furniture belongs to an earlier era, it's a bit like what they had in Chandrapur. There's a dining table and chairs of dark wood, a dressing table with a swivelling mirror which stays at a leaning angle since the screw has come out, a rocking chair like her father's...

'Ma said if you don't want the furniture, we'll have it removed. Do you have a lot of stuff...?'

'Only my books, clothes, my laptop and...that's about all. Let this stay.'

'We can remove the pictures of course.'

A whole lot of pictures have been put up on the wooden screen that separates the living room from the dining space.

Family pictures, obviously, posed for during happy times, as if the people, aware of how ephemeral happiness is, had captured the moments to prevent them from being lost forever.

'No, let them stay too. They have a greater right to be here than I have. But listen, why are we talking as if the place is mine?'

'Ma said, if you like it, it's yours.'

'I love it.'

'Then it's settled. When would you like to move in?'

'My God! You don't mean I can move in right away?'

'Yes, doctor. Just give us two or three days to clean it up.'

Something is not quite right, Aparna thinks. Nobody gives a house for rent this way – letting a kid talk to the tenant and allowing her to take an instant decision. There must be a catch somewhere. Maybe the house is haunted. Or leaking. Or maybe the rent is impossibly high. Hesitantly she asks, 'how much is the rent?'

Mira mentions a figure Aparna thinks most reasonable. 'And a year's rent as advance.'

Which is not a problem. But she's still hesitating when Mira asks, 'Would you like to move in this Sunday?'

She looks at the girl's face and is ashamed of her suspicions. 'Yes, I would. But don't we need to draw up the lease? I can give the advance, but...'

'No hurry, doctor. You can talk to Ma about all that. Or even better, you can talk to Deepumama, my uncle, he's the owner of this place. He lives in the US, he's coming here in a month or so.'

Aparna had never imagined that moving home would be so easy. Two trips in Madhu's SUV carry all of Aparna's worldly goods, Aparna and Madhu following in Madhu's little car with the more fragile objects. Taimavshi comes a little later with two large bags – kitchen stuff and food, she tells them. 'And pots and pans. In case, Apu decides to have a cook. But first we have to boil the milk and have a cup of tea.'

The milk, as always when watched, takes a long time to boil. When it does, the three women sigh in relief. Aparna thinks of how her father would have scoffed at them for believing in this ritual of boiling milk in a new home. Taimavshi says, 'Now this has become Apu's house. Madhu, make us a cup of tea. I'll put the food in the fridge and get the kitchen in order. If you have a cook, she will be able to find things easily.'

There's not much work to be done. The place is spotless. Aparna sees that the family has taken the trouble to make the place clean and comfortable. She thinks there was a TV in the living room, now it's gone and there's a brand new one on the wall in the bedroom. Their work done, they have a wash and Taimavshi says, 'Time for lunch. Then I have to go back.'

'Lunch? Here?'

'Where else? I told you I've got us food from home.'

'But, Aai, I've also got food for us at home. Abbas rang up to say he's got beer cooling in the fridge for us.'

'But what about the food I've brought?'

'Put it in the fridge. Apu can eat it for two or three days.'

'But, Madhu…'

The mother and daughter argue. Aparna knows that Taimavshi's reluctance to go to Madhu's house unless she has to, exasperates Madhu. 'I know you don't want to come because Sada doesn't like it. But how can you give up coming to your daughter's house, Aai? I have as much right to you as he has. Isn't it enough for him that I no longer visit your house – my house too by the way – because he doesn't like it? But, of course, I forgot, he's your son and I'm only a daughter…'

Finally, as Aparna knew she would, Taimavshi relents. She has a bad conscience about Madhu having given up her visits to her mother's house because of Sada's threat that if she does, he will no longer visit her.

'He's nursing his grief,' Madhu often complains to Aparna. 'Aai shouldn't give in to his unreasonableness.'

But there's Anil, Sada and Anju's son, Taimavshi's only grandchild. Madhu knows her mother will do anything to avoid a rift in the family for his sake.

The breach between her two children (not of my doing, Aai, remember that, Madhu always reminds her mother) has disturbed the even tenor of Taimavshi's life. Aparna always thinks of how strange it is that of her two children, Sada had been the steady and responsible one while Madhu had been wayward and rebellious. She had refused to go to college after she passed out of school (I'm not interested, Aai, why listen to lectures which will bore me to death!), she had taken up dancing instead. She was not consistent there either, starting with Bharatanatyam, then moving on to Kathak and finally ending up with film dances, which were not as acceptable and popular as they are now. To her family's horror, she'd begun dancing for films, one of a crowd at first, then, when she'd caught a choreographer's appreciative eye, getting a little more visibility and prominence, appearing for a few seconds, a few steps, along with the heroine. And then she'd met Abbas, a director considerably older than her, a married man with two children. They'd fallen in love and married. Taimavshi had been apprehensive, equally because of his age as because he was a Muslim and a married man with children. Sada, always protective of his sister, had been just as anxious for her. And then Sada's wife Anju had been killed, she had died when the hotel where she worked was attacked by terrorists. Sada had changed into a silent and bitter man. A hating man. All Muslims had become the enemy; his sister, married to a Muslim, was a traitor to her country and religion.

Whereas Madhu, after marrying Abbas, has turned into a mature and sedate woman, no longer a reckless girl. For Aparna, a teenager when Madhu and Abbas got married, their love story has been the ultimate romance. She notices now, how Abbas pulls Madhu to sit by his side, how Madhu nestles against him.

'Sit down, all of you. You must be tired,' he says.

'You talk as if we've been hauling heavy crates and furniture up the stairs. You know how heavily Apu is burdened by possessions.'

'Now, where's the beer I was promised?' Taimavshi asks.

'That's like my Aai,' Madhu says and is getting up when Abbas stops her. 'My job. Sit down.'

Taimavshi is the first to leave. Abbas and Madhu, who are going out later, drop Aparna home.

'Come and see my home.'

'Next time, Aparna. And you keep coming.'

Aparna switches on the lights, enjoying the feeling of being by herself. She knows she is not a natural homemaker like Sulu was, or Taimavshi or Madhu are; nevertheless, neatness and orderliness matter to her. I will be comfortable here, she thinks, but has a pang, wondering whether all her life she will live like this, in homes that belong to others, among the possessions of strangers. The one place she remembers as a home was in Chandrapur. When she sold it after her father's death, she became homeless. 'Sell it, don't keep it,' Baba had told her. 'Don't be sentimental about it. I know you will never come back to Chandrapur.'

She had not been sentimental, not then. But recently it has been haunting her, reminding her of the life she has lost. She stands in front of the array of pictures belonging to her landlords. 'If you want to put up your own pictures, we can take these away,' Mira had said again. But Aparna has no pictures to put up. She does have a few pictures of her parents, but thinks it's hypocritical, well, not exactly that, but wrong, somehow, to put them up together, giving an illusion of a togetherness which had so abruptly ceased. Ended without dignity, which is what she minds the most. Even to hang them separately on two different walls would be wrong, because she has no right to make a show of filial devotion, considering the way she had behaved with her father. She's more comfortable with these pictures of nameless strangers (later Jyoti will identify each one of them for her); she has no shared history with them, there is nothing about them that can disturb her.

She has a bath and goes into the bedroom which Taimavshi has made comfortable with clean sheets and pillow covers. She sees her mobile on the bedside table, her personal one. She had forgotten to take it with her. She opens it now and is horrified to see a long list of missed calls and about a dozen messages, all from the same number. They are all from one person – Shree Hari is the way he writes his name in the messages. Today was the day of his programme. She had forgotten, completely forgotten. She wonders whether to talk to him now. But it's too late, he will be sleeping, best to do nothing, to leave it alone. She quickly deletes the messages, noting that the last two are both angry and despairing. I don't want to get into anything that might become a problem, she thinks, I'm good as I am. I don't want anything more, I don't want anything else. Anyway, what right does he have to expect anything from me, how can he make any demands on me? she asks herself. Since her divorce, and even before that, she has been able to fend off men very comfortably; why does this man make her so uncomfortable, as if she owes him something?

Aparna has a sense of déjà vu, though it's not as late as it was the last time and there are still some patients waiting in the room; none for her, though. Once again, when she is on her way out of the hospital, he stands up, as abruptly as he had done earlier, and moves purposefully towards her. There is the same sense of being taken by surprise, of sudden shock that makes her heart stop.

'You didn't come,' he says abruptly. 'For my programme.'

'I'm sorry, I…'

'I waited for you. I kept waiting until almost the very end.'

'I was moving house.'

He does not seem to hear her, intent as he is on what he wants to say. 'Each moment I thought you would appear. I was so sure you would come, I never thought…'

She has been walking as he talks, forcing him to follow her. When they get outside, she stops and says, 'Can we talk later?'

'No, I can't wait. I must know. I went to your home and they told me you no longer live there. It was a shock, such a great shock.'

'I told you I've moved out of there. I moved on Sunday.'

She walks briskly, but even at her fastest he can overtake her, he is so much taller. At times, people come between them, forcing them to separate, but he manages to keep pace with her, he always comes back to her side.

'You could have told me, you could have sent me a message. Why didn't you tell me you were moving?'

She could say, 'None of your business.' But she does not, she has to take his distress seriously. She suddenly stops, making him stop as well. 'We can't talk here. Come home with me,' she says.

He stares at her for a moment, controls himself with a visible effort and then says, 'All right. Shall we take a rickshaw?'

'No, we can walk. This house is very near, it's just round the corner,' she says, unconsciously echoing Mira's words. 'I told you I've moved,' she repeats and the exasperation in her voice makes him smile for the first time; he holds up his hands as if in surrender.

'All right, let's walk.'

She speaks next only when they stand before the building. 'This is where I live now.'

'Lift?' he asks, when they enter the foyer.

'No, let's take the stairs. I'm on the first floor.'

Unlike the last time, she unlocks the door and stands aside to let him enter before her. 'Sit,' she says. 'I'll get you a glass of water.'

'Not fridge water.'

'I know. Room temperature.'

He drinks the entire glass in a few gulps, puts it down and looks around him.

'Why didn't you tell me you were moving?'

'Should I have?' He looks so stricken that she quickly adds, 'It happened in a rush. I was offered this place, it was ready for occupation, I liked it and so I moved in the first Sunday after that.'

'Doctor… Doctor Aparna…can I call you Aparna?…don't do this to me again.' He stands up as if the fervour of his feelings cannot be expressed sitting down. 'When you didn't come I thought – I don't know what I thought, I had such confused and negative thoughts. I kept looking for you, thinking each moment that you would enter the hall. It was madness, I didn't know what I was doing. I have never sung so badly in my life. And I've been singing in public since I was twelve. I was ashamed of myself.'

'I'm very sorry your programme didn't go off well.'

'Oh, I did better in a while. I thought of the people – not many, but each listener is important – who had come all the way to hear me, I thought of the money they had paid…' He suddenly goes back to his frenzied tone. 'I went to your house the next day and when they told me you had moved out, I thought I had lost you forever.'

Lost me? What is this? This is madness. She must stop him, tell him that she scarcely knows him, that she forgot about his invitation, she did not take it seriously, she wants to say that there is no reason why she should worry about his feelings. But she can't, he looks so vulnerable and hurt.

'Stop,' she says. 'Please stop.'

They stare at each other.

'I was married earlier,' she says baldly.

'I know.'

'And I've been divorced.'

'I know that also.'

'And I'm no longer young. Children, rickshaw drivers, bus conductors call me auntie. Sometimes,' she amends hastily.

He laughs. 'What do they know? You look like a girl. And everyone calls everyone else auntie or uncle these days.'

They are silent again. 'I'm hungry,' she says suddenly. 'I haven't had lunch today.'

She hopes he will take the hint and go away. But instead he says, 'Can I take you out somewhere for dinner?'

'No, I'm too tired. I can't face the thought of going out anywhere. My Taimavshi brought me some food the day I moved – masala rice with *tondli*. I'll heat it and have it for dinner.' He looks so crestfallen she has to say, 'There's enough for two, enough for four, really. Would you like to join me?'

He hesitates for a moment, then says, 'Yes. If it's okay with you.'

'Would I have asked you otherwise? Sit down. I'll have a bath and then I'll heat the rice – it won't take a minute.'

'Microwave?'

'Yes.'

He looks horrified. 'You can't heat rice in a microwave. You have to heat it in a cooker.'

'Cooker? I don't know if I have one. Yes, I think Taimavshi brought one the other day. Now, where did she put it…?'

She goes into the kitchen and looks vaguely at the storage shelves. He laughs at her. 'Go and have your bath, I'll do the heating up.'

'But you don't know where things are.'

'You don't know either, so what difference does it make whether you do it or I do?'

She comes back, the fragrance of talcum wafting in her wake. She is wearing an old cotton salwar kamiz; she has deliberately squashed her desire to wear something better, something that would make her look good. She finds him peacefully chopping tomatoes, whistling as he works, while he waits for the cooker to cool down.

'Making a salad?'

'*Koshimbir*,' he corrects her.

'Okay, *koshimbir*. So you don't like to speak English, you're one of those "our language" faddists.'

'No, but salad means something quite different. The vegetables are not cut, there's a lot of oil...'

'You shouldn't be working in my kitchen.'

'Why don't you set the plates? By that time the cooker will be ready.'

He seems surprised by her ineptness in the kitchen. Watching her clumsily blunder about, he asks, 'You're not used to cooking?'

'No, I never learnt to. My mother didn't want me to enter the kitchen. You study, she used to say. She herself was so efficient and quick, I think she didn't want me getting in her way. And once I went to the hostel, I had nothing to do with cooking and kitchens. I was too pampered,' she says thoughtfully.

'Only children always are.'

'How do you know I am an only child?'

'Gavi Dandekar had only one daughter. Everyone knows that. Now we're ready.'

She's startled when, before beginning, he folds his hands and says the before-meal prayer, *Vadani kavala gheta*... She stares at him in amazement, but makes no comment. Prayers, religion, these are private matters. When they start eating, she asks him, 'How did you learn to cook?'

'My grandmother taught me when she fell ill, so that my grandfather and I wouldn't be totally dependent on cooks. I can manage most everyday food – except chapattis. I think it's a special gift given to women, the way they can roll out chapattis to an exact shape and size.'

'The gift was not given to this woman. I can't make a chapatti to save my life. And I don't think it's any great gift. All it needs is practice.'

'How do you manage? I mean, do you have a cook?'

'I'm trying to find someone who can cook at least one meal a day. Breakfast is easy – there's cereal, there's bread, I can make a fairly good omelette, or scrambled eggs. *Pohe* is the one thing I can make easily and well, and when I want to pamper myself, I make it for breakfast – only on Sundays, of course. I don't eat lunch, just a banana, an apple or something like that. I need a proper meal only at night. I'll soon have to start looking for someone who can give me that.'

'And until then?'

'I'll manage. Taimavshi is always agitating to send me a dabba every evening, but I won't allow her. She shouldn't be doing things for me at her age.'

He has been listening to her intently, as if she's telling him a story that fascinates him, imbibing every word she says. 'Your mavshi is a good cook,' he says. 'This rice is good.'

'Oh, she hasn't made it herself. Her maid, Kusum, has been with her for years; she taught her to cook and now Kusum has become almost a proper chef! Taimavshi's husband was an Air Force officer and they lived in style – they always had a cook. When her husband died, she started working with All India Radio, a full-time job, and she had no time to cook. My mother, poor thing, had to work hard. Baba was only a college teacher and she did all the cooking herself, though she had a full-time job, she worked in a bank. Baba and I were useless at home, we did nothing, I mean, Baba had his teaching and writing and I had my studies. But otherwise, she did everything for us.'

She has stopped him from saying what he had wanted to say. Once said, she knows, it can never be unsaid, it would be there between them, taking up all the space there is. Later, she wonders whether, if she had not stopped him, he would have burst out, like any classical lover, into words of love, into declarations and promises. But we are no longer of the age to do such things, she thinks. Later, however, he will tell her that he could not sleep at night because his mind was full of her, that he was haunted by her image, her face, that he had fought with himself, knowing, guessing, that she was not ready to hear his words of love. But she will never know, because he has not told her, he will never tell her, how long he sat in the waiting room among patients who wondered what could be wrong with this seemingly healthy young man, she will never know how long he waited for her in the midst of patients and their families, holding his love in his hands like a flaming torch, like a showy, colourful flower.

Aparna is much more circumspect than he is, she has the burnt-child-dreads-fire kind of wariness. And he, even if more reckless, is quick to understand her feelings, to respond to them. He has come, not only to remonstrate with her, but, hungry for a sight of her, to get a glimpse of her, if nothing else.

When he changes the subject and talks of ordinary things of families and food and cooking, the edginess between them disappears. He speaks of his grandfather, who was a Sanskrit and Marathi teacher in a school – 'whatever I know of these languages is because of him, not because of my teachers in school' – but gave up his job to become a purohit, a priest who performed weddings. He gained a reputation for performing it in the correct Vedic style, all the mantras and rituals intact. 'He was in great demand,' he says with a naïve pride she finds touching. He tells her that his grandfather also earned recognition for the strange fact that most of the marriages he performed turned out to be happy ones. But for him, the most important fact is that his grandfather was his partner in his dream of a life in music. 'Without him, I would have been nowhere. He himself sang well – though he had no formal training – and he was my first teacher.'

She realizes that his name is Shree Hari – he spells it Shree Hari, making two words of it, the 'H' of Hari a capital letter – and that the Shree is not an appellation as she had thought. She remembers that his friend had called him Shree the time they first met.

'And when you're a Pandit, will you be Pandit Pandit?' she asks.

'Long way off, Dr Dandekar.'

He sounds modest, but Aparna will learn that, where music is concerned, he is full of confidence in himself. Though he has times of total despair as well. 'It's so easy to remain a second-rate musician, I would rather give up music than be that,' he will say to her. They speak of the play during which they had first met. She tells him that she now remembers that evening, she remembers being there with her father and her friend, Emily. He tells her of the accident that gave him entry into the play, the boy who was to play the main role having broken his arm. 'Because of that I met your father,' he says, making it a momentous event in his life. He speaks in Marathi, the language conferring an immediate intimacy on their talk, though he is careful to call her *tumhi*. Once, only once, he slips into the intimate *tu*, but he quickly retrieves the word and replaces it with *tumhi*.

His first outburst has died down, almost forgotten, but it still lies between them, quiescent, yet with the potential of making its presence felt once again. It does not happen, he is careful to see that it does not. Dinner is long over, conversation peters out. They look at the time and are astonished to find that they have been conversing for over an hour. She has a sense of great fatigue; the battle between the tumult of her feelings and her attempt to behave as just an acquaintance has tired her out. When he says, 'I must go,' she does not demur. She is reluctant for him to go, but she wants to be on her own, to think of what is happening to her, what she is doing, what she is getting into. She thought she had learnt to do without love, men and all that, but this man...? How is it, she wonders once again, that she who has become so adept at keeping men at bay (after all she has been single for nearly seven years), how is it that she has been unable to brush off this man the way she has many others? When he leaves, it is with the confidence that they will meet again. The very moment after he goes, her phone gives a ping and she knows it is a message from him. I won't read it now, I need time, I have to think with a cool and calm mind. She has a sense of a force she cannot control and she thinks she will have to counter his impetuosity with her composure. Next time, she thinks, I will handle it better. For she knows, as well as he does, that they will meet again, that this is not the end, that this is only the beginning.

The new place is working out much better than she expected. What had seemed to her the most difficult and tiresome problem, that of finding help, has been quickly solved by Mira, who comes to her with Saguna's suggestions. So now she has a girl who cleans and washes – she's quick, slapdash, but good when she is in the mood – and a woman who comes and cooks for her four times a week. Taimavshi will be pleased, she thinks. And, the thought sneaks in, Shree Hari Pandit as well. The uneasiness she had felt at the thought of getting close to a patient, the awkwardness of socializing with her, the hazards of being approached by the family when she was at home, of being disturbed at all times, at any time: she had worried about these. But the family has kept aloof. Except for Mira and Saguna, who came to help, she has been left alone. The door of Jyoti's apartment remains closed most of the time, only the slippers left outside the door tell her that they have visitors. Aparna had imagined that Jyoti's 'long list of volunteers' would be translated into many callers, but obviously they have taken her advice to curtail guests. Not only is it tiring, Aparna had warned, but Jyoti's immunity is very low and she should not interact with too many people. Once Mira comes to her saying Jyoti has fever. 'Bring her to the hospital if she's not better by tomorrow,' Aparna tells her. But they did not come, so obviously she was better.

Hari and she have met rarely since the evening he came home. Her workload is heavy, her schedule tight. He is busy as well, with his students (he teaches in a music school twice a week and has students at home once a week) and his own riaz. In addition, he goes to Pune once or twice a month to spend a day with his guruji. However, even when they don't meet, he is present in her life through his messages. He is an avid texter, one of those to whom his mobile is an extension of himself. The messages are in Marathi, but written in the Roman script. It takes her some time to learn to read these two-language communications, some words seem so odd it takes her time to understand what is meant but she does finally catch on. The messages themselves are prosaic and short, feelings and emotions are never mentioned. Yet it is very clear that he is pursuing her. To what end? To have an affair? She has met many men who wanted just that in the years since her divorce. But this man is not the type, she has come to know that. Brought up by his grandparents, he has been imbued with the values of an earlier generation. And she senses something in him, which makes him different from all the other men she has known – an intensity of feeling. She has glimpsed, even in their short time together, that music is not just a profession for him, it's a passion that lights up his entire life; obviously, she thinks, he will bring the same passion into a relationship. And, therefore, she remains wary, trying to keep her distance. They meet once or twice in a small café near the hospital to have coffee. Each time he goes back with her to her home, as if he thinks she needs to be escorted, though he never makes any move to go inside. They go for a play once. 'I thought we could see one of your father's plays, but I couldn't find even one on the entire page of play listings.'

'Nobody stages his plays now.'

'That's strange. Why?'

She shrugs. 'I don't know. Maybe there are fashions in these things as well.'

It's a long time since she entered a theatre, something which was so much a part of her life when she was a child. As soon as they get in, there is such a strong reminder of her father that she thinks she can't bear it. But it passes and she understands when the play begins that this is another time, another generation of actors, another generation of spectators. Though, perhaps, this playwright is, like her father was at one time, one of the rising stars of Marathi theatre. And he was good, Aparna thinks, he was a thousand times better than the man who has written this inane play. How could anyone think this worth staging?

Hari apologizes for the play when they come out of the theatre. 'My friend who sees plays thought you might like it. Women like it, he said. It's a feminist play.' He uses the English word 'feminist', handling it carefully, clearly a word he is not very familiar with.

'Your friend doesn't know much about women.'

'He's married.'

'That makes no difference.'

If he hears the bitterness in her voice, he ignores it. He laughs. 'Maybe you're right.'

In their few meetings she has seen that he has a tunnel vision, his life dominated by his passion for music. History is to him the history of his gharana, the greats of the world are the great musicians of all time. Music runs in the family, he has told her. His grandfather's grandfather was a kirtankaar, a very popular one. 'Ajoba told me he was a very handsome man, he was fair and had those light grey cat's eyes. And when he wore his red silk *uparna* on his shoulder, he looked so handsome, women flocked to see him as well as hear him. He was a beautiful singer and a wonderful storyteller. His son, my grandfather's father, wanted my grandfather to become a teacher, a more respected profession he thought, but Ajoba also went into music in a different way. People loved the way he chanted mantras during a wedding ceremony. He taught me Sanskrit so that I could chant the mantras with understanding.'

Listening to his seemingly artless confidences, she begins to wonder whether he is trying to build a link to her through this information, whether the confidences are indeed a substitute for the word 'love' which he never utters. Or whether he is the same with everyone, easily opening his life to another's gaze. Though, eventually, she comes to know that there is more to him than what he reveals to her; he never talks of his father, for example.

'And your father?' she asks once, hesitantly.

'He's in business. A travel agency.'

He is so dismissive that she is surprised to find later that the agency, called 'Carousel', is one of the biggest travel agencies in India. He does tell her, though, that his mother died when he was less than two years old and that he was sent to live with his grandparents after that. And though his father got married again, he never went back to live with him. But the most important thing about him, she learns, not from him, but from someone else: that he is regarded as one of the rising singers of the Kirana gharana, that his reputation is slowly but steadily growing. She comes to know this only by chance and, oddly enough, in Jyoti's house.

Mira comes to her on a Sunday afternoon, to ask her whether she can come home. 'Ma's aunt Kamalamavshi is here, she says she'd like to meet you. I believe she admired your father. Was he a writer? And it's a little difficult for her to climb the stairs. But if you're busy, it's okay.'

Aparna reassures her she's doing nothing, she will come. Jyoti greets her languidly, she looks low. Mira, Aparna notices, keeps a watchful eye on her mother and looks at the old lady, whose talk seems inexhaustible, with exasperation, but she controls herself and remains silent. Kamala, like many old people, goes straight into names and events, uncaring of whether her listener knows what or who she is talking about. After a few references to Gavi (he was so handsome, such a hero to Baby and me – Baba handsome? Baba a hero?) and the plays she and Baby saw, she goes on to speaking more about 'Baby', who, Aparna soon realizes, is Jyoti's mother. She and Kamala, the last two of a large family (we were five sisters, *panch kanya* we were called, and two brothers) were very close. Until she married Jyoti's father, that is. She goes on to tell Aparna that he came to 'see' her, Kamala, she was the proposed bride, not Baby. 'But he liked Baby better and made an offer for her. She saved me from that terrible man. But poor Baby, he ruined her life.'

'Kamalamavshi doesn't know words like tact and diplomacy. Here I am, my father's daughter, and look at the way she speaks of him.'

'You know you never got on with him, you got married early to get away from him.'

'Now you know all the family secrets, doc.'

Aparna is a little alarmed by Jyoti's peevishness; is something wrong? But Jyoti can't stop the old lady. She goes on to tell Aparna that her two brothers, twins, are doctors, like their father was. 'You're a doctor yourself, you must have heard of them? Dr Ram Kirtane and Dr Laxman Kirtane? Rambhau was a physician and Laxmandada is a surgeon.'

'Kamalamavshi, she's too young to know them,' Jyoti demurs, more gently now, as if aware she has not been very kind to her aunt. 'How can she have had anything to do with them? They're of a much earlier generation.'

'But everyone knows them. And Laxmandada had so many students.'

Aparna finds her attention wandering as Kamala goes on to speak of their mother's illness and how anxious she was to get her two youngest girls married. Of how, after Baby's marriage was settled, she had no peace until Kamala's marriage too was fixed. And then she hears Jyoti and Kamala speaking of Laxman's 85th birthday. 'What's happened to the music programme, Kamalamavshi? Have you found someone to sing that evening?' Jyoti asks.

'Nahi ga, they haven't got anyone still. The other day someone was talking about a young man who sang in Dr Bhagat's house. He was good, they said. But no one knows him, they can't even remember his name.'

'Shree Hari Pandit?' Aparna interrupts her.

'You know him?'

'Yes.'

'Just look at that now. Such a coincidence. Do you have his number? Give it to Mira. Someone will ring him up.'

But it is Aparna who gets a call from a man who introduces himself as Dr Jayant Kirtane, Dr Laxman Kirtane's grandson. She gives him Hari's number, but the man suggests she talk to Hari first, find out whether he is free, and then he will talk to him.

She rings Hari at night. His voice comes to her strong and joyful.

'Do you know this is the first time?'

'First time what?'

'That you have rung me. Each time it's I who ring you. There must be a reason, otherwise you wouldn't have called me.'

She tells him about the music programme. Suddenly he becomes professional and says, 'Ask them to call me. There's no need to trouble you.'

'Dr Kirtane said he will call you.'

'Dr Kirtane?'

'Jayant Kirtane. One of the family is my patient.'

'I'll do it, not a problem. One more private baithak.' There is a tiny pause, as if he is sighing. 'I'm a little tired of them, but I can't turn anything down anything at this stage. And this one comes from you. How can I refuse? I'll say yes yes yes.'

'One yes is enough.'

'Not when the invitation comes through you.' Once again she has a sense of a force she cannot control. Then he adds, 'Such a coincidence.'

Kamala had said the same thing. 'Yogayog' she had called it. Aparna had wondered then that, even at her age Kamala could still find life's twists and turns intriguing. Coincidence, she had said. But if you think that everything has been plotted and planned, there can be no coincidences; what you think is a coincidence is a part of the scheme. Her father's words. She herself had been naïve enough to believe in the marvel of coincidences when, on her first day in the hospital in the US, she had met the man who had been in her college, a few years ahead, so popular there was no one who did not know him. No girl who didn't fall for him. What a coincidence, she had thought. Homesick, still smarting from the things that had happened to her – the death of her mother, her alienation from her father – she had been ready to fall in love with someone. She had gone to him and said, 'Do you remember me? We were in the same college.' And so…

No, she no longer believes in coincidences. Things happen, but it's what we make of them that matters, she thinks. That was a disaster, I don't want any more disasters, no, never!

'Are you coming for the music?' he asks.

'If I am invited, I will.'

In fact she is invited by the great man himself, Dr Laxman Kirtane, Dr LK as he is called in his professional life, a legend among surgeons, as she now comes to know.

We are five sisters and two brothers, Kamala had said. Aparna, when she gets to Dr Kirtane's house, is overcome by the number of people. And everyone there, it seems, is family. There's a subdued buzz of sounds in the house, the smell of flowers and of food (there was a puja and a lunch in the morning), and an aura of wealth, wealth which has been with the family for so long that it is taken casually and easily. Overcome by being among so many unknown people, she stands a little lost, wondering whom to look for, when a man of about her age detaches himself from a group and comes to her.

'Dr Dandekar?'

'Yes.'

'I'm Jayant Kirtane. Thank you for coming. And for helping us find a singer. Please come and meet my grandfather.'

He's an orthopaedic surgeon, he tells her, and as the evening goes on and she meets more people, she realizes that it's a doctor's family, that they have almost all the specialities among them. The 'birthday boy', as the younger generation irreverently calls Dr LK, is sitting in state, cherubic, a halo of white hair round his face. He speaks to her of her father, he did something remarkable to Marathi theatre at the time, he says; he speaks of Dr Bhagat, his student (she realizes that many of the prominent surgeons are his students); of the cancer hospital where she's working; and then lets her go. Mira takes her around and introduces her to her mother's uncles and aunts, her mother's cousins. She feels as if the people in the pictures in her house have walked out of there, have come alive. It's an eclectic crowd. People have come together for this occasion from all over the world. Though the younger crowd speaks English, the brothers and sisters speak to each other only in Marathi. Appellations fly about the place – ajji, ajoba, kaka, kaki, mama, mami, atya. Obviously they believe in defining a relationship clearly; no 'uncles' and 'aunties' here. The older women are all dressed in the traditional nine-yards sari and the older men in dhoti and kurta – a planned effort, clearly. But the younger generation has gone its own way, wearing all kinds of clothes, even jeans. Mira is wearing a long skirt that trails behind her like a train with a

T shirt on top. Aparna watches a very young girl with very short hair, like Jyoti's when she began her chemo (but, God forbid, not for the same reason!) with a stud in her nose and a very short top that plunges at the neckline, above which is the face of innocence. She remembers her own mother's rules about clothes, about not revealing any part of her body. 'You should wear a burqa, the kind which covers everything but the eyes. Only then your mother will be happy,' her father said. The girl, who exudes a sophistication beyond her years, sees Aparna staring, gives her a tremulous smile and Aparna thinks, Why, she is only a child!

The music is to take place in a large community hall on the top floor. When Mira takes her to the place, Hari and his accompanists are already seated on the slightly raised dais. Hari is bending over his accompanist's taanpura, his ears cocked to getting the right tone. As if something has alerted him to her presence, he suddenly turns round, sees her and smiles. Not the polite meaningless smile of an acquaintance, but the full-bodied, full-blooded smile of a lover. Her heart suddenly starts thudding in her chest (I must see a cardiologist!), he doesn't believe in concealing his feelings, she thinks. And then – he's going too fast, what am I going to do? She smiles back, no more than a polite smile, she hopes, and takes her seat. He goes back to his taanpura tuning, then has a brief conversation with the tabalji. In a while, a young man goes to Hari, bends down and says something to him. Hari nods. There is a sudden hush in the hall. The man straightens and begins to speak. While he introduces Shree Hari and his team, Hari sits in the padmasana pose, cross-legged, erect, hands lying in his lap, palms upwards. Even after the introduction is complete, he continues to sit in the same pose, eyes closed now, as if he is meditating, taking a journey into himself. He is beautiful, Aparna thinks, he was born for this, so that he could sing. And then chides herself, don't be stupid.

He opens his eyes and with a deep bow and a namaste to

Laxman he announces, 'I will begin with the raaga Malkauns – Doctor saheb's favourite, I am told.' There is a distinct loud 'Wah!' from Laxman. Then Hari begins, in a low deep voice, so deep that it seems to be coming out of the great depths he had gone into a little while back. The alaap is almost tentative, his voice opening up slowly, like the Brahma Kamal flower, opening petal by petal, letting his music waft into the audience the same way the flower releases its heavenly fragrance. And then, suddenly, his voice emerges with a tremendous force, like a clap of thunder, and she realizes its splendour and strength.

Aparna listens, conscious of nothing but the man and his music, the man who himself is aware of nothing but his accompanists and his music. Hari's singing reminds her of a surgeon at work, a precise meticulous search for the place he has to get to, finally getting there with marvellous skill and finesse. The tabla and harmonium players, the taanpura accompanist – they are like assistants and theatre sisters, giving him what he wants, responding to his wordless demands with the right instruments. When he comes to the end of the first raaga, the major one, she gets her breath back. She remembers her father then, remembers his love of music, the radio always tuned to music, the tapes he played whenever he was at home, she remembers him shaving as he listened, humming along with the music and suddenly pausing, his razor poised in the air, calling out to her mother, 'Sulu, Sulu, come and listen to this.'

And her mother coming, though she was busy, she had a thousand things to do before going to work herself, her mother standing and listening with him. Then, with a shared smile, they would go back, he to his shaving and she to her work in the kitchen. She remembers her father occasionally singing – his voice was not good, but he sang fairly well for an amateur – and saying to her mother, 'Sulu, I must write a musical play one day. I have the music and I have the words, I just need to bring them together.'

As she listens, the past seems to merge with the present, the years between disappearing like a bubble touched by a finger. Then Hari asks the crowd, 'Shall I go on, or do you want a break?''

'Go on, go on.'

In the background they can hear the muted clatter of plates – the tables are being readied for dinner – but someone hushes them and there is silence again in which Shree Hari asks Dr Kirtane, 'Sir, what would you like me to sing now? Bhavgeet? Abhangs?'

'Natya sangeet,' a chorus of voices cries out. 'He loves natya sangeet.'

'I don't know many of those songs, but I have heard some. And if you can suggest any song and I know it, I will try my best.'

The young man goes to Shree Hari and whispers something. Shree Hari nods, speaks briefly to his harmonium player, who brings out a little book, flips through the pages, finds what he wants and shows it to Hari. Hari swiftly glances at the page and nods. He then tells his audience, 'Doctor saheb wants us to sing Bal Gandharva's *Nahi mi bolata.* If you will forgive me for trying such a great singer's song, I will begin with it.'

A much loved song, sung by a much loved singer during the glorious time of Marathi theatre. And, obviously, it has a special meaning for these people, for a ripple of laughter runs through the room when Hari announces the song. Laxman, aware of the younger people's ignorance, tells them, 'My mother used to sing this when she was angry with my father. It was like a signal... My poor father didn't know what to do.'

This time it is the harmonium that takes the lead, the man briskly getting into the heart of the song, without any prelude. Hari, his eyes closed, nods and at the right moment, the tabla player joins in, Hari following exactly on the next beat. They do it with such precision, and without any rehearsal, that Aparna marvels at them. After that comes another request, then another, songs of an earlier era, songs which were loved by an earlier generation. Women's songs, sung by a male actor, who so submerged himself in women's roles that he became a role model for the women of his time. Shree Hari ends with an abhang which reduces them to silence. Then it is over. Shree Hari comes down and touches Laxman's feet. 'May you achieve greatness, boy,' he says. 'You're only a few steps away from it, these are the tricky steps, be careful.'

Aparna does not catch Shree Hari's reply. She gets up with reluctance, but is now engaged in conversation by Mrinal Apte, the doctor who had come to the hospital when Jyoti was having her chemo. She meets an old classmate from college, then someone who was in medical college with her. There's a woman who identifies her as Taimavshi's niece, Anandi and I were in college together, she says. She speaks of how religiously she used to listen to the women's programme Anandi conducted on the radio in the afternoons. 'She was the first to introduce something more serious in those programmes: discussions, poetry readings, issues that mattered. Otherwise it used to be only cooking, recipes, beauty and all that. Our lives were supposed to centre round these. But Anandi very cleverly moved away.' Aparna treasures this, she stores it up to tell Taimavshi, she gets the woman's name and phone number. And there are many of the older generation who come and talk to her as Gavi's daughter…

Hari and his team pick up their instruments. They are ready to leave, steadily refusing the invitation to have dinner. Finally, at Laxman's urging, they have some shrikhand puri. Hari looks around for Aparna but she is in the midst of a crowd, having dinner.

Mira is to take Aparna home, but Aparna, reluctant to drag the girl away from a family gathering, tries to persuade her to stay back.

'I can't, doctor. I've left Ma alone for too long. I'd better come with you. I'll see if the driver is ready.'

In the car, they are silent. Then Mira asks, 'We're going to have a lot of visitors now. Everyone will want to come and see Ma. Is it okay, doctor?'

'As long as you don't tire her. And as long as her visitors are all right. You know her immunity is compromised.'

'Yes, doctor.' Silence again. Then suddenly she bursts out, 'I'm frightened, doctor. Do you think Ma will be able to make it?'

'So far so good, Mira. She is responding well to the chemo, so let's see. I am hopeful.'

'I'm scared, doctor. When Papa died, Prabhaajji was there for us. Now there will be just Tejas and me.'

'You have a large family.'

'It's not the same.'

'I know. But why are you even thinking of her not surviving? Cancer treatment has been revolutionized in the last few decades. There are so many new drugs, so many newer drugs are coming, the life expectancy of patients is so much more now than it ever used to be.'

Yet, it's always one step forward, two steps backward, she thinks. The disease is just too wily, too tenacious, too protean. But she does not say these things to the girl beside her. Besides, Mira is following the train of her own thoughts.

'It's not fair, doctor, it's not fair. Why do these things have to happen to us? First my grandfather died…'

'He must have been old.'

'No, he was not that old. Then my Papa – he was so young.'

'What happened?'

'He was returning home from Pune, driving himself, when he met with an accident on the highway.'

'I'm sorry.'

'Then Prabhaajji. And now Mama…'

'Don't think too much, Mira. Just be cheerful and do all you can to help your mother. Which you are doing. And don't blurt out your fears to your mother. It's not good for her.'

'I never do that,' she says fiercely. 'I don't even let Tejas know how I'm feeling.'

By this time, Aparna has realized there is a problem with Tejas, Jyoti's son. He is rarely seen, even today he was not part of the family crowd. Or, perhaps he stayed behind so that Jyoti should not be alone.

'You are carrying a heavy burden, Mira. When I was in school, the nuns used to say that God gives burdens to those he loves. I used to get furious. I used to think – what kind of a god is he to make those he loves suffer! I would not want people I love to suffer.'

She thinks of her mother, but does not want to talk of her to this child, for it will confirm her fears that this illness can end only in death. In fact, she does not want to bring the word death into their conversation. Luckily Mira herself goes on to another track.

'Do you believe in prayer, doctor?' she asks.

'Not really. But perhaps it helps the person who prays, you feel you are doing something. Maybe it gives you courage as well.'

By the time she is ready for bed, there have already been two messages from Hari. After she gets into bed, he calls up.

'Did you like it?

'It was beautiful.'

'I sang for you, only for you.'

'You know I don't like this kind of talk. But thank you, you brought my father back to me.'

'I am glad I could do something for you.'

'Good night, Shree Hari Pandit.'

'Good night, Dr Aparna Dandekar.'

Why am I doing this? she asks herself yet again. I must stop encouraging him. I will not encourage him, she resolves, but she knows that when the time comes she will not be able to be hard and forbidding with him.

Aparna rings up Taimavshi when she finally signs the lease. 'My landlord is here, Jyoti's brother, Deepak. All the formalities are over, I'm safe here for two years.'

'That sounds good. But Bala,' she says, 'you shouldn't be paying so much rent when you have your own house waiting for you. You know your mother would have been so glad if you lived here, she bought this flat for you.'

It was Taimavshi who had persuaded her sister Sulu to buy the apartment next door when it was up for sale. 'Apu will never live in Chandrapur, you know that, Sulu. There's a greater chance of her living in Mumbai. Buy this, it'll prove useful to her.'

To tell Sulu to do something for Aparna was to make sure Sulu would do it. She bought the apartment, though it almost wiped out her savings; it was for Aparna. Sulu had never imagined that she would herself find it useful one day, that she would spend her last days in the place and die in it.

'This place is just a few minutes from the hospital, Taimavshi. Think of the time and energy I'll save.'

'That's true, Apu. And it's a good place, I liked it. I hope you will be happy there. I also hope you consulted a lawyer before you signed the lease.'

Why would I? she wants to ask, but desists. Taimavshi has not met Jyoti or Deepak. Aparna has, and she knows that they are not people you can mistrust. Deepak has come on a visit both to be with his sister and to complete the formalities of the lease. Their meeting has been businesslike and brief. But he rings her in the hospital one day, saying, 'I would like to meet you, doctor. What time can I come to the hospital?'

'Is it about Jyoti's health?'

'That's one of the things. But there's something else as well.'

'Then we'll meet at home. I'm rather stretched for time here. Come after seven. You'll know when I'm back.'

The first question he asks is, 'How do you think Jo is doing, doctor?'

She knows it must have been a shock for him to see his sister the way she is, totally bald, emaciated, trying hard and pushing herself, yet finding it difficult to be active.

'So far so good. There's nothing very alarming about her response to the chemotherapy.'

'Right now she's suffering from sores in her mouth, it's very painful.'

'That's part of her immunological vulnerability. Once the chemo is over, she'll pick up.'

'She doesn't eat, doctor.'

'I know, Mira told me.'

'Mira gets so agitated, she's ready to shove the food down her throat. I wish she would…' He pauses and goes on, 'But let me not waste your time over these trifles. I'll get to the point.'

He's come to talk about the money for Jyoti's treatment. He knows the treatment is expensive, the cost of the drugs exorbitant. 'Jo is very conscious of the amount of money they are spending, she's unhappy about it. The money should be for the kids, she says, they have all their lives ahead of them. Mira and she argue about it all the time,' he tells her. 'So Mira and I have agreed that the rent from this house should be used for Jo's treatment. The money will be lying in the bank here anyway. If more is needed,

Mira will come to me. On no account is her treatment to suffer because of money. Can you make sure of that?'

'I have very little to do with money and payments, you know that's another department altogether, but tell Mira to come to me if there's a problem. I will see that there is never any pause in the treatment.'

Aparna is a little surprised by this talk of money. She had imagined that money was no problem for Jyoti. After seeing Jyoti's family, her mother's family, rather, she was even more convinced about it. There was no ostentatious show of wealth, but the air of ease and casual elegance about them showed they didn't have to think of money. Jyoti has the same air of confidence and ease that she saw in the family, something that comes from always having enough money. But she can understand Jyoti, for she remembers her mother's anxiety. 'Don't spend money on me,' she said. 'It's of no use, it's like throwing it down the drain. We all know how it will end. Keep the money for Apu's future.'

'Yes, of course, I'll never be able to earn for myself, I'll never be able to support myself, I'll live all my life on your hard-earned money! What's wrong with you, Aai?'

How hard she worked, both in the bank and at home. Waking early to make breakfast, the lunch boxes for herself and for Aparna (Baba, if she gave him lunch, forgot to eat it, brought the box back with the food uneaten, or often didn't bring it back at all), getting Aparna ready, plaiting her long hair, making sure that her school uniform had been ironed the previous night, leaving home after breakfast, with Aparna pillion riding on her scooter, so that she could drop her at her school. Shopping on the way back in the evening, tidying the house, preparing the evening meal. And always thoughts of Aparna – she should go to the best school in Chandrapur, the convent school, the best college later, she should achieve her dream of becoming a doctor. 'She's doing all this,' Baba would joke, 'so that you will take care of us in our old age.'

Not that they were short of money, but Sulu was always conscious that she had to be thrifty, that Aparna should have enough; she was constantly thinking of Aparna's future. Gaja was different, he did not worry about her as much. 'She's a bright girl,' he told Sulu. 'She will do well, we don't have to buy a medical seat for her, you can be sure of that.'

Though he had once confessed to Aparna, 'I wish I wrote novels instead of plays, I'd make some money from my writing then. If I earned more, I'd keep Sulu in comfort, make sure she didn't work so hard. But I write plays – who buys books of plays? And if they perform, they don't give the writer the royalty, they think, hey, who is he, anyway? The haramkhors wriggle out of it somehow. Or they don't let you know about it at all.'

Baba had a huge repertoire of abuses, and when he spoke about theatre groups who didn't pay him his royalty, or about publishers who dodged payments, or his college administration, he used so many expletives, not even conscious of what he was doing, that Sulu had to warn him, 'The child is here, you can't use these words in her presence.'

'Apu? Are you listening? Don't. Be a good girl and cover your ears.'

'Apu, cover your ears' became a kind of announcement that he was angry and that he would be using foul language. He knew that she didn't really shut out hearing, because he once told her, away from Sulu's presence, 'You have to let these words in one ear and out of the other. You are never to use these words, understand? I don't want any foul words in your sweet mouth.'

I didn't do anything for him, Aparna thinks. Sulu, yes, she looked after her in her last days, in fact, she gave up college for six months at the end. But I did nothing for Baba, she thinks, the father who loved her so extravagantly. She has never seen a father, no, not in all her life, so demonstrative in his love for his daughter as her Baba was.

Now she tells Deepak, 'Your sister is lucky in her family, specially in her brother.'

'Don't say that. Jo is…' He hesitates and then says, 'It's not just me, even Mel, my wife, loves Jo, although we're now divorced. In face she's coming here next month, and our son Jai after that. We're taking turns so that Jo will have someone with her over an extended period and Saguna and Mira won't have three guests at a time to struggle with.'

How odd it is, Aparna thinks yet again, that none of them speak of Tejas. She's seen him only very occasionally, glimpsed him, rather, a hooded and cowled figure running across the road in the early morning, Mira just a little behind him, giving the feeling of protecting him. Brother and sister. Aparna has never regretted not having a sibling, it was wonderful to have all her parents' attention and love for herself. But since their death, she has felt a gap in her life. To some extent Madhu has been able to fill the gap. And so, when Madhu rings up Aparna asking her to come home, Aparna immediately agrees. Aparna is in a very confused state. She has always taken her own decisions, about her marriage, her divorce, her jobs. But this time…

She knows that she can no longer deceive herself, she can no longer ignore the fact that Hari is steadily pursuing her. No words of love have been spoken between them, but it is clear he is serious. He has been out of town for a week now, working for a programme with his guruji, and his messages have been coming so thick and fast she wonders when he has the time to type them out. She once attended a wedding in which one of the rituals had five married women passing a thread around the couple, unspooling it as they passed it from hand to hand, finally encircling the couple in a complete circle. She feels if these messages are encircling her in the same way.

'Come on Saturday and stay the night,' Madhu says. 'Abbas has gone to Delhi for some work. I'm alone.'

'As if you can ever be alone, Madhu.'

'You will be my excuse for shaking off everyone else. You have to come.'

Madhu's is a welcoming house. Ever since they demolished the family bungalow and got three apartments in a high-rise building built on the site, the crowd and the chaos have moved to Abbas's eldest sister's house; nevertheless it's unusual to find only Madhu at home. No one else, not even a visitor or a protégé of Madhu's.

'Now talk,' Madhu commands her after dinner. 'What is it?'

'Shree Hari Pandit.'

'Who's that? And what about him?'

'He a singer, Hindustani classical…'

'Oh yes, I've heard someone mention him.'

'Soon everyone will know his name.'

'Oho, it's like that, is it! Where did you meet him?'

Aparna tells her about their meetings. When she's done, Madhu asks, 'So have you come for my blessings?'

'Don't jump to conclusions, Madhu. There's nothing like that.'

'Like what?'

'I mean – yes, he's attracted to me…'

'And you?'

'I…well, I…I'm attracted to him as well.'

'Then what's the problem, silly. Boy loves girl, girl loves boy – happy ending.'

'We're not boy and girl. That's the problem.'

'But if you love each other, why should your age – and for god's sake, don't talk as if you're fifty – be a problem?'

'I don't know, Madhu, I really don't know. I'm totally confused.'

'All right, let's start at the beginning. Tell me about him, this Hari Pandit.'

'Shree Hari Pandit. His name is Shree Hari.'

'And?'

'He's a Hindustani classical singer.'

'You already told me that.'

'He belongs to the Kirana gharana.'

'Already deep into music, are we?'

'But Madhu, that he is a singer is the main thing about him. That's his life. He was born with music in his genes, he grew up with music in his ears.'

'Anything else?'

'He was brought up by his grandparents, he idolizes them, he's always talking of his ajji and ajoba. His grandfather was his first guru, he learnt Tukaram's bhajans and the Geet Ramayan from him…' Madhu makes an awed face. 'See? I told you it's not so simple. He is old-fashioned. He calls me *tumhi*, at least he used to until recently, he speaks of older people as *aapan*, he speaks beautiful Marathi – I could listen to him all day, both the language and the voice are so wonderful…'

'Oh Apu, you are besotted.'

Aparna, ignoring her, goes on, 'And he speaks English with a Marathi accent. He says vherry vherry nice.'

'Are you judging him by the way he speaks English?'

'What do you mean, Madhu? I love the way he speaks it.'

'You're a gone case. And is he in love with you?'

'He's a more gone case than I am. He is open about it, he doesn't try to hide it.'

'In which case, children, you have my blessings.'

'Madhu, don't!'

'What is it, Apu?' Madhu is serious now. 'What's the problem?'

'I'm frightened, Madhu. What if it doesn't work?'

'Why won't it work?'

'I don't know. Look at my parents. Look at me. If it doesn't work this time, I won't survive, I promise you, Madhu, I won't survive.'

'Apu…'

'If people can change, the way my parents did… I never imagined Aai would walk out on Baba, or that Baba would do what he did.'

'It's true, Apu, people do change, equations between people change, relationships change. But change doesn't always mean the end of a relationship. We shift, we move on, we take in the changes.'

'But look at Aai and Baba, the way she devoted her life to him.'

'I admired her. You know, for a long time I never knew that she wrote out his manuscripts.'

Madhu learned this from her mother, who in the outpouring of grief after her sister's death, told her that Sulu sat up nights, painstakingly converting his messy manuscript into a tidy one. Only she could read his terrible handwriting.

'And Baba too, the moment he came home it was – Sulu, where are you? Sulu this and Sulu that.'

'But that was them, Apu. And this is you and your Shree Hari.'

'That's the problem – he being what he is and I being what I am. He talks about his grandparents and I think – maybe he expects his wife to be like his grandmother, calling her husband "Aho" serving and looking after him all day, and wearing a mangalsutra all the time.'

Madhu is laughing. 'And glass and gold bangles and silver toe rings. You're mad. If he loves you and he knows you, why would he expect you to be like that? He knows you are a career woman.'

'Okay, not exactly like that. But a proper wife.'

'And god knows what that is! We just have to muddle along, Apu, because we need each other and we have to put up with the entire person. You can't get only what you like in any person. Go ahead and marry him, woman.'

'He hasn't asked me.'

'Then *you* ask him. Or start sleeping with him.'

'He will never do that.'

'Seduce him, then. You don't know how attractive you are, Apu. It's all Sulumavshi's fault. For some reason she was frightened of your good looks and tried to make you look as plain as possible. Remember those two tight plaits of yours?'

'I didn't need anyone to tell me about my looks. The mirror tells me the truth.'

'Sulumavshi must have cursed the mirror.'

'Don't be mean about my mother.'

'I'm not. It's just that she loved you so much, she was terrified your beauty would make you vulnerable. Anyway, Apu, marry him. Love is worth taking a risk for. And forget about your marriage. Anyone can make a mistake once.'

'If once, why not twice? I'm frightened.'

Aparna is aware that things are not in her control, that Hari is taking them inexorably to the point from where she may not be able to return. When he gets back from Pune, there is a difference in his tone, his behaviour. Once they quarrel and she thinks, But this is like a lover's spat! However did we get to this point? When did we become so intimate as to quarrel?

The spat had been about an evening when he came to meet her and, after waiting for a long time, had rung her up to find out that she was out with some friends.

'I didn't know you were coming. Am I supposed to wait at home every day on the chance that you might come? You expect too much of me.'

'That's the worst thing you have said to me so far.' He sees her face and hastily goes on, 'I'm sorry, Aparna, but when I get into this state, when I feel I must meet you, I don't think straight.'

'Hari,' she says more gently, 'don't you think you're going too fast? We don't know each other well enough. I don't even know where you live.'

'What do you want to know about me? Ask me and I'll tell you. I can give you my grandfather's name, my gotra, my nakshatra, I can tell you how much I earn each month, how much money I have in the bank. If you want, I can put all the information, including my school and college achievements, on paper and give it to you. Or to your Taimavshi, if you'd prefer that.'

'Don't be ridiculous. You know that's not what I meant. And do you know I'm older than you?'

'Six months.' Neither of them is in the mood to smile at the thought of the research the other has done. 'You look ten years younger. And you're a very stubborn woman. But I'm just as stubborn, Dr Dandekar. I won't let you go. Watch out! And the truth is, Aparna, you're the reserved and secretive one. You keep things to yourself.'

'See! You already have a problem with me.'

He smacks his forehead with the palm of his hand. 'What shall I do with this woman?'

At which point she had wondered – how did we get here? I thought I had kept my distance.

Perhaps it's in response to her casual remark that she does not know where he lives, that he invites her to his home one Sunday morning. He has his students on Sunday, 'but the class gets over by ten. Come a little after that.'

It's a modest apartment block. While she is waiting for the lift to descend, she hears footsteps clattering down the stairs. Young voices. When they come to her level, she guesses that they are his students, rushing off, poor things, to the next thing on their Sunday schedule. When she reaches his apartment, she sees that the door is open. He is in the hall, putting away a taanpura in a corner, while tidying the rucked carpet, a blue and red striped one, with his feet. This, obviously, is the place where he conducts his classes. There is a sofa, two cane chairs, two plastic ones and a central cane table at the other end of the hall. He sees her and gives her his joyous open smile. 'Aparna…'

'Right on time. I met your students as they were leaving.'

He makes a face. 'They're so eager to get out.'

'No good?'

'Most come because their parents want them to learn music, either to know about "our culture" – you know how people are about that – or because the parents themselves had musical ambitions at one time. Many of them come to be trained for the talent shows, they hope to have a music producer hear them and give them a break as playback singers for films. Once they learn the basics, the *sa re ga ma*, they and their parents think they're ready. Musical geniuses.'

'Madhu says it's the same in the dancing world. Everyone is looking towards the talent shows.'

'Anyway, I earn a regular income, thanks to them. Will you have tea?'

He goes inside to make it, leaving her in the hall, telling her he needs no help. 'You sit and read the paper,' he says. When he comes out with the tea, she is looking around with curiosity. 'What are you looking at?' he asks her.

'The way you live.'

'A very ordinary, less than middle-class life. I haven't added sugar. I know you doctors are careful.'

'It's not about being a doctor. It's about being a woman and afraid to put on weight.'

'Put on weight! You need a few more kilos. And, Aparna, however poor this seems to you, this is my own house.'

'I never said it was poor.'

'I saw your face. But yes, it's mine. I sold my grandfather's house which he left me when he died and this is all I could get for what I got from the sale.'

'I was born and brought up in Chandrapur. In a small house. It was not a palace.'

'But when it's a man, it makes a difference. I remember the father of a girl came to see me once, someone had suggested me as a possible groom for his daughter. After he saw my house, he was so confused he didn't know what to say to me.'

Later, much later, she will learn from his brother Krishna that his father had offered to buy him an apartment in Bombay, but Hari had refused. By that time she will have already come to know about his difficult relationship with his father. He rarely speaks of him, and his stepmother, Krishna's mother, he never refers to at all.

'I'm not considered a good match,' he is going on. 'I am a very ordinary man living a very ordinary life.'

Your voice is extraordinary, she wants to say, you are extraordinary. But before she can speak, he adds, 'It doesn't matter to me. But what *you* think matters to me. Music was the only thing in my life. Now there's you. But you won't allow me space in your life, you are afraid of my coming closer to you. Is it because I'm not as well educated as you are? Because I went to an ordinary Marathi school, not to a convent school? Because I don't have much money? Because I live this way? I can't change other things, Aparna, but I promise you I will make my mark in the music world one day. I know I will. And I will never earn my living any other way. My father forced me to graduate. My Ajoba agreed with him, so I did a B.Com. I worked in a bank after I graduated, because my father said I should be able to earn a living. He said there is no guarantee music would give me a living. Ajoba said I had to respect my father's wishes. So I worked in a bank for two years. Those were the two worst years of my life.'

Is this a proposal of marriage?, she wonders.

'See, Aparna, I'm not concealing anything from you. I'm only a poor ambitious man, grandson of a poor Brahmin schoolteacher.'

'And I'm the granddaughter of a maharaja. And my father was the President of India.'

'Don't joke.'

'I'm not joking. If you want the truth, my grandfather was a clerk in the Railways and my father a college teacher in a small town. So…?'

'Aparna, I'm serious. I want you, I want to marry you.'

Now he's said it. But she does not know what to say, how to respond.

'Aparna, say something. Say anything.'

'Hari,' she clears her throat, 'I can't say anything right now. Give me time, give me some time. Please.'

'Okay. Am I allowed to ring you, to send you messages?'

'Hari, please!''

'Just asking. I don't want to make any mistakes.'

'Don't be angry with me, Hari.'

His face clears. 'No, Aparna, I'm not angry with you. I can never be angry with you.' He adds with a touch of sadness, 'I've never felt this way about anyone before. What have you done to me, Aparna?'

'No girls?' she asks, trying to bring their conversation to a lighter level.

'Nothing serious.'

'I don't believe you.'

He shrugs as if to say, it's up to you. She has a feeling he might say something more, but he doesn't. She leaves it at that.

A blonde woman sitting by Jyoti smiles at Aparna. 'I'm Melinda,' she says, which Aparna has already guessed. Jyoti opens her eyes and adds, 'My brother's ex-wife.'

'I know.'

Jyoti has closed her eyes again and does not respond. 'I can't take any more of this, doctor,' she had said to Aparna the last time. But here she is again going through it. Fortunately it's the last session. (But, who knows?) Aparna wonders for the nth time when they will find a better way of dealing with this disease, when they will stop pumping toxic drugs into patients. We tell them to put up with it, to endure the ravages of the drugs on their bodies, we try to minimize the ghastly reactions they suffer, and they go through it because their lives are at stake. But no one should have to go through what they do.

A little later Mira comes to her to tell her they're leaving.

'All done? All the paper work?'

'Yes, doctor.'

'The follow-up schedule?'

'Yes, doctor, I got that. We're waiting for Ma to finish talking to her friends here. And doctor, Mel auntie wants to know whether she can come and see you in the evening.'

As Aparna hesitates, Mira adds, 'She wants some photographs from your place.'

'Yes, of course, she can come. You'll know when I'm home.'

Melinda rings the bell a while after Aparna's return. 'I'm truly sorry for troubling you, Dr Dandekar,' she says as soon as Aparna opens the door. She pronounces the name correctly.

'Why? They're your photographs, this is your house…'

'Was. Not any longer. And we scarcely stayed here when we came to visit Jo. We left our bags here, that's all. I won't take up much of your time, just pick out a few pictures – Deep wants one or two, and I want to give Jai, our son, some of them.'

She is true to her word, quickly makes a selection and is ready to leave, when she turns back and asks the question Aparna does not want to answer. 'Doctor, how is Jo doing?'

'Good, as you can see. Now that the chemo is over, she'll improve, there will be a remission.'

'Amen to that. You can't imagine what a blow this has been to all of us. The family has gone through a great deal…' She is silent. 'Well, thank you for letting me come and take these pictures. I'm astonished you let them be here.'

'I have very few pictures of my own. I don't have a family – not like this one.'

'Overwhelming, aren't they? When I came here for the first time after marrying Deep, I was bewildered, dazed almost – there were so many people, mamas and mamis, mavshis and kakas… Lord, it was crazy. And just as I was getting to identify them, our marriage was over. We are no longer together, I'm sure you know that?'

'Yes, I do.'

'Well, I must go. Thank you, doctor, for your courtesy. Sorry to have taken up so much of your time.'

It doesn't matter, Aparna thinks, because Hari is not in town; the evenings are her own. He has gone to his guruji for his monthly visit and from there he is to go to Sangli for a programme. But before he left, he gave her a CD of his programme in the Kirtane home, which becomes a substitute for his company. He had come with two CDs, one for her and one for Jyoti. 'Dr Kirtane wanted me to give it to Jyotitai since she couldn't come that day.'

The day after Melinda leaves, Aparna goes to visit Jyoti with the CD. Jyoti opens the door herself. 'I'm alone,' she says in response to Aparna's look of surprise. 'But come in. I haven't had a chance to talk to you. Is everything all right? In the apartment, I mean.'

'Yes. Mira has been very helpful. Mira and Saguna.'

'I'm glad.' She takes the CD and says, 'Laxmanmama rang me up, he told me you'd be giving this to me. It's just like him to remember. He lost his wife last year. And his twin brother the year before. He doesn't show his loss, but I know something was scooped out of him, there's an emptiness in him. Anyway,' she shakes herself and goes on with a determinedly cheerful manner, 'Laxmanmama says it was a wonderful evening. He was very impressed by the young man you recommended.'

I didn't recommend him, Aparna wants to say, it was your aunt who spoke of him first. But Jyoti goes on, giving her no chance to speak, 'Laxmanmama says that once he finds his own style – the shadow of his guru still hovers over him – he'll be on his way to greatness.'

Impossible not to be pleased, impossible not to smile.

'Is he an old friend of yours?'

'No, I got to know him only a short while back.'

I must go, she thinks, before I give myself away. But Jyoti will not let her. 'Have a cup of tea with me,' she says.

'Do you have to make it yourself?'

'Why not? Didn't you tell me I need to go back to whatever my normal life was? And I am feeling better today.'

'Where's Saguna?'

'Gone shopping. I sent the kids away as well. I wanted to be alone. I haven't been alone since the diagnosis. Somebody has always been with me. I suppose I should be grateful, I am grateful, but I never knew what a luxury being alone is. Come and sit at the dining table while I make the tea. With milk and sugar?'

'Yes. Desi chai. Strong.' Aparna notices a book on the table, obviously something Jyoti was reading.

'You've been reading this?' she asks Jyoti when she returns with the tea.

'Yes. Everyone says I shouldn't. They say that reading about cancer is morbid, it will depress me.'

'It doesn't?'

'No. Help yourself to sugar. No, it doesn't depress me. For one thing, it's so well written, it reads like a story. For another, it's good for me to know what it is that has entered my body, my life. I've noticed that people are afraid even to say the word cancer. They say Big C, or the Crab or "my problem" – anything to avoid the word cancer. I thought if I know it better, the fear will disappear. And it's not just me and my problem, it's all humans, it's the scientists, it's the doctors constantly trying to find a cure.'

'Know your enemy, huh?'

'Exactly.' She laughs. 'Do you know, doc, how many of the words you doctors use are connected to warfare? To the army? Enemy, you just said. My report said my special enemy was *invasive.* You also say *infiltrating.* And there's *sentinel node.* I like that. I like to think of it saying to a malignant cell that's trying to enter, "Halt! Who goes there?" and stopping it from entering. And *adjuvant* therapy – that's so like adjutant.'

'Same thing.'

'Yes. And *cohort.*'

'What does that mean – in non-medical language?'

'It was a unit of the Roman army.'

'Oh! You remind me of my father. He was fascinated by words. But he was a writer.'

'I wanted to be a writer, I hoped to be one. I gave up that dream.'

'What happened?'

'It's a long story. No, it's a very short one. I realized I was no writer. But I was, I am, a good reader. There's much in this book I don't understand. Some of it I do. And I've understood this much, that this is a conflict in my body between the bad cells and the good cells. It's like all the fairy tales, all the stories in myths and fables – a battle between good and evil.'

'That's an interesting thought.'

'Yes, and what it proves is that our idea that good always wins is in the end wrong. You know, the myth that a good fairy who comes to undo the curse of the bad fairy. In fact, it's the bad cells which ultimately win, don't they, by going wild and growing all over the place? This book calls them rebels and outlaws who don't follow the rules, the laws of nature. They go berserk. And ultimately, unlike in the stories, it's they who win.'

'Not always and not easily.'

'But they do. All that you doctors do for your patients is to buy them some time. Death is waiting patiently round the corner.'

'So it is for all of us. The only difference is between the knowing and the not-knowing.'

'Don't give me that bullshit, doc. Pardon my language, but there's a world of difference between knowing and the certainty of it. And how can you say *only difference* doc? The difference between knowing and not-knowing is the biggest difference there is in the world. The way I thought about my life before I was told I had cancer and the way I think of it now – there's no comparison! Once the knowledge enters you, it becomes a part of you. You go to bed with it and you wake up with it.'

'Jyoti, you're saying things that are beyond me. I only know that today patients are expected to do much better than they did before and for some cancers there's the certainty of survival…'

'Not for mine, not for TNBC.'

'It will come.'

'It will be too late for me.'

'But even today there are TNBC patients who survive ten years, fifteen years. And there are those who think of each day as a gift, each day matters.'

'Sorry, doc, I get carried away. As long as the treatment was on, I thought of nothing else but coping with it. I've always been fighting the demons inside me, this was the same thing, only this time the demons came in a new avatar. All my energy was directed to fighting them. Now I have time to think and I've begun brooding over that most pointless question of all – why me? Why do my children have to go through this? They have already lost a parent…'

'Jyoti, don't…'

'Be positive, huh?'

'Absolutely. Be positive. And don't ask yourself questions for which there are no answers. And I promise you one thing – they're constantly getting newer and better drugs, we have a much better understanding of the disease now – look at this book – and I'm confident that in time we will be able to do what we really need to do, which is to tackle, to destroy the malignant cells without harming the good cells.'

'I like your confidence, doc.'

I need it, Aparna wants to say, but doesn't.

When she goes home, Aparna thinks of how rare it is for her to talk so openly to a patient, to discuss with her her own disease, her mortality, the inadequacy of Aparna's profession. We have no time to sit with each patient and talk, Aparna has often told herself, we have no interest in the patient's story. She is surprised that she has gone this far with Jyoti. How did it happen? She does not realize, or if she does, she puts the thought away, that by letting Hari enter her life and her thoughts, by letting emotions, which she had been so wary of, take her over, she has become open to other people's feelings and emotions. The distance she has maintained between herself and others since her father's death, since her divorce, seems to have dissolved.

At night, after dinner, Aparna inserts Hari's CD into the player. She enjoys listening by herself, without the distraction of people talking or of their movements. Hari's voice floods the room. Pure and strong. There's nothing else, only his voice and her. Singer and listener. Voice and ear. Like the gopurams of South Indian temples, his voice soars, seems to touch the skies. She knows she can no longer pretend to herself: she *has* entered the world of emotions she had wanted to stay out of. Thank god I live alone, she thinks. Anyone would wonder why I listen to this one CD over and over again. Do these things wear out?

Should I get a copy made? Should I ask Hari to do it for me? No, I can't let him know my weakness, I would be embarrassed to let him know what his music means to me. She can't fool herself, though. It's not just the music; it's the man. She wants to see him, to have his physical presence with her. What have I got myself into? she asks herself. Her father comes often to her mind now. She had raged against him for what he did to her mother, she had hated him for what he did to their family. She has often asked herself – knowing Sulu as he did, knowing her as well as he did, how did he take that terrible risk of losing her? Or, perhaps, the truth is that he could not help himself, perhaps it was out of his hands. Does love make us strangers to ourselves so that we don't understand what we are doing and why? I never imagined I would get into the state I am in now. That I would once again succumb so wholly to my feelings for a man. She thought she had gone through it once and that it was over for her. That she had acquired immunity, as if love is like the measles. Yet here she is, behaving like an adolescent fool, ready to fall into his arms when she opens the door early in the morning and finds Hari at her door. She controls herself, uncomfortably aware that she must have revealed her feelings to him in that first moment.

'When did you return?' she asks, hoping she sounds casual. Indifferent.

'Last night. I wanted to come right away, but I thought you would be sleeping. Aparna, can you give me a cup of tea? I came to you the moment I woke up, without even having a cup of tea.'

'Sure. Sit down, I'll get it.'

Thank god she has brushed her teeth, she thinks thank god her hair is neat and tidy. Should she do something to her face? Is it greasy from last night's cream? She splashes cold water on her face and rubs it dry before going out with the tea. He is sitting at the table, drumming on it with his fingers, as he usually does.

'Did you miss me?' he asks.

'Yes.' She can't help herself, the word comes out before she is aware that she has said it. His face flares into a fierce joy.

'Hari, I haven't added any sugar. Help yourself.'

'Do you know, Aparna, you are the only one who calls me Hari?'

'What do the others call you?'

'My grandparents called me Bal,' he tells her, making a face that implies the infantile name was not to his liking. 'My brother Krishna calls me Dada. My friends call me Shree. Hari is special. It's yours.'

'Shree Hari. And is Krishna Shree Krishna?'

'Yes, of course. Our grandparents named both of us. So that, they said, when we call out to you we'll have god's name on our lips. Ha! You should have heard Ajji call us by our names when we'd done something wrong! Even god would have been scared, the way she said our names.'

'Have your tea, Hari.'

'Yes.' He pulls the cup towards him, but before drinking, he picks up her hand and kisses her palm, a gesture so totally unexpected – and from him! – that a tremor goes through her.

'Thank you, Aparna.'

'For what?'

'For telling me you missed me.'

'Yes, but you have to drink your tea and go. I have to get ready and leave in…' she looks at the time, '…forty-five minutes.'

'When can we meet? In the evening?'

'I'm not sure. Call me after six.'

'Shall I come to the hospital? Or here?'

The questions 'when?' and 'where?' so occupy Aparna that she realizes only later that she has agreed to meet him. From then on, it becomes a regular matter, their meeting in the evenings when she can get away early and he is free. They walk from her home to the sea front, his strides so long that he has to stop every now and then when he finds her lagging. They sit on the sea wall, facing the sea, their legs folded under them and it seems that the sea makes him talk of things he has not spoken of until then, like his long-dead mother.

'Both my ajji and my mother were from the Konkan, they were both brought up near the sea. In fact, they came from the same village. My ajji and my mother's mother were great friends, that's how the marriage happened. Ajji took me to their village every summer, during the vacations. She thought I should get to know my mother's family. After Ajji died, it came to an end.'

He speaks of his brother (stepbrother, she knows, but he always says brother) Krishna, who is working with their father in the travel agency business. She sees the pride on his face when he tells her it is Krishna who has made the agency as big as it is now. Their father began by organizing yatras, the only reason why people travelled earlier; now it's 'customized tours and global holidays', he tells her.

They begin to learn about each other's professions. Cancer doctor, he called her, until she corrected him and told him she was a medical oncologist. He is awed by her work, by the calm authority she exudes among her patients, by the way her patients look up to her. He thinks she is the boss. 'Who, me? No way. Dr Patel is my boss, but he is on leave, right now he's sick.' It makes no difference to him, she is still for him a figure of authority in her profession. When they go out together, there is an air of effervescent excitement about him, which she finds incredibly touching. If they meet someone he knows, he proudly introduces her as Dr Aparna Dandekar. For her, it's like coming out of the depths she had plummeted into after her failed marriage. He wants to know everything about her.

'But why did you go into cancer?' he asks her once.

'Because of my mother. When she was diagnosed with cancer, I was a medical student, I knew very little, the doctors didn't tell us much. I was so frightened, I felt so helpless… Maybe I thought that if I became an oncologist myself, both the fear and the sense of helplessness would go. Too late for my mother, of course, but there would be others I could help…'

His world fascinates her as much as hers interests him. She realizes he has tunnel vision, that he sees little beyond his music; but his involvement with it, is absolute. She sees him one day with a tabla-playing friend of his, working on something, shaking his head as if saying no, no, at the different beats the man produced. And then suddenly he is smiling, saying, 'That's it, you got it.' And she knew that it was that little space of time, like a missed heart beat, that he was chasing, she realizes that there is something almost mathematical about the precision he had wanted. (She is not surprised when, later, he tells her he was good at maths.) She learns that he has a strong bond with some friends from his school in Pune who support him in different ways. One of them, now in the US, who is doing very well, has created a website for him, he has got him on Facebook. Another friend, Abhay Tambe, manages his programmes, coordinates with the organizers. He takes these things for granted, to him it seems right and natural that others should look after some part of his professional life.

Aparna and Hari are, like all lovers, cocooned in a world of their own. That there is a world outside, watching them, come home to Aparna when Jyoti asks her, 'Isn't that Shree Hari Pandit who comes to see you?'

'Yes.'

'Can you ask him to come and see me? Just for a few minutes? I want to thank him for the CD. It has given me so much pleasure.'

Hari is as pleased as a child when she tells him this. But when he is with Jyoti, he is poised and serious. 'You have to thank your uncle, Dr Kirtane,' he tells her. 'It was his idea to make this CD for you.'

'But the music is yours, the singer is you. How I wish I could have been there.'

'I'll sing for you any time you want me to.'

'Really?'

'Certainly.'

'But I'm not sure I can afford you. I've heard that singers want a lot of money, in fact, the meter starts ticking the moment they open their mouth and say aaaaa.'

He laughs. 'Only the veterans. And anyway, even if I was a great singer, I would not charge you, Jyotitai.'

'Are you always so kind to your admirers? Or am I special because I am a cancer patient?'

'Come on, Jyotitai, what a thing to say! All right then, I'll take money from you. Right now.'

'How much?'

'Let me see…' He sees some coins in a brass bowl on the table and picks up a ten-rupee coin. 'This is it.' He gives it to her and says, 'Now you give it to me. There, it's done!'

'That's all?'

'A special concession because you are Aparna's friend.'

It's like the kiss on the palm of my hand. I wish he wouldn't do this to me, I wish he wouldn't spring these things on me.

'Are you my friend, doc?'

'Of course.'

Aparna speaks without thinking, then realizes its true. It's been a long time since she had a friend. She'd left all her friends behind when she went to the US and after her marriage ended, she had no desire to get in touch with anyone. Now she's back home, but most of her friends, the women, are absorbed in their families and work, there's no time for anything else. And the men are running all the time, just to stay abreast of others in their profession. The only friend she now has is Freny, who is a pathologist in her hospital; but she lives so far away they can never meet outside their workplaces. That Jyoti and she are becoming friends is mainly due to contiguity. They have to make no effort to meet. And there's Jyoti's personality. She surprises Aparna with her openness, with the way she plunges into intimacy. Like the time she suddenly said, 'I was an unloved child.' She said it in English which made it even more stark.

After seeing the family, Aparna knows that they are not just rich, but old-rich. She imagined Jyoti's life as one of privilege – going to clubs, tea on the lawn, swimming, drinks, dates and dancing. (Jyoti, when Aparna tells her this, will laugh at her.) She will learn later from Jyoti that her father's money came from owning a company that sold traditional medicines for babies, packaged and sold under a brand name that quickly became famous. Innumerable babies had, like little baby birds, opened their mouths to imbibe the gripe water produced by them. It became a must for all babies; mothers fervently believed in giving it to them several times a day. This, and the powder which was supposed to assuage the pains of teething, laid the foundation for the family money, which gave Jyoti and her brother a good life as well as good schools and good colleges. Later, the company launched into beauty products, being one of the first to use traditional ingredients like haldi and amla, and became even more prosperous.

And Jyoti says *I was an unloved child*. 'My father didn't even look at me, his focus was Dada, the Son of the family, the Heir. And for my mother, Dada was the love of her life, she had no eyes for anyone else. So I was left to Saguna's mother, Tarabai, who plotted and planned, like a woman in a TV serial, to get me away from my mother, to keep me in her clutches. Imagine, she told me my mother didn't want to see me, she didn't want me troubling her, she said don't go to her, she'll get angry. Dada saved me, he showed he cared for me. If not for him, I would have remained a little savage.'

'I could have gone abroad to study, like Dada,' she tells Aparna another time, 'but I got married just to defy my father, to show him that I didn't want anything he gave me. All that he wanted was to dominate us. My poor mother couldn't call her soul her own.'

Aparna thinks of her father, of his love for his wife and daughter, of his tenderness, his teasing, his playfulness. To him, women were superior creatures, he said it openly. 'I don't know how Sulu agreed to marry me,' he often said. 'I looked like a monkey and I sometimes behave like a monkey.'

As for Aparna, he called her his jewel, his star, his moon, his sun, his piece of gold, of silver. Extravagant words, but she always knew they were truly meant.

And then he destroyed everything, he dealt a mortal wound to his marriage, to their family, to Sulu's and Aparna's love for him. And this for something as ephemeral as a woman's beauty. Not that she was very beautiful, either. Aparna saw her once and wondered what he saw in her that he abandoned everything that he had treasured for her.

If that is what love is, if that is what love does, I want no part of it, she had thought. But here she is, languishing for a man like any adolescent. 'The madness passes.' Baba had said that to her when she went to see him the last time. The madness passes. What remains then?

It is one of those days when Aparna does not want to be alone at home. The faces of the parents who came with their nineteen-year-old son, imagining that now he was in the right hospital, he would recover, are still with her.

'Didn't you tell them the truth?' Aparna had asked her old classmate Sudhir, who had brought the boy and his parents from their home town. Sudhir had been a quiet and reserved young man in college; now, practising in his home town, he is more confident. And, Aparna can see, very involved with his patients. 'I got to know you're here. This boy needs immediate attention, Aparna, you have to help me,' he had said bluntly to her. The patient had a glioblastoma.

'Didn't you tell them the chances of recovery are very slim? I can't bear the way they look at me, as if I'm a saviour.'

'How do you tell the parents that nothing can be done, that he's going to die? He's their only boy, Aparna. There are two younger sisters, they all adore him. He's very bright. And who knows…? Let them hope as long as they can. Remember, Aparna, on our first day in college, our anatomy professor asked us the question: why did you decide to become a doctor? And most said, to help people. If he had asked me, I would have said, because my father was a doctor and he wanted me to become one. Now, I would give a different answer. I believe that as a doctor I can give my patients hope. It's like god; when there's nothing else, there's always the hope that god will help. Hope is what we doctors really deal in, we are the greatest sellers of hope. Specially you oncologists.'

Aparna is touched by the way he associates himself with his patient, with the parents.

'What about the money for his treatment?'

'Oh, we'll manage that somehow. You just get us an early appointment. I have to go back tomorrow. See what you can do.'

Aparna was able to get an appointment with the surgeon, who decided that the patient would receive neoadjuvant radiotherapy first. The tumour needs to be shrunk, he said. The radiologist had agreed to start the treatment in a week. It's a kind of pyrrhic victory, they can only stave off the end, but Sudhir is profusely thankful. He comes to thank Aparna before leaving.

'It's part of my job, Sudhir. I haven't done anything special. It's you, giving up your work, coming all the way here…'

'Part of my job,' he grins. 'To tell you the truth, I hate coming to Bombay. The crowds, the noise, the traffic…'

Their talk becomes personal after that. He tells her of his twin sons, eight years now and 'shaitaans, both of them. At the end of a day, my poor wife is so tired I have to wake her up when I go home.' Suddenly he asks, 'How is your husband?'

'Who?'

Her tone, her stare, make him apologize. 'Sorry, I thought you were married. Someone told me you'd married that hero – what's his name? The one who was two years ahead of us and had girls running after him…'

'I'm still Dandekar. Yes, I married him, but I divorced him.'

He surprises her by saying, 'Good for you. He was such a vain fellow, always showing his best profile to girls.' She laughs. 'I was surprised that a sensible girl like you had married him.'

'We all have our moments of foolishness, Sudhir, moments of madness.'

She tells him she is not the chief. 'Dr Patel is, but he's very ill. And they are reluctant to fill the post.'

'Won't you get it?'

'Not enough experience. And what power do doctors have in the hospital set-up anyway? Everything is in the hands of professional managers. All that they want us to do is hold on to our patients, get lots of investigations done…'

It's so rare for her to have someone to speak to in this way, she is sorry when he gets up to go. They exchange cards. 'You know, Aparna,' he says when leaving, 'you should have taken obstetrics. I remember you telling me once that that was what you wanted to do. Always good news, you said. And boxes of sweets at home.'

Aparna laughs. 'There's good news here also, Sudhir. Twenty, thirty years ago, it wouldn't have happened.

Jyoti is the good news right now for Aparna. She is recovering well, she goes out for walks, the lymphedema has subsided and she is hoping she can drive herself soon. Her hair is growing, she has a skull cap of tight little curls on her head, giving her the look of a Shakespearan male actor in a female role. Aparna knows what a boost it is for patients to see their hair grow back.

'Your enemy has retreated,' she tells Jyoti. Jyoti is alone. Deepak's son Jai is visiting and the kids, she tells Aparna, have gone to Goa. 'I have a cousin there – I have cousins all over India and abroad) – who's been asking me to visit them for a break. I sent the kids instead, I wanted Miru to have a break. She takes her responsibilities very seriously. She was only nine when Aakash died, and she changed overnight. I feel we – I took her childhood away from her.'

'So you're alone.'

'Blissfully alone. Two of my friends were to come, but I put them off. I don't want to talk to anyone.'

'Shall I go away?'

'Don't be silly, doc. I didn't mean you. The problem with my friends is that I can see them thinking – she's a cancer patient, she's going to die, or she might be dying and what do we say to her, how do we talk to her? You're different. You know how it is. You know, doc, I was thinking – I'm forty-three and they say I'm too young to die. Still a fairly youngish woman. But there was a time when forty-three was ancient. Women would have had a dozen children, dozens of grandchildren, many of the women would be dead at my age. Do you remember that rhyme, Solomon Grundy…'

'Solomon Grundy born on Sunday…'

'No, born on Monday.' And she recites the entire verse to Aparna. 'I'm like Solomon, whizzing through life. Born on Monday, married on Tuesday, widowed on Wednesday – that's an extra dimension to my life, good old Solomon didn't have that – ill on Thursday, worse on Friday, died on Saturday, cremated on Sunday…' She holds up her hand, palm facing inwards, as if stopping herself. 'Okay, okay, I know what you're going to say. Be positive. Right?'

'I say, let's change the subject. I don't like to talk shop on Sunday.'

'Sorry, doc. No more morbid talk, I promise.'

And then she talks of Jai – spelt Jay – and how his parents are so devoted to him that, in spite of their divorce, they manage to keep the façade of good feeling between them. 'Not that I ever saw any overt hostility myself. They never had problems of culture or race. I think it's Dada's love for his mother that makes him incapable of giving himself wholly to any woman. Dada was so protective of our mother! He left home because he couldn't bear to see the way my father terrorized her. Families are strange, aren't they? And talking of families, I met your cousin Madhuri last week.'

'You did? She never told me.'

'I think she came to see you. You were not at home, so I asked her to wait in here. But she had no time. She told me that you spoke to her of Shree Hari's offer to sing for me?'

'Yes, I thought she could help to organize it. She's good at such things.'

'She'd come to tell you that she's going to have it at her home.'

'Oh! I must talk to her.'

It is two days before Aparna gets Madhu on the phone. 'Yes, that's right, Apu, I've decided to have Shree Hari's programme at home. But I'm very busy right now. My kids have a big programme coming, we're rehearsing like mad. Fifty kids. Imagine! So we'll talk about Shree Hari's programme after this is over. And by the way, can you visit Aai some time this week? I haven't been able to go for a while. I'm feeling guilty…'

'Not a problem, I'll go.'

Aparna had stayed for two years with Taimavshi after she left Chandrapur to do her premedical studies in Mumbai. Even after she joined medical college, she spent almost every weekend in Taimavshi's home for the first year or so. Then her visits tapered off, specially when she began her clinical terms. After Sulu came to live in her own house, and was diagnosed with cancer, Aparna was with her much more. Now her visits are rare. It's not just that she is busy; the house has changed since Anju's death. It is filled with Sada's sorrow, with his never-ending mourning for his wife, with his hatred for her killers. For Taimavshi, the worst thing has been his complete alienation from his sister Madhuri, and only because she's married to Abbas.

'His own sister,' she said to Aparna, 'who stood by him those three days, shoulder to shoulder, outside the hotel. She was with him all the time the shooting was going on inside. Madhu is the one who went from hospital to hospital, from morgue to morgue, searching for Anju's body. She saw such terrible sights in that time, for months afterwards she could not sleep. And Sada decides she is responsible for his wife's death because she married Abbas, Abbas who did so much to help us then.'

When she visits Taimavshi, the talk is mainly about Hari's programme. Taimavshi, as the founder of a group that organizes a music festival in the suburbs every year, is interested. She's thinking of inviting him next year, she says. 'How is he, Apu?'

'He's very good.'

'Madhu tells me he's a friend of yours.'

'Yes.'

'Anything special?'

'I don't know, Taimavshi.'

'If you don't, who does?'

'I'm confused. I like him – yes, a lot. But I'm also frightened. I don't want to get into something and then find I've made a mistake.'

'You can't go on like this, Bala. If you like him, take the risk.'

'I did once and look what happened!'

'It can't happen again. I remember how Sulu dreamt of your marriage. She thought you were so good only a prince would do for you.'

'And I got a frog.'

'But we don't really want a prince, do we, Apu? They are full of themselves. This man…?

'He's crazy about me. So he says.'

'Are you sleeping together?'

'Taimavshi, you shock me.'

'Why?'

'Imagine my Aai asking such a question.'

'Sulu had a thousand good qualities, but she had some queer ideas, specially about sex. We grew up on a farm, we saw animals mating, cattle being taken to be impregnated – she should have looked at sex as a natural thing. Maybe then she would have forgiven Dandekar and all that happened need not have happened. So, Apu…?'

'What?'

'The answer to my question?'

'No, Taimavshi, we are not sleeping together. It's not because of me, it's him. He's very old-fashioned, he's been brought up by his ajji and ajoba.'

'Hmm. Don't wait too long to decide. Living alone is very hard. I should know. I've spent most of my life without a partner. But I had the children, they were the purpose of my life. You know, Apu, I've been thinking – my mother had four children, Sulu and I between us had three, and now between the three of you, there's just one child, Anil. Madhu says she has decided not to complicate Abbas's life by having children. But her argument makes no sense. How can a child complicate anyone's life? His two children by Nilufer will continue to be Abbas's children, he will love them just as much. It's like Sulu deciding not to have any children after you. I can't give attention to two children, she said. I thought she was stupid. Do you give all your love to one child so that when another is born, they have to share and get only half of your love? I think the real reason was that she was afraid Dandekar would give up his job. You know how he kept talking about it. And if he didn't earn, the burden would fall on her. How could she both work and look after home and children? I thought that, on the other hand, having another child would steady Dandekar. Oh, let that go. All that I really want to say to you, Apu, is put your past behind you and look ahead.'

A wise woman, Taimavshi, Aparna thinks.

Jyoti is overcome when she hears about the plans for the programme Hari is having for her. 'You're very generous,' she says to Hari when he comes home to speak to her about it.

'Madhuritai is generous. I'm not. You paid me, remember? And this will be a request programme. Tell me what you would like me to sing. The patron can command the singer.'

'Not this patron. I would not dare to command an artist.'

'Right then. Leave it to me. I promise you a special programme.'

It is. It is something they will remember for long. Madhuri's living room has been emptied of furniture and a raised dais for the musicians arranged at one end of the room. There are more than the twenty-five or thirty people earlier envisaged; Madhu has invited some musicians and music lovers, as well as friends. Jyoti, surprisingly, comes with all three children in tow – Mira, Tejas and Jai.

Hari begins with the raaga Bageshri and then goes on to Basant. 'Although it is still not the right time for Basant, I have a special reason for singing it now.' Jyoti had expressed her fondness for it. It's so joyful and lilting, she had said.

The event is informal, Hari speaks to his audience in an intimate way. For the first time Aparna sees that, besides being a superb artist, he is a very good performer, he knows what the audience expects, he knows how to communicate with them.

During the break, people move to the table where Madhu has arranged tea, coffee and some snacks, but the moment Madhuri says, 'Interval over', they move with alacrity back to their seats. 'It's the custom to sing bhajans and thumris after the chhota khayal,' Hari tells them, 'but I always sing abhangs in memory of my grandfather. He couldn't pursue music as a profession, but he loved music and he was a devotee of Tukaram Maharaj. So I will end with Tukaram's abhangs. But before that, if any of you have any requests…? Jyotitai? Anandibai?' He looks at Jyoti and Taimavshi.

'Natya sangeet?' Jyoti asks tentatively.

'Why not? I don't know many songs, but like I told your uncle, if you suggest any, I will try my best.'

Jyoti mentions a song and Hari nods. He speaks softly to his accompanists and they try out a few notes, nod at one another and then begin, the harmonium player starting first. After that, Taimavshi asks for a song, then someone else makes a request. Finally he goes to the abhangs. Hari is now at his best, as if the entire programme has been moving to this climax. He is emotional, devotional, meditative. Looking at him, Aparna thinks, he is not an ordinary person, he's an artiste. And when he sings, he is not Hari, but an instrument giving his music to the world. For some reason the thought disturbs her.

After the programme is over, Taimavshi, who is talking to Hari, beckons to Aparna. 'Shree Hari says he would like to have some texts of natya sangeet. Didn't Dandekar have a book of them? Do you have any idea where it is?'

'Madhu and I just pushed everything into two trunks, perhaps they're in the flat.'

'Can I see them?' Hari asks.

'Sure. Taimavshi will find them and I'll get them to you.'

'I'm not going to open your father's trunk by myself, Apu. You have to come.'

'Okay.'

'How soon?'

She thinks Hari is being pushy. 'How soon do you want it? Now?'

'If possible.'

'Sorry. Not possible.'

He laughs. 'Whenever you have the time.'

He goes off, as usual declining the offer of dinner. 'I never eat after a programme, Madhuritai.'

He calls at night.

'How was it?'

'Good.'

'Not very good?'

'Okay, very good.'

'Not very very good?'

'Yes, vherry vherry good,' she says, mimicking his accent.

'Don't you dare criticize my English. Our English teacher was the best in Pune.'

'Really?'

'And Aparna, I've been thinking. Those songs are running in my head, I know I won't be able to sleep tonight. I wish I could start practising right away, but this is not Pune. There, our neighbours loved Ajoba's singing, whether he sang at night or in the early morning. This is Mumbai, they'll call the police. I thought I'll make these songs part of my programme. Something different. Depending on the audience, of course. What do you think?'

Aparna listens, gives the right responses, finally tells him she has to sleep. But she can't. She thinks of her father, who, as a writer, was so different from what he was in daily life. She remembers him at his table in his room, the room they, Sulu and he, Sulu mainly, had got built on the first floor and furnished as a study for him. She thinks of how, when she went to him with a cup of tea, he, scarcely looking up, said, 'Put it there,' and went on writing. The room was a space Sulu had created for him, a place where he could be alone, where he could write undisturbed. She'd bought all the furniture in the room with her own money: a rocking chair, a chair and table, a glass-fronted bookcase for his books, a wooden bench he used to spread his papers on, because the table was never enough. And there was the huge world map, almost covering an entire wall. She often found him standing before it, not really seeing it, she knew later. 'It helps me to think,' he would say. 'I like to see the vastness of the world and the smallness of us humans. And yet without us the world has no meaning.' Everything in the room was bought for him by Sulu because he would not allow her to spend her money on the household. 'That's my job,' he would say. And so she spent it on him and on Aparna.

And there is Madhu, who gave up her dancing, her choreography about which she had been so passionate, after Abbas's illness, gave it up so that she could support Abbas, give him the assistance he needed, be the person who would do things for him without having to be told. Now she only goes to municipal schools to teach boys and girls to dance, something that gives her great joy. She takes no money for it. No, I can't be like Sulu and Madhu, Aparna thinks. It's not in me to be selfless. I can love. But selfless devotion?

'You're a spoilt brat,' he had said to her, the man she had married, the man she always thought of as X. (Ex without the E, she had explained to Madhu on the rare occasion when she spoke of him.) 'You've been spoilt by your parents.'

Maybe I have. No, I was. Baba was not only a doting father, he had the words to express his love. I knew he loved me, I knew how much he loved me. And Sulu, perhaps she didn't have the words, but even the most mundane things she said showed her love. Yes, I was spoilt, maybe that's why I can never be like Sulu or Madhu. Self-effacing. All love. Expecting nothing in return. Gaja took all of Sulu's services, her devotion to him, for granted. Can I be like Sulu with Hari? God knows. But I can look for the book he requires, yes, that's something I can do for him.

And so it begins, the search that ends in the discovery of Ahalya.

In the event, Madhu who had promised to go with her, can't make it. So it's only Aparna and Taimavshi who open the trunk. Aparna has to make an effort to enter the place. It is darkened for her, not only by memories of her mother's suffering and sorrow, but also her father as he had been when Madhu had brought him to see Sulu. His clothes crumpled, smelling of stale sweat, his unshaved face with a grey stubble that looked like ashes. This is not my father, she had thought, this man in unwashed clothes and with an unbathed body is not my father. This man has no dignity left. It was the loss of his dignity that she had minded the most.

'You start, Apu,' Taimavshi said. 'I'll join you in a few minutes.'

She goes out, leaving Aparna alone with her memories. Madhu and she had hastily packed these things, mostly Baba's books, papers and manuscripts, when they had to vacate the house after his death. Yes, it was all here. Long notebooks with hard covers, the name of the play on the first page with his name, Gajanan Vidyadhar Dandekar, in her mother's hand. Everything that he wrote, every word, was copied out by her. No one can understand his handwriting, she had said once. It's as if a spider has climbed out of an ink bottle and walked over a blank page.

She thinks of her father telling her, 'Your mother made me a writer. Just like there can be no god without devotees, there can be no artist without believers. Your mother was my echo, my mirror, I saw the writer I was in her.'

This was during the last few days she spent with him, when he shed all his inhibitions and spoke to her as he never would have earlier. As if he had forgotten she was his daughter. As if she was a stranger to whom he could unburden himself. 'She made me believe I was doing great work. I fooled myself into believing that as well. Now when I look back, I think – what have I done? There's this great big drama of life going on around us and I couldn't get even a pinch of it.'

He spoke of Sulu as if he had gone past the bitterness of her desertion, the grief of her death. Even when he said, 'Your mother believed in capital punishment. She would not take money from me for her treatment. Tell me, did I deserve that?' he had been passionless, asking the question as if it was a theoretical one and had nothing to do with him.

When Taimavshi returns, she finds Aparna sobbing bitterly.

'What is it, Apu? Don't cry, Bala. It's all over, they are both at peace now. And you have to put it away, you must go on with your life.'

She wipes Aparna's face with her sari as if Aparna is a child and says, 'Come on now, let's finish this, then have our tea. I've made sabudana khichadi for you. Apu-special, Madhu still calls it.'

Aparna laughs. 'Taimavshi, I'm no longer a kid. It's you who are living in the past.'

'Am I? Well, mothers like to look for the child in their sons and daughters. Did you find the book?'

'It's not here. Maybe in the other trunk.'

They find them finally, not one, but two notebooks filled with the texts of all kinds of songs.

'Take them. Let your Hari sort it out.'

'My Hari! No way, Taimavshi.'

'But he wants you. He can't take his eyes off you.'

Hari rings up later. 'Did you find the book?'

'Books, not book.'

'I want to see them. Can I come now?'

'I'm tired, Hari.'

'Aparna, what's wrong? You sound – different.'

'Just tired.'

More than her mother's suffering and death, it is her father's tragedy that still tears at Aparna's heart. Why can't I tell Hari, she thinks, that she has been weeping for the tragedy of her father's life, for his self-hatred, for his utter loneliness when he died. That she has been weeping at the thought of how little remained of a life rich with friends, students, books, ideas, family. She has been weeping for the scant notice he got after his death, for his final stoical acceptance of the fact that he had failed both as a man and a writer. He never got a major award – he pretended it didn't matter, 'they don't think of drama as literature', he said – but Sulu and she knew he minded, they knew it hurt. To hate yourself, never to be able to forgive yourself, to carry a load of anger against yourself – what kind of a life is that?

'Have you read Hardy's *Mayor of Casterbridge*?' he had asked her in those last days.

'No. It wasn't a text for us. Only for the Arts students.'

'I taught it, you know. Each time I came to the end, when I got to the point of Michael Henchard's will, I felt something I can't describe. I found it hard to read it. Now I think that's because this was waiting for me; like Henchard, I would die unmourned, unloved.'

She had read the book after Baba's death, she had read the words of the will, and had known the extent of her father's despair. '…that no m(o)urners walk behind me at my funeral…that no man remember me…' She thinks even now that there can be nothing worse for a man to wish for. And she also thinks of the irony of it – there is not a single day when she does not remember him and his despair, not a day when she does not remember how much he loved her and how she failed him.

Hari comes to her on Sunday morning and finds her still in her night-gown sitting cross-legged on the floor, Gaja's dusty notebooks strewn all around her.

'I thought you would have finished sorting them by now.'

'No, I…no, Hari, each time I begin, I get distracted by something. Look at this – he translated two of Shakespeare's plays, *Macbeth* and *King Lear*. I remember him saying that they were Shakespeare's best plays, the tragedy of ambition and the tragedy of old age.'

'Shall I help you? We can do the sorting together,'

'No, don't! You've had a bath.' His clean body emanates the fragrance of soap, the pleasing aroma of washed and ironed clothes. 'You'll get dirty. I haven't had a bath as yet. Just look at the dust the books have collected!'

Despite her words, he sits down opposite her, cross-legged as well, pushing the books a little to a side so that he can get closer, now their knees are touching.

'Never mind that,' he says. 'I've come to talk to you.'

She knows, she thinks she knows, what he wants to say. She knows too that she can no longer stop him, that he will say what he wants to. But he surprises her by speaking of something quite different from what she'd expected.

'You were crying that day.'

'What day, Hari?'

'The day you brought these books home. When I rang you, I could make out you were crying. But you wouldn't tell me why. What is it, Aparna? What are these things you can't talk to me about?'

'Does it matter now?'

'Yes, it matters to me. When you refused to share your grief with me that day, I felt so left out, it was as if you were pushing me out of your life and closing the door on me. Don't do that to me, Aparna, I can't bear it.'

'It had nothing to do with you, Hari.'

'Everything you do matters to me. Everything that makes you happy or sad is important to me. What was it?'

'It was my father. Seeing his books, his manuscripts, everything came back to me. His life. His death. I wanted him to come and live with me in Mumbai, I told him I was coming back from the States, that I was looking for a job in Mumbai and that when I found it, he should leave Chandrapur and come to me. He'd just had a myocardial infarction, it was bad and I didn't want to leave him alone. But he refused, he wanted nothing from me. I don't blame him, I was cruel to him…'

'You cruel, Aparna?'

She ignores him and goes on, 'He told me to get on with my life, to leave him to himself. Ring me up once in a while, that's enough, he said. I'm not worth your attention, he said. He had become such a bitter and unhappy man. And he had been always so cheerful, such a loving father. Why didn't I help him? Why couldn't I help him? I'm so ashamed of myself, I just took from him, I gave him nothing.'

She is silent for a while, then continues, 'I had decided that when I came back, I would take him away with me, I would not leave him alone. But he died just as I was leaving.' She is silent again.

'Apu...'

She goes on as if she has not heard him, 'I was packed and ready to leave, the taxi had arrived. He came with me to the door. When I got to the gate and looked back, he was still standing in the doorway and the next moment I saw him crumple, I saw him fall... When I got to him, he was dead. Hari, the memories of the days I spent with him hurt. I was so indifferent, so dutiful, just a daughter doing her duty. He saw that, he saw through me. Few children are loved the way I was. And I was so cold. Why didn't I help him, why couldn't I help him?'

He has been listening to her in silence, his eyes focused on her face.

'If he loved you so much, he would have forgiven you.'

'But I can't forgive myself.'

He wipes her face as gently as Taimavshi had done the day they opened the trunk.

'Let it go, Aparna, let it go.' He smoothens her hair and his fingers very gently touch her face, so delicate a touch it is like a blind man trying to see. And then he leans forward and kisses her, a kiss so gentle it's as if he is merely touching her lips with his own.

'Hari, what are you doing?'

'I've been wanting to do this since the day, since the moment I saw you in Dr Bhagat's house. You were wearing something yellow, it was a little crushed, not properly ironed, but it made you look like a golden chafa flower with the petals wilting a little. Something happened to me when I saw you. I had never seen you before, but you didn't seem a stranger, you were already a part of my life. I never thought I would feel the way I did. Marriage, yes. I knew I would marry some day, I wanted to, I wanted a wife, children, I wanted to be a father. But when I saw you, I forgot everything. There was only you, only you, my Aparna.'

He puts his arm around her and pulls her very gently towards himself. She does not resist, her body is pliant. When he kisses her, firmly this time, her body moves backwards and he tightens his hold, brings her closer. Then suddenly he draws back and says, 'Stand up, Aparna.'

'What?'

'Stand up.' He gets up and pulls her up so that they are standing face to face. 'Listen to my heart.' Once again he puts his arm around her and drawing her to him says, 'Listen to my heart now. Here, here.'

'I know where the heart is, Hari.' Her voice comes out muffled. Is she crying? Or laughing?

'Can you hear it? Can you hear what it's saying?'

'I can hear the normal sound. Rub dub, rub dub. It's in good working order, thank god.'

'Put away your stethoscope, doctor, and listen with your heart. Then you'll hear your name, you'll hear the song in my heart. It's Aparna, Aparna, Aparna.'

She tries to free herself, but he won't let go. He bends down and whispers in her ear, the song, the abhang he had sung in Madhu's house. '*Sweet is your form, sweet is your name. Give me your love for all time.*'

'Hari, oh Hari, you're mad.'

'Yes, I am, Aparna. My ajoba would have whacked me if he had heard me singing this song to you, making you my god, my Vithala. Or maybe not; who knows? Don't move, Aparna, let me hold you. I've been wanting to hold you like this since the moment we met. Each time we met, I wanted to hold you, to kiss you. But I told myself – hands off! She's a big doctor, she'll slap you. Remember how stern you were when I came to the hospital to see you the first time? What are you doing here, you asked me.'

'I was frightened. I thought you'd come as a patient.'

'And you frightened me. I thought I would go away and never come back. But I couldn't, I can't stay away from you. I think of you all day, I think of you as soon as I wake up in the morning, I think of you when I go to bed. Ever since I saw you, you've always been with me, you are here…' He puts his hand on his heart. 'Say something, Aparna, why don't you say something?'

'I don't know what to say. You say such beautiful things, you speak such beautiful Marathi, I could listen to you all day. I don't want to speak.'

'But I want to hear you, Aparna. Do you feel like I do? If you don't care for me, tell me so.'

'No, Hari, it's…'

'Is it because of your marriage? Was the divorce such a tragedy for you? Did you love him very much?'

'No! No!' she cries out, eager to refute the idea. 'That has nothing to do with my life now.'

She is so vehement he does not pursue the subject. But she will tell him later how humiliated, how ashamed she was, that she had imagined that the man she married could fill the huge gaps left in her life by her mother's death, by her father's alienation. She was angry with herself; how could she ever have thought he could be a companion, a companion for her entire life? They are now sitting on the divan, his arm still around her. Suddenly she pushes him away. 'Hari, I want to be by myself, I want to think, I want to have time to think.'

He is silent.

'Please,' she says, pleading this time. 'Please don't rush me.'

'All right, I'll go. But I'm coming back, I'll keep coming back.'

'Not for a week, Hari. Let's stay away from each other for a week.'

He demurs, he protests, but she is firm. 'No phone calls either,' she adds. 'And no SMSes.'

Finally he goes, leaving her so shaken it's like she's lived through an earthquake. She has no idea how she gets through the day. She thinks that the chaos in her mind, the tumult, will make it impossible for her to work, but miraculously, once in the hospital, her working self takes over. When she goes home in the evening, everything comes back. His presence. The taste of him on her lips, the light flitting touch of his fingers on her face. She remembers seeing her parents locked in an embrace once, her mother on tiptoe, her arms around her father's neck. She was twelve then and she had thought: is this the great secret of the world, is this what nobody wants to talk about, but everyone thinks about? Later, she knew that this was what knitted a man and a woman together and isolated them from the whole world, even from their only and much loved child. Now she thinks: Is this the world I've missed for so long, is this the world that is waiting for me if I say yes to Hari? But it will not last, the world will intrude, the world will make its presence felt. She remembers Baba saying: the madness passes. And then, what remains? There was nothing left for Baba. He was a lost man even before he died. It was as if, when Sulu left him, his life was over.

'This girl,' he had said to Aparna, speaking of Sulu, his wife and Aparna's mother, 'you should have seen this girl when we got married. With her long hair, her dark inscrutable eyes and silences, she was like Meena Kumari.' And her mother, pretending she could not hear him, turned her back on them, but even her back showed her embarrassment, her pleasure.

'Your mother,' he told Aparna another time, 'must be the only woman in the country who calls her husband by his surname. Dandekar, she says. She used to call me Dandekar sir at first. Then, thank god, she dropped the sir. Now I'm trying to make her call me Gaja, but she won't. How is it that the whole world can use my name, but my wife can't?'

She did call him Gaja, but only in private; Aparna had overheard her once or twice and it had seemed to her strange and disturbing. Erotic. She did not know the word then, all she knew was that it was disturbing. Now she knows that what had disturbed her was the eroticism she had felt between her parents.

She listens to Hari's CD every night. She listens to his voice and sees him, sitting erect, his hands in his lap, eyes closed, drawing the music out of himself. She thinks of the feel of his body against hers, she remembers she had felt his arousal that night. What if I had asked him to stay? Would he have stayed, would he have made love to me? Perhaps, with sex the madness is spent, and I – no, both of us can be free.

Sweet is your form, sweet is your name. 'I sang it for you, Aparna.'

I never thought I would get this kind of love, I never imagined I would feel this way for a man. So why am I hesitating? What am I afraid of? What is it that keeps pulling me back, saying *Take care, take care?*

Let's not meet, she had said, but she had never thought he would keep his word. Remarkably, he does. He does not come to her or ring her or even message her, showing her a side of him she has not seen. She is restless, disturbed, unable to settle down to anything. The week is over and there is still no sign of Hari. She knows she can't sit at home waiting for him to come, waiting for the phone to ring. She decides to visit her boss, Dr Patel. She has a strong sense of guilt that she has not seen him for a long time. His quiet announcement of his own diagnosis had shocked her, as it had everyone. 'Seems to be a professional hazard for oncologists to become patients themselves,' he had said with a wry smile. He had surprised everyone with his decision to be treated in his own hospital, by his colleagues. The thought of treating him had unnerved Aparna. But he had been a good patient, he had submitted without questions to everything, he had been like any other patient. He had recovered well after the surgery and chemo. He dropped in at times, apart from his check-up and treatment visits, he rang her up occasionally, and she knew she could consult him on difficult cases. But the last six months there has been a drastic deterioration. This time she has a case to discuss with him, she wants to talk to him about the international conference the hospital was to hold next year, and which Dr Patel had been so enthusiastic about. He barely nods his head when she speaks. His physical deterioration is shocking, he is frighteningly cachectic. But it seems worse to her that he knows he is close to his end, that he has accepted it. He is detached and aloof, barely listening to her. She sees the same detachment in him with his wife and even with the daughters he so adored. Now he seems to be saying, Leave me alone. What have I to do with these things? She remembers the day she found him in his room, back from his surgical examination. He had looked up at her, his face blank.

'I don't want to go home,' he said. 'I don't want to face my wife with this news.'

'Sir, we still don't have the biopsy result, the path report…'

'No, Bhagat knows and I know Bhagat is right.'

He had three daughters who were, his wife later told Aparna, 'Papa-crazy. I don't matter at all, I'm just a cipher in this house.'

Now they had all become ciphers to him. At first he had been phlegmatic and matter-of-fact about his predicament. Aparna remembers him on his rounds, cheerful, encouraging, always leaving some hope behind, even in the most despondent patient. He had come back to work after his radiation and chemo sessions were over. However, within a month he decided to stop working. 'I want to spend time with my family, I want to read,' he had said. To Aparna he also confessed that it would do his patients no good to know that the man who walked among them, the man who held their hands and promised them they would be better, was himself suffering from the disease. If he could suffer, what hope was there for them?

Nevertheless, when leaving he had been cheerful, warning Aparna, 'Don't think you can occupy my chair. I'm coming back.'

'You had better come, sir, before I make a mess of things.'

Now he is waiting for the end. His wife, he told her before she left, had promised him they would let him be at home until the end; his old friend Gandhi was looking after him. That was the only thing her mother had asked for as well. Let me die here, she had said. Aparna has seen enough of deaths in the hospital to know why people want to die at home. In a hospital, death is often deprived of all meaning, it becomes the commonplace, it is something of a defeat. Therefore, it remains the unspoken, it is concealed behind screens, it happens in ICU wards where the other patients are too sick to care about the final drama that is taking place in their midst. And death, when it happens in a hospital, is immediately erased, the bed filled up, the files banished into oblivion. She had, many years ago, visited the Viet Nam wall, she had seen how even the beautiful surroundings and the flowers left at the foot of the wall by people for their dear ones could not sanitize and beautify the ugly face of war, the suffering and needless young deaths. We can never accept death, she thinks.

Aparna returns home in a sombre mood in the evening. When she is fishing for her key in her bag, she suddenly hears Hari's voice call out her name. She is so startled she cries out, the key falls from her hands. She has not seen him, he has been sitting on the stairs that lead to the floor above, sitting close to the wall, in the shadows. He picks up the key, opens the door and with his hand at her back, gently ushers her in. He switches on the light. She is still shaking.

'Come and sit down, Aparna. Did I frighten you? I am sorry, I never thought…'

He is still holding her, not in a lover's embrace, but as if to reassure her, to calm her down.

'When did you come?'

'Some time back. I thought I would wait for you. '

She looks at him for the first time. He has cut his hair short, shorter than she has ever seen it. It gives him a shorn, vulnerable look.

'You've cut your hair. Why have you cut it so short?'

'People in the south go to Tirupati, they offer their hair to god and ask for something. I went to the barber's and asked for my Aparna's love.'

He rubs his face against hers and she makes a small exclamation, his end-of-the-day stubble scratching her. 'I am sorry, I am so sorry.' He gently rubs her cheek with his hand and puts his forehead against hers.

'Aparna…?'

'What?'

'Nothing. Just Aparna.'

'Why didn't you come all these days?'

'Why did you ask me to stay away?'

'I don't know. Yes, I know. I wanted us to be sure. What if all this is – a passing thing, what if it doesn't last?'

'I promise you, for me this is for a lifetime.'

'You might promise me everything now. But later?'

'You're insulting me, Dr Dandekar.'

'I don't know what I'm saying, Hari. I must – I want to have a bath.'

'All right then. I'll go.'

'No, don't go. Stay. I'll be back soon. Make yourself a cup of tea if you want.'

'No, I must go. I'll come tomorrow.'

'Oh Hari, don't go, don't go.'

'I'll come back tomorrow, Aparna. I promise.'

And so he does. And so begins their love affair.

This, the time of getting to know each other, is, though they don't know it, the best time for them. There is a sudden slip into intimacy, an intimacy which eliminates all barriers that exist between humans; it gives Aparna a heady feeling, 'as if I've drunk champagne,' she says.

'You drink champagne?'

'Occasionally. You don't approve?'

'I approve of everything my Aparna does. All I want is that she should love me always.'

Lovers' conversations are of no consequence to anyone but themselves; at times, not even to themselves. The words don't really matter. To speak is to affirm that you are with your beloved, each word is like a caress, it is a promise of love. And with the questions which they, like all lovers, ask of each other, *When did you…? Why did you…? How did you…?* they are actually bridging the gap between their earlier separateness and this present togetherness. In a while the earlier time is left behind, it's forgotten, it's always been this way, they've always known each other, they've always been together. This is their time of revelations, discoveries, coincidences. 'I worked in the branch of the bank near your college,' he tells her.

'I had an account there. Why didn't we meet?'

Their first meeting is revisited, looked at from all sides, and like a prism it changes colours, they see colours they had not seen earlier. She has a vague picture of his youthfulness, his exuberance when he sang, of his innocent face. And his voice – it was beautiful. He had just found his true voice at the time, he tells her. He remembers her more clearly. 'You and your friend were waiting impatiently for your father to finish talking. Both of you looked bored,' he says. He had thought then that she was very sophisticated, he tells her, frighteningly sophisticated. So he says. And she marvels that anyone could have thought her, a callow Chandrapur girl, sophisticated.

Hari is passionate and open about his feelings, he is

demonstrative; he is unashamed even to employ the banalities of love. 'One thing we will not do,' she tells him firmly. 'We will not say, we will never say *I love you* and *I love you too.'*

'But I like it, it's such an easy way of speaking of your love. I can't find the words. We are always singing of love – love of god, or of woman. But when I want to tell you about my love, I can't find the words. They are locked in here.'

He thumps his chest and the dramatic gesture brings back the boy she had seen on the stage, the boy who, not knowing how to act, had employed loud gestures, coming into his own only when he sang.

Once he even brings her a red rose. 'What is this, Hari?' she asks, laughing.

'I thought of all the things I want to say to you, but can't. Then I thought, maybe these kids who go around giving roses to their girlfriends are right. This can say all that I can't.'

'You must have said the same things to your girlfriend,' she says.

'What girlfriend?'

'You told me there was a girl, but she was not right for you.'

'I was never serious about any girl. Not until I met you. Only once, I thought… But I was only a boy then. What did I know of love?'

He laughs at himself, easily, comfortably, as if at something forgotten, long left behind. For some reason, she has, once again, a sense of his leaving something unsaid, but she does not pursue it.

She has made a rule that they will not ring each other when they are working. At times he flouts the rules.

'What are you doing?' he asks.

'Working. I thought we agreed we won't talk during working hours,' she says, trying to be stern.

'I thought this is your lunch hour.'

'I'm working.'

'Liar, I bet you're thinking of me. Like I'm thinking of you.'

'Liar. I bet you are in your *sa re ga ma* world.'

'A pair of liars, eh, Aparna? Made for each other, huh?'

They meet mostly in the evenings, when she comes back from work. They go to the sea face, already *their* place, their favourite place and sit, hands entwined, the thundering of the sea a constant background to their talk.

'I can talk to you about everything,' he says and speaks to her of his ambitions, his frustrations. He tells her how slighted he feels when someone not as good as him gets the attention he does not, because he himself has no connections. She thinks of her father, who was constantly tormented by a sense of not being given his due. She is surprised, disappointed that Hari feels the same way. She had imagined that his world, the world of music, was one of beauty and light, of life and creativity. While her own is one of suffering and darkness.

'Don't run down your profession, Dr Dandekar,' he says. 'I waited for you in your waiting room twice, I sat among your patients and I know how much you do for them.'

His profession, she learns now, is like any other, with people trying to get to the top by promoting themselves, by using others. A world of big egos. 'The best time is when you are singing,' he says. 'That's the real thing, that's the only thing that matters.' But you can't go far unless you do the other things as well, networking, self-promotion – he does not say this, but it is implied and she understands.

Two different worlds, two different professions – each finds the other's world fascinating and esoteric. She goes to his house on a Sunday evening and finds him with two friends, the three of them working on something, engrossed in it, Hari humming a few notes, beating out a tala with his two hands, while the other two listen. Then they see her and Hari, getting up with the awkward haste of a young boy, comes to her and calling out her name, holds both her hands in his. Everything out in the open, nothing furtive or concealed. His friends are ready to get up and go, but he won't let them. 'No, don't go, let's go on. Come and sit here, Aparna,' he says. 'Sit by me.'

His friends are a little awkward with her, a little awed by her. Though they accept her, they are unsure of what to call her, fumbling between doctor, Doctor Aparna, Aparnatai, Aparnaji. But Hari is composed, he wants her as part of his life, he makes it clear that she belongs where he does. It's the same when they go out together; he is exuberant, happy, proud to be with her, to be seen with her. He has changed the ringtone of his mobile and now when she calls him she hears him singing, *Goda tujhe rupa, goda tujhe naama*. Their song. It's as if he's announcing his love to the world.

'I'm in love with your face, your body, your heart, your soul,' Hari says to her once. And then asks in sudden anxiety, 'Have I left out anything?'

'No, you've added an extra factor. The soul. I've done so many dissections, but I've never seen the soul.'

'How can you? Only lovers can see each other's souls. I can see yours. It's beautiful,' he says and she is suddenly stricken by her own unworthiness. Don't say such things, she wants to say, don't think such things, one day you will be disappointed. But she does not say this; the silences of love, she is learning, are as valuable as the words of love.

Aparna is a little puzzled about Hari's careful avoidance of any kind of physical intimacy between them (except for the kisses with which he had declared his love) which is such a contrast to his verbal exuberance. In this one matter he is an enigma to her. But she is glad they haven't rushed into sex. She remembers how it was in her marriage, how the precipitancy with which they had moved into a physical relationship had masked the hollowness of their feelings. It had given her a totally mistaken idea of his feelings for her. Small-town girl that she was, in spite of her years in Mumbai, she had felt that to have a sexual relationship was a prelude to marriage, she had taken it for granted that they would marry. For a reason she did not know then, he had agreed. She wonders whether, brought up as he was by people of an earlier generation, Hari believes that sex should come after marriage, that it has to be sanctified by marriage. But she does not speak of this. Some things, she has realized, are best left unsaid.

These lovers have yet to learn that there is always a ghostly twin of each, an imaginary beloved, walking between them. That, only if the imagined and the real meet, can there be perfect love. But this never happens, the two never meet: this is the truth that lovers can ignore only at their peril, indeed at the cost of love itself, this is the truth, these lovers will learn in time.

There's talk in the hospital of appointing a new head for the medical oncology department. Freny, Aparna's pathologist friend, tells her that the man who is being spoken of as likely to get the post is supposed to be quite a stickler for rules, 'not like your Dr Patel'.

Aparna is worried about the possibility of change. There is also a tentative offer from a hospital in Nagpur which would give Aparna full control, she would be head. But she can't see herself moving away from Mumbai, partly because of Madhu and Taimavshi, but mainly because of Hari. She has shackled herself to a man, she is anchored to Mumbai because of him; if he is here, I have to be here. And for Hari, this is where he has to be, his work is here, his students are here; for him, this is where everything happens. And, yes, his friend Bhide, who manages programmes for him, is also here. I'm becoming dependent on Hari, she thinks. And she remembers how she and the man she married had lived apart for most of their time together, almost the whole continent between them, she on the East coast and he on the West. 'I'm trying to find you a place in my hospital,' he'd said to her at first, he kept saying this for a few months. And then it was dropped, never spoken of between them. For by then, they knew it did not matter any more.

But with Hari it's different. When he goes out for his

programmes, or to be with his guruji, she has a sense of loss. What will I do in the evening, she asks herself and then chastizes herself: I can live a few days without him, I must not get into this clinging state. Yet when Madhu invites her home for a weekend when Hari is away, she snatches at the chance. Madhu tells her Taimavshi has gone to Kolhapur to attend a family wedding.

'Why didn't you go?'

'I wasn't invited. I've married a Mussalman, don't you know that? Not that I would have gone. I've been telling Aai she should stop doing these things, she should slow down. But you know her sense of duty – she's the eldest in the Rajwade family now.'

Aparna has always enjoyed her evenings with Madhu and Abbas. It's peaceful being with two people so much in harmony. They create a world of peace and quiet between them. 'We've had enough of excitement and turmoil,' Madhu says with a shudder, and Aparna knows she is thinking of Nilufer, Abbas's first wife. She had said she would kill herself when she found out about Madhu, she rushed to the terrace to throw herself off the building, 'making sure the others got there before she climbed the parapet,' Madhu said wryly. After this, Abbas went back to his wife and marriage and Madhu disappeared, driving Taimavshi and Abbas frantic. It was Gaja who found her and brought her back. By then, Nilu had found her millionaire, a man who fell for her victim image, who saw in her (so he said) all the beauty and helplessness of women, and who wanted to marry her, to protect her. And so the problem was solved. But Nilu, though she has accepted Madhu, still occasionally uses her wronged-wife story to dramatize herself. Fortunately, Madhu no longer finds Nilu a threat, she's friendly with her and the children as well.

With Madhu, Aparna often reverts to her old Chandrapur self, the girl who had looked up to and admired Madhu. With her marriage to Abbas, Madhu became what Aparna thinks of as the epitome of sophistication. And Abbas, when he opens up, is a person she loves to talk to, to listen to. To be with them is like becoming part of another world, a more sophisticated and civilized world.

Today she is eager to talk to Madhu on her own. She has not told Madhu that Hari and she have come together. Her feelings seem to her too fragile, too delicate; like the parijaat flower, handling would leave them bruised and crushed. Nevertheless, like any adolescent girl in love, she has an irresistible desire to say Hari's name. And so when Madhu, as usual, comes to her room to see if she has everything, to say goodnight, she holds her hand and says, 'Come and sit with me for five minutes, Madhu. I have something to tell you.'

'About Shree Hari.'

'Yes, how do you know?'

'I have my spies. Oh you stupid Apu, it's written on your face. So when are you getting married?'

'I thought at least you wouldn't ask me that question. I know Taimavshi will. But don't you start, Madhu.'

'Why not? Any sensible person would ask that question. You're both single, independent and over eighteen…'

'Eighteen!'

'…no one to object, so what's the problem?'

'The problem? I don't know. But I'm not sure I want to jump into marriage right away.'

'Then when? When you're sixty?'

'Don't be like this, Madhu. I'm really scared. What if it doesn't work?'

'So how and when do you make sure it works?'

'We can be together for some time.'

'Live together, you mean? Will he agree to that? And why won't it work?'

'We're so different.'

'All couples are two very different people. The difference adds zing to a marriage. People *are* different, Apu. Remember Gajakaka saying, no writer can get anywhere close to the variety of people in this world? Only that great man, no, he always called Shakespeare *mahapurush*, great man doesn't sound the same, does it? – he said that only Shakespeare came somewhere close.'

'But our differences could become important. His work, for example. He needs a woman who will look after everything, who will make him comfortable and leave him to pursue his music. I'm not sure I can do that. I can only give him a part of my time. I'm not the nurturing kind.'

It comes to her mind then, what her father had said when they were estranged, when she had turned against him. 'We've made you selfish, we've given you everything you wanted.'

And he, the man she had married, had said it too. 'You're a selfish brat. Your parents spoilt you.'

'But he wants you, not that imaginary woman who will look after him. Love works miracles, Apu. Remember how I was before marriage? Aai was sure I would never be able to work at my marriage.'

Yes, they had doubted her, Taimavshi and Sulu. They had wondered how a rebellious girl like her would adjust to living with a man, who not only had a wife and two children, but who lived in the midst of a large family of mother, two sisters and their families. But she had coped, she had learnt to become part of them, she had even managed to bring his two children back into the family, into his life.

'You gave up everything, Madhu. I can't do that, I can't imagine being without my work.'

'You don't have to, I'm sure he doesn't expect you to.'

'You should have seen him when I didn't go to one of his programmes. He was so upset, so angry.'

'Apu, these little tiffs will happen. You can't insure your

marriage against all possible problems. And I didn't give up my work because of Abbas. I gave up because I was disgusted with what they call dance these days. Music has gone out of dance, there's only rhythm. And what is dance without music? As for Abbas, I'm only his sounding board, I let him talk to me. That's all you need to do, take interest in what he does. I know you keep thinking of your parents. But stories don't repeat themselves. Everyone told me when I married Abbas that, since he had abandoned one wife, he could easily abandon me as well. I knew it would not happen. And he didn't abandon her, she walked out on him into the arms of a millionaire husband.' Suddenly she leans forward and rubs a finger on Aparna's cheek, then looks at it as if she has picked up something from her cheek. 'You're blooming,' she says. 'Are you sleeping with him?'

'No.'

'I can't believe this. No wonder you're confused. Once you sleep together, everything falls into place, your relationship becomes pukka.'

Aparna laughs. 'Personal experience?'

'Of course. Abbas was reluctant, he thought I was too young, he didn't want to *take advantage of me* – that's what *he* said. So I took the first step. Don't tell Aai, by the way.'

'What do you mean? Of course, I'm going to tell her. By the way, Taimavshi, I'm going to say, do you know Madhu slept with Abbas before marriage? And that it was she who took the initiative? Really Madhu!'

'Sorry, Apu. But tell me, don't you want to have sex with him?'

'I'm dying for it.'

'And he?'

'Dying for it too, I think. I hope. But he's exercising self-control. He obviously thinks that sex comes only after marriage.'

'For god's sake, Apu, not that old *suhaag raat* stuff. You're not a virgin, you were married.'

'Tell him that.'

'You should tell him.'

Aparna shakes her head in vigorous denial.

'Then I guess there's no other way. You just have to buy a sheer black nightie and seduce him.'

'You have such a filmy mind, Madhu. *Suhaag raat* and sheer black nighties...and dancing like Helen? I know you are part of the film world, but Abbas's films don't have these clichés.'

'I think it's time for me to go to bed and stop being insulted by my little sister. Good night, Apu. And by the way, let's spend an evening together, you, your Hari and Abbas and I. I've got some good wine.'

'He doesn't drink.'

'What! And he a singer! What's happened to them, they were so colourful, they drank like fishes and sang like angels. Do they live drab lives like the rest of us now? Anyway, bring him along.'

'And you'll interview him?'

'Of course. Ask him his income and how he's going to support you. Someone has to act the family elder, though Aai will do a much better job than I can. I might just ask him though, what's the matter with you, why don't you sleep with Apu? Aai will do the family bit.'

'Oh, she'll love Hari's pedigree. His grandfather was a purohit who performed marriages, he was also a teacher of Sanskrit and Marathi, and his ajoba's grandfather was a keertankar...'

'Holy cow! You have all the information. I'm impressed. No wonder he doesn't drink. Well, good night, girl.'

Madhu is leaving when Aparna suddenly remembers. 'Madhu, there's something else I wanted to ask you. You know we opened Baba's trunk to get Hari the natya sangeet songs?'

'Yes.'

'All of Baba's manuscripts are there. What do we do with them?'

'You have to preserve them, they're important. Don't throw anything out, or give it to the raddiwala.'

Aparna makes a sound of exasperation. 'Doctors are not ignorant fools, Madhu. I know they matter. That's why I'm asking you what I should do. I'm his daughter, remember?'

'I don't know. Maybe I'll ask Prof Mohite, at the university.'

'And that's not all. I found a notebook among the books I brought back. It came along with the other books. Baba has written 'Ahalya's story' on the first page, I recognize his handwriting. But the rest of it is not in his hand.'

'Sulumavshi's?'

'No, not hers either.'

'I can't imagine what it could be. Give it to me, I'll have a look.'

'Right, I'll give it to you the next time we meet.'

'Fine. I'm wondering, Apu, whether this is *the* novel. The novel he was going to write.'

'But he never wrote novels.'

'He wanted to write one. He said so.'

'He did?'

'But this can't be his novel if it's in someone else's hand.'

'And the notebook looks very old.'

'A mystery. Well, we'll solve it when we see it. Good night again, Apu.'

When she's gone, Aparna thinks, he wanted to write a novel? He spoke to Madhu about it, but he never spoke of it to me? She's surprised that the old jealousy can surface so many years after Gaja's death. 'You like Madhu more than you like me,' she used to charge him. 'Apu, you are my darling daughter. How can I like anyone more?'

But it's true, Madhu was close to him. And she stayed loyal to him when Sulu turned her back on Gaja. Taimavshi and Aparna were with Sulu, they were on her side. But Madhu never let her connection with Gaja cease. She stayed in touch, she brought him home when Sulu was close to death, she rang him up as soon as she died, she continued to meet him after that when he had sunk into the depths. Whereas I…?

'You are your mother's daughter,' he had said to her when she came back to be with him after his heart attack, and told him that her marriage was over. 'I'm not going back,' she told him. 'I'll have to go back to wind up everything, but I'll be back soon.'

'What's wrong?' he asked her.

'He's not the man I thought he was.'

'How many people are what we think they are? Give him another chance.'

'No. It's over.'

'You are your mother's daughter,' he had said then. 'You don't know how to forgive.'

Will I be the same with Hari? Unforgiving. Hard. Love works miracles, Madhu says, but can we ever escape our own selves?

When Jyoti had first come to Aparna, Aparna had never imagined that this patient, this woman, would find a place in her life, that one day they would be friends. Aparna, like most doctors, rarely thought of the final outcome when she first saw a patient. The treatment that she was going to start the patient on, the results of the investigations, the patient's physical condition, to some extent her state of mind – these were what mattered, these were the things she took into account. Yet with Jyoti, looking through her file on her first visit, the thought had suddenly flashed through her mind: this is not going to be easy, I might lose this patient. She had, however, quickly pushed the thought away; she believed that negative thoughts had no place in her dealing with patients. In any case, they would meet only on professional ground; Aparna always made sure of that.

Mira had broken this rule by guilelessly offering Aparna a place to live in, something that Aparna had badly needed at the time. A place so convenient that Aparna knew it was a stroke of luck to come across something like it, she knew she would deeply regret it if she did not take it. In any case, she thought, I can always keep my distance.

And she had. They had not intruded either, except for Saguna, who had got her the help she needed and Mira, who, feeling responsible perhaps, stayed in touch to make sure Aparna was all right. Mira's occasional bouts of panic, her courage in hiding these from her mother, had brought back to Aparna her own younger self, the girl she had been when her mother had been diagnosed with cancer, the daughter who was constantly fearful for her mother. She had thought of that girl when Jyoti, unusually for her, spoke to Aparna about Mira. 'She gets so agitated if I don't eat. How do I tell her, doc, that I can't eat?'

'She's frightened for you.'

'I know that. But I can't take her anxiety. When I see her face, I feel as if I'm being pierced with knives.'

So must my mother have felt seeing my grief. Grief? No, it was a desperation, a desire to do something that would save her mother, keep her alive. She, who had never prayed in her life, had prayed to all the gods there were to save her mother.

As if Jyoti sees into her mind, she speaks of prayer. 'I've gone back to prayer, doc. As a kid I believed in prayer, the nuns brainwashed us into believing that God, the bearded guy sitting up there, listens to our prayers; or, if he doesn't, the saints do. Then I met Aakash and forgot about god. After that it was a constant prayer for my children, they were so little, so fragile, I was terrified something would happen to them, I used to wonder how other mothers coped. You know that hollow babies have on the top of the skull, what do you call it?'

'Fontanelle.'

'It seemed so dangerous to me, I couldn't believe Nature had left them so vulnerable. I wanted to cover their heads all day, sit by them watching them, protecting that lethal opening. God, it was scary! And then Aakash died and I gave up god. Now in spite of my I-don't-give-a-damn attitude, I am praying all the time. I pray that I don't suffer too much, I pray that my children don't see me suffering, I pray that they have the courage to live without me. But I don't know who I am praying to. There is a blank, an empty niche, a pedestal without a statue. Maybe I should pray to you doctors. You are our gods, we think that only you can help us go on living.'

'We are too busy praying to some unknown entity ourselves to listen to your prayers.'

They laugh. Aparna and Jyoti have moved way ahead of the doctor-patient relationship. Perhaps it's the right time for them to meet, perhaps each fills a need in the other's life. For Jyoti, Aparna is a woman who knows her illness, who is able to look at her without pity, or the slight sense of fear that the disease always arouses. Aparna takes Jyoti's illness matter-of-factly, something to be tackled as and when the need arises. Aparna, too, finds in Jyoti a companion who, not being family, does not bring the baggage of her own past into their relationship. Taimavshi's and Madhu's concern for her, their anxiety about her being alone, their great desire that she marry again, loom over their relationship. There's Hari, of course, but that is an all-consuming, at times even an exhausting, bond. Besides, Jyoti also reminds Aparna of her father Gaja. Her mind is quick and agile like his was, her curiosity about the world huge, like his. And like him, unlike most people, she is more excited by ideas than by facts. Aparna remembers Gaja saying, 'A writer is like a bird building a nest. You pick up facts, ideas, stories, all kinds of things – and then knit all these together with your imagination.'

Aparna has come to know that Jyoti is a great reader. 'I read everything and anything I could lay my hands on,' she'd said to Aparna. 'All that I wanted was a story, a story about people who would interest me. Now I think I've wasted so much time in my life. If I had known I was not going to have much time, I would have been more careful with it. I wouldn't have read all the rubbish I read as a young girl.'

Now she tells Aparna about a book launch she had gone to, 'a book written by a cancer survivor,' she says, putting invisible quote marks around the word survivor. 'It was awful. He spoke in such a cocky triumphant way, he seemed to be announcing loudly *I've defeated cancer.* If I was him, I'd have touched wood. You don't speak of such a formidable enemy in that way! It's so cunning, so protean, it lulls you into a false sense of security – how could he speak of defeating it? To me, the nature of cancer is condensed in the words *Vita mea mors tua.* My life your death: that's what the malignant cells are telling us. The man obviously couldn't hear. Or maybe he thought that if he crowed loud enough, he could drown that voice.'

Aparna has never met a patient like her, one who moves away from the personal, from her own problem, to an abstract discussion of the disease. Her detachment abandons her, however, when she speaks of her children. 'I get so angry when I think of them. Why have they – whoever or whatever it is that arranges the world – done this to my children? First their father, now I. Miru was only eight when her father died. The poor little thing grew up in a day after that. She took on burdens children shouldn't even know about. She took on Tejas, just four years younger than her, after my mother died. I want more time, doc, I want to see my children grow up, I want Miru to be free of responsibility, I want to see Tejas a happy person.'

'We're trying to give you that time.'

'But so much is outside your control, doc. I know that.'

'You're in the safe zone now, think only of that.'

'Think positive, huh?'

'Absolutely.'

'And good will ultimately triumph over evil?'

Aparna is puzzled until she remembers Jyoti's talk about good cells and bad cells. 'Yes.'

'Thanks, doc. That's great, doc, keep up the pose. But I know the truth. And I will give this crab credit for making me understand what my priorities are. I know what I want – I want to spend time with my children. I've given up my job. They'd given me leave, now I've resigned.'

Aparna knows by now that Jyoti was the editor of a women's magazine, one published by a millionaire's wife, to funnel their black money, perhaps. But with Jyoti as editor, it became something more than a glossy magazine full of models and advertisements. It became a sensible magazine, with the information women need to have. There was lighter stuff, of course. Fiction. 'I don't look down on romance. It gives women the escape they need. After all, which man can be a lover like Mr Rochester or Darcy? We need them in fiction to make up for real life. I used to think, we don't need these things now, the world has changed, women have changed, but, doc, you'd be surprised to know how much remains unchanged.'

Later Aparna will come to know that Jyoti wrote some of the stories herself; under a pseudonym, of course. There were also experts writing for the magazine, giving legal, medical and financial advice. 'I thought of what I went through after Aakash's death. I was so ignorant, I thought no woman should be ignorant,' she tells Aparna.

'What will you do now?'

'At one time I thought I would write. Now? I don't know. Maybe I'll just read. I remember my mother became a great reader when she came to live with me after my father's death. I still have her books, the magazines. Maybe I'll try to read them, get back my Marathi.'

'You read Marathi?'

'Yes. Why?'

'Most of us who are English convent-educated don't.'

'Marathi was my second language. At one time, I could read it well.'

Aparna tells her then about the notebook she has found among her father's papers. 'I can read Marathi myself, but I'm slow and I don't have the time. Do you think you can read it and tell me what it is? Madhu and I are very curious.'

'With great pleasure.'

'Shall I get the book?'

'Now?'

'Yes.'

'Why not?'

Jyoti passes her hand over the cover. 'It's very old,' she says with awe. 'Ahalya's story. That's your father's handwriting.'

'Yes.'

'And you don't know who Ahalya is?'

'No.'

'Fascinating. Must be someone in the family.'

'So you'll read it?'

'Of course. Though I may take some time.'

'No hurry. You can take all the time you want.'

'All the time in the world,' Jyoti says and pumps her fist in the air. 'Yes, think positive.'

Aparna has to laugh.

'When are you giving me the notebook?'

'Notebook? What notebook, Madhu?'

'Really, Apu, do you have to be such a classical lover? Lost in your love and the world lost to you.'

'You mean Baba's notebook? The Ahalya's story one?'

'That's it.'

'I'm sorry, Madhu, I gave it to Jyoti to have a look. She hasn't yet given it back to me. I'll remind her.'

'Never mind, let her take her time. But I'm very curious about it, I'm hoping it's Gajakaka's novel.'

She's right, Aparna thinks when she puts the phone away. Madhu was making fun of me, but the world *has* receded. Aparna is moving between her work, her routine and Hari, like a cat walking on a narrow wall, delicately keeping her balance. Right now, Hari is busy, he has a programme in Nagpur in two weeks.

His mornings and evenings are occupied with his preparations. He comes to meet her in the hospital in the afternoon and waits patiently for her. When she is free, they go out and have lunch in a place across the road, trying to talk in the midst of a hungry lunchtime crowd. Some evenings she goes to his place and sits with him, while he works at putting his programme together. 'It's a morning event,' he says. 'I'm glad, because almost always it's in the evening and I go back to Darbari and Malkauns.'

Here, in his house, when he is working, she does not have to speak, she has only to listen to him and his friends talking, listen to their discussions which she finds fascinating, to the little bits of music which they hum, the taala they beat with their hands. To look at him, to listen to his voice is such bliss... She laughs at herself. Lost indeed! Madhu is right, she thinks.

Full of contrition at having forgotten Madhu's request, she speaks to Jyoti and learns that Madhu has forestalled her. She has already contacted Jyoti and she's coming to visit the next evening. Aparna agrees to join them. I'll try to get back early, she says. But she is late. In fact she had forgotten about the meeting, having had to spend time with the parents of a girl who has had surgery but refuses to have chemotherapy because she does not want to become bald, she says. As if she has transferred her terror of the disease to the loss of her hair.

Jyoti opens the door to her and says, 'Madhuri is here.'

'I'll join you in a few minutes. I need to have a bath.'

When she joins them, they are in the middle of a discussion about Gaja.

'I was telling Jyoti that I remember seeing the notebook on his table when we'd gone to Chandrapur, you and I. Remember, Apu, we went to get Sulumavshi's things?'

Aparna does not remember seeing the book, but she remembers the occasion. Sulu had walked out of home with only a suitcase, she had no intention of going back. When Taimavshi was absolutely sure Sulu would never go back, she had sent Madhu and Aparna to get some of the stuff she would need: documents, like her bankbook, her certificates, a few clothes. Aparna remembers her father opening the door and coming out, alerted by the sound of a rickshaw stopping. Perhaps he had thought it was Sulu come back. When he saw them, hope and happiness died out of his face and he went back in, leaving them to follow him. They went in and found him, newspaper in hand. Aparna had thought he would ask them about Sulu, say something about her. But all he said was, 'Why are you here?'

'We've come to take some of…' Madhu suddenly stopped and Aparna completed the sentence, 'Aai's things.'

'Are you staying tonight?'

'No, we're going back by the night train.'

At which he'd lost his temper. He had flung the newspaper away from him and said, 'Take anything you want, take everything there is in the house. Or burn it down, it makes no difference to me.'

Aparna had been shocked. She had never heard him speak this way, never to her, certainly. This angry, bitter man had frightened Aparna. She had rushed inside and come out after a bath to find Madhu and Gaja having a peaceful conversation, as if the fit of temper had never happened. They were sitting at his table, which as usual was piled with books. One of them, Madhu says, was this notebook.

'I don't remember it. What's it about?'

Jyoti tells her that she has only just begun reading it. 'It's not easy reading. The writing is small, some of the letters seem unfamiliar, written differently, the ink has faded. But it looks like it's an account of her life by someone called Ahalya. Madhu doesn't know who that is. Do you have any idea, doc?'

Aparna doesn't. 'Maybe we should ask Aai,' Madhu suggests.

'Well, whoever she is – we'll get to that later – it looks

fascinating. I've just read the first few pages and I found a reference to Tilak in it. I'm intrigued. How does Tilak come into this woman's life?'

'The Swaraj-is-my-birthright man Tilak?'

'Right. I think the beginning is perfect, she knows how to tell a story, this woman, how to hold your interest. I thought it was crying out to be translated, I found myself mentally translating it as I read. If you give me permission, I'd like to translate it.'

'Permission? Who, me?'

'It's your property, doc.'

'Is it? In which case I give you full permission. You can do what you want with it.'

'What if it becomes a bestseller and earns pots of money?'

'We'll share it. Fifty-fifty.'

'Poor Gajakaka, he always groaned and moaned that his writing never earned him enough money. Apu, does anyone stage his plays now? Do you get any royalty?'

'Nothing.'

'Strange, how quickly writers are forgotten. They say writers go on living in their works, but once their physical presence is gone, even their works become shadowy, orphaned.'

Actually, Gaja's eclipse had begun even before his death. At one time he had been the rage, he was lionized, he was the young rebel who brought freshness into Marathi theatre, who did away with the sentimental three-act play, with adaptations from English. He was a popular teacher, he was Dandekar sir, he was a man who could galvanize a class of students. And then it ended. His plays flopped, his creative powers declined. He tried a musical, which was a disaster on a large scale.

'It's not fair. We should do something for him,' Madhu says. 'At least three or four of his plays are excellent.'

'Which ones?'

'There's one he wrote during the Emergency about the

Railways. Remember, the Emergency started with the railway workers going on strike? Gajakaka combined that with the British during the war time, the way they turned all trains into troop trains, resulting in a famine in Bengal. That was an excellent play. Very powerful.'

'I must get hold of his plays.'

Madhu ignores Jyoti and continues. 'I owe him so much, he was the one who encouraged me to go on with my dancing, he introduced me to books and theatre…'

He was the only one from the family who had been present at her wedding. Both Taimavshi and Sulu had been angry with him for supporting Madhu, but it had not deterred him. There he was, cap on head, ready to sign his name, to be a witness. 'He'd brought some pedhas, a few grains of *akshada* and a pair of gold bangles for me. I will never forget that, never,' Madhu had once said to Aparna.

'We must do something for him, Apu. I'm ashamed we have not done anything.'

'What can you do, Madhu?'

'I'll think of something. Apu, you have to be part of it.'

'Whatever you say.'

'These doctors! Such Philistines.'

'Don't you say anything against my doc, Madhuri. She deals with human lives. Compared to that, the rest – music and theatre and literature – is trivial, they are the frills of life.'

'Artists can be very businesslike, Jyoti. I remember my college drama society asked me to tell Baba they wanted to stage his play. And he said, tell them they have to pay me the usual royalty. Just because my daughter is in the college, they can't get it free. These sons of bitches try to avoid paying the author. They spend enough on themselves. Cups of tea and packets of chivda and cigarettes. But when it comes to paying the writer, there is never any money.'

As they laugh, she thinks of Hari, who leaves it to his friend Bhide to see that he gets his due. Why didn't Baba have anyone?

She listens to Madhu speaking of ways of bringing Gaja's writing back and thinks sadly that it's like keeping someone alive on a life-support system. If people stage his plays, he will live. If they don't, nothing can help. She says none of this to Madhu. But when Jyoti asks as they are leaving, 'So can I start the translation?' she says vigorously, 'Yes, do'.

It is much later, after they have read a good bit of her translation, that Madhu comes to know that Jyoti had written a novel in response to a publishing house which had asked for light romantic stories set in India. 'I meant it to be like that, frothy syrupy stuff, but halfway through it became something quite different. So I gave up.'

But this is later. Right now Jyoti tells them that she has already translated a few pages. 'I'll email them to you. You can tell me what you think about my translation.'

Aparna laughs. 'I, to judge a literary work!'

Before parting Madhu reminds Aparna of her promise to bring Hari home. 'Bring your boyfriend home,' she says.

'Boyfriend? He's my lover.'

'You mean…?'

'I mean boyfriend doesn't sound dignified enough. We'll come after he returns from Nagpur.'

'Music programme?'

'Yes, he's singing at a medical conference. You know, the usual cultural evening. He knows he won't get a good audience. But even if a handful understand and enjoy, it's enough, he said.'

'The life of an artiste is hard. Don't I know that? Missing him?'

'My god, yes. Oh Madhu I'm totally out of control. It's frightening.'

Madhu pats her as if she's a restive horse. 'You'll settle down in a while. That's why I say, get married. Nothing like marriage to take the bubbles out of a relationship.'

'Have you settled with Abbas?"

'No, Apu, not as yet.'

'And he?'

'He was married once, he had his youthful fling. Or flings. I don't know, I don't want to know. A pair of fools, aren't we?'

'I guess we are.'

'And tell Aai about Shree Hari. It's hard for me to keep secrets from her.'

'I'll tell her.'

'And Apu, I'm truly truly glad for you. You've had some bad years, a rough time. You should get a taste of happiness, don't you think?'

'Says who?'

'Says I.'

'And is anyone listening to you?'

'You got me there. But we can always hope, can't we?'

AHALYA'S STORY

After months of thinking, of not being able to decide whether I should or I should not write, I now begin to write my story. Why am I doing this? No one will read this, not even Durga, for I will destroy it before I die. Why then am I writing it? Maybe I have a hope that by writing about my life I will make some sense of it. Maybe I want to see my life from a distance and try and understand what it was all about. I first got the idea of writing the day Balasaheb (*Translator's note: she means Bal Gangadhar Tilak*) died. Even here, in our little place, we heard of his death, we heard of the huge crowds that followed him on his last journey, we heard of the way people mourned his death. And I thought, yes, he was a great man. One of the few humans who can change the lives of people, even of a country. I found it hard to believe that our lives had touched, even if briefly. No, not mine, it was 'his' life that had touched Balasaheb's, 'he' had stood up against Balasaheb twice. When I heard how Balasaheb was honoured and mourned, I thought, how had 'he' dared! I knew the answer then, I know it now. 'He' dared because of the kind of man 'he' was.

Let that be. I am not trying to take away from Balasaheb's greatness. That will remain for all time, he will never be forgotten. Whereas 'he' remains unknown, will always be unknown. Yes, now I know that I am writing about my life because I want to write about 'him'. I am not the main character in my book. 'He' is. By writing, I will remind myself that a man like 'him' existed, a man very different from Balasaheb, but to me as great as Balasaheb was. It is 'his' life, the life that I shared with 'him', the kind of man 'he' was, and how 'he' changed my life forever – these are the things I am going to write about.

I have to hurry. It's strange, now that I have retired, I have a lot of time on my hands. At the same time, I know my time is limited. I don't know how long I will be able to live by myself. Ever since I retired, Durga has been asking me to go and live with them. But I will not go, not as yet. As long as I can manage myself, I want to be here in my own house. Yes, I would like to die in my daughter's house, with her and my grandson by my side. I know the time will come when I will have to go. My eyes are giving me trouble, at times it seems as if there is a *mulmul* curtain between me and the world and my strength is no longer the same. Therefore I have to hurry. I will begin right away. In a way, it will be like living my life all over again, tracing my footsteps from the day I was born. Maybe, by looking back from this distance, I will be able to see a pattern. Or let me admit that by writing about 'him', I will be able to bring 'him' back into my life, even if it is only for the little time I spend in writing.

For that pleasure I will have to pay a price. I will have to write about things I have tried hard to forget. Yes, if I am going to write about my life, I have to write all of it, I cannot leave out anything, I cannot change anything. We can't change our stories, our stories are us. I never thought of this when I decided to write. I was afraid of other things. I was nervous about my eyesight. Of my memory. Would I be able to recall the things that happened to me years back? But, most strangely, memory awakens as I write and things come back to me. Sometimes I see only the picture, sometimes the sounds come with the pictures. I can hear the sparrows chirping in the backyard of our house in the morning when I woke up, I can hear the cows mooing, calling to Pandu (how did that name suddenly come back to me?) to relieve them of the weight of the milk in their udders. This was what Pandu said. But my mother differed, she thought they were calling out to their calves to come and drink milk. 'It's for the calves, Pandu,' she would say to Pandu, pleading with him to leave more milk for the calves. 'This milk is not really ours.'

'How can you say that, bai? We feed them, we look after them, they owe us their milk.'

Once again something strange is happening: I thought I would write about my life with 'him', instead I see pictures of my childhood. I see that I have to go back, because, wasn't it the child I was who became the woman who lived with 'him'? Who became what I now am? Yes, I have to go back.

This part about my childhood is easy to write about. What is hard is knowing that I will have to keep moving until I get to the point in my story when a cloud of grief will come down on me and drench me in sorrow. I am fearful, I draw back, but I understand I have no choice. I have to move forward. As children, we were told that the feet of ghosts pointed backwards. This was how you recognized ghosts, because, though they often disguised themselves as ordinary humans, their feet would give them away. (I remember there was a time when I looked first at people's feet, then at their faces.) We humans have feet that point forward, so we have to move ahead. You can turn the pages of a history book, you can go back a few years, or a few hundred years, or even a thousand years. But in life you can't go back even a step, you have to move forward. And so I have to go on, in spite of knowing I will suffer sorrow all over again. I have also come to realize that I am burdened by my past. The burden is greater because I have never been able to speak to anyone about it. Nobody knows the truth of my life. The painter knew, but he never referred to it, not once, and I respected him for it. But if I can't speak, I can write, and I know I will die lighter after I have written the things I have never been able to speak about. I think that death may be waiting for me to shed this burden before it comes to me. You have to give up everything – possessions, emotions, relationships, even memories, to be able to meet death.

Many times I wonder: what if things had been different? *What if?* Writers, real writers I mean, not scribblers like me, must be asking themselves this question 'what if?' when writing their stories. And the answers that they get to the question 'what if?' are what they finally write about. It now occurs to me that writers have complete control over the world they create. I have none. I have to put my feet in the footprints I made when I walked the road so many years ago. I cannot make fresh footprints. And, however bad it was, I do not want to change my life, no, not even on paper. To do so would mean no Kashi and no Durga in my life. I can't imagine my life without them.

Mine has been a most unusual life. I have lived three lives and died two deaths. When I die now, it will be my third and, I hope, final death. I gave up my religion when I died the second time, so I have given up a belief in many lives or in rebirth. It is a very happy thought that I will not have to go through this thing we call life all over again. In any case, I have had three lives in this single one. My first life, my life in my parents' home, my life as a child, ended when I got married. Everything changed after that, even my name. Like all women, I thought that this married life was forever, but that too came to an end for me and I began my third life. I began this life with fear and sorrow and anger. I didn't want it, I wanted to put an end to it. But, like humans always do, I finally came to terms with it. And I have to admit, it has been a quiet and peaceful life, without any of the drama of my earlier life. It has been more useful too, because I have taught girls, many of them, through the years and I hope I have made some difference to their lives. At home, in the early years, most of the time it was just my girls, Kashi and Durga, and I. I cooked, I washed, I cleaned, the girls helped as much as they could, and then we went to school, the three of us, they to learn and I to teach. In a way it seemed to me that life had come full circle. I began life as a teacher's daughter (my father became a headmaster later) and I became a teacher myself. I also became a headmistress in the last few years of my service. It made me proud, not for myself, but for my father; how proud he would have been for me! But I could not say this to anyone. As a child I loved playing school-school; my father used to tease me and call me Headmaster-bai. My brothers and I were always spoken of as the headmaster's children. I don't know about my brothers (boys are strange creatures) but I was very proud of it. My father was also a very unusual man – so I think now. I wish that I had realized it then.

Now that I've got to my family, let me write about them. My father was the eldest of three brothers, one of whom had a job in Mumbai. The third brother and my father lived together with their families on our land. We also had my father's mother at home and a widowed sister. Plus we seven children. And there always was one or another poor boy, a student who either had no home, or was too poor and so lived with us. It didn't matter because our family lands, which my uncle farmed, were fertile, yielding good crops. We always had enough to eat, there was nothing lacking. I was the youngest of four, the only daughter and much petted, specially by my father. My favourite companion was the brother next to me, Mukund. We were great friends.

I lost them, I lost that entire life of mine. It remained a great grief for many years, that not only would I never meet my family again, I would never know about them, never know whether they were alive or dead, never know how my nephews and nieces were growing up. It was like losing a novel when you are halfway through reading it and not knowing what happens afterwards to the characters. But these were not people in a book, they were my family, my blood relations, my brothers and their children. The connection was completely severed and even today I know nothing about any of them. Let it go. If I am going to complain, I will never finish writing this. I must keep moving.

One of the things I have begun to see as I write is how little control I have had over my life, which has been shaped by other people, by their thoughts, their actions. I could call it Fate. When 'he' decided to marry me, my mother said it was 'Fate'. But 'he' did not believe in Fate. We control our own lives, 'he' would always say. Life is a Karma kshetra, 'he' said. 'He' made 'his' own life a field of action.

I was very young then, I had not learnt to think for myself and, even if I had, I would never have argued with 'him', I was so awed by 'him', so influenced by 'him'. But if I had thought then the way I do now, I would have asked 'him', 'That is all right for a man. What about women? Look at me!' Yes, look at me! I was to get married, in fact it was my wedding day when I got my periods for the first time. My father was a very honest man, he told the bridegroom's people what had happened. And they called off the wedding. I am sure my father never expected that. But they had their reasons. How did they know this was the first time? Perhaps I'd begun earlier, perhaps I was older than what they'd been told I was? How could they trust our family? I can remember the dismantling of everything, the dispersing of people who had come for the wedding, the atmosphere of gloom, my grandmother blaming my father all day long. Why did he have to be a Satya Harischandra?

And then 'he' came. 'He' sent word through a friend of 'his' that 'he' was ready to marry me. It was as if god himself had come to our aid. At first our family was suspicious. Why did 'he' make an offer for a girl who had been rejected? Did 'he' have a wife already, bad habits, vices? But no, there was nothing wrong. 'He' was a well-educated man and 'his' family was well known in Pune. They had money, they had a good reputation. 'He' was also good looking, better than me, actually. There was one thing, though, which 'he' spoke of to my father himself, that he had twice been almost engaged to girls who died even before the engagement ceremony. My father did not hesitate. Not because he did not believe in omens and stars and bad luck, but because he had to get me married. Dearly though he loved me, he decided I would have to take my chance. A dead daughter was better than an unmarried daughter. 'He' of course did not believe that it was 'his' bad luck which caused the deaths of the girls. 'He' said girls were so badly looked after, their health was so neglected, it was not surprising so many of them died. Whatever it was, we got married. There were very few guests and much less fuss, but there was much happiness around.

Now what control did I have over either of these happenings? 'He' had control, 'he' made a choice. Later, when we were able to talk to each other, 'he' told me that 'he' had seen me when 'he' had come to Wadgaon for his friend's sister's wedding. By chance, 'he' had seen me playing 'school-school' with other children. I was, as always, the teacher. 'He' thought it was most unusual for a girl to play at being a teacher. Most girls played at being mother, cooking, scolding the children and such things. 'His' friend told him about my father, how he believed in education, in educating girls. Perhaps that was one of the reasons why, when 'his' friend told 'him' what had happened to me, 'he' decided he would marry me. Everyone called it Fate, but 'he' did not believe in Fate. 'He' said we control our own lives, not something called Fate. To believe in Fate, 'he' said, means you make no effort yourself; it's a lazy way of thinking, 'he' said. We need to know where we are going, we need to swim, not to let ourselves float. I tried, as I always did then, to think like 'he' did. But I knew even then that there are times when we have no control over what is happening to us.

Have I written this earlier? My memory plays tricks on me now. So often I can't remember whether I have done something, or said something earlier. Another problem I am realizing as I write is that it is hard to know what to write about and what to omit. What is important and what is trivial. Let that be, I will try my best to overcome these problems. And if I don't, nobody will read this – that's a comfort.

To go back – and so I was married. I think I will stop here with the sound of the shehnai in my ears, my sobbing as I realized I would have to go away from home and my mother telling me I was now a married woman and married women did not cry. I heard it for the first time that day, the words which would be the key to my life, the key to all women's lives: what will your in-laws say if you say or do this, that, or the other? Yes, what will they say? The question that shapes the lives of all women, the question that keeps all women under strict control. Enough for today.

Tr. note: It was difficult to decide how to translate the way Ahalya speaks of her husband. Always only a pronoun and always in the plural. But imagine calling a man 'they' and 'them' in English. So I've made it as 'he' 'him' etc. I never knew that in translation even simple things become difficult. I'm learning.

I'm enjoying this. Even reading Ahalya's handwriting is easier now. Her handwriting is like that of a child who has just learnt to write, each letter shaped with care, each one distinct and clear, the line at the top of the letters absolutely straight.

Let me know what you think of the translation.

Excellent, Jyoti, it's really excellent.

Thanks, Madhuri. And you, doc?

Silence. Your doc is in her own world. Never mind. Keep going, Jyoti, I'm eagerly waiting for the next instalment.

Jyoti has come to Aparna with the results of her tests. It's like the first time, but now Mira is with her. And it's a different Jyoti. Last time she had been brittle with fear, but had put on an act of bravado. She had been slightly hostile as well as if the doctor, not the disease, was her enemy. She is humbler this time. She has confessed to Aparna how reluctant she was to go through the tests. 'I'd much rather not know at all than get bad news,' she had said. But all is well, as Dr Bhagat said. 'He was pleased with me,' Jyoti says.

Yes, surgeons love their patients when they say they're fine. But if the patient has a problem after they've done cutting them up, the surgeons don't want to know about it. Of course, Aparna will not say this to Jyoti; why spoil her mood? Or Mira's? In any case, the mother and daughter, sitting opposite Aparna, look wary and guarded. There is absolute silence while Aparna goes through the reports. Finally she puts them down and smiles. 'All well. You know that.'

'I wanted you to say it, doc.'

'You're doing fine. Nothing to worry about.'

But it's only a reprieve, both Jyoti and Aparna know that. The danger is still waiting. Jyoti speaks to Aparna openly, later, when they are on their own.

'I'd read somewhere that when Anne Boleyn...you know her,

she was beheaded by Henry, the wife-killer?' She looks inquiringly at Aparna, who nods. 'Well, when she was going to her execution, she kept looking back, thinking that a messenger would come with a pardon for her. I feel a little like that. Only it's the other way round. I've got a pardon, but I keep thinking a messenger will come and say, *sorry, that was wrong, you're not let off, you're going to lose your head.*'

Jyoti has been close to the edge; she has moved back a little, but she is still close enough to the brink, still suffering a sense of vertigo. And something has gone out of her, a confidence, a trust that we have in life, that we will go on living, that, after today, a tomorrow will come. She asks Aparna something she had not dared to ask with Mira present. 'How long do you think this good behaviour will last, doc?'

'You want the statistics? I'll look them up and let you know.'

'Oh, let it go, doc. I know you doctors don't like to be pinned down. Leave it vague is your motto. But if someone asks me, how much time do you want?' I'll say, ten years more. Even five will do, at a pinch. That'll be a great boon for me and my kids. I know that when I'm not here, my family will do all they can for them. But it's never the same, is it?'

Then she goes on to talking about her mother, whom she and Deepak call by her name, Prabha. 'I always felt that my mother didn't love me like I thought a good mother would. Saguna's mother, Tarabai, had full charge of me, she did everything for me. Later, when Prabha came to live with me, I found out that Tarabai had been playing her own game, deliberately alienating me from my mother. And, of course, there was my father. Daddy wanted Mama to be a memsaheb, a society woman, to dress well, go out with him; he encouraged her to leave me to Tarabai. When Prabha came to me after my father's death, I felt I'd suddenly found my mother. It was for a very short time. She didn't live long. I always regret that. Something goes out of you when your parents die – I know that now.'

'I should know. I lost both my parents.'

'Sorry, doc.' And then she asks her whether it's all right for her to go away on a holiday.

'Where?'

'Goa. Remember, the kids had gone to my cousin Manoj, who lives there? He's been after me to spend some time with them. We were great pals as kids, we're the same age, almost, and both of us were hell-raising brats. The children are insisting I go.'

'Go, then, go. How long?'

'A fortnight? Depends. I'm not sure.'

'I see no problem.'

'Can I ring you up if I feel I want to talk?'

'Sure.'

'Don't you think, doc, we must have met in our past lives? I feel so comfortable with you, as if I've known you forever.'

'You believe in past and future lives?'

'No! But it's a good game to play sometimes.'

Suddenly, before going, she asks, 'Did you get my mail? You know, the one with an attachment? My translation of Ahalya's story?'

'Oh, I'm sorry. I haven't read it as yet. I've saved it to read when I have the time.'

'Whenever, doc. No hurry. Don't push yourself. But it's fascinating. I hope to do some work on it in Goa.'

'Don't work too hard.'

'No. And I hope you won't mind my sending you the bits I do?'

I will read it this weekend, she thinks. Hari is not here, he'll be back on Monday and then I will have no time, I will not be able to think of anything but Hari and my work. But her weekend is full of chores left undone through the week, of trying to go through a paper she has written for the quarterly meeting of the Oncologists' Association. And then it's Monday, the day Hari is to come back. Aparna is full of expectation, almost choking with impatience. She rushes through her work, wanting to finish on time, to go home early. She looks at her patients and thinks: Please, please don't get into any complications today. My Hari is coming back after a week, he's coming to me in the evening. I want to go home on time, I want to have a bath and be fresh and sweet-smelling when he comes. Smelling of flowers and sandalwood, not of hospital disinfectants and sickness. She thinks of him, his face glowing with joy, telling her about his programme, unconsciously playing a beat on the table as always, she thinks of his presence, his voice, his face…

When he comes, she is bathed and fresh, but he has obviously just got off the train and come to her the way he was. She is swallowed in his arms and for a few moments they don't speak, just enjoy feeling each other.

'I missed you,' he says. 'Oh, how I missed you.' He is holding her so tightly it hurts; she winces but he does not notice. 'And you?'

'What do you think?'

'What's happened to me, Rani? I'm lost, I'm really lost.'

'Let me get you a glass of water.'

'No, don't go.'

But a moment later, he is the one who lets go of her suddenly and says, 'All right, get me some water. Then a cup of tea? After that I have to go, I must have a bath, I'm feeling filthy. I'll come tomorrow morning.'

Why did you come then if you wanted to go away so soon? Don't go, she wants to say to him, stay with me tonight, make love to me, I want to feel the pressure of your body on mine, I want to feel you inside me. But she can't say these things to him. I'm a woman, not a girl, and yet I find it hard to say them. And he…? She wonders at his self-control, she knows he goes away so as to not succumb to his desires. How long, Hari, how long do we go on in this way?

'You are your mother's daughter,' her father had said to her. No, Baba, she tells him now, I am *your* daughter, I hunger for Hari the way you hungered for the woman you left my mother for. She thinks of Gaja telling her during her last visit, 'Nature has not been kind to men. They have to carry the yoke of their libido almost all their lives. And a man's libido is very strong. At times it becomes so loud that it drowns out a whole orchestra of emotions. What remains is only that one tune, that one instrument.'

But Baba, she had wanted to say, we have our minds, our will, we have been given these things so that we are not all animal instincts. As if hearing her unsaid questions, he had gone on, 'No, no, I am not trying to excuse myself. I'm telling you as it is. You are not embarrassed, are you?'

She had wanted to protest, to stop him, she had wanted to say to him, Baba, I'm your daughter, don't speak to me of your sexual life. But she knew that for him, at that point, she was just a pair of ears, someone to listen to him. When she was silent, he went on, 'You are a doctor, you know Nature's demands, you know how strong they are.'

For women, too, Baba. I know, now I know, Baba, perhaps I can understand how you felt and why you did what you did. And she remembers too what Taimavshi had said when she told her about Hari. 'Marry him, Apu, marriage gives you stability, it leaves you free to live the rest of your life without worrying about loneliness or sex. And the greatest boon – you can have children. Life is transformed when you have children.'

Aparna is picking her way delicately through her father's words and her aunt's advice, trying to know what it is *she* wants. It is now very clear Hari wants marriage. She has noticed a change in him, she can see he is more sure of himself and their relationship, more confident that both of them are committed to being together for the rest of their lives. He tells Aparna his brother Krishna wants to meet her. Shall we have lunch together, he asks, the three of us? It's not really a question. Krishna and he have decided on the day, the time, the place. She hesitates, then agrees, thinking she will not make an issue of such small matters. If he wants her to meet his brother, why not? But to her it smacks too much of showing her off to his family, of making an announcement about their relationship, about a future togetherness. He has moved to a different level, taking her with him, though she is not ready.

But she is glad she meets Krishna, for watching the brothers together, she sees a different Hari, she sees him as the elder brother, the fond brother.

'Your father was a dramatist, wasn't he?' Krishna says to her when they are introduced. 'I remember seeing a play of his.'

'Don't take him seriously, Aparna. I'm sure this boy has never seen a Marathi play in his life. He's completely English, he knows what's happening in New York or London, but don't ask him what plays are running in Mumbai.'

'That's not fair, Dada. Sometimes I think you've joined the *we-Marathis* gang.'

Listening to them, she becomes aware of the affection between them. And she thinks of the strangeness of human relationships. That Hari, who has for long kept a distance from his father, has resented his remarriage, and who never mentions his stepmother's name, yet has so much affection for Krishna, the fruit of that marriage. She listens with pleasure to them talking of their childhood (Krishna spent every vacation with Hari and their grandparents in Pune), of their childhood games, their friends, of how strict their grandmother was. She sees that Krishna admires his brother, she's surprised at his knowledge of music, something he has obviously learnt because of his brother's passion for it. A discordant note is struck when Krishna speaks of their parents' impatience to see their sons married. Hari's face becomes stern, it's like he is rejecting their concern.

'I keep saying Dada has to get married first. I can't think of marriage until he is married.'

'Listen, Krishna, I've told you many times, you're ready for marriage, you have the money to start your own life, Maya is waiting for you – why do you bring me into the picture? What do I have to offer a woman?'

'Listen to him! Women fall for him all the time. I had to hide my girlfriends from him. They only had to see Dada with his taanpura and a soulful look on his face, singing *Aao sajaniya*, or *piya nahi aaye* – and it was all over for me. I knew I didn't stand a chance.'

While they argue, Aparna thinks, I've let things drift for too long. Hari thinks I'm hesitating because he doesn't have enough money. That's not true. I'm hesitating because…because… She stumbles, trying to find the words to tell Hari clearly about her feelings. Instead of words, she sees Madhu bringing her father to see Sulu, who was nearing the end of her journey. Madhu had been the only one with enough courage and love to bring Gaja home. Hearing Taimavshi's startled tone and Madhu's sharp response, Aparna had come out of her mother's room and seen her father, looking as if he'd never seen this place before, as if the three women, even his own daughter Aparna, were strangers to him.

'Come,' Madhu said to him and when he hesitated, she took him by the hand as if he were a child and led him into Sulu's room. She came out almost immediately, closing the door behind her, and at first there was only silence. Then they heard the terrible sounds of a man sobbing. Taimavshi turned round and went back into her own room, Madhu followed her and Aparna stood where she was, wanting to go but unable to stir, when Gaja came out. He walked past Aparna, as if he could not see her. She went in to her mother, who was lying, her face to the wall, seeming to be asleep. But the tremors of her shoulders gave her away; Aparna knew she was sobbing. She had gone out herself and thrown herself on the sofa, sobbing with a grief that seemed to tear her body apart.

So much suffering, she thinks now, both of them wounded and bloodied, both of then dead not very long after. 'He's not like other men,' Sulu would say proudly of Gaja, excusing his many weaknesses. 'These writers,' she would say, but with pride, 'are not like other people. We can't judge them like we judge others.'

Why, then, did she refuse to forgive him in the end? Why did all those years of being together, of loving and being loved, not matter at all? And how could he have dealt their marriage, their life together, how could he have dealt Sulu, whom he had loved so much, such a mortal wound? Does marriage mean tying two people in so tight a knot that to live together is difficult, and to separate is death?

Hari, I want you, she longs to say, I want you in all ways, I want you badly. But I know you won't go ahead without marriage. And I'm afraid of marriage. I had thought once that I would destroy the fear by jumping into marriage; instead, my fears came true. What if it happens again, Hari? I won't survive it, I won't. I'm not a besotted young girl. Besotted all right, but I'm not young enough to make it an excuse for foolishness. This time, if something goes wrong, it will be the end for me.

To me, marriage is…marriage is… Finally she gets the words: Marriage is a site of possible betrayal.

AHALYA'S STORY

After Bhausaheb left me and went away (I have decided I can call him Bhausaheb, I no longer have to call him Mamanji, because he is no longer my father-in-law. Is he not the one who said that I had no connection with his family any more?) I knew what grief really meant. Grief is too small a word to contain my feelings. I had thought until that moment that I had experienced the greatest sorrow any human can bear, I had lost everything. But I did have some hope. I had my son, I would live for him, I would watch him grow, I would tell him about his father, I would see his father in him and try to make him a man like his father was. And who knows, perhaps I could become a teacher like Miss Simpson, I could be of some use in this world.

What a fool I was! How could I have hoped for such things? How could I have imagined they would allow me to go out of the house and become a teacher? I myself had thought Miss Simpson a strange creature when I first saw her. A woman who was not married and had no children, a woman who lived by herself – what kind of woman was she? And how could she have left her home and come alone, so far away, to another country? I asked her when I came to know her better and when we had begun to converse, I, in my terrible English and she, in her Marathi which never sounded like Marathi – I asked her whether it was easy being an unmarried woman in England. I asked her, a little hesitantly, whether she had ever wanted to get married.

She answered my second question first. Yes, she said, she would have liked to get married, but only to the right kind of man, a man whom she could respect. I thought this a strange idea then. Right man? The right man was the one who was already waiting for you. We believe that Brahma himself has tied the knot, we believe that marriages are destined, I said to her. She smiled at that and said, 'Yes, I know that.' Then she answered my other question: Are unmarried women respected?

'Not as much as married women are,' she said. 'A woman who is not married is often pitied, people think she must be lacking something because she could not get a man. It is not a failure of the family as it is here, but a failure of the girl, of the woman herself.'

But she was so educated, so intelligent. Was she not respected for that, I asked her? 'He' respected her enormously.

'Your husband is an unusual man. And don't forget, in your country I belong to the ruling race, I am a white woman, and therefore superior. I don't get this respect back home. There, I am only a spinster. Though I am better off than many women because I have some money of my own.'

She told me that an aunt of hers had left her all her money when she died. Not much, but enough, so that, along with what she earned from a teaching job, she would never have to ask anyone for money. It was like a miracle, she said, this money coming to her. And it was a total surprise. 'I didn't know my aunt very well, as a matter of fact. But she seemed to know my desire for independence. And she knew money was the one thing that could give a person independence.'

She is right; money makes much possible. If I had money I could have taken my son with me and lived somewhere on my own with him, I could have…

What am I thinking of? Can a woman live alone in this country? A young woman? Women don't even have a name they can call their own. I was forbidden by Bhausaheb from using the name that had been mine for almost half my life, the name 'he' had given me on marriage. It was Indutai who told me that not only was Bhausaheb not going to come back for me, henceforth I would be staying in this place with other widows and abandoned women. And she gave me Bhausaheb's letter which told me I could no longer use the name that became mine when I married his son. It was as if I was dead. I had no family, no name. He had put me on the pyre and gone away, leaving me to burn.

It was a shock. The earth opened up under my feet like it did for Sita. But I had no mother to take me into her arms, to comfort me for the loss of my name, my family. The worst thing was that I had lost my son, I would never see him again. 'I have done what I promised,' Bhausaheb wrote. What had he promised and to whom? And what right did he have to give anyone a promise which deprived me of my son? I had given him birth, I fed him, I watched him as he slept by my side, seeing, with great joy, his little chest rising and falling as he breathed. 'I set you free,' Bhausaheb wrote. What kind of freedom was it to lose everything, to lose my son who was everything to me?

It took me a long time to come out of it. But I did. At first I thought I would die, I wanted to die when I thought I would never see my Sonya's face again. I would not be able to live without him; how could I, when almost every moment of my life for the past three years had been spent with him. I wanted death, but death did not come to me. I survived. Life matters above everything else. Even when your mind wants to give up life, your body craves food, nourishment, it makes you walk back to the path of living. Survival is the main goal of life, I heard Miss Simpson say during her conversations with 'him'.

Stories within stories. To think of Miss Simpson is to remember that she came to our house to teach 'him' what 'he' called life sciences. It is to remember that Bhausaheb had prevented 'him' from doing what 'he' wanted most to do – become a doctor. 'You are a Brahmin,' he had said. 'You cannot touch dead bodies, you cannot touch people of different castes, low castes.' It is also to remember that Bhausaheb loved his son, his only son, so much that he agreed to his learning life sciences at home. And so Miss Simpson came to us. I had to be with them, they could not be left on their own, a man and a woman. So 'he' suggested I learn English from her. I did, but above all I listened to 'him' and Miss Simpson talking, I admired the way they conversed, I marvelled at the things they said. The old gurus must have taught their shishyas in this way, I used to think. Question and answer. Listening to them was like entering another world, like getting a glimpse of a different world which existed outside our petty world of rituals and festivals, of cooking and feeding, of rules for fast days and feast days, of time measured through pregnancies and menstrual periods, of children and lack of children. Through their talk I came to understand that we humans are part of a much larger world, a world that contains life other than human life. That we are only a part of this world, we are not the centre of it. 'He' spoke of Galileo (I was hearing the name for the first time) and said that after reading Darwin, 'he' felt like Galileo who found out that we are not the centre of the universe, and that the planets revolved, not around our earth, but around the sun. As in that universe, so in this life, 'he' said. They both agreed that we would one day learn to accept our place on this earth with humility and give up the arrogance of thinking of ourselves as superior creatures.

This was a difficult thought for me to accept. After all, were we not superior to all other creatures, because we could think and talk and understand? 'But how many of us think?' 'he' asked. 'And being superior also means being more responsible, responsible for other living creatures. But are we?'

Miss Simpson herself confessed that it was not easy for her to see human life as part of a larger whole. To her, human life was central, the most important.

'That is because you arc not a Hindu,' 'he' said. 'We Hindus do not think of ourselves as the beginning and end of creation. There is so much more outside us, so much more inside us – it's an amazing philosophy which comes closer to understanding many of the questions we ask.'

Miss Simpson was not a missionary, she was a teacher. But she could not entirely shake off the ideas that Christianity had given her. 'He' never spoke against her beliefs, but I remember 'he' said to me once, Christianity has a very neat idea of creation and of the world. Hinduism recognizes the chaotic quality of the world and of creation. That's why we have so many gods and goddesses.

This is hard, this is too hard. I should not have begun this. I feel as if something is being torn out of me when I write. I thought that to remember bad moments, times of grief would be hard; but even the good moments, the wonderful moments, come with daggers and sharp knives. I am also learning that when you are writing you cannot change things to make it easier for yourself; you have to stay with the truth. What *you* know is the truth.

I will go on with my story. I remember that 'he' and Miss Simpson spoke of reproduction. Thank god, I didn't know what the word meant. And when I did, I wondered what Bhausaheb, what the women, would say if they knew 'he' was talking of such things with a woman, a strange woman. This was the time when there was much discussion about the Age of Consent Bill. The law, as it was, required a girl to be at least ten years old before her husband could consummate the marriage. Then a little girl died, torn to pieces by her twenty-five-year-old husband. The girl was eleven when this happened, which means her husband could not be punished. And some people wanted the age of consent of girls to be raised to twelve, others, including 'him', wanted it to be even higher. But Balasaheb disagreed. Must our culture be destroyed by the British, he asked. This was what the Age of Consent Bill would do, according to Balasaheb.

'He' was very angry at that, so angry that Miss Simpson asked 'him' to write a reply. And 'he' did. 'His' question was: what has marrying little girls to men much older than themselves to do with any culture? Where is it written, 'he' asked, that girls should be married to men twice their age, at times even more? This is nothing but a cruel custom. 'He' spoke of the cruelty of little girls having to endure the passions of grown men. 'He' asked the question – does a thing become sacred because it has been happening for a long time?

'He' himself had waited for me to be fifteen before we became husband and wife in every way. Our son was born when I was sixteen. By then the women in the family had begun to despair, they thought I was barren, there was even a whispered conspiracy to get him married again. Then our son was born and the family came together to rejoice.

To go back to 'his' article, 'he' said that science has proved that girls' minds and bodies had to mature before they were ready to become mothers, that little girls who are not ready to become mothers only produce weak babies. Which is why so many babies die in our country, which only means women have to go on bearing more and more children. If we reject science, 'he' said, we are going to be left behind in the world.

This article came out in a paper. And 'he' was abused, people called him the white man's slave, they said 'he' wanted our women to become immoral, they called him the gora saheb's slave, they said 'he' was part of the conspiracy to replace our great Hindu culture with Christianity, they even said 'he' was being converted to Christianity, something that frightened the family more than anything else. Such foolishness. 'He' is forgotten today. Nobody knows 'him', or what 'he' tried to do. I wonder whether 'his' son, our son, has any of 'his' father's qualities. I wonder whether they told him about his father and the kind of man 'he' was. Or did they keep that a secret? I know Bhausaheb was not happy with 'his' ideas, so maybe they told his son nothing about 'him'. And what did they say about me? Did they tell him that I was dead? Yes, Bhausaheb must have said that, because in his letter he wrote, 'To us you are dead.' Did they perform my funeral rites then? I am thankful my son was too little to do any of the rituals, otherwise they may have made him go through the pain of performing his still-living mother's shraddha.

Tr. note: I have to stop here. Doc, I get so lost in your Ahalya, that when I could be sitting in the balcony with my morning cup of tea, watching the ocean, I am in my room instead, with my laptop and your grimy notebook (don't worry, I got it cleaned) and enter your Ahalya's world. By the way, Madhuri told me that her mother has identified Ahalya and that you too remember that Durga was your father Gavi's mother's name. So Ahalya is your father's grandmother. Not so distant a relation then, is she? That solves some of the mystery. And Bhausaheb is Ahalya's father-in-law, Miss Simpson, I suppose, one of those enlightened Englishwomen who were great teachers. But why was Ahalya deprived of her son and who is the painter she talks about?

I expect I'll soon find out. I'm trying hard not to skip, not to peep at the end as I used to when I read mystery novels as a girl. Sadly, once I knew the end, I did not find the book very interesting. So I cured myself of this habit. And now I know it's not the end that matters but the story. I will therefore go steadily from page to page. In any case, this is not a novel but an account of a woman's life. How can it end except with her death? And how can she write about her own death? Let me see what happens.

Doc, you'd find the markings your father Gavi made in this document very intriguing. At least, I guess he's the man who's scribbled in the book. Madhu and you will be able to recognize his writing. There are comments in the margin, sentences underlined, occasional question marks. It's clear he wanted to do something with this document. But what? It gives me a glimpse into a writer's mind and I am fascinated.

Gavi has made some pencilled notes in the margin mentioning three names: Shakuntala, Vasantsena, Vasavadatta. I know these are heroines in Sanskrit drama. Children? He has written after their names. And quoted the number of a shloka in Shakuntala. I read that shloka. It is about Shakuntala's burgeoning breasts. Obviously Gavi was trying to say that she was an adolescent, not a child.

I checked up on the Age of Consent Bill as well. It's pathetic, all that they were doing was raising the age of girls from 10 to 12 for the purpose of consummation of the marriage. Below that age it was rape, above that, it was okay, the husband could 'enjoy' his conjugal rights. I think it's ironic to call it the Age of Consent Bill. Whose consent? Little girls of 12? What would they know of sex, or what they would be consenting to? Some day I will tell you both about my mother, a story which came to my mind when I was reading about this controversy.

Have a look at this some time, doc. I know you are busy with your patients, holding their hands and leading them into the chemical inferno of chemo. But find a little time and read this. After all, Ahalya is your great-grandmother – right?

There's something I should have made clear earlier (this is for Madhuri as well). I am not translating the entire book. I am choosing pages. There is stuff about the family, about family relationships, family events. I'm leaving much of it out. I am conscious, Madhuri and doc, that you are my readers and that I don't want to bore you, to lose you. She obviously has a great emotional attachment to houses, because she has described both her early homes, her parental home and the one she went to after marriage, in great detail. But, curiously, she has not referred to many of the family members, as if she wanted to ignore that part of her life. She says it herself, that the important thing in writing is to know what to include and what to exclude. How fast she was learning about writing, this woman with her failing eyesight, sitting alone in her village home and writing an account of her life, no, of her life with 'him'. It is amazing.

There's a phone call from Abhay, Hari's friend. 'Aparnatai, can you come to see Hari today?'

She is alarmed. 'Now?'

'No, some time, whenever you are free. But today.'

'Is he unwell?'

'No, no, there's nothing wrong with him.'

Aparna waits for him to go on. Finally he gives in and says, 'He's in a bad mood. I can do nothing with him.'

'I'll come after work.'

'Not earlier?'

'No, I can't.'

'All right. I'll try to be there, but I'm not sure.'

Abhay is the one who opens the door for Aparna. There is relief on his face when he sees her. He makes a shushing gesture, finger to lips, as if warning her not to let Hari know he had asked her to come.

'Aparnatai,' he says loudly. 'Come in.'

'Aparna? Did Abhay ask you to come? No, Abhay, don't tell me lies. I know you did. Why did you disturb her? You know she's a busy woman.'

'I'm off. See you later, Aparnatai.' He picks up his bag and walks out, closing the door behind him.

'What did Abhay tell you?

'I want a cup of tea. I've come straight from the hospital.'

'What did Abhay tell you? That I'm dying? Or no, he must have said, this fellow is behaving badly, come and make him see reason.'

'Hari, will you give me a cup of tea or shall I make it myself?'

By the time he gets the tea, she's had a wash. He waits until she finishes her tea before he says, 'Now, tell me.'

'No, you tell me. What is it?'

He and two others have been invited to a programme organized by a cultural centre. It's supposed to be for young singers, he says. 'Young singers! One of them is nearly fifty!' But that's not the problem. 'After all, like politicians, we are young even at fifty.' But in the programme details he has just been given, he has found that while the other two have been given an hour each, he has only forty-five minutes. And he will be the last to sing.

'It's an insult to my music, to my guruji, to me.' He tells her that the other two are very mediocre singers, one of them less than that, but since his uncle is one of the top singers today, he gets the support of sponsoring companies. 'This is a joke, Aparna. It makes me so angry I have decided I won't go. But Abhay says I must go. He says it doesn't help to alienate people at this stage. The programme gets a good audience, they get sponsors. But why should I put up with the humiliation? By the time I begin, the other two will, of course, have taken more than the time given to them and the audience will be ready to go home – if they haven't already gone.'

She has never seen him this way, angry, scarcely aware of her presence, uncaring of it. She thinks again of how different his profession is from what she had thought it would be; there is the same ambition, envy, frustration, competition in it as there is in any other profession. She remembers her father, his fury when critics spoke badly of a play of his, of the string of abuses he had for them. She remembers his response when another playwright, one of his own generation, was praised or got an award. First he would be angry, then would come the depression. 'I'm no good, Sulu,' he would say, 'I'll never be able to come up even to my own standard.' And how hard her mother had to work to get him out of that mood. How did she do it? she wonders now. What do I say to Hari? Ultimately, she only says, 'If you don't go, you gain nothing, except a reputation for sulking, for jealousy. If you sing, you can make your point, show how much better you are.'

'I'm tired of compromising, Aparna, I'm tired of singing in makeshift halls, I'm tired of baithaks in people's houses with the furniture moved out, I'm tired of dealing with the sound system myself, with making arrangement for my own accompanists, of insisting that they should be paid enough. Sometimes I keep nothing for myself, I give it all to them, though they guess and refuse…'

'It will end one day.'

'But when? I know that Abhay spends his own valuable time to help me, he leaves his shop to a stupid assistant so that he can arrange my programmes. I know that Datta plays the tabla for me because we are friends, he can get more money playing for big names.'

'Hari, it's your profession, you have chosen it, or it has chosen you. You decide whether you think it's worth going through all these petty irritations.'

'You're right,' he suddenly gives in. 'I have to decide. And I will. Now shall we go and have dinner somewhere? I'm hungry.'

'Where?'

'I know. A South Indian place I always enjoy going to. Datta took me there and I loved it. Come, let's go.'

'Do you like this food?' he asks in sudden doubt when they are seated. Not at a table of their own but long tables with benches to sit on. 'This is not *Madrassi* food, by the way. I have friends in Bangalore who told me the difference. This is Udipi food.'

'Call it what you want, I love it.'

'Good. This is good food. Much better than Krishna's expensive coffee shops.'

His anger seems spent, he is back to his usual self, though like all the rest, they are silent when eating. This is not one of those places where people talk as they eat. Both the servers and the clients are silent, respecting the food, it seems. They walk out of the silent dining hall into a night blazing with headlights, noisy with the thundering of trucks, the hooting of cars. Abhay wanted me to calm him down, she thinks, but I have done nothing. He would have got here without me, because he is a practical man where his work is concerned, he knows that he cannot afford to throw tantrums. But when he becomes a success…? She smiles at the thought of the tantrums he will throw then.

'What are you thinking of?'

'You,' she says.

She does not ask him whether he will accept the invitation or not, nor does he tell her. It is from Krishna that she learns he has decided to go.

Krishna's call is a surprise. He wants to meet her, he says, he has some things he wants to say to her. She agrees, more out of curiosity than anything else. He takes her to a coffee shop in a five-star place, a new hotel that has sprung up, incongruous and arrogant, in what was once a lower middle-class area of mills and mill workers, on a street where poor workers had bought everything off the pavements, from fresh and dried fish to clothes and gadgets. She smiles, thinking of Hari's comment on his brother's fondness for such expensive places. Krishna, as if he has seen her smile and sensed her thoughts, says almost apologetically, 'We can talk undisturbed here.'

'Of course.'

She has wondered what he wants to say to her. She is taken wholly aback when he begins by apologizing to her.

'To me? What for?'

'For my behaviour that day when we met with Dada. The thing is, I was nervous. Dada is a very important person in my life and I've come to know how important you are to him, Aparna, I've never seen him this way about any woman before. I want us to be friends. But that day I guess I tried to impress you.' He gives a wry smile. 'I know I didn't succeed. About your father – that was a lie. I'd heard from Dada that your father was a dramatist, but I don't think I saw any of his plays. I'd seen one or two Marathi plays and I thought, maybe one of them could have been your father's.'

'That's honest. My father used to have people come to him and say, I believe you're a writer? And then ask him, what do you write? He used to tell me, if one day you hear I'm arrested for murder, you can be sure it's one of these creatures I have killed. If those – well, I won't repeat his words – if those creatures don't know what I have written, why do they talk to me about it?'

Krishna laughs. 'But I was speaking the truth when I spoke of our grandparents and Dada and how I loved going to Pune and being with them during vacations. It was such an easy life in that house. But there was no need for me to go on about it, boring you, I'm sure, and giving you no place in the conversation.'

'I enjoyed listening to the two of you.'

'You did?' As if encouraged, he begins to talk about Hari's hostility to his father. 'They were never very close, but when Baba said he wouldn't allow Hari to take up music as a profession, Hari stopped speaking to him.'

She likes him much better the way he is now, anxious, affectionate, rather than the brash, annoyingly complacent self he had presented to her when she met him with Hari. He is silent for a few moments, then goes on, 'My father was the first in his family to do well in life. I guess he didn't want his son to go back to the world he had left behind. Finally, it was Ajoba who persuaded Hari to graduate and to take up a job in a bank. I know Hari hated it. And then Ajoba died and Hari was – he just disappeared. I traced him through one of his friends and after that I was able to stay close to him. I helped him to sell Ajoba's house in Pune, to find this apartment he now has.'

She has gotten used to thinking of Hari as having no one but his grandparents. For the first time she sees Hari as part of a family. He has this brother who cares, a father who wants to help him…

'Both Baba and I would like to help him more, sponsor a programme for him or something. He won't take anything from us, from my father, actually. I wish he would accept some help. Baba wants to buy a larger apartment for him. He says no, this suits him fine. Now that he has you – and thank god for that, I can't tell you how good I feel about it – I thought he'd be more practical.'

Suddenly it hits Aparna that this is why Krishna wanted to talk to her, this is what he wants to say to her: that she should be the means of reconciliation between Hari and his family. Women are supposed to be good at that, aren't they? There's Madhu, who managed to find a place for herself in Abbas's chaotic and complicated family, who managed to bring his children back to him. But I'm no use, she thinks. I could not bring my parents together, I didn't even try, I just took my mother's part and made Baba the enemy.

'Anyway, Aparna, I'm glad you managed to persuade him to sing at the Cultural Festival.'

'Is he doing that?'

'Yes, he rang me up just a while before I came here.'

He told you, not me: the thought flashes through her mind and stays in it. However, when Hari calls her up at night and tells her his decision, he says he rang her earlier but she didn't take the phone. 'I'll come to you tomorrow morning and tell you about it.'

'No, not in the morning. I have to go early to the hospital.'

'Evening then.'

But he doesn't come. He rings up to say he is busy, that he is working out his programme with his friends. 'We're trying out a new programme. Come and sit with us, Aparna, I like that.'

But she has no time either, she has a conference coming, a paper to get ready, a patient to discuss with a colleague...

In the event she meets him only on the day of his programme. Abhay is waiting for her near the entrance. There's still time for Hari to come on, he says, the singer who's singing now is good for a half hour at least. He takes her into the hall where he has kept a seat for her. The hall is not full, but the crowd is restless, she can feel it, she can hear rustling sounds, chairs scraping. She can almost hear a collective sigh of relief when the singer, the 'fifty-year-old young singer' she guesses, comes to an end. There is the scraping sound of chairs being pushed back; people are beginning to get up, to go away, perhaps. Oh don't, please don't, she thinks, please don't go, sit down and listen to my Hari, he's good. The compere rushes in and requests people not to go away. 'We have one more singer, a young man who's making a mark in the world of Hindustani classical music. And it's only for forty-five minutes. Shree Hari Pandit.'

Aparna hopes Hari hasn't heard this announcement. Pleading with people to listen to him? Assuring them that he will sing 'only for forty-five minutes'?

As always her heart gives a jump when Hari enters, the others following. While the introductions are on, he sits silent, in the padmasana pose, hands folded in his lap, palm facing upwards. His face is serene and composed, very different from the angry man who had spoken to her about the invitation.

When the introductions are over, he draws the mike to himself and says, 'I have been given forty-five minutes. Forty-four minutes now.' He's being wicked, Aparna thinks with a tremor of apprehension. 'And I don't know what I can do in this time. I can sing two short raagas, maybe, but raagas don't let you decide for them, they can't be hurried if they don't want to be hurried. There's no such thing as a *jhatpat* raaga.' There's a ripple of laughter in the room. 'And so I decided to sing some abhangs. My grandfather…' he touches his ears, 'was my first guru and a great devotee of both Tukaram Maharaj and his Vithala. So I will sing Tukaram's abhangs and let us see where these three great souls – Vithala, Tukaram and my grandfather – take us. I can only go the way they show me.' He ends with the usual appeal to switch off mobiles, something the compere hasn't done. Hari, when he says this, is stern, but he has a smile. Already the performer pleasing his public, Aparna thinks.

He introduces his accompanists, says that his saathi will be singing with him and then nods at his team. They nod back, they are ready. There is silence for a moment. Then the tabla player plays a little beat on his tabla as if declaring he is ready. But it is neither the tabla, nor the harmonium, that begins. Just two strong young male voices. None of them are prepared for the explosion of sound that bursts upon them. The two voices seem to be trying to reach the skies, shattering the roof and leaving them with fast beating hearts and racing pulses. It is the cry of the *varkaris*, the pilgrims who walked to Pandharpur to get a sight of their god Vithala. The voices stop as suddenly as they began. Before silence can make its presence felt, Hari begins the first abhang.

He's got them, Aparna thinks, as the team, smiling at one another, gets into the heart of the songs. They give the audience no respite. There is a sense of being caught by the words, the music, the rhythm emphasized by the relentless, almost desperate clanging of cymbals. They've worked at this, Aparna knows, they've worked very hard to achieve this effect. But the effort never shows. It's a joyous flow of devotion and love, of tune and rhythm.

Hari stops, looks at his watch to confirm the time and lays down his taanpura to applause, to voices clamouring for more. He shakes his head, then speaks into the mike, 'I don't want to exceed the time given to me.' They can see someone talking to the compere and the compere edging from the wings on to the stage, signalling to Hari to continue. But Hari shakes his head, stands up, bows low, and with a namaste walks off the stage.

She meets Abhay on her way out. 'Do you want to meet Shree?'

'No, not now, not today.'

'Hari said to drop you home.'

She makes a pushing away gesture and says, 'No, I don't need that.'

As usual, she gets his call when she's in bed.

'How was it?'

'Vherry vherry nice.'

'Dr Aparna Dandekar, you are being wicked.'

'Like you were.'

He laughs. 'I wanted to show them.'

'And you did.'

'We worked hard, but it was worth it. I wish you were here, Aparna, or that I was with you. I want to talk to you, I can't sleep, I could talk to you all night.'

'But I have to sleep, I have to go to work early tomorrow morning. And Hari, I think you were wonderful. Your voice, your music, they're still with me. I can go to sleep with that.'

'Arre wah! Dandekarbai, you are improving.'

'Am I? Maybe. But I need to sleep now.'

'We'll meet tomorrow.'

'Let's see.'

He is with her early in the morning, so early that for a moment she mistakes the doorbell for her alarm. She washes her face, opens the door and says sternly, 'Now sit down here like a good boy. I'll be back in ten minutes.'

When she returns, he has tea ready for her. She takes a sip, then says, 'Now you can talk. How can you wake up so early?'

'I couldn't sleep, I didn't sleep at all. You know Aparna, I was singing Tuka's words, I was addressing Vithala, but I could only think of you. Bhakti, Ajoba said, is another face of love. I understand it now. I've sung these songs all my life, but I understand what they mean only now. Only because of you. You are my light, my world, my music.'

Stop, Hari, stop, she wants to say. I'm a very ordinary woman. When we start living together you will see that and what will happen to your love then?

'I want to be with you all the time. Let's get married, Aparna. Today, tomorrow, any time you say. But soon. Soon.'

So easy to say yes, to go along with him, to tell him that she too wants to be with him all the time, forever. So easy to submit, to stop thinking.

'Hari, we can't take such a big step in a hurry.'

'We've known each other for nearly a year now. I knew the first moment I saw you that I wanted you. I've been waiting since then, I've been very patient. Now I can't wait any more. What's the problem, Aparna? Is it because I'm not earning enough money?'

'No! I told you once, I've told you often that it doesn't matter to me.'

'Don't think I will feel bad about it. A girl said it to me once. She was the daughter of a musician, she said she did not want the uncertainty of a musician's life, she'd seen enough of it. I am so glad she said no. What if I had met you after marrying her?'

'Imagine that! But, Hari, this is not the time, this is the wrong time for such a discussion. I have to get ready, I have to go to work.'

'Then when? Give me an appointment, doctor. I need to see you, when are you free?'

'Hari, please don't be like this.'

'Oh Aparna, Aparna, how else can I be? I want you so badly and you…'

'I just want time, Hari.'

'How much? And tell me, is there someone else?'

'Hari, we'll talk, I promise. But not now, not with my eyes on the clock. And no, there's no one else, there's only you, Hari, that's the truth.'

'If that's the truth, why can't you say yes? Why do you want more time?'

'I don't want to quarrel with you, Hari. Please!'

'Okay. But give me another cup of tea. With sugar. I need some sweetness in my mouth.'

'I'll give it to you on your lips.' She gives him a kiss and before he can do anything, she moves away.

'That was jelabis, boondi ladoos, shrikhand – all in one. Who needs tea now?'

The door bangs and he is gone.

Jyoti is back from her holiday. She looks better; it's not that she has put on weight, but she is much more animated. The house seems to mirror her well-being and liveliness. It's alive, conversation flows out of the open door, the bell rings often and Aparna can hear Jyoti's voice calling out to her children, to Saguna, talking to her visitors. Aparna has no idea of the kind of person Jyoti was before she was diagnosed with cancer, but she thinks that maybe the old Jyoti is coming back. Yet Jyoti herself says she has changed, that she can never go back to being her old self again. She confesses to Aparna, when they meet, to a constant sense of wariness. 'As if, you know, once your house has been burgled, you're always suspicious of strange sounds, of strange voices, you're always alert. It's terrible the way this disease takes over your whole life, your whole self.'

'People who're suffering from kidney failure, from serious cardiac problems, would perhaps say the same.'

'Thanks, doc, for reminding that I'm not the only sufferer. And that reminds me, I have to thank you for being so good to my kids.'

'What did I do?'

'You took them out to dinner twice – or thrice? And that's not the only thing. You haven't seen my family at work. They can be overwhelming, over-solicitious. Miru appreciated you for not being like that.'

'We never value what we have, don't we?'

'I know. I'd have felt so good if my mother had fussed over me. I used to hear girls in my class complain about their mother's interference, their over-protectiveness. I wished my mother would do that. The only piece of advice she gave me when I was a child was – hold your breath, doc – never to leave my underwear for anyone to wash.'

They laugh and then Jyoti says, 'I have another thing to thank you for, doc.'

'What's that?'

'For giving me Ahalya's story. You haven't read it,' she says, rather than asks.

'No, I...' Aparna begins a little apologetically, shamefacedly.

'Never mind, doc, I'm not accusing you. But you must read it some time. It's so surprising, so astonishing to find a woman of that time having the kind of thoughts and ideas she had. She gives her husband all the credit, of course. But she must have been an exceptional woman herself. I can't tell you how much pleasure I am getting out of working on it. I sometimes think it's giving me back something I had lost.'

Before they part, Jyoti tells Aparna that her aunt Kamala has told her that there was a bit about Hari in a Marathi paper, 'a review of his recent programme, she said.'

'Which paper? What did it say?'

'Praises him highly, she said. If you want to read it, I'll ask Kamalamavshi to give me a cutting.'

'Do.'

Jyoti looks at Aparna's face and asks, 'Are you in love with him, doc?'

'Yes, Jyoti, I am.'

'And he?'

'Yes, he too.'

'So, are you getting married?'

'I don't know.'

Jyoti's face asks the question 'why?'

'I've been married before.'

'I know. Surely you got a divorce?'

'Yes, but…it was such a disaster.'

'What happened?'

To her surprise Aparna finds that she can talk to Jyoti about it. Easier to tell Jyoti than speak to Taimavshi or Madhu. Maybe because they're too close to her, too involved with her life, too concerned about it. Whereas Jyoti… 'What happened?' she asks, but Aparna knows that if she says nothing Jyoti won't press her, she will drop the subject immediately. She has never really told anyone what happened to her marriage. It's more possible to speak of being a victim than a fool, which is what she thinks she was.

'I was raw and sore from my mother's death, from my separation from my father, I hadn't spoken to him after my mother's death. Nor had he tried to contact me. When I got to the States, I was lonely and homesick for the home I had lost forever. Then I saw this man on my first day in the hospital; it was my first job in the States and I was nervous. He had been in my college, a few years ahead, two or three, maybe. And he had been very popular, all the girls were a little in love with him. I went and spoke to him and he seemed to remember me (he didn't, I found out later, it was another lie) and I was so grateful I was almost clambering up his legs like a puppy. We began to see each other, we went out on our off days. He seemed to want my company and I was so pleased. And of course we began sleeping together. He laughed at my hesitation, he called me a small-town girl, still living in Chandrapur; so I slept with him. He didn't seduce me, I was more than willing. But I *was* a small-town girl and I thought it was a prelude to marriage. We did get married a month or two later. In a week I knew I'd made a mistake. There was nothing to him, he was like a movie set with nothing behind the façade. He was shallow. No substance to him.'

'*Shape without form, shade without colour,*
Paralysed force, gesture without motion.'

'Who said that?'

'T.S.Eliot. *The Hollow Men.* But go on.'

'He must have met my X. A hollow man – that's right, that's what he was. I soon found out that he married me only because his mother was arranging his marriage with the daughter of a family friend. He wanted to escape that.'

'It never worked?'

'Never. We were soon working in different hospitals, we almost never lived together. Both of us knew it was no good, both of us knew we were wrong for each other. Our marriage kind of petered out. But we gave ourselves a last chance. We went to Paris for a holiday together. I was there when I got the news of my father's heart attack. I came back home, Baba died. And I never went back.'

'That's it?'

'Yes.'

'Men are such asses.'

'My Hari is not. He's a race horse, a valuable and precious race horse.'

'Race horses are supposed to be incredibly stupid.'

'My Hari is not.'

'Oh doc, you've got it badly, haven't you? What are you going to do?'

'I don't know.'

'Marry him. I don't understand you, doc, I just can't. When I met Aakash, I jumped into marriage with both feet.'

'How old were you?'

'Eighteen.'

'There you are! I'm double that. And we're so different, Hari and I. He's such a Brahmin.'

'And you're not?'

'My mother was not a Brahmin. And my father didn't believe in caste, he flouted all the rules. But Hari…he's the only person I know who chants *Vadani kavala gheta* before eating. I almost expect him to do that thing Brahmins do – you know, sprinkling water and putting little morsels of food around the plate – what do they call it? Chitra something?' Jyoti shakes her head. 'Anyway, he's such a pure, such a strict vegetarian. While I love an omelette for my breakfast, I love fish curry, I love the Kolhapuri mutton curry Taimavshi and Madhu make…'

'Oh, what a greedy doc.'

'I am, am I not?'

'What else?'

'I'm earning more money than he does, quite a bit more. And I'm almost sure he won't touch my money, he won't want to live in my house…'

'Practicalities.'

'I'm a practical woman, Jyoti. Like my mother. My father used to say – you are your mother's daughter. Except, of course, when he was pleased with me. Then he would say – you're my daughter. You know how couples use children in quarrels.'

'I don't know. I was never important enough to my parents to be used in that way.'

'Yes, I'm practical. I think of where we will live and whose money we will live on, and about the food. I enjoy varan-bhat, but if I have to eat rice and dal all my life, I'll go crazy.'

She leaves it at that. She has not been able to talk of these things to anyone and perhaps it has helped her to bring them out. But there are things she cannot speak of even to Jyoti. She can't speak of the baby she aborted when she came back to India, a baby conceived in Paris in the most loveless way during their week of supposed reconciliation. She had told no one about it, she had gone instead to a doctor she did not know and had the abortion as soon as she realized she was pregnant. Poor baby, she now thinks, you chose the wrong parents. She quakes when she thinks of telling Hari about these things, but how can she keep anything from him, when he is so open and pours out everything he feels to her?

'Don't call me Madhuritai.'

'Sorry, it's a habit.'

'I know. But for me Tai means my mother. She was Tai to Sulumavshi and umpteen others, she was Taimavshi to Apu, and Gajakaka called her Taisaheb. He admired her, but he was also pulling her leg when he said that, she was so much the family elder. There was always some mischief in Gajakaka. And to all the listeners of her programme and to everyone in the radio station, she was Ananditai.'

'All right. I get it. But I'm not used to calling women by just their names, specially if they're older than me.'

'Makes you safe, eh? Adding the *tai* puts them out of bounds.'

'You have some of your Gajakaka's mischief in you, Madhuritai, I mean Madhuri.'

'That's better. Clearly you don't belong to the new generation. Look at the way you called me an older woman! Shree Hari, I could have taken offence.'

'Sorry again.'

'And look at how you don't call people by their first names. Today you call everyone by their first name. American style.'

'My brother Krishna is like that.'

'I bet he's Krish to his friends.'

'How did you guess?'

She laughs. They are meeting in Hari's home. Hari had rung her up, he said he wanted to meet her and hesitantly asked whether she would come to his home. To his surprise, she had immediately agreed. The truth is that she is curious to know how he lives; the way a person lives speaks much about her or him. She remembers her surprise when she saw Abbas's house for the first time; the chaos, the number of people, the constant babble of talk – none of it had reflected his quiet and thoughtful personality. And she was right. The place was tuned to his sisters' personalities, to his then-wife Nilufer's garish ostentation.

Looking around her, at the hall of Hari's home, she is struck by the starkness of it. A few magazines on a table are the only signs of any interest apart from music. Most of the hall is occupied by a blue-and-red carpet, the taanpuras and the tabla and harmonium in the centre dominating everything. Knowing that Hari's family owns a well-known travel agency, and that they are quite well off, she guesses that the extreme simplicity is his choice. It worries her a little. She cannot imagine Apu in this house. From what she can make out, there is only one bedroom. On the other hand, why not? Gaja and Sulu had lived a very austere life as well; they did not need too many comforts, leave alone luxuries. And ultimately, it's the woman who sets the tone for the way a couple lives. Abbas and she now live very differently from the way he had lived with his first wife Nilufer.

'Can I get you a cup of tea?'

'No, don't bother.'

'I make good tea. Aparna likes it.'

'Later perhaps. Now I want just a glass of water.'

She takes a few sips, puts the glass down and says, 'Now, Shree Hari, what is it? What do you want to talk to me about?'

'I want to ask you something about Aparna.'

'Do you think we should talk of her behind her back?'

'It's not gossip, Madhuri. I need your help.'

'All right. What do you want to know?'

'You know about us, about Aparna and me.' She nods. 'I had thought that once I spoke of my feelings to her, there would be no barriers between us. But, somehow, she makes me feel she's still not willing to open the door, that she's unwilling to commit herself.'

'Why do you say that?'

'We are so close, but if I say the word marriage, she retreats. It seems odd to me that she should resist marriage, even the idea of it, even the word. Madhuritai, I want to live my life with her, I want to share my life with her. But if she does not want marriage, where do we go from here? And yet she loves me, I know she does. So what is it, Madhuritai?'

'Madhuri,' she corrects him automatically.

'Sorry, Madhuri. This is hard for me.'

'Okay, I won't correct you again. Call me what you want.'

'Madhuri, I want to know what's wrong. Is it her marriage? Was it a very bad break up? Did she love him very much? Did he abandon her?'

Madhuri is silent for a moment. Then she says, 'She never talks about her marriage, not even to Aai or to me. In fact, she and I were not very close earlier. She is much younger than me, there are eight years between us. She used to follow me about when she was a kid, you know how little girls hero worship older girls. When she came to live in Bombay after her 10th, I was in the midst of my affair with Abbas, I was self-absorbed, no time for anyone else. And she too, once she became a medical student, she had little time to visit us. But when her mother left Gajakaka and came to live in her apartment next to ours, Apu and I came closer, specially when we knew that Sulumavshi had cancer. Apu stayed for as long as she could with her and I too was there much more often.'

Hari is watching and listening with a painful intensity. When she stops, he prompts her. 'And?'

'Well, what I'm trying to say is that she never confided in me about her marriage. She wrote that she was getting married and after that there were occasional phone calls. Just *hello hello, I'm well, how are you?* – that kind of thing. I rang her up when Gajakaka had a heart attack. She came at once, she told us that her marriage was over and that she wasn't going back, except to wind up and get all her stuff. She said she was looking for a job, preferably in Bombay, and that she would try and get Gajakaka to come and live with her. I asked her what was wrong, whether her husband was having an affair. And she said, no, if he had she wouldn't have minded.'

Suddenly she asks, 'Has she told you about her parents' separation?' He shakes his head. 'I think that's what hit her really hard, that's what changed her, made her a different person altogether.'

She thinks for a moment, then, obviously having taken a decision, tells him the story of Aparna's parents' break up. It is clear from her talk that she is an admirer of Gaja. Even when she speaks of his dreadful mistake, Hari can sense her reluctance to condemn him, he can hear the unsaid words of justification.

'Have you seen any of his plays?' she asks.

'Only one. About a joint family which disintegrates.'

'That was his first one, it made him known. And popular. It was unpretentious, straight from the heart. Gajakaka himself was young, energetic, rebellious, and a good teacher with a sense of humour – his students loved him. But after a time, maybe after five or six plays, he began to lose ground. He wrote one brilliant play, with the Railways as the background – his father had worked in the railways, he knew that world well – which connected the Emergency to what happened in 1942 when the British diverted all trains to carry troops and people died for want of food in Bengal. By the way, I must revive these two plays. I keep saying that, but I do nothing. I must do it and soon. Do you know, Shree Hari, what I like best about Gavi's plays? He writes about women without any sentimentality. Even in life, he was one of those rare Indian men who could be easy and comfortable with women. That kind of man was even rarer in those days. He loved and admired women. In one of his plays, a character says, *Women are the magic, the miracle and the reality of this world.* I don't know whether it was his own idea he put into a character's mouth, but he thought women were wonderful. And then... What was I saying? I've forgotten.'

'About Gavi sir's plays.'

'Yes, of course. Unfortunately for him, he was soon overtaken by another new playwright and relegated to the background.' This dramatist quickly and unobtrusively occupied Gaja's place, he was media savvy, he lived in Bombay, knew the right people, he had a very good troupe performing all his plays. 'While Gajakaka, poor man, had to make do with his students. Raw amateurs. The moment they're out of college, they have no interest in the theatre, he used to say. Give me a group of professionals, give me a good director and I'll show them. He had two or three flops and he decided he needed to give up his job and write full time. Sulumavshi was against it. She thought that he needed the pressure of time to write, that if he had nothing else to do, it would not be the same. They already had a disagreement about Apu coming to Bombay after her 10th, he didn't want it, but Sulumavshi had her way. Then this... Maybe Sulumavshi had a point. But he began to blame her and finally he gave up his job. He had such a lively active mind, we never understood what happened to him.'

'And then?'

'He became ambitious. He decided he would write a musical, he would revive the old kind of musical, adapt it to contemporary times. He had to go to Bombay to work with a singer/composer. There he met this woman, this actress. She could sing, so they cast her in the main role. And so it began. Gajakaka went crazy about her, nothing else mattered, not even Aparna, who had been his world until then. You know, I'd never have imagined Gajakaka would succumb to a *grand passion*.' She says these two words in English. 'He was always so light-hearted and humorous. I've read all his plays in the last year or so, now I can see the capacity for intensity was there in him, all right, but it was channelized into his writing. Even in his first play, when the father, the Gandhian, the ideal man, speaks of his affair with a woman when he was a boy, you can sense that passion. There's something about the way the man speaks of her – to his wife and children – that gave me goosebumps.'

She tells him the rest of the story in a few words. This part is harder for her. Hari can see her grief and anger when she speaks of the way Sulu came to know about his affair. 'I never thought Gajakaka could be so insensitive, but he made his passion for that woman clear in his play. By that time they had begun their affair. Sulumavshi was surprised that he hadn't asked her to copy the play for him as he usually did. She came to know about the woman only after the play was first performed in Mumbai. She questioned him when he returned, he didn't deny it. Sulumavshi left him, came to live in her apartment in Bombay, Gajakaka's play was a flop, the woman left him. And then came Sulumavshi's cancer. Actually, she had been unwell for some time, but she hadn't spoken to him about it, she didn't want to disturb him when he was writing his play. She never went back, she died here in her own apartment.

'And Aparna?'

'Apu took it very hard. When Sulumavshi's cancer was confirmed, Apu turned totally against her father. She refused to meet him or speak to him. We had to go once to Chandrapur to get some of Sulumavshi's things and she scarcely spoke to him the few hours we were there.'

Gaja was a man who had lost everything – his job, his reputation, his wife and daughter. 'It is so strange, but his life became the kind of melodrama he had so scrupulously avoided in his own plays. When we saw him, he looked so terrible, I couldn't bear to look at him. I hoped that he and Apu would talk, that there would be a kind of reconciliation. But Gajakaka only asked, *Why are you here?* And she said, *To take Aai's things.* And he said, *Take whatever you want, take everything, burn down the house.* What hope was there for any conversation after that? Apu and I found out after his death that he had burnt everything personal: Sulu's letters, Apu's letters. Only his manuscripts were left. Perhaps he didn't have the heart to burn those.'

Both of them are silent. Madhu resumes, with an effort. This journey into the past, an emotional journey, seems to have exhausted Madhu. 'I don't know what these things did to Apu. I'm no psychologist. But I think that whatever happened is still simmering in her. She was so loved, so protected and then the family disintegrated as if in a flash, her parents died, her marriage broke up. I worry about her, Shree Hari, I worry about her.'

Madhuri falls silent. She is remembering Gaja's words: 'Marriage asks for the impossible, it demands the ungivable.' Does Aparna think the same way? Should she say this to the man sitting before her, anxious and humble, the man who loves Apu so much? Ultimately, she says the only thing she thinks Hari can take. 'When Apu loves, there are no limits, she goes to the extreme edge. She turned against her father, but when he died, she cried so violently we were frightened for her. I have not seen grief like that. She did the last rites herself. I think it helped that a local politician came all afire to give Gajakaka a state funeral – he had only just heard that he was a very famous writer, that there was a huge crowd gathered at his house after his death, most of them students. He thought he'd take advantage of that. Apu came out of her grief then, she sent everyone away, until only his few friends, some students and the family were left. She was like a flaming torch. After that she decided to sell the house and we, she and I, packed up the house and she left Chandrapur forever.'

She picks up her glass and drinks the rest of the water. Her fingers, Hari notices, are trembling.

'Thank you Madhuritai, thank you for telling me.'

She shrugs. 'I don't know how much this will help you. But I hope it does. I want Apu to move on, to live a happy life.'

Madhu gets up and goes to the door, then lingers at the head of the stairs. 'Don't come down with me,' she tells Hari. 'No, I mean it, I'll go by myself.'

'You have your car?'

'Just round the corner.' She still waits, as if there is something more she wants to say. Finally she says it. 'Wait for her, Shree Hari, don't give up on her.'

I wonder whether I have helped Hari by telling him these things. Apu may not like it, but he has a right to know. She wonders whether she should tell her mother about Apu, but decides not to. Aai is looking very frail, Madhu thinks with a little clutch of fear at her heart. And why did she say to me the other day, 'Be good to Anil, Madhu. Always be good to him'? What was she trying to say? Preoccupied with her thoughts, she has gone past her car. She walks back, gets into it and drives away.

Hari goes back into his house and closes the door. He looks at his watch, it's been less than an hour since Madhuri came, but he feels as if he has gone through Aparna's entire lifetime in that time. Wait for her? Of course I will wait, I can wait all my life. He has asked himself a hundred, a thousand times, why Aparna and no one else. What makes a person stand out in the crowd of humanity so that he can see her and no one else, so that he wants her and no one else? He has not found the answer. He is sure he never will. I don't know what I will do with my life if I can't get

Aparna. But I will, I am sure I will get her. I will never give up. I know she loves me, but maybe I frighten her with the way I show her my need of her?

He thinks of his grandparents, of their life together, of its simplicity and how they complemented each other, how they formed a unit that made their lives so much richer and more meaningful. That kind of marriage is no longer possible: he knows that. He thought he had armoured himself sufficiently against unreal expectations. Then he met Aparna. She had overturned everything in his life – his ideas, his dreams. Nothing mattered but to make her a part of his life.

Hari, a man who has lived a simple uncomplicated life, finds himself suddenly caught in a web of longing and desire. He thinks of Aparna's father, Gaja, of the madness that overcame him so that he risked everything in his life for a woman. And then he lost it all. Perhaps, he thinks, it is not marriage, but love itself that Aparna distrusts? How do I help her to get over it?

AHALYA'S STORY

This house, when the painter brought me here, reminded me of my childhood home. It's a much smaller house, of course, just two rooms and a kitchen. And a shed, which he converted into a bathroom before he brought me home. But there is the same sense of openness, of spaciousness, because of the large backyard which stretches to the fields. Of course, the fields were not ours, they belonged to his patron. But we were free to go into them, and I knew then how much I had missed this kind of living in Pune. His patron gave us some bajra every year after harvesting was over. I felt very awkward taking things from him. My father had been a landlord and donor himself and 'his' family of course, were wealthy; I did not know how to take from others. But the painter did not think it was wrong, his patron helped him in many ways, and he accepted it gratefully. I learnt from the painter to accept things with grace; there was a kind of innocence in him which helped him to do this. We had a vegetable garden in our backyard in which I worked in the evenings. Durga followed me about ever since she could walk and later, she helped me with whatever I was doing. Kashi was eager to help, but she soon got bored and went away to do something she found more interesting. How different human beings are, even those born of the same parents!

To go back – I felt at home, comfortable in this place from the first day. We were accepted by people around us. The painter was known to everyone, and though he never stayed long, they had good feelings for him; he had a good reputation. He had been abandoned as a baby and brought up by a couple who worked in the temple. He showed his skill at drawing very early. Everyone admired his work. As for me, he had told Indutai and me that his patron was going to start a school for girls and wanted a teacher. He was sure I could get the job. This was, in fact, one of the reasons why I married him. And so I became a teacher, which I had long dreamt of. It made me, it made us, respectable. Some of my students' mothers asked me to teach them to read and write, which I did with pleasure. They looked at me as if I was Pandita Ramabai herself! When our daughters were born, we became much more part of the community than before; children not only dissolve differences, they create bonds like nothing else can.

Can I say I was happy? It's so hard to know when we are happy; we know we were happy only when we have gone past that time. But yes, after the girls came, I was happy. Not the kind of happiness I had known – for such a brief time – after my son was born. But my life was full, I was busy, I was working, and I had my daughters. I can say I was at peace with myself and my life. To the girls, of course, this was home, they never knew any other home. The painter was not always with us, he came and went as and when he pleased. It was true that he needed to travel for his work; but by nature he was restless, a wanderer, he could not stay in one place for long. He had asked me earlier whether I would be able to live on my own. I said I could and I managed very well. I wanted to ask him in those early days, 'If you like your freedom so much, why did you marry?' Though I did not ask him the question, I think I got an answer in the years that we lived together. And when, later, I did ask him, I knew my guess was right, for he said, 'I wanted a home to come back to, I wanted a woman in my home. And I wanted children, children above all.' An honest man. I have never seen a father who loved his children as much as he loved his daughters.

But even his daughters could not keep him home for long. Nor, when he came, did he disturb the pattern of our life much. After Kashi was born, he built a room for himself at the back of the house, where he kept his painting paraphernalia, so that it would not get in our way in the house. That's what he said, but I think he wanted to keep that part of his life private and separate. He spent as much time as he could with the girls when he was home. But at night, he would go off to his room. The girls and I slept in the main house, my two girls on either side of me. Durga, a neat and tidy sleeper, would be in the same position in the morning, but Kashi turned and twisted all night, her skirt* pulled up to her knees, flinging her arms about as if, like her father, she was trying to get somewhere else.

At some point after the girls fell asleep, I went to the painter's room. Always on the first night after his return and, after that, occasionally. At first it was very awkward, because he told me that he left it to me to go to him whenever I felt like it. How could I do that? To go would be like admitting I wanted to be with him. When I stayed away, he told me, 'You don't need to feel shy. You can come to talk to me. Or let me talk to you.'

Which was what happened more and more often. He liked to talk to me of the places he visited, of the work he did. He had begun by painting temples, pictures which were cherished by those who could never visit the temples in their life. After our marriage, he had begun painting people, rich people mainly, among whom he was becoming known. (It was getting him more money than he had earned before, he now had a room for himself in Mumbai, half a room actually, for he shared it with another man). He told me about the rich, of their houses, of the way they lived, of their fears that they would one day cease to exist and there would be nothing left of them. That is why they want to be painted, they want their children to put up their paintings on the walls of their homes, so that they will continue to exist, he told me. They want to be remembered, he said. Everyone wants to be remembered, I replied. Even you, through your paintings. Which is why you put your name in a corner of the painting. He laughed at that. You know me so well, he said. Later when we could talk to each other freely, he said to me, 'When I paint some of the rich women in their grand saris and jewellery, I wish I could paint you. Just the way you are. To show that there is beauty in simplicity. I would like to paint you some time.' Both of us knew he never could. I had to remain unknown, unseen, faceless, nameless. I was a dead woman.

I liked listening to him, sometimes arguing with him. But it was very awkward for me to go to him on my own.

'You tell me when you want me to come,' I suggested.

'In that case, you will be here every night, all night,' he said. He was laughing as he said that, laughing, I knew, at himself. I think it was at that moment I knew I had done the right thing by linking my life to his. I had been so reluctant, I had been so afraid, so sure what I was doing was a sin; but his laughter was reassuring. It was like the way 'he' had first explained to me this business of men and women coming together. 'He' did it without any awkwardness, making it seem simple and natural. And, therefore, when I heard 'him' and Miss Simmons talking of reproduction, part of the study of animal (and even plant) life, I did not find it wrong. They spoke a great deal about Darwin, a name I soon became familiar with. 'He' was a great admirer. Miss Simmons was also an admirer, but she seemed a little troubled by his theories. I soon came to know that the Church was against his theory because it left no room for god. And Miss Simpson's faith in god was very strong. 'He' never spoke against her

Christian belief, but he told me once that he found it surprising that Miss Simmons, such an intelligent and well-educated woman, could believe that god created the world in seven days, that he created Eve out of Adam's rib and so on. 'He' thought that the Upanishads came closer to dealing with the question 'who created the world?' by asking questions, the Rg Veda through poetry and Darwin through knowledge, experience and observation. But finally, Nature and we humans have to solve the great riddle of life between us, 'he' said.

I could not understand most of what they spoke about Darwin's work, the language was too difficult for me. 'He' explained it to me later, when we were on our own, in simple words, and I could understand a little bit of it. 'He' said that according to Darwin, there is something called a struggle for existence and that this is part of the life of all creatures and plants. Darwin believed that there was something called natural selection, which made sure that the strongest survived. Darwin called it – I can write this only in the English words 'he' used – 'survival of the fittest'. And it was not only survival, the fittest do what is more important – they leave healthy progeny behind them; the females choose the strongest as mates for this purpose. Actually, I am not sure I have this right. It is so long back and I have forgotten so much of what 'he' told me. I had written it in a book, I remember, so that I could read it again, but the book remained in 'his' house. How was I to know that I would never go back?

To go back to what I was writing, after 'he' told me about Darwin's theory, I thought it over, then I asked 'him', 'But how is it that this does not apply to humans?' I told him about the sickly child in Wadgaon, who everyone said would not live even for a year. Bit his mother cared for him so much that he lived for years. 'For any mother,' I argued with him, 'survival of her child is more important than her own survival. Selflessness and sacrifice are part of human nature, aren't they?' I asked.

'You have given me an idea,' 'he' said. 'Let me think it over.'

That day 'he' was pleased with me, so pleased that it seemed I had given 'him' a great gift. 'He' said, 'Now you know why science is so wonderful. You can ask any questions of science. Religion does not allow questions. It says – this is how it is, don't ask any questions. But science needs questions, science knows that knowledge comes through asking questions, through doubts.' He added, 'I don't have to worry about you now that I know that you can think for yourself.'

Why did 'he' say that? Did 'he' have some premonition? I don't know. But I know that 'his' words came back to me on the worst day of my life. 'Think for myself' – what myself was there without 'him'? The only thing I could think of then was that I wanted to be like Savitri, Savitri who had followed the god of death to reclaim her husband from the dead. I knew I could not do that, but maybe I could embrace death myself? It is very strange to remember that Miss Simmons and I had spoken of Savitri's story some time earlier. She was eager to know more of our stories and she had asked me about Savitri. In turn, she told me a Greek story of a man, a musician, who loved his wife so much that he went to the underworld to bring her back. He charmed the king of the underworld with his music and won the right to take his wife away. There was one condition – that he should not look back. He was careful until he came out of the underworld into the sunshine. Then, to make sure she was following, he looked back. And she was gone, he could never get her back.

I think both the stories are false. They give us hope that we can bring back those who have gone, that the dead can come back to us. We like to believe this, though we know it is not true. We have to accept, and we have accepted, that death is a part of life, that it is the one great truth of life. Those who are gone can never come back and death, which we humans fear more than anything else, is the final power. The living have to go on, they cannot look back. But is that right? Have we not been given a wonderful gift in exchange for the loss that death causes? Does not our memory make sure that nothing is lost forever? Sometimes I wonder whether animals have the gift of memory too. I remember how the cattle in our home would come back without anyone leading them or driving them; unerringly they went back to their places in the shed and stood there, happy, it seemed, to be back where they belonged. And now, look at me, bringing back memories of all those who were part of my life, feeling them around me as I write. The moment I stop writing, they are gone. But then life itself is only a flicker, a blink of an eye.

**Let that be. I think I have found out that there is only one way to save yourself from grief – it is never to love anyone. Because what we fear is not death itself but the non-existence of those we love. Yet, is there anyone in the world who can live without loving others? If they can, they are not human. If there is no one else, there is love of our own selves. After I lost 'him', I thought I had lost everything and that I had nothing more to fear. Then I lost my son and it seemed to me that I would never again in my life care about anyone. But my daughters came into my life. And then my Kashi died. I wept for my restless little girl, my grief poured out in endless tears. Durga brought me out of it. 'Aai, I am here, don't I matter to you at all?' I stopped grieving then, though in private I continued to grieve, I still do, for my two lost children. Two out of three lost to me. But there is Durga. And her husband. And my little Gaja, who has reconnected me to life.

In all my times of sorrow, I did not pray. Which god would I pray to? After I lost my son, I lost my religion and I knew I would never be reconciled to god. I went to the temple for my daughters' sake; why should they be deprived of this support even if I no longer believed in it? And why should they be different from the others? I knew how hard that makes life. I lit the lamp every evening in the small niche where I kept a painting of Rama and Sita, which the painter had painted. I liked this ritual, mainly because evening is a time of peace. It felt good to sit there for a few minutes and feel peaceful. And to light a lamp before it gets dark is meaningful, it is to say that we can keep away the dark. The painter went along with me in this one ritual that I observed, though he, abandoned as a baby, had grown up without parents and had no idea of a father-like god or a mother-like goddess. Earlier I had prayed to the goddesses. Like most women, I thought that as a woman I had a special right to their protection, their favour. After I gave up prayers, I realized that these goddesses were subservient to their husbands, the same as us. So what could they do for us poor ordinary women?

When the painter died, I accepted it as if it was something I had known would happen. A stranger came to the village looking for me and I knew immediately what had happened. Durga and I went back with him to Mumbai. There was nothing to be done, they had already cremated him, they could not wait for us, but Durga wanted to see the place where he had lived. It was a small room (Kholi No. 19, Ganpati Chawl, we used to write on the letters) shared by him and another man who was a supervisor in a cotton mill. There was nothing in the room, only a mattress rolled in a corner, a few pots and pans, and his paintings. When I saw them, I realized he had moved from temples and people to posters of films. He spoke a lot about films, he was fascinated by them. And here were the posters they put up on the roads, inviting people to go and see them. 'He was looking for an answer to the question, why so many people come to this city,' the man who had taken us to Mumbai told me. 'I think he found their dreams in these films.' Yes, there was something unreal, exaggerated about the posters, the people looked superhuman somehow. 'These paintings won't get us much money,' the man said. *(Tr. note: I am sure they would today. Sure you've never seen or heard of them, doc?)* 'But I will hold an exhibition of the paintings and sell as many as I can.'

I told him there were some paintings in his room at home too. He sent a man and took them to Mumbai. He did hold the exhibition and sold many of the paintings. The money I got from that helped me to send Durga to a school and hostel in Pune so she could do her teacher's training. Her father's blessings, she always says.

Tr. note: It is getting clearer that 'he' and the painter are two different people, that she had two daughters by the painter and a son earlier who was, for some reason, taken away from her. But it only gets more mysterious: could she have been married twice? A Brahmin woman? It was a time of reform, a time of widow remarriage, but she doesn't say anything about that. Curious.

*Skirt sounds odd, it sounds like it is a – yes, a skirt. So should I say a long skirt? Or the Marathi parkar polka? Or the word that has become so common now, lehnga? Ladies, suggestions are welcome.

**I like the way she says 'Aso!' at the end of a chain of thoughts. Aso. Let it be. I can almost see her delicately, deliberately, putting the earlier thought aside and turning to another.

Madhuri, doc, this woman is teaching me that translation is not just converting a word from one language to another. Because of her, I had to go to Darwin (thank god for Google) and then I found myself thinking about her question. I'm almost sure 'he' had some of the same ideas I have. Are natural laws upset by civilization? Love and self-sacrifice may not be part of Nature's plans, but humans have developed them to a great degree. So do they work against the natural law of evolution by helping the unfit to survive? Or do they make us evolve in a moral sense? Or is Nature always present behind the veneer of civilization, which is why, when we reach the point where it is 'your life or mine', the savage instinct takes over?

Another thought: If life, survival, matter above all, then death is wrong, it is fearsome. It goes against what I am trying to convince myself about – that death is but one stage in human life, inevitable, not fearful, though unavoidable.

They come back from their walk to find Hari in the foyer, phone held to his ear. Obviously he has dialled Aparna's number, for her phone rings at the same time. They see each other and smile.

'There you are! I just rang you.'

'I know.'

'My fault, Panditji,' Jyoti says. 'I made her come with me for a walk. She needs the fresh air.'

'And the exercise. My father was a diabetic, I need to remember that.'

'I'll see that you walk every day – at least two miles. Namaskar, Jyotitai.'

'Whoever brought you up did a good job, Panditji. *Namaskar, Jyotitai,* not hello Jyoti, or hi Jo.'

'My grandparents taught me to respect women.'

'Bless their souls. I was like a ragamuffin, no idea of polite behaviour at all.'

'Tch tch.'

'You may well say tch tch. Anyway, I haven't met you since your programme which got such a good review. I believe it was great.'

'Well…'

'Good to be modest. But you're getting there, Panditji. And I believe you have been invited to sing at an important Sangeet

Sammelan? The one held in the suburbs? It's a very prestigious event for musicians, isn't it?'

'I'm invited? Who told you?'

'Madhuri. I believe her mother Anandibai is one of the organizers of the event. You don't know? Was it supposed to be a surprise?' She looks from his face to Aparna's, then says, 'I'm sorry if I spoilt the surprise. Sorry, doc.'

They walk up the stairs in silence, a silence that continues even after Aparna opens the door and they get into the house. Only then does he ask, 'What is this, Aparna?'

She tells him, hating herself for sounding apologetic, for being intimidated – no, for being apprehensive about his tone – that she herself has just heard from Taimavshi.

'Am I not supposed to know? Or to be asked? Do they think that I will be so overwhelmed by the honour that I won't refuse?'

'Hari, listen…'

'Did you ask Anandibai to invite me?'

'No, she mentioned it herself when she read the review. If I'd known earlier, I'd have included him in this year's event, she said.'

'And?' he prompts her.

'And I asked why not now and she said the programme was full, that if someone dropped out, she would invite you. And someone did drop out. She rang me a little while back.'

'Aparna, promise me one thing. Promise me you'll never ask anyone to do me a favour like that, never again.'

'But I didn't. Didn't you hear me, Hari?'

'I don't want you to make yourself small for my sake. And I don't want to be invited anywhere as a favour.'

'There's no question of making myself small, Hari. Taimavshi is like my mother, she has been my mother since my own mother died. And she's not doing you a favour. They want good singers for their Sammelan, they like to invite promising young singers…'

'But if you hadn't spoken, she would not have thought of me. I want to be invited for myself alone, for my singing, not because someone says – why don't you invite him?'

Hari's anger can no longer be concealed. She should have known, she has seen him this way before, the time they had spoken lightly of going away together somewhere, of having a holiday.

'Paris,' he had said. 'I believe that is the city for lovers. I believe it is a very beautiful city.'

'Not Paris, Hari. Anywhere but Paris.'

He had laughed. 'I was only joking, Aparna. I'm not serious.'

'But I am. Both about going somewhere and about not going to Paris.'

'How can we go anywhere? Where do we get the money from?'

'Don't worry about money, I have enough of it. The money I got from Baba is lying in my bank.'

'What are you saying? You can't throw money about like that.'

'Like what?'

'Carelessly. Your father must have struggled to earn that money.'

'He would be very happy to know that I'm having fun with it, that I'm enjoying myself with the man I love.'

'I can't take your money.'

'Don't be silly. Your money, my money – you're not serious, Hari!'

But he was. Brought up by his grandparents, shaped by his grandfather's austerity, by the strong belief that a man does not take money from a woman, he is serious. From Hari's conversation, she has begun to imagine how their home must have been like, a home in which all festivals were celebrated, pujas and rituals part of their daily life. And always the buzz of people who came to consult his grandfather about auspicious days and right times for anything, of women who came to ask his grandmother about rituals. Whereas her father had been an atheist, a rationalist. They had neither pujas nor rituals at home. Even her mother was a minimalist in matters of religion. She had a Ganapati and a Balkrishna on a little shelf in the kitchen, where she lit the lamp and folded her hands morning and evening. That was all.

It seems to her that she is constantly stubbing her toe against the differences between Hari and her. She thinks of people who have arranged marriages, of the way they ignore the differences. And, yet, most of them work. Why am I so obsessed with the differences between us? Can't love surmount these obstacles? Look at Madhu and Abbas.

Hari rings her the next day to tell her that he has received a formal invitation from Anandibai. She admitted to him that the invitation was rather late, that it was because someone opted out at the last minute. Aparna does not ask him about his response. He tells her himself that he has accepted it, mainly because 'Anandibai was honest with me.'

'I'm glad,' she says.

He comes to her that evening, back, it seems, to his normal self, the dark cloud behind them. He tells her he has to sing on the last day, the day they reserve for younger singers. And that the finale, with a very famous and popular singer, will come after his session is over, 'which means people will wait until I finish. With luck, I should have a decent audience.'

All, it seems, is forgotten, but they both know it is not. It lies between them, the issue of his reluctance to take anything from her, something she will have to be careful about. It's going to be tightrope walking, she thinks, balancing myself with a pole in my hands. Now I know that that's what my mother did, what she had to do. Which is why she did not spend money on the house, or on necessities, only on gifts to Baba. Anything for Aparna was, of course, justified, there was never any problem with that. But she remembers Baba's feelings about the apartment Sulu bought in Mumbai, his refusal even to have his name on the nameplate; it's Sulu's, he said, she's bought it with her hard-earned money, I have no right to have my name put up along with hers. And, whenever he came to Mumbai, he continued to stay at Konkan Lodge, even though the apartment was kept ready for him, or for anyone else, to live in for a few days.

Male pride, she thinks. And then, that's one problem I never had to deal with in my marriage. She remembers their trip to Paris, how he had made sure that she bought her own ticket. 'I'll pay for the hotel room,' he'd said, with a sense of showering largesse on her.

She should have known then that the trip would be a failure. It was to be a holiday, to spend time together, to try for a reconciliation, to bridge the growing gap between them. But for him a holiday meant drinking, reconciliation meant sex. It sickened her finally, their coupling, growing increasingly loveless, more and more mechanical. 'No,' she said one night when they got home after a late dinner. 'No, you're drunk, go to sleep.' He had insisted, kept savagely groping at her, tugging at her clothes. Ultimately she had locked herself into the bathroom, she'd come out only when the silence told her he was sleeping. He lay sprawled across the bed, still in his outdoor clothes, his face flushed with alcohol, leaving little room for her. She sat on the one chair the little room provided, pulled a cover off the bed and tried to sleep. But sleep evaded her. I've made a mistake, I've made a mistake: the thought thudded through her mind. At some time, when she was on the brink of dozing, the phone rang. It was Madhuri, her voice as clear and distinct as though she were in the next room. Aparna was so muddled with sleeplessness and futile thoughts that she wasn't surprised to hear Madhu's voice in a hotel room in Paris.

'Apu, thank God, we've been desperately trying to trace you.'

'What is it?'

It was her father. He'd had a heart attack and was in hospital. Madhuri and Taimavshi were with him in Chandrapur. 'You have to come right away,' Madhu told Aparna. She told her that a cousin of Abbas's, who was in Paris, would come to her with a plane ticket. 'I'll give him this number. He'll call you and tell you which flight and at what time. Pack up and wait for him.'

Aparna was wide awake by then. She got up, bathed, packed, dressed and then tried to wake him up. 'Damn you, let me sleep,' he mumbled, obviously still full of his last night's grievance, of last night's drink. She gave up finally and waited in the foyer, her suitcase by her side.

The man who came to pick her up was youngish and mercifully silent. He said nothing except, 'Are you ready? You have your passport?' And when he dropped her he said, 'Try to sleep on the flight. You need to get some rest before you reach home. I'll ring Madhuri and tell her you've left.'

She didn't want to sleep. She thought she had to stay awake, she was afraid something would happen if she slept. She thought, superstitiously, that as long as she was awake nothing would happen. They were flying just above the clouds, not white and fluffy like you'd think they would be, but thick and seemingly heavy. Chaotic thoughts tumbled and revolved in her mind, thoughts of her father dying, of her disastrous marriage, of what a mess she'd made of her life…

Sada was waiting for her at the airport. 'Is Baba…?'

'Yes, he's okay, I spoke to Madhu just a few minutes back.'

When she got to the hospital, Baba was awake and alert. 'Why did you come all the way? You didn't have to come for my sake,' he said. But she could see the relief on his face. He needed a bypass, the doctors said. She, Taimavshi and Madhu wanted him to go to Mumbai for the surgery. He steadfastly refused to go anywhere, to undergo surgery.

Aparna stayed with him for a fortnight after he came home. 'Don't worry about me, you go back home,' he said.

'I'm going back, Baba, but I'll return as soon as I've wound up everything there.'

'Why?'

'I don't want to live there any more.'

'Both of you? He's coming back too?'

'No, I'm coming back alone. Our marriage is over.'

'Why? What happened?'

'He's not the man I thought he was.'

'Which one of us ever is what others think we are? Don't make such quick decisions. Give him another chance.'

'No, Baba, it's no use. I'm coming back.'

It was then that he had said to her, 'You are your mother's daughter.' He added, 'Your mother believed in capital punishment. She didn't believe in mercy. She refused to forgive me even when she was dying. Don't be like that. And don't come back for my sake. Don't change anything in your life for my sake. I'm fine. I'll be fine.'

'I'm going to look for a job in Mumbai, Baba. When I get it and when I have a place to live in, you'll have to come and live with me.'

'It's too late for that, far too late.'

It was indeed. On the day she was to leave, the taxi waiting at the gate, she had said goodbye to him, picked up her bag and was getting into the taxi when the taxi driver's face alerted her to the fact that something was wrong. She had looked back and seen him lying on the floor in a crumpled heap.

History won't repeat itself. It won't happen that way, not with Hari and me. Spoilt brat, my X called me. But I have changed, I no longer expect the world to shape itself to my needs, my desires.

And yet, I'm not good wife material. I don't know what being a good wife means. I thought my mother was a good wife, but when I think of what happened to her…

This is the first time Aparna is attending Taimavshi's sangeet sammelan. She and two other music lovers had started it, in a small way, after her retirement some years back. In the years since then, the festival has grown and become one of the important music events in the city. Aparna, when she enters the place, finds crowds both outside and inside, a subdued buzz of voices, and understands that for a singer to sing here matters. Abhay is waiting for her, he tells her that Shree wants to see her before he begins. She follows him to the back of the building and through a side door into a corridor which takes them past the stage – suddenly the music comes loud and clear to them. Abhay puts his finger to his lips and Aparna nods. A little ahead is a door which he opens, and the people in the room look up at them. Hari and three others, are grouped around a taanpura. He gets up, gently closes the door behind him and takes her to a backyard full of cartons and empty bottles clustered around a dispirited looking tree. He pulls out a plastic chair for her and sits opposite her on a stool.

Aparna has felt burdened by her anxiety for Hari, afraid that his displeasure about the programme would disturb his concentration. To her surprise, he is cheerful and confident.

'Ready?' she asks.

'Now you're here, I'm ready. It's the waiting that's always hard. Aparna, my guruji is here.'

'Come from Pune?'

'Anandibai invited him and got him here. I'll take you to meet him later.'

'Your hands are cold.'

'I know. Strange, isn't it, my body is nervous, but my mind is not? It seems to me that I've been preparing for this for years. Where are you sitting?'

'I don't know. I haven't gone into the hall as yet. With Madhu and Abbas, I suppose.'

'Never mind. I won't see you, anyway. But as long as I know you're there, I'm okay. Aparna, I have to go. We need to change one of the taanpuras.'

He takes her hand and kisses it. She gently caresses his cheek and they smile at each other.

When she enters the hall, the singer who was on has just finished. She is putting her taanpura down and, hands folded in a namaste, smiles at the audience. She's a plump woman, with pearls round her neck and flowers in her hair. Aparna has heard of her, she has heard Hari say she is good.

'How was she?' she asks Madhu, nodding at the singer on the stage.

'Good, but not at her best. I've heard her sing much better.'

The formalities of thanking the singer and her team are over and they are walking off. Easier to talk now.

'Where's Taimavshi?'

'Running around. I tell her to sit in one place and let the younger ones do all the running, but will she listen? A stubborn woman, my mother.'

'Like her daughter.'

'Abbas! What do you mean? When I'm Aai's age I'm going to sit like a queen and make the others run around. Watch me. Apu, are you nervous?'

'Yes, a little bit.'

'It's somewhat like waiting for Gajakaka's play to begin, isn't it?'

Yes, it is like that. Aparna too has been remembering herself as a child, sitting in the audience with her mother, waiting for the curtain to go up, excitement clutching at her throat so that she feels a little nauseated. Waiting to see the magic transformation of the actors. She'd seen the actors a little earlier when she'd gone backstage with her mother, she'd seen them squabbling, flipping over the pages of the script to look at their lines yet one more time, some of them wandering about, touching things, impatient to begin, looking in the mirror to make sure their make-up was all right. And when the curtain went up, there they were, different selves altogether, no connection at all to the people she'd seen a short while back. Only she knew who these people really were; she felt privileged, set apart from the others who didn't have her special knowledge. Baba was never in the audience, or even backstage. He would disappear, she knew he would be wandering around somewhere, and then suddenly turn up when the play was over and the curtain came down, rushing into the midst of the actors, bursting with questions, arguments, sometimes angry, at times laughing with pleasure. And Sulu, watching them, would say, 'Let's go home, Apu, your Baba will be here for much more time.' When he got home, Aparna still awake, the excitement of the evening keeping her from sleeping, would hear him call out, 'Sulu, how did it go, what did you think?'

'Shh, Apu is sleeping.'

Then there would be murmurs, sometimes laughter, at times Baba would hum a song. And she would fall asleep, feeling safe and enclosed in her parents' happiness.

Taimavshi joins them, bringing Aparna out of her reverie; strangely, she too speaks of Gaja's plays, as if she is happy at this resumption of their connection to the stage. 'This is like waiting for Dandekar's play to begin, isn't it?'

The announcer comes to the mike and, waiting a moment to catch the attention of the crowd, says, 'Now we go on to our next singer. Shree Hari Pandit, one of our finest young singers today.'

He introduces him and his team and then adds, 'We have Shree Hari Pandit's guruji with us today.'

There is loud applause at the name and a man sitting in the first row gets up and makes a namaste to the audience. Shree Hari and his team come in and take possession of the instruments already in place. Before sitting down Shree Hari bows low to his guruji. There is the usual settling down, arranging of instruments, checking of mikes, something Aparna has got used to and which she always finds exciting; it's like watching a surgeon and his team preparing before starting surgery. The tabla player taps the mike in front of him, his fingers try out a few tentative beats on the tabla, he sprinkles a little powder on it and then, nodding, as if satisfied, he sits back, arms folded across his chest. Aparna feels a little flutter inside her when Hari, after a whispered conversation with his taanpura accompanist, goes back to his usual pose, cross-legged, eyes closed, hands limp in his lap. Each time she sees him this way, she thinks, this is his world, this is where he belongs. The throat clearing and the coughing in the audience ends and there is a silence into which Hari's voice enters. Not to sing, but to say, 'My pranam to my guruji. With your permission, guruji, I will now begin.' He waits, for a response perhaps, nods to the tabla and the harmonium player, gives a backward wave to the taanpura player behind him and then begins.

He starts off on a low note, so low that it is as if he is whispering to himself. He seems to be coaxing the notes out gently, caressing them as they appear. The audience has settled into an absolute silence, there is neither sound nor movement. When the alaap is over and he moves into the khayal, the tabalji, whose hands have been hovering over the tabla, his fingers flexing and unflexing themselves, joins in. Not with the usual flourish, or the joyous abandon of the tabla, but gently, as if tiptoeing into the world the singer has already created with his voice. The harmonium enters in the same hushed manner and the three of them, the singer and his two accompanists, smile at each like old friends who have met and are starting a new journey together. As always, Aparna is fascinated by the way they communicate with one other; the smallest of gestures, a nod, a look, a small turn of the head is immediately picked up by the person it is meant for. This is perfect communication, Aparna thinks, this is how communication should be, this is how Hari and I should be able to communicate. The group on the stage creates a tight little circle, a small world of their own, closed to the rest of the world. Suddenly she is conscious of a great loneliness, she knows this world of Hari's will always be closed to her, she knows they will never be able to understand each other as perfectly as he and his team can.

And then she shakes herself and gives herself up to the music. There is something meditative about the way he is developing this raaga, even she who understands so little can see that. He is following not just the notes or the raaga, but a thought, an idea. He had faltered for a few notes during the alaap, but now he is in full control, he knows he is in control. Taimavshi will tell her that he had taken two popular raagas, but the treatment was completely new. 'I wanted to try something different,' he tells Aparna later. 'I knew it was make or break with an audience like that and with my guruji listening. I knew I had to take the risk. If I didn't, I would stay where I was.'

Aparna knows nothing of the technicalities of music, but she understands what it is doing to her: it brings her whole life back to her. She thinks of how inadequate words are to speak of music, of how you can speak of music only through music.

Hari ends, as always, with what has become his signature, a Tukaram abhang. As soon as the compere ends his speech of thanks, Hari descends from the stage and goes straight to his guruji. Taimavshi joins them and then Hari looks around as if searching for someone. Madhu raises her arm to catch his attention and he smiles, gets to Aparna and says, 'Come, I want to introduce you to my guruji.' He takes her by the hand, as always making his feelings for her clear and public, and says 'Guruji, this is Dr Aparna Dandekar.'

Should she bend down and touch his feet as they all do? She feels awkward, it's not something she is used to, not something she is comfortable with. Finally she does a namaste, bowing low, almost a Japanese bow, Madhu says later.

'Chhoti hai,' Guruji says. She can feel his hand on her head.

'Lekin badi doctor hai, Guruji. And Gavi sir's daughter.'

'Yes, and my niece,' Taimavshi adds.

'All good connections. Look after this boy, child. He's going far.'

What has Hari told him about her, about their relationship?

'Come, Guruji, your car is waiting.'

Taimavshi leads him away. Hari is swallowed by a crowd. He looks back at her, gesturing, finger and thumb on his left palm and Aparna knows he is saying he will text her.

Abbas and Madhu are waiting for her. They try to persuade her to go home with them, at least to have dinner with them, but she steadily refuses. She is eager to go home, to be by herself, to reflect on her emotions, to understand her feelings.

'I have to go early to the hospital tomorrow,' she tells Madhu.

'Have you got any dinner at home?' Madhu asks her.

'Yes, don't worry.'

But when she gets home, she finds there's nothing. She had forgotten that Shaku had told her she would not be coming today. She finally eats the two bananas left, black on the outside but quite edible, she assures herself, as she forces them down her throat.

She can't sleep for a long time. His voice throbs in her ears, it seems to be plucking some strings inside her, she feel so taut and tense. He is a genius, I am a very ordinary woman. How long before he sees me for what I really am? The magic will vanish one day, the glitter will fade, the gloss will rub off. *The madness passes.* But I am incomplete without him, I want to be with him, I want him near me, his body close to mine, lying on top of me. She moves restlessly, uneasily, then tells herself sternly, 'Control yourself, Dr Dandekar.' She tries to think of other things, of the conference preparations, she thinks of the boy, just sixteen, eager to start on his chemo. What did Jyoti call it? 'The chemical inferno of chemotherapy.' But the boy thinks that the sooner he begins, the faster he will recover. He's confident because he came out of his surgery so well, so quickly. But that's because he's young. And, except for the monster lurking inside him, healthy. She thinks of his parents' faces, of his mother's eyes, rarely moving away from his face. The boy has never known sickness until this struck him, the father had said. Don't love him so much, she wants to tell the parents. People are not ours, we can't have them for a lifetime, they have been loaned to us, some time we have to give them back. Love doesn't help, she thinks, it makes the suffering worse. And yet Hari had once said to her, 'Aparna, don't you think that this illness, terrible though it is, brings out the best in people, brings out love and courage, which we would never see otherwise?' A patient's mother had said, 'If only I could take her illness and suffering on me, I would happily do it.' But if there's one thing I have learnt in this life, it is that we cannot take on another's suffering. We have to bear our own.

The phone rings. She switches on the light and looks at the time. Who could it be at this hour? She looks at the phone and sees Hari's name.

'Hari?'

'Open the door, Aparna, I am at your door.'

'Here?'

'Yes, yes. Open the door, Aparna.'

He enters with a rush as soon as she opens the door, as if he had been leaning against it. He immediately puts his arms round Aparna and closes the door behind him with his body. He picks her up, off the ground, holds her face close to his, breathing deeply as if he is inhaling her very presence and lets her down.

'Hari, are you drunk?'

'With love, Aparna, drunk with love, my pyari Aparna. I couldn't go home, Krishna said he would take me, but I didn't want to go home. I wanted you, I wanted to be with you, to talk to you, to hold you like this, to drink from your lips. I was thirsty, Aparna, I am so thirsty for you.'

His lips are on hers, his hands are roving over her back. He lets go of her and unhooks the single hook of her nightdress, puts his hand inside and cups her breast, first one, then the other.

She stops breathing, she feels she is suffocating. 'Hari…'

Again he puts his lips on hers, a kiss that lasts so long, they move away from each other, breathless and laughing.

'I want you so much.'

'Here I am, Hari, here I am.'

He smoothens her hair off her face, gently, tenderly, a gesture more erotic than the kiss. This time it is she who reaches with her lips for his, she who says, 'Hold me, don't stop Hari, hold me'.

'You're so beautiful Aparna, you're so beautiful.' He bends down and tenderly kisses her breasts, her nipples. He exclaims, an exclamation close to anguish, when she touches him. They move to the bed and he speaks only when he is poised above her, only to say her name in a questioning way. 'Apu…?'

'Yes, yes Hari, yes yes, yes, oh Hari, oh my sweetheart.'

Like his music, she thinks, like his music, as she feels his hands, his lips move over her body. Then she lets thought go and gives herself over to sensations, skin against skin, lips touching, tongues probing, hands demanding, claiming. She calls out, 'oh my god, oh my god,' as he reaches the climax and falls slack on her. He moves away and begins to laugh.

'What?'

'You speak English even in bed.'

'What did I say?'

'My god, my god. But there was another word you kept saying to me. Say it again, say it my Rani, my Apu rani.'

'What word?'

'Sweetheart. Say it again.'

'Sweetheart.'

'Oh Aparna,' he says to her in a kind of wondering delight, 'I can't believe we are really together. I've been searching for you, waiting for you all my life.'

'Why didn't you come earlier?'

'I don't know. Even after I met you, I was afraid, afraid that you would look down on me, I was afraid of what you'd say.'

'What else but yes yes yes, like I did today.'

'Why didn't you come to me?'

'How could I? I thought you would think I was an immoral woman, that I was free and easy…'

'Shh. Stop.' Suddenly he sits up. 'I'm hungry, I'm starving, I haven't eaten since lunch. Have you had dinner?' She shakes her head. 'Come on then, let's see if there's anything to eat in your house.'

'There's nothing,' she says in a small voice.

'What do you mean there's nothing? There has to be something. This is a home.'

He looks at her accusingly after a futile search which does not take long. 'What kind of woman are you, Dr Dandekar? Keeping a Brahmin starving? How can you do that?'

'Sorry, sorry. Though, actually, they may give me an award for that. A Padma Bhushan, perhaps. And now you know what kind of woman I am, do you want to get away?'

'Get away? I have something more important to do. I have to find something to eat.'

Luckily he finds a sachet of milk. He boils it, watching it like a hawk, and heaves a huge sigh of relief when it boils without curdling. She has, in the meantime, got out mugs and spoons. 'There's no sugar. Is honey okay?'

'Wonderful. And here's a packet of biscuits. Great.'

'Baby food,' she says, making a face when they sit down at the table.

'All food is good food. Tomorrow you had better get some food, stock your house. I'm a man who needs to eat.'

'Ji huzur.'

'And always have milk and dahi in your fridge.'

'Ji huzur.'

He's talking as if he will be with her again the next night and the night after and…

They go back to bed and with the urgency gone, they explore each other's bodies slowly and with joy. It's like she's known him always, she thinks; everything is familiar, the touch of his skin, the odour of his body, the taste of it.

'I have been searching for you all my life,' he says again. 'I didn't know what I was looking for, but the moment I saw you, I knew it was you.'

'Oh Hari, I was so alone, so incomplete without you. I am complete now, now I am whole.'

He says some words in Sanskrit. 'Shree Hari Pandit, don't talk to me in Sanskrit.'

'It's a shloka, you stupid woman. One of my grandfather's favourites.'

'Then say it again, no, chant it like a shloka.'

He chants the lines in his beautiful voice, his pronunciation of the Sanskrit words clear and perfect. 'Understood?'

'No, nothing, except the word *poornam*. A whole.'

'It's about wholeness. And now,' he says, 'we have to go to sleep.'

When she wakes up, he is gone. There is nothing to show that he had been there, except the feel of her own body to herself. But he has left the imprint of his presence everywhere in her life, he has entered her home, her life, her body. *Poornam idam poornam adaha*… I must learn the shloka from him, she thinks.

She rushes through her bath and breakfast. By the time she leaves the house, there are already three messages from him. She goes straight to her room, responds to his messages, and determinedly opening her laptop, sits at her table, working.

She goes through the day in a kind of daze. There is such an acute longing to be with him, for their bodies to meet, she thinks she can't bear to wait. For Aparna, like it is for all doctors, the act of sex had been demystified, divested of its secrecy by her knowledge of the human body; it was only one more function of the human body, it became just what it was meant to be, an act for procreation and to satisfy a basic human need, the various parts involved created with meticulous care to provide both. As a student, she had learnt the mechanics, the physiology of copulation. As a woman, she learnt the huge ignorance and mistaken ideas men have about sex, their ideas of right and wrong, their inability to understand a woman's desires, her needs. Now this emotional upheaval, this huge surge of love and happiness, the joyousness of desire without guilt, stuns her. She has learnt in one night that it can yield the greatest joy a human can experience, that it is a kind of union that goes beyond physical coupling.

She is so eager to be home, so afraid of being late, that she forgets the shopping. She remembers when she gets home and wonders whether to go out and shop or to have a bath. Ultimately she decides to have her bath. She is bathed, fragrant with talcum, when he comes, shopping bag in hand.

'What's that?'

'Food. I knew I couldn't depend on you. Did you do any shopping?'

'No, I forgot.'

'I knew that. Take this, put it away and come to me. Oh my Aparna, I've been waiting for this moment all day.'

'Me too. That's why I forgot to shop.'

'I didn't. I want to be with my beloved, but I want us not to starve.'

'Oh Hari, what a strange lover you are, more concerned with food than with your love.'

'Let me show you what I really care about. Come, Dr Dandekar, let me see whether you're as good as I've been imagining you all day.'

'Better,' he says, in English, later. 'Much much better.'

'Really? Much much bay-ter?'

'Don't you make fun of my English. And stop talking.'

This time they come together with a sense of ease and intimacy. There is something light-hearted and joyful about their lovemaking, Aparna thinks. She had never known such a thing was possible. She is surprised at his comfort with a kind of sexual badinage.

'I never thought you could talk like this.'

'What did you think I would be like?'

'Serious. Panditji-like. Or you would say – *my ajoba told me…*' He stops her mouth with his. When he lets her go, she goes on determinedly, 'Or, I thought, you would speak in Sanskrit, call me *Priye…*'

'Shall I recite a shloka?'

'No, no.'

'I can sing film songs as well. Want me to sing one? No, I'll sing you a Pankaj Mullick song – *piya milan ko jaana...*'

'No, no Hari, just this, just this.'

'Dinner,' she announces, when they move apart.

'I don't feel like getting up. I want to stay this way forever.'

'Something so beautiful can't last for too long.'

'Why do you say that, Apu? Don't say such things.'

'You're taking it seriously. I didn't mean anything serious. We'll always be together, I promise you. Always. Forever.'

When they are having dinner, he tells her he has already had two calls, tentatively asking him whether he'd come for a programme. Fairly prestigious events, he says. One in Delhi. 'And I have to go to Pune tomorrow to talk to Guruji, he asked me to.'

'Oh no, Hari.'

'Just a day, Rani, I'll be back at night. I'll come straight here. Why don't you come with me to Pune?'

'No, I can't. Another time. Give me enough notice.'

'All right,' he says, but she sees his disappointment.

Later, when he is sleeping – and she so envies him his childlike ability to fall asleep the moment his head touches the pillow – she thinks of how her mother had shaped her life to her father's needs. She refused to do the Bank Officers' exams because she might be transferred elsewhere. She never spoke of her work at home, yet she never took leave unless it was absolutely necessary. Home and work, work and home – her life consisted of only these two. And yet she walked away from both, as if they meant nothing to her. She realizes only now what it must have cost her to do that, how strong she must have been to be able to do that. But how could anyone change so much, change so completely? She remembers that she, who had signed as Sulabha Gajanan Dandekar, always the entire name, squeezing it into a small space if that was all there was – she decided to go back to her maiden name, Sulabha Patil, when she left home. To get rid of the 'Gajanan Dandekar'. But her illness overtook her and she died as Sulabha Gajanan Dandekar.

'Anything so beautiful can't last.' Why had she said that? She had frightened him and when she realized what she had said, frightened herself as well. But if there's death, there's also life. Cells die each moment of our lives, but there is also renewal, there is also birth. And she thinks of how Hari, like the sea carrying all the debris from the shore with it, has taken her past away, leaving her clean and lighter. There's only this, only the present, only Hari, only Hari and her.

In the morning she gets his message even before she goes to work. He says he might be late, but he will come.

Come Hari, come any time, but come, come to me, my love, my sweetheart. And then she thinks, I must give him a key, I must get a spare key for him.

Even as she is pulling the door shut, preliminary to locking it, she hears footsteps clattering up the stairs, Mira's voice calling out, 'Doctor, Aparnamavshi…'

Fear grips her. Mira climbs the last few steps and stands panting, trying to get her breath back.

What is it, Mira?'

'Ma is… Please come, come quickly.'

They run down the stairs, Mira standing back when they reach the door of her home, letting Aparna enter first.

'Go in, Mavshi, she's in her room.'

It's not as bad as she had feared. Jyoti is lying on the floor, a pillow under her head, Saguna anxiously bending over her with a glass of water in her hand. She sees Aparna and moves away with relief.

'Jyoti, Jyoti…' Her eyes slowly open and take in Aparna's anxious face.

'Hello,' she says.

'Hello.' Aparna smiles at her.

'What happened?'

'You tell me.'

Jyoti looks around, sees she is lying on the floor, takes in their anxious faces. 'I guess I passed out.'

'Do you remember anything?'

She shakes her head. She is struggling to sit up. Aparna stops her. 'Don't get up. Lie down. Mira, will you get my stethoscope? It's in the bedroom, here's the key.'

'I'm fine now, doc. I can sit up.'

'Wait a few moments.'

'Where's Tejas?' Jyoti asks Saguna.

'He's outside.'

'Call him in.' The boy comes in reluctantly and stands at a distance, not looking at Jyoti. 'Tejas, I'm fine. Don't worry. Doc, tell him I'm okay.'

'You're fine,' Aparna confirms when she checks her after Mira's return. 'You can get up now.'

Saguna and Mira help her into a chair, but Aparna says, 'Let her lie down on the bed. And, Saguna, get Jyoti a cup of milk. Or would you prefer tea?'

'Tea.'

'And some biscuits.'

When leaving, she tells Mira to bring Jyoti to the hospital.

'What for?'

'Let me have a proper look at you – for my satisfaction. Ring me after twelve, Mira, I'll tell you when to come.'

'Doc, is this serious?'

'I don't think so. Just a vasovagal – a fainting attack.'

In the hospital, after checking her, Aparna suggests Jyoti goes for a scan.

'Again?'

'Maybe you should see the neurologist first. Don't worry, Jyoti, these are all routine things. We don't want to think we missed out on anything.'

When Aparna visits her in the evening, Jyoti is in the little enclosed sit-out outside her bedroom, reading. Rather, holding a book in her hands. She sees Aparna, puts the book down and asks, 'Come to see if I'm still alive?'

'That's not funny. What if the children heard you?'

'I'm sorry, that was stupid of me.'

'How do you feel?'

'I wish I could tell you. State of great confusion. Imagining all kinds of things. Above all, feeling that my disease has tapped me on the shoulder, telling me, hey, remember, I'm still here. Sit down.' She says this in Marathi, using the intimate *tu* for the first time. 'Are you in a hurry to get home?'

'Not really.'

'Panditji not around?'

'He's gone out of town.'

'Then stay and have dinner with us.'

'No, I'll have a cup of tea. Don't bother, I'll go and tell Saguna to make me a cup. You?'

Jyoti shakes her head. When Aparna returns, Jyoti says, 'When you're with me, I feel safe. I feel you're keeping the crab at bay.'

I wish, how I wish, Aparna thinks, but doesn't say it.

'So what does it mean, doc? My fainting spell, I mean.'

'Honestly, I don't know. Anyone can faint. We had a girl in my class in school who used to regularly fall down with a thud.'

'They didn't take her to the neurologist?'

'No.'

'You know they don't use the word victim these days? They say survivor. Isn't it funny? You're facing death and they call you a survivor. What difference does a word make? It doesn't change the truth.'

'The truth being...?

'That I'm facing death.'

'Have you changed your doctor?'

'No. Why?'

'How come I don't know you're facing death?'

'Keep it going, doc, keep the fiction going.'

Saguna comes with the tea and a plate of chivda. 'Tai, anything for you?'

'No. I'll have dinner straight off. Tell me when Miru and Tejas return.'

When Saguna is gone, Jyoti resumes her conversation with Aparna. 'I was hoping to have some good years after the children grew up. Even find a companion for myself, maybe.'

'Why didn't you get married again, Jyoti?'

'It's a long story. Or rather, a short one, with one reason. Tejas. I was on the brink of it when Tejas found out, and he turned so hostile, I had to give it up.'

'Not fair, is it?'

'I know. But when you have children, your first duty is towards them. Specially when they don't have a father. And I think he came to know in a rather shocking way. Shocking for him. He found us together...' She says no more and Aparna leaves it there. She tells her that, as far as her experience and acumen can tell her, Jyoti is fine.

'As yet.'

'Yes, as yet.'

'Thanks, doc. You don't know what a relief it is. I make wisecracks, I'm sarcastic, nasty, but the truth is I'm scared. Who wouldn't be? This life is all we have, there's nothing else beyond.'

The house is silent except for the sounds of Saguna working in the kitchen. Tejas comes in, sweating and panting.

'Finished your run?'

He nods. 'All right, go and have a bath. Saguna will call you when dinner is ready.'

Where's Mira?' Aparna asks when he has gone out.

'I sent her out. She needs to get away from me and all this...' She waves her hand at the paraphernalia of the sick strewn about the room. 'And I'm glad we are alone, there's something I have to talk to you about. It's about me.'

'Go ahead.'

'It's about my future. My future! Ha! Anyway, I've been thinking that this time I've been lucky, it was only a scare, but some day the thing is going to come back. When that happens, I'd like to be left alone. I don't want to go through the treatment all over again.'

'What do you mean?'

'I mean, if there is a metastasis, I won't be pumped full of chemicals all over again. It's no use trying to stop the flood by putting a finger in the breached dam. And spending money which should be for the children. So I've decided – no further treatment. The money is for my children.'

'Your children need you more than they need money.'

Jyoti ignores this and goes on, 'So remember, doc, you have to back me when the time comes. Support my decision.'

'Sorry, I have a very poor memory. I've already forgotten what you said.'

'Don't be like this, doc.'

'How else do you expect me to be? My job is to heal and that's the only thing I can do.'

'But you can't put off death forever! Why are you doctors so afraid of the word death? Start using it and you'll find it's not so terrible after all.'

'Death is the enemy we're fighting. We don't want to shake hands with it, no, never!'

'But, doc, if you face the enemy, you'll find it's not so much of a bogey, after all.'

'Should we tell our patients – you're not going to live, you're going to die, in spite of all our knowledge and experience we can do nothing for you? Should we say that?'

'No, no, doc, not like that. Just let it become part of your vocabulary. Death is part of life, it's built into the system.'

'For us death is defeat.'

'So you won't support me?'

'Sorry, Jyoti, it's not something I can do. It's for you and for your children to decide, they have as much of a right to decide as you do.'

To Aparna's surprise, Jyoti drops the subject. But she persuades Aparna to stay on, to have dinner with her and the children. While they wait for the children to come, Jyoti talks to Aparna about her parents' marriage. 'My father was an abominable man, he lived his life with an *I'm the Emperor of the world* attitude. We were all his subjects. It was worst for my mother, of course. You know, doc, Kamalamavshi told me something about her that I've never been able to get out of my mind. She told me this after Prabha died. I believe my father slept with her every night of their married life, every single night, except perhaps when she had her periods. My mother – Kamalamavshi told me this – said, I didn't know I could say no, I thought it was my duty to do what he wanted, but I felt like a prostitute. Kamalamavshi told me that Prabha even thought of scratching her face and spoiling her looks, so that he would leave her alone. I tell you, when I heard that… But I'd hated him anyway. I married Aakash to get away from him.'

Aparna has seen this before, it happened to her mother. A woman reserved to the point of taciturnity, she spoke to Aparna in her last days as she had never done before. She spoke to her as one human being to another. She told Aparna of her early childhood, of the sudden death of her parents in a car accident and how Taimavshi's parents took her into their family and made her one of them. She spoke of Aparna's childhood and her dreams and ambitions for her. All her talk only about the past, no word of the present or the future, no word at all of the man who had been her life and her world for so many years. It was as if he had ceased to exist for her.

And here was Jyoti speaking of her marriage, of her own immaturity. 'I thought, even after marriage things would be as they had been before, our feelings for each other would remain at the same high pitch. But things changed. For him, once he had me, it was as if he no longer had to think about me. We fought, oh god, how fiercely we fought! Both of us had bad tempers. It was only sex that saved us; sex is the one drug that brings about complete forgetfulness, amnesia almost, even if it's for a few moments.'

She is silent for a while, then goes on, 'Ultimately, the children took me away from my Aakash obsession. I was besotted with them, specially Miru when she was born. My first baby. I thought she was a miracle. And I was no longer infatuated with Aakash. I almost thought I'd fallen out of love with him. Then he died and I fell in love with him all over again. I could do nothing but brood over his death. Why? Why? I kept asking myself. At that time I wrote a novel about marriage. I killed him in it – or, rather, I killed the husband figure. I think it helped me a lot.' She laughs.

'Where is that novel?'

'I thought, when I wrote it, that it was a masterpiece. But when I read it, I realized it was bad. I shredded it,' she says cheerfully.

Aparna tells her how her mother saved every little piece of paper Gaja wrote on. When he thought of something, he wrote on anything that came to hand – the margins of magazines, white space in newspapers, old bills. 'Aai used to collect all those bits and put them carefully on his table.'

'Your father was a real writer. Not a sham like me.'

They can hear Mira's voice calling out to Tejas. She comes into Jyoti's room and seeing Aparna asks, 'Are you okay, Ma?'

'Yes. Why?'

'Aparnamavshi is here.'

'She's come to tell me that all's well. Go and see if dinner is ready.'

As soon as she's gone, Aparna asks Jyoti, 'I wanted to ask you – can I have another key to my place? Is there another?'

'There are two – one is with us and one with you.'

'Can I make another one? Only if you agree, of course.'

'Doc, it's your house now, you're paying us rent for it. You can do what you want. But wait a little. I think there is a third key somewhere. I'll look for it…'

'Don't take any trouble.'

'No trouble at all, doc.'

'Thanks.'

'And, doc, now that we're on this subject, I must tell you that the watchman was telling me that a man comes out of Doctor saheb's house in the mornings.'

'Oh shit!'

Jyoti laughs. 'Don't be upset, doc.'

'I'm sorry.'

'And don't be sorry. What for? It's nobody's business but yours. We're all adults here. Go on, doc, go on loving your Shree Hari, forget everything else.'

Aparna.

If I write your name, only your name, all the words of love in all the languages come into it. I talk to you on the phone so many times a day, I keep messaging you; this is the first time I am writing a proper letter to you. I have lost the habit, I can't remember when I last wrote a letter and sent it by mail. But now it seems that I can communicate with you only in this way – no short forms, each word written out complete, each sentence with all the words in it. And I have to write to you in Marathi, only then can my heart find its way into my words. I don't know whether you have the Marathi software in your laptop. If you don't, I'll install it for you when I am back.

You may find it hard to believe (or maybe not), but I bought a copy of your father's plays in Pune. There are five plays in this collection. I've been reading the plays since I got the book. And as I read, I have been thinking how different words are when spoken. The words in your father's plays are meant to be spoken, only then is there life in them. And, yet, it's only when the words are written that they become so clear that there can be no misunderstanding. Strange, isn't it? But perhaps that is why I am writing. Because I know that when I spoke to you this morning about postponing my return, you were disappointed, annoyed, you did not want to talk any more. I said I was here for a friend's sister's wedding, but I will admit I am using this as an excuse to stay away, to think of some things. I'm going to write to you about these things.

I went to Pune to meet my Guruji. I thought I would stay for a day, but he had no time for me that day, so I stayed on (as I told you). I also wanted some quiet after the noise and din of my last performance. I thought I was becoming a little too satisfied with myself. I need to get out of that state. I need someone to tell me honestly whether I am on the right path. I also need to think about us, about you and me. About what we are doing, what I have done. I have been very uncomfortable with myself since our relationship became physical. I am not so stupid or old-fashioned (I know you think I am very old-fashioned) as to think that what we did is a sin. So many young people have sex before marriage today. I know Krishna has had some relationships, I know Maya and he are together in the physical sense also. I am uncomfortable with myself because I lost control over myself. It was as if a cyclone had hit me; I could do nothing but go the way it forced me. I want to say this to you, my Aparna – I did not do it light-heartedly, casually. It was my great love for you that drove me into loving you through your body. I don't want you ever to think that I came to you only for sex, for your body. I came to you because of my love, because of my desire to express my love for you through our bodies. Your body is sacred to me.

When I asked you to marry me, you said you wanted time. I agreed. But how much time, Aparna? There has to be a limit, we can't go on this way. I know you are a very independent person, that you live your life the way you choose, that you have taken your own decisions. I promise you it will continue to be this way even after our marriage. I will never interfere with your choices, your life. I know I am not what they call 'a good prospect'. I do not earn very much, my earnings are not steady; I have a career in which I can never be sure I'll make it. I have no good home to offer you. I know you have your own home, I know we can live there, but I cannot live with you in your home unless I am sure I am able to contribute equally to it.

These, however, are small matters and I know both of us will be able to compromise a little. What is important is how we feel about each other. When I met you, I knew that what I felt for you was something I had never felt before. And when I came to know that you loved me, I felt my life was fulfilled. I felt as if I had been given a key to heaven. Now I have become greedy. I want all of you, I want us to live together, I want to go to sleep with you beside me, wake up with your head on the pillow beside mine, I want us to have children, to bring them up together. I want to walk through life's journey holding your hand in mine. I know you will laugh at this kind of language, or smile, because this is the language of all lovers. But let me quote to you a few lines from your father's play. One of the characters says:

We don't write our love on a clean slate, on a blank sheet of paper. There's already much written on that paper – stories, songs, poems, ideas, beliefs. They become part of our love story as well. Which is why all the songs sung through time, of stars and moons, of cool breezes and hot sighs, become part of our own love stories.

Madhuri-not-tai has told me about your parents, about how deeply their separation affected you. (Don't be angry with her, I made her tell me.) But why do you think we will repeat their lives? I would like us to be like my grandparents were, but I know that will not happen, either. I am sure they did not ever say the word love, but when my ajji died, Ajoba became half the person he had been, he lived only for my sake. We will find our own way, and I am sure it will be a way which will bring us both happiness.

I came here, to Ratnagiri, two days back. I am staying with my younger mama, my mother's second brother, Vasant. My oldest mama lives in Pune. I met him this time, I don't know why, because I had not gone to him for years. He was happy to see me, but not so happy at my choice of music as a career. I did not argue with him, what's the use? And I think he finally understood I have made my choice. I hoped to find better company in Vasantmama, who was very close to my mother and I was not disappointed. I must tell you about a talk I had with him yesterday. For some reason, I don't know why, I had always thought that my mother committed suicide. I don't know where the idea came from, I once even asked my ajji about it. She was angry. Who told you such stories, she said, but she did not deny it. And I continued to think that my mother had killed herself and that it was because my father had made her unhappy. I asked Vasantmama, not whether my mother had committed suicide, but how she died. And he told me she had had a pregnancy which started in the tube. You will know what it is. It is dangerous, he told me, and they could not get her to the hospital in time and she died. This happened when she had come home for a visit in summer. Vasantmama also told me something else, that my mother was an excellent swimmer, she swam like a fish, he said. Her ambition was to swim the river from bank to bank. The last time she came home, she told him that she was going to try it before going back to Mumbai. Then they discovered that she was pregnant and she said, 'all right, next time'. The next time never came. For the first time I thought of her death, not in connection with me, not as my loss, but hers. She died young, she could not do the things she must have wanted to do. But I feel good that she had an ambition; no unhappy person can have an ambition.

I am coming back to you with a lighter heart; the thought that my mother committed suicide had been like a stone on my heart, her unhappiness came back to me at times like a dark cloud. I can't tell you how relieved I am that this is not true. I suppose I should change my ideas about my father, but it is not easy. He and I are very different people and his wife is someone I am most uncomfortable with, she is so false.

So, my Apu Rani, I will come home a little lighter than when I went. I think we should avoid a physical relationship for some time until we decide about marriage. Marry me, Aparna, I swear I will love you all my life, I will try my best to make you happy. I will be thinking of you every moment until we meet.

Your own and always yours and only yours,

Hari

Aparna carefully refolds the letter the way it had been folded, pressing on the creases, and puts it back in the envelope. My first love letter, she thinks. She remembers the bunch of letters she had come across in one of Baba's table drawers. Sulu's letters to Gaja. They were nowhere when Madhuri and she cleared the house after his death. Burn the house, burn everything in it, he had cried out to them angrily. Perhaps he had burnt the letters himself. What happened to his love? And Sulu, who after years of loving and living with Gaja, walked out like a character in a movie or a TV serial, with only a suitcase. And Jyoti, who wrote a novel in which she says she killed her husband. Was she joking? Can you joke about such things?

She passes her fingers gently, tenderly over the letter and thinks again, My first love letter.

Let's go back to the way we were, he had written. But it is not possible. They are addicts, they are like alcoholics, unable to control their desire for a drink. She thinks of the smokers with cancer, of the way their physical suffering is exaggerated by their huge consuming desire for a smoke. Just one, they say sometimes. Just to hold in my hand, I won't smoke it. If I could just inhale once, doctor, they say. But they know, and their doctors know as well, that nothing but constant smoking will ease their torment.

She remembers a patient, only thirty-six, who had known he was dying, who hated himself for what he had done to himself. And yet he told her once that he would sell his soul, give up all his future days, for a smoke.

Hari and she decide that they won't meet at home, they will meet outside to avoid temptation. She often finds him waiting for her when she comes out of her room. I'll walk back with you, he says. And when they reach home, he comes up with her. I'll see you in, he says. I'll sit for just a few minutes… It never happens that way. Once she comes home to find him waiting in the house for her (yes, she's given him a key), dinner ready and on the table. 'I'll have a bath, then we'll eat,' she says. But he joins her in the bathroom and by the time they get to the table, the food is cold. Another time, she wakes up at some time of the night to find him sitting by her, his breath warm on her face. She is startled. 'Don't be afraid,' he says, 'It's me.' And he puts his mouth on hers, such a demanding, fierce kiss that it brings her out of drowsiness into instant arousal.

They are now familiar with each other's bodies, yet the need to explore does not stop; it seems never-ending. Sated, she is still not free of the constant need for him. The need remains just as urgent, it keeps growing. It's no longer a simple need, but a demanding, ferocious hunger. It's a hunger now, not only for sex, but for the innumerable intimacies that come with sleeping together. Lying face to face without talking, legs entwined, inhaling each other's very being. Lying side by side, hands linked. Speaking in the coded language of lovers, to which the key is always love. Lying in a silence that is full of their love. He hates their truncated time together. I want to spend all my time with you, he says. He tells her he is going to Bangalore, that he has a programme there, arranged by friends of his, and asks whether she will go with him.

'But you'll be busy.'

'We'll stay two extra days if you come.'

She asks for the dates. I have to check whether I am free, she tells him. But she knows she wants to go, she wants to be with him for those three or four precious days. Jyoti's words about her marriage come yet again to her mind: And then I fell out of love with him and I wanted to kill him, but he died. And then I fell in love with him all over again.

Is love always so whimsical, so incalculable?

AHALYA'S STORY

It seems to me that my days of living in this place are coming to an end. I am finding it hard to do the things I did so easily earlier. But now this child, my student's daughter, comes to help me both before she goes to school and after she finishes school. I manage with her help. She is good, but she is impatient to finish her work and go out, to be with her friends, to talk and do the things that girls of her age do. She is so eager to move out of girlhood into womanhood, I want to tell her – enjoy this time, this is the best time of your life, your mind is fresh and eager to learn, your body is strong and active, enjoy this time. But she won't listen. Youth has its own urges, its own desires. And we have to walk the path ourselves, nothing others say can change the way we live our lives; we can learn only through our own experiences. But the child makes me feel good. Each time she leaves me, she says, '*Majja kara, Ajji.*' Have fun? At my age? But that she says it to me is enough to make me smile, to feel good. *Majja*? Have I had any fun in my life? As a child, yes, it was wonderful. I lived in the midst of plenty – our fields were fertile, the yield was most often good and we had plenty of cattle. Above all, there were my parents, my brothers, my uncle, aunt and their children. And yes, there was school.

When I look back I can see that I was truly lucky in the early years of my life. I moved from the plenty of my childhood home to plenty of another kind in 'his' house. There, wealth could be seen in the jewellery the women wore, the silver plates brought out for festivals and weddings, the grand way festivals were celebrated. In this house the painter brought me to, I have had wealth of a different kind – I have been free, I had my daughters, and I found work for the first time. I needed nothing more, except the painter's company at times. I had plenty of women's company, but a man's company is different from a woman's, there is a different texture to it. The conversation is different. And a man has a very different way of looking at things. I need that at times. I am also proud that I have kept my word – kept? No, I did not give my word, it was taken from me. I had to agree never to use their name. And I never have. I have had different names here. The painter never called me by name, it was always 'aapan' very respectfully. Outside the home I became 'masterinbai', later 'Headmasterinbai.' Now I am ajji to everyone. Yes, I kept my word, I never reclaimed my name 'Ahalya'.

And yet, I think of this, what I am writing, as 'Ahalya's story'. I wonder why. My last act of defiance? After our marriage, when 'he' and I could be by ourselves, when we could talk freely, 'he' told me 'he' named me after the great queen Ahalya. Ahalyabai Holkar. I later came to know that there was another Ahalya as well, a not-much-talked-about Ahalya. The wife of Gautama Rishi, she was a disgraced woman. The story goes that Indra desired her and tricked her when her husband was away by disguising himself as her husband Gautama. And she, thinking he was her husband, succumbed to him. For which she was punished. I find this very hard to believe. There is something wrong with this story. How can anyone believe she was fooled by Indra's disguise? Women have become so skilled at concealing their thoughts, they can live all their lives with a man and never let him know what is in their minds. But how can a woman not know her husband? How can she not recognize his feel, his touch, his skin, his smell? How can she not recognize the way he comes to her, the things he does to her, what he says to her? *(Tr. note: My god, this woman is brave! She follows a thought, uncaring of where it is going to lead her.)* Perhaps, I thought, she pretended she thought he was Gautama, when she knew he was not. Perhaps she knew it was Indra, the king of gods, she was flattered that he had come to her and so she remained silent. Whatever it may be, the story goes that Gautama returned, found them together, cursed her and turned her into a rock. Indra was also punished, a very ugly punishment – if it is any consolation. *(Tr. note: I must read this story.)* Ahalya remained a rock until Shri Rama came and the touch of his feet turned her into a woman again. What does this teach women? A man does you wrong and you need another man to deliver you from the punishment for that wrong? It makes no sense to me.

When I began to live with the painter, I began to look at the body very differently. We women were always made to think of our bodies as unclean – unclean during our monthly periods, unclean after childbirth. We could never think of our bodies as a source of pleasure, it was always a burden. The painter saw it differently. He found the symmetry, the lines of the human body, amazing. He appreciated even the flaws, the asymmetry, because these were the things, he said, which made us different from one another. There is no such thing as perfection, he said, but there is a glimpse of perfection in every body. He loved the quick movements of children – he drew many sketches of our daughters. 'He', on the other hand, admired the human body for the way it functioned, the way it had been created, each part meant to perform a certain function and doing it so well that we never even thought about it. 'He' taught me to enjoy the human body; but for me all its beauty was in 'his' body. 'He' used to ask me to massage 'his' neck and shoulders when 'he' had been working at 'his' table for too long. I used to think that 'he' didn't really want a massage, 'he' wanted the touch of my palms on 'his' back. For me, too, it was such a wonderful thing to feel 'his' body, 'his' skin under my hands, I could have gone on forever. 'He' had such a beautiful body, 'his' chest, 'his' back…

What am I doing? This is old-age madness, writing such things at my age. Thank god no one will read this. *(Tr. note: Hello, Hello, there are three of us here reading you, enjoying what you are saying. Two of us, really, maybe the third will read it some day. What do you say, doc?)* But it was my babies who taught me the beauty of the human body. My son and two daughters. I could look at them for hours, watch how they opened and closed their little palms, how they spread their five fingers wide, how their legs moved endlessly in a kind of cyclical movement.

Now I know all human bodies are a wonder. But we misuse our bodies. We misuse our minds even more. And where does the cruelty that lies inside us come from? Could the same creator who made these wonderful bodies have made the mind what it sometimes is – crooked, cunning and cruel? I can never think of Bhausaheb without anger, even now, even after so many years. To take my only son away from me – or, rather, to take me away from my son. He will be a grown man now, older than Durga. I never saw the process of his growing up, one of the greatest joys of a parent. Whenever I saw a young man, I used to think of my son. Young men are like untamed animals; there's so much energy in them, so much joy in life. They look down at the world from the lofty heights of their young manhood. They are so sure of themselves, so sure of their ability to shape the world to their wishes and desires. I remember my brother Mukunda, how much fire there was in him. My son must have had that fire in him as well; being his father's son, he could not be a dull man. I lost him. I lost all the different avatars of his life – as a child, as a growing boy, as a young man steering his way between being a child and a man. I lost all these.

I wonder whether Bhausaheb knew what he was doing, I wonder whether he was comfortable with himself. I wonder whether, when he was dying, the thought of what he had done troubled him. I have been able to forget Bhausaheb and his cruelty at times, but thoughts of my son never ceased to torment me. What kind of man is he? What is he doing now? Who looked after him and who brought him up? I accept the fact that Durga has a son. But that my son, even older than Durga, may be having children of his own, is hard to believe. I see him as a baby, as a child – I can't go beyond that.

Now it is time for me to leave this house and live with Durga and her family, time to spend the last stage of my life in my daughter's house. She has been getting irritated with what she calls my 'stubbornness'. She does not understand that it is not that I don't want to go to her. But I have lived alone for so long, it will be strange to be among people again. And I am a little afraid of going to a new place. I am so familiar with this house that I can move about it easily in spite of my poor vision, I am able to 'see' it even at night. But in Durga's house, the unfamiliarity will make me more dependent. And I know that once you lose your independence, it is hard to get it back. But perhaps I have also begun craving human company, for so often these days I dream of my time in the place where Bhausaheb left me, a place for widows and abandoned women. All of us slept in the hall at night and all night I could hear the sounds of women sighing, women sobbing quietly, women speaking in their sleep, one or two occasionally suddenly crying out as if someone was attacking them, so that they had to be woken out of their nightmares. It was always a very uneasy, disturbed sleep for all of us. It was as if a cloud of sorrow and cruelty and suffering hung over all of us in that room. I have never forgotten those women. Each girl I teach, I think – let her not become one of those women. I try to tell girls they must have some control over their lives. I know it is hard, I know it will not happen in my lifetime, perhaps not even in theirs. But we have to keep working, hoping that some day women will be able to live without fear – the fear of not marrying, the fear of not having children, the fear of widowhood, the fear of men.

Let that be. I have done what I could. Now I have to go to my daughter. But I have to finish this first. I am not free until I complete it. I have a strange feeling that I will die only when this story of mine is done.

There is much that I have not written here. Much that I am unable to write. I cannot even think of the last moments of 'his' life. I was kept away from him; he insisted on it because of our son. He knew TB is dangerous, he did not want to expose me or our son to that dreadful disease. I can never write of those first moments, of those first few days after he was gone. I can't even remember much of that time. Memory returns when I was told that I had to go with Bhausaheb. I did not know where he was taking me. When I thought of it, I expected he wanted to make me a shaven widow, that he didn't want to have that done at home and therefore he was taking me away. Memory brings back the house he took me to, of being left alone while Bhausaheb went inside. I waited for him to return. He never did return, I never saw him after that. Instead there was a woman who came to me and saying 'Indutai wants to see you,' took me into a room where a woman told me the truth, that Bhausaheb had left me here and that I would never be able to go back home.

My son? I asked her. Over and over again I asked, my son?

She could not answer. I saw the answer in her eyes, on her face. I got my answer in the letter he had left for me, the letter I refused to read for a long time. I have kept my promise, the letter said. What promise? Had Bhausaheb promised his son that I would not be made a shaven widow? Had 'he', who had abhorred the custom, made 'his' father promise they would not do that to me? And, Bhausaheb being what he was, deeply conservative and traditional, the family being what it was, could not fulfil his promise and at the same time let me live at home. And therefore this solution?

But my son, my son?

It took me a very long time to come out of this greatest sorrow of my life. Even 'his' death had not hit me so hard. I had wild thoughts of running away – where? Of going to Miss Simmons and asking for her help in recovering my son. Ultimately, I gave up. Indutai asked me to think of my son's future. Was he not better off in the midst of his father's family than with me, who had no one and nothing? And so I gave up hope. I turned my thoughts to educating myself. Bhausaheb had left some money for that. I knew I had every right to it. I studied, I did my teacher's training. Indutai kept coaxing me to marry. The world is hard for a single woman, she kept telling me. You can't live alone, she said. You will be like a deer in a jungle of wild animals. She suggested the painter to me, she thought the painter was an ideal choice because he didn't care for the customs and rules of society. And so I married him and came here to his place. He had promised me he would get me, through his patron, a teacher's job and he kept his promise.

I have been happy here, yes, I can say that now. My one great grief is that Kashi died, she had typhoid and died after ten days of the fever. But I had Durga. And when the painter died, it was a quiet kind of mourning. I mourned him because he had been such a good man, he had been very good to me. He died in Mumbai, in the room which he shared with another man. A friend of his came to tell us what had happened. Durga and I went to Mumbai, I wanted to see where he had lived; Durga needed it much more than I did. She loved her father, she found it hard to accept his death. When we saw the bare room in which he had lived, she sobbed, she knew he had spent little on himself, he had given most of his money to us. He married to have children, he wanted children more than he wanted a wife. I was glad his daughters loved him so dearly. I came to understand that there had been some women in his life, but it never affected me, because he never spoke of them, he never brought them into our life. Just as he never brought my past into our life together. He knew about it, Indutai had told him – with my permission. But he never spoke a word about it.

I made no attempt to find out anything about my son. How would I explain my curiosity? I have sometimes thought I should tell Durga, I should tell her she has a brother. But what good will it do her except, perhaps, change her idea of me? Of our family? She does not need to know my past. The future is more important and the future is with her in her son, Gaja, such a bright, active little boy. I will quickly finish with the past and go to be with them, my daughter and my grandson.

Her annual visits with Sulu to Mumbai had been the high point of her year for Aparna. The joy had been, not only in knowing that Madhu and Taimavshi were waiting for them at the end of the journey, but that Mumbai, the most fascinating and amazing city, was waiting for them. There was also the journey itself, the rails unrolling before them, the rhythmic song the train and the rails sang together. And the long hoot of the whistle when they came into Mumbai, the hoot that became even more strident when the train began snaking its way through the city. A hoot that announced – here I am, get out of my way. Travelling with Hari to Bangalore is different; it's not the destination or the journey that matters, it's being with Hari, it's knowing that for the next four days they will be together, that they don't have to look at the clock and prepare themselves for the moment of separation.

She had been at the airport before him. 'Wait for me,' he had said when she rang up and told him she was there. 'We'll check in together.'

'Just one bag?' she asked in surprise.

'It's only four days.'

'I thought you travel with your taanpura. Like cricketers with their bats.'

'Carry that huge thing? That's for the instrumentalists. I have my voice, that's easy to carry.'

She sleeps through the flight as always and wakes up with a jerk when the plane touches land. As they walk out of the gate, Hari waves at a man, who holds up his hand in reply.

'Rohit!'

'You're on time.'

'Yes. Rohit, this is Aparna, Dr Aparna Dandekar.'

Aparna knows he is the friend who has arranged Hari's programme.

'Arundhatitai?' Hari asks him.

'She's got things to do at home. You're coming home for dinner. I'll drop you at the hotel. Call me when you're rested and ready.'

In the hotel, he speaks briefly to the man at the reception and leaves them. The man smiles at Hari, addresses him by his name and seems to know that Hari is the musician for this year's festival. Aparna is surprised that they have only one room. She had imagined Hari would book two rooms, she had already decided that she would pay for her own room. She goes to Hari's side, but he is turning away.

'Excuse me,' she says to the man at the desk, 'I need to sign for my room.'

'Sir has signed…' the man is saying, when Hari holds her by her arm and hastily takes her away saying, 'Rohit has looked after it.'

'No reason why he should pay for my room, Hari.'

'He has booked only one room for us, Apu. I told him to do that.'

Now, she thinks, there is no longer anything secret about our relationship. The man at the desk knows that Hari is with a woman who is not his wife. Or perhaps he thinks I kept my maiden name like so many women do. Or maybe they think that musicians, like all artists, have lax morals? But why does it matter to me so much? Or at all? But it's not what the man thinks that troubles her, it's Hari who puzzles her. He's always so careful for her sake. She has not even spoken to him about the watchman's comments, afraid that he will stop coming to her. Why, then, is he flaunting, almost, their togetherness?

Everything is forgotten when they get to their room. For a hotel room it's large, with open windows, a wooden double bed and a chest-of-drawers with a swinging mirror on it. And, yes, a wooden parquet floor.

'This is beautiful,' Aparna says, when the man who brought up their luggage has gone.

'Rohit tells me this was a zamindar's home – or palace. He's part of the team that renovated it.'

'Hari,' Aparna calls out from the open window, 'come and look at this. Such a beautiful garden.'

He comes to her obediently and says, 'Nice garden' without looking out and she laughs. He puts his arm about her and asks, 'But why are we talking about rooms and gardens, Apu?'

'I don't know. And we have to get ready. Rohit will be here to pick us up.'

But there is something so intoxicating in knowing that time and space are theirs, so hard to discipline their bodies, that they have to scramble to get ready when Rohit rings them from the lobby.

Aparna is quiet in the car, listening to the two men talking.

'Have you been here before, doctor?' Rohit asks her.

'Call me Aparna. Yes, I've been here once. With my parents. Long back. My father was invited by the local Marathi association. I remember nothing.'

'In any case, there's such a disconnect between this city and the city of yesterday, your memories will get lost in this new city.'

When they enter the house, there is the happy sound of children's voices. Rohit's wife comes to greet them, he introduces her as Arundhati. It is when the woman is talking to Hari that something goes click in Aparna's mind and the thought flashes through it: this is the woman Hari has not told me about, this is the woman I have met in his thoughts. She does not know why the thought comes to her, but it is a certainty: this is the woman he was attracted to when he was a boy. 'They have two children,' he had said casually, when he spoke of his friends. She had imagined the woman, if she had thought of her at all, as a plump middle-aged woman with spreading hips. But this woman is as slim as a wand, she's erect and has a face that you want to linger on. Aparna learns that she is a lawyer working in the family courts and that this beautiful home was built on the site of her family home. Aparna likes it that she formally introduces her to the children, a boy and a girl, the girl very dignified and yes, bossy, the boy boisterous and trying his mother's patience. And then, suddenly, the ghost in her head disappears and she sees a woman involved with her family, her children.

Aparna, on Arundhati's suggestion, joins the men 'until these brats are fed'. A young woman moves in and out, the help, most probably, Aparna thinks; but she is friendly, not servile. Rohit, in charge of the drinks, has got Hari his strange concoction of hot water, lemon juice and honey; it shows how well he, how well *they* know Hari, how familiar they are with him. For Aparna, Rohit gets out a bottle of wine. The children's talk, their laughter, their occasional raised voices form a pleasing background to their conversation. When the children have gone to bed, Arundhati joins them.

'Shree Hari was part of our marriage,' she says, smiling at Aparna. 'His grandfather was the priest who married us. He knew my mother's sister, she's a gynaecologist in Mumbai. Do you know her? No, what a stupid question, Mumbai is such an ocean. Here's a picture of Shree Hari with us,' she says, picking up a small framed picture from the table. Aparna can recognize Rohit and Arundhati in their wedding clothes. There's an older man who presumably is Hari's grandfather, the first time she is seeing him, a portly man with a broad smile on his face. 'We were married right here, we still had the old house then. Shree is behind his grandfather,' Arundhati points out. The couple is laughing, as is Hari's grandfather. Only Hari is serious. He is plumper than he is now, his face a little sulky. Both his body and face have been pared down over the years, chiselled, giving him a distinguished look. In the picture, he too is wearing 'priestly' clothes, his sacred thread prominent on his chest, the head clean shaven, with only the tuft left at the back.

'My father wanted me to graduate. I wanted to take up music full time. Just to defy my father, I said I would become a priest like Ajoba – I knew my father would hate it even more than music, he had got away from his background, he didn't want me to go back to it. So I said I would become a priest. And when this wedding came up, Ajoba said, if you're going to be my assistant, you had better come along with me and assist me properly.'

'Ours was a simple wedding. Both of us wanted it that way,' Rohit says. 'Besides, Aru's grandmother was dying, she died soon after we got married.'

'And Shree Hari was such a surprise. He came in his jeans, T-shirt and baseball cap. Like any other kid of his age.'

'And then he turned up for the wedding, trailing behind his grandfather in a dhoti and bare chest, a shaven head with that shendi wagging behind him. A nice thick tuft. It was such a transformation. And then he sang the mangalashtaka.'

'I had to show them I was serious about becoming a priest. I never fooled my ajoba, though. He gave me such a shock in the morning. He said, Balasaheb – when he called me Balasaheb, I knew I was in the danger zone – Balasaheb, he said, you are going to sing the mangalashtaka.'

'Who had written the mangalashtaka verses, Shree?'

'My ajji. It was like a – what do you call it – you make others from it...?'

'Template.'

'That's right. You could use it for any couple, you only had to change the names. When Ajoba told me I had to sing, I went blank. I always used to refuse whenever anyone asked me to sing. You know how, when they know someone is learning music, they say, *sing something*? I used to get angry. What do they mean, *sing something*? I'm not a performing monkey! Ajoba scolded me once. He said, you have a gift. You have to sing to an audience, otherwise your music is dead. And that day he gave me such a shock when he told me I had to sing the mangalashtaka. I was sure I would make a fool of myself.'

'He sang beautifully, so beautifully. His voice was like a flute. Even the birds in the trees were silenced.'

'Arundhatitai, you're exaggerating.'

'I mean it, I'm serious. Ours was such a simple, small wedding, but Shree transformed it with his music.'

'When I stood there, I was blank. But when Arundhatitai came into the pandal, it suddenly came to me. I knew I could sing it, I knew how I would sing it. But for me the best thing was that, after that day, Ajoba supported me. But he said I had to graduate, I had to give my father's wishes that much respect.'

The three of them are weaving their memories together to make a story, a story in which she sees a different Hari. A sulky boy with a glorious talent, intent on carving his own path in life. And perhaps, because they are all addressing her, she does not feel left out. She is their audience, the story is for her, they know that she has a role to play in the story. She also thinks that this is perhaps the first time that he has spoken of his father so naturally and easily.

There is a sense of mellowness that comes with good wine and conversation. Arundhati gets up often to go into the kitchen, the dining room, or into the children's room. Each time she returns, Rohit looks at her as if welcoming her back after her brief absence. Aparna has a fleeting thought that perhaps Hari has brought her here to see this family idyll, to see that it is possible for two busy people to create this kind of life. Then she dismisses the thought; it is too tortuous and cunning a thought for Hari. He would never think of it.

Before going back to the hotel, Hari has arranged with Rohit to go to their house in the morning to meet his accompanists. We have an empty flat upstairs, my father-in-law is away, you can use that, Rohit tells him.

'And you and I,' says Arundhati to Aparna, 'can go out in the morning, I've kept myself free. Shopping, sight-seeing, whatever you'd like to do.'

For the first time Aparna and Hari have the whole night ahead of them, for the first time they see each other's going-to-bed routine. Hari's consists of doing the pranayam.

'So late?'

'Good for the voice. Good to induce sleep as well.'

When he is done, he lies in bed, lazily watching Aparna going through her routine, and when she comes to bed, he suddenly sits up and holds her in his arms as if he will never let go.

'We have the whole night,' he says. But he falls asleep within minutes after they move apart. Maybe I should try pranayam, she thinks wryly, knowing that sleep will not come to her so easily.

When she wakes up the next morning, he has already left. Arundhati comes for her very early as well, soon after breakfast, in a chauffeur-driven car. 'I'm feeling very grand today, being driven around,' she tells Aparna. 'And very uncomfortable as well. I'm not used to it. But my aunt Devaki insisted I take her car and driver. She doesn't like me driving myself. Honestly, neither do I. The city has become a nightmare. I was planning to take a rickshaw.'

She tells Aparna that they have to go to her aunt's sari shop at first to deliver something. 'Why don't we go in and have a look?'

she suggests. 'My aunt has one of the best sari shops in the city. You can look at the saris.'

'I wear saris so rarely, I think I have more than enough of them.'

'You can buy for someone else.'

Aparna is ashamed she hasn't thought of it. But once the idea enters her head, she is enthusiastic about buying saris for Taimavshi and Madhu.

'What colours do they like?'

'Colours?' Aparna is blank.

Arundhati laughs. 'Ring up and ask them.'

Once they have the colours – 'Any colour is good for me,' Madhu says, 'I love getting gifts, unlike my starchy mother' – everyone in the shop, the sales girls, Arundhati, even another customer, get enthusiastic about choosing saris for Aparna's aunt and cousin. The search for the right saris becomes something of a celebratory group activity. Aparna has never done anything like this before. Everyone wants to know how the two women, for whom she's buying the saris, look, what they do, there's a kind of admiring gasp when Aparna says Madhu is a choreographer for the movies, Hindi movies, that she's married to the director Abbas. Seeing Arundhati fielding innumerable calls while being part of the conversation about the saris at the same time, Aparna gets the sense of a life lived in a network of relationships. Like a spider's web. Getting a glimpse of the various demands being made on her, Aparna thinks, if I were to live such a life, I'd feel… I'd feel shredded.

Later they have coffee in a place that has, Arundhati tells her, the best coffee in the city. The waiter who brings them their coffee seems to know her; he inquires about Rohit, or so Aparna guesses, for they speak in Kannada. Aparna admires the way Arundhati belongs to the city, she's as much a part of it as she is of her home, her family. Whereas I, since I left Chandrapur, I have been drifting, not belonging anywhere. Except, now, to Hari. As they drink their coffee and talk, the bells of the temple just across the road keep ringing, she watches through the window the flower-selling women selling strings of mogras to devotees, she admires the way one of the women casually tucks the string into her long plait.

It's a long morning, because Arundhati decides they will end their sight-seeing with lunch. Over lunch, they begin to talk with the intimacy of old friends. They find they share some things; both their fathers were teachers. 'Your father taught English?' Arundhati asks Aparna in surprise when she tells her that. 'I thought he wrote in Marathi.'

'He did. But his father was in the railways and in the early years he was posted somewhere outside Maharashtra. Baba had no choice but to go to an English school. He went back to Marathi in high school. He never regretted his few years of schooling in English, though. How would I have read Shakespeare otherwise? he used to joke. It was Shakespeare who inspired him to write drama.'

Arundhati is fascinated by the fact that Aparna's father was a writer. 'I've always admired writers, I've thought of them as superior human beings. Must have been wonderful having a writer for a father.'

'To me, he was just my father. Only after his death I've begun discovering the writer part of him.'

She tells Arundhati that he was always crazy about drama. She tells her the story Gaja had told her of how, as a boy, when he sat, like children did then, on the carpet, waiting for a performance to begin, he would be so excited that he would move forward on his haunches and raise the curtain to get a glimpse of the magic behind it. Someone would yell at him and he would quickly move back. In a while the sounds of the harmonium playing a quick sa re ga ma would float out from behind the curtain. At which he knew it was starting and… 'He never had words to speak of his excitement,' Aparna says, 'he would only go *aaahaha* in a rapturous tone.'

She falls silent, thinking of his passionate response to life and how at the end he turned bitter and cynical.

'I like that kind of madness. That's what makes the world such an amazing place,' Arundhati says.

They realize that both of them lost their mothers early.

'My mother died in an accident,' Arundhati tells Aparna. 'Our family life went to pieces after that.'

Idyll? Did I think her life idyllic, Aparna thinks, as she listens to Arundhati telling her about the time. No one's life can ever be an idyll. Aparna comes to know that some time after Arundhati's mother's death, her father got into a relationship with another woman. 'I hated him and I hated her. We had been estranged even earlier, but after this I thought I'd lost my father. Luckily we were able to reconcile and the woman, Kasturi, became my friend, she is my friend.'

Aparna learns that both their children are adopted. 'We waited nearly seven years. I was getting desperate, then we decided to adopt. Are you and Hari getting married soon, Aparna?' she asks casually.

'I don't know.'

'Sorry, I shouldn't have asked.'

'No, that's okay. It's I who am the problem. I'm afraid of committing myself to something that seems so forever, so binding.'

'I felt that way myself. But Rohit was persistent. And I know Shree is crazy about you.'

'I know that. So am I crazy about him. It's just marriage…'

'My father and Kasturi are still together, they didn't get married. But they've had their lives, they have children…' Arundhati leaves it at that, for which Aparna is thankful.

When she gets back to the hotel, Hari is waiting for her in their room. 'Where were you? Why did you take so long?' he asks.

'We had lunch. What about you?'

'I was waiting for you. Come and sit with me while I eat.'

She is seeing Hari for the first time before a performance. He is agitated, restless, he starts eating, then gives it up, finally settling for a little curd and rice. He sits drumming his fingers on the table while they wait for the waiter to bring their check to sign.

'You go on, I'll do it and then come up.'

When she gets to the room, he is lying on the bed, eyes wide open. 'Rohit has gone out of his way to give me this chance. What if I disappoint him, Apu? Do you think I'll be able to do well, Apu?'

'Remember last night you told us how terrified you were of singing the mangalashtaka for Rohit and Arundhati's wedding, but how when the time came, you were able to find yourself? Isn't it always like that?'

'Not always. I hope it will be like that, but sometimes it doesn't work. I'm wondering how I'll manage with these new accompanists. I'm so used to my own team… And this time I want so much to do well for Rohit's sake. Come here,' he says suddenly. 'Come and lie down by me.'

It is a frenzied lovemaking, so rapid and so brief that it leaves Aparna with a sense of dissatisfaction. For the first time she finds herself unwilling, but his demand is fierce and her body plays its role, it does what is needed, participating in the act so that he has no clue. But she is wrong, for he immediately says, 'I'm sorry, Apu, I'm so sorry.'

I should tell him it's okay, she thinks, because he will be singing in a few hours and I should not disturb him. But she knows there is a small seed of resentment in her, a seed which will grow if left unspoken. 'I was not ready,' she says.

'I know, I saw that, but I... Sorry, Apu, I promise you it won't happen again.'

Lovers' promises, she thinks, the frailest and the most dangerous of promises because, if broken, the most destructive.

When she comes back after a wash, she sees that he is fast asleep. Sex as a sedative, she thinks cynically. But she orders the tea, ginger tea which she has learnt he likes to drink before a performance and then gently wakes him up. He comes back after a bath and opening his suitcase, takes out a plastic bag, the clothes he's going to wear for the performance neatly packed in it. He takes them out gently so as not to crease them, smoothens down a little crease at the hem of the kurta, frowning at it, asking Aparna, 'Do you think I should send this for ironing?' She is smitten by compunction, thinking of him getting his clothes ready, making sure his clothes are ironed, carefully packing them. She remembers her mother packing her father's bag when he was to go out of town, she remembers how her father had nothing to do but pick up his bag when leaving.

The reception rings up to say that the car has come for him. 'Don't be late, Apu,' he says. 'You know I'll be waiting for you.'

'It depends on when Rohit sends me the car.'

'Oh, he'll make sure it comes on time.'

So it does. When she gets to the venue, Rohit is waiting for her. 'Aru is not here as yet,' he says. 'In the meantime I thought I'd show you the place. It has been nearly seven years of work and to see it being used this way is like a dream come true for me,' he says.

When the tour is over, he takes her back into the hall and to her seat. Arundhati is there and she introduces her to more people than she will ever remember, a vast number of family and friends. Once again she sees the network, the spider's web in which Arundhati seems to live and once again she's – no, not jealous, but wonders how she manages. She sees the curiosity in some of them when she is introduced as Dr Aparna Dandekar. She's come with Shree Hari, many of them know that, but if she isn't his wife, what is she? One man addresses her as Mrs Pandit, and she immediately corrects him, but later wonders why she did that. This will keep happening, she thinks, I have to get used to it. And then the performance begins. A young woman makes the introductions. As always Aparna's heart gives a leap and she gives herself over to listening to Hari. She senses his initial nervousness, she guesses he is missing his usual accompanists. But in a while they get into a rhythm and he is lost in his music. She can relax.

When the music is over, she waits patiently for Hari to be free of the people who surround him, she waits while he goes backstage to collect his things.

'Tomorrow and the day after are ours,' he says to her when they get into the car. And so they are. It is when they are on the flight back that it occurs to Aparna that Hari perhaps brought her here to give her a glimpse of the life he wants with her. She thinks of the last two days, when they were on their own, doing what they wanted. Hari was at his most passionate, most tender, erasing the memory of the afternoon before his programme.

She has no regrets about having come with Hari to this place, no regrets at having met Arundhati. She knows that she meant something to Hari, at some time, if not now. She knows that she was the shadow she always sensed in Hari's mind. And it troubles her that he has never spoken of it to her. Suddenly she decides to speak, to take the arrow out of her body, even if the blood gushes out.

'You were in love with Arundhati,' she says abruptly.

'What?' he asks, startled. He looks at her and sees she is serious. 'How could I, Apu? She was getting married when I first met her, I was one of the priests marrying her to Rohit.'

'Still,' she urges.

He hesitates a moment then says, 'I thought she was an ideal woman, for a long time she was an ideal woman to me. Maybe I was a little attracted. But I was only a boy, Apu. I was waiting for you. I still did not know what love meant. It was you who taught me that.'

She accepts his statement, she knows it is the truth.

'Jealous, Apu?'

'A little,' she tells him.

'We have both lived for many years before we met each other. We've met others we liked, there have been feelings for others, but none of it matters now.'

'I know,' she says.

And she does. Ideal woman, Hari called her, and she understands what he means. The woman is steadfast, steadfastness and courage shine through her like a light. While I...? I'm being stupid, she thinks. She knows it is not jealousy that is troubling her; that ghost, that shadow, is no longer in her mind. What remains is her own inadequacy, her doubts about her ability to meet the kind of commitment that marriage asks for. Handcuffed, he had said immediately after they were married, the man she had married and now calls her X. She had thought he was joking. Later she knew he was not.

Aparna finds a crisis waiting for her when she gets back. A patient died during the course of his chemotherapy. He suffered a myocardial infarction with all the classical symptoms, the nurse saw his distress and immediately alerted the doctor, but by the time he came, the man was dead. Nevertheless, it became a police case, and the family was agitating, speaking of negligence and criminal liability.

Aparna knows that their department is under fire, she knows that she will have to answer questions, even if she was not there. Dr Mishra has already been questioned by the Administrator, he's assured them that all the tests had been done. Aparna, when she is questioned, asserts her confidence in Dr Mishra and in Sister Molly Joseph. They did everything right, she says. There is to be an internal inquiry soon, but for the moment the administration accepts her word and prepares to face the patient's family and the media.

Aparna thinks she would rather deal with the family than with lawyers and the media, whose ignorance of procedures and medical problems is appalling. This ignorance permeates everything that the media purvey to their viewers, talking glibly of negligence and the casual attitude of doctors. Outwardly she keeps her cool, she tells the patient's family, who barge into her room, that it is very possible for a person to have two major diseases, that the presence of one does not rule out others, and that what killed him was, in layman's terms, a heart attack. It had nothing to do with the drugs he was being given for his carcinoma. No, it was not an allergic reaction (the lawyer must have coached them on this one). She does not add that he could have died anywhere, at any time, that it was unfortunate that it happened in the hospital, when he had just been started on his CT.

Of all the things that are happening, Aparna regrets most the erosion of trust between doctors and patients. She knows how long it takes to build that trust and how much longer it will take to rebuild it. She knows she can't work without that trust and that, while the accusations of negligence and a casual attitude are often true, they are also as often not. There is a meeting of doctors, the administration, the public relations department; they decide to wait for the findings of the autopsy. The findings are as expected: there was a blockage and a left ventricular myocardial infarction.

The matter will soon die down, Aparna knows, but the sense of guilt that she was away at the time stays with her. When Hari, who has not come to her for the last two days, rings up, she wants to tell him about what has happened, to share the burden with him. But he is eager to tell her *his* news. Maya and Krishna have officially announced their engagement, he says. They will be having the engagement ceremony in a few days.

'He wants us to meet them. He wanted to take us to one of his fancy places, but for once I was firm. I've asked him to bring her home. You will come, Aparna, won't you?'

'When?'

'Today evening.'

'Today? I'm not sure…' she is beginning, when she realizes she can't opt out of this. 'All right, but I may be a little late. We've had some problems here.'

'Try to come by 6.30. I need you, Apu. You know my place. I want you to make it look good.'

'I'll be there.'

But there is a sense of uneasiness among patients, a kind of fear, and Aparna has to spend some time with those scheduled for their CT that day, to reassure them that all will be well. It delays her and she is late. When she gets to Hari's home, Krishna and Maya are already there. The room has been cleared of everything but the chairs and a table in the centre. There are flowers on the table and the smell of food comes to them from the kitchen. Krishna immediately introduces Aparna to Maya. The brothers look hopefully at the women, as if expecting them to get intimate straightaway. But Aparna smiles and says, 'I need a wash. I've come straight from the hospital.'

Hari comes to her when she is tidying her hair.

'Sorry, Hari. I tried my best to be here earlier, but we had a problem…'

'It's okay. Krishna came in the afternoon, he brought their cook, got the place cleaned up, he's the one who got the flowers as well. He didn't want Maya to look down on me and my house. He promises to be a good husband.'

They smile at each other in the mirror. 'He's a good brother.'

'Come on, the *pohe* is ready and the tea. Let's get it over with.'

Unfortunately, the atmosphere never lightens. Krishna keeps the conversation going. Aparna does not speak much, Maya responds only to Krishna, and Hari is busy trying to act the host. I hope we don't have to meet very often, Aparna thinks. And then they speak of the wedding.

'Maya's parents want a big fat wedding,' Krishna says.

'A normal wedding,' Maya adds.

'When will it be?'

'It's up to you, Aparna.'

'To me? What do I have to do with it?'

'You fix the date of your wedding and then we are free to plan ours.'

'What's the connection?'

'Dada is older, he has to get married first.'

'Krishna, I never knew you could talk like Ajoba. Never mind, Aparna, don't take any notice of him.'

'But Dada, you're the one who told me that Aparna would decide your wedding date!'

'That's not true. We haven't even decided to get married.'

She looks at Hari's stricken face and realizes what she has said. There is not much conversation after that. Krishna and Maya leave first, Krishna asking Aparna whether he can drop her. She says 'no' and he goes away, imagining, perhaps, that they need to talk about what has happened. But Hari is silent, he says nothing. He lets her go by herself, refusing her offer of help to clear up. She knows she has hurt him deeply. She would do anything to take the hurt away, to go back and do things differently. But how could she go along with Krishna's assumption that she was ready for marriage with Hari?

She is miserable the next day, specially when she does not hear from Hari. It is the day of the patient's funeral and a kind of cloud seems to hang over everyone. She notices Hari's message only when she's winding up, sent some time back, telling her that he will be waiting for her at home. She hurries home, ready to apologizc for being late, for keeping him waiting, for blurting out what she did yesterday.

He is standing by the window when she enters. He turns round at the sound of the door opening and for a moment she thinks she is seeing the face of a stranger.

'I'm so sorry, Hari, I saw your message only after I finished my work. I'll be with you in a moment.'

'Take your time,' he says. 'I'll make tea in the meantime.'

When she returns, the tea is waiting for her. 'Thanks, Hari, this feels good. Now,' she says, never one to draw back from anything unpleasant, 'are you very angry with me? Have you come to scold me?'

'No, Aparna, I've come to ask you to marry me. Will you marry me? Do you want to marry me at all?'

She puts her mug down and looks at him in astonishment. 'What is this, Hari?'

'Yesterday, when you said what you did to Krishna, I was very angry. Later I thought – yes, I did ask you once to marry me. But maybe I should ask you again. Properly. So here I am asking you – will you marry me, Aparna?'

'Hari, we've already spoken of this.'

'Have we? I thought you asked for time and I gave it to you. Now I must have an answer.'

'Must have? Must have? I don't like to be threatened, Hari.'

'Call it what you want, but I want a yes or a no. Now.'

She's not prepared for his tone, for the curt and businesslike way he is speaking.

'Hari…' she begins and can't go on. He says nothing, offers her no help. 'Hari, I love you and I want us to live together. I am as sure of that as I am of anything else in this life. But I am not sure about marriage.'

'Do you mean you want us to go on like this, I living in my home and you living here? And I come to you at night, sneaking in like a thief and we…'

'Hari, it's not the way you put it.'

'How do I put it then? I don't want us to meet only for sex, I don't want to come to you only for sex.'

He uses the English word 'sex'.

'But Hari, we do so many things together. We talk, we laugh together, we eat and drink, we go for walks, we go out for coffee…'

'But it's mainly sex, isn't it?' Once again he uses the English word. 'Admit it, Aparna.'

'No, not for me.'

'Then you're lucky. I had told myself I wouldn't do this before marriage. But I lost control over myself and I came to you. Since then it's getting harder and harder to stop. I tell myself, I won't go to Apu tonight, but when the time comes, I find myself at your door. And I hate what I'm doing, I hate myself.'

'You don't think our love makes any difference?'

'I don't know, Apu. I know I'm doing wrong when I come to you and we sleep together. I feel terrible. The security man downstairs tells me, showing me his teeth, Madam ghar mein hai. He knows what I'm here for, his smile cheapens what we're doing, it cheapens you. I want to bash him, to knock out his teeth, but I control myself. That won't make things better. Apu, let's get married.'

She is silent.

'I'm good enough to have sex with, not good enough to marry – is that it, Aparna?'

'You know that's not true. How can you even think such a thing?'

'You tell me how it is, then. I could see Maya looking at my home yesterday. I'm sure you feel the same way.'

'For me, it's your home, Hari.'

'Will you live there with me? See, you can't say yes. Yesterday Krishna did everything he could to make the room look good, poor fellow, he brought flowers, the carpet, he brought even the cups and plates. But I could see Maya looking around and I'm sure she thought that it was a shabby little home.'

'I'm not like that, Hari, you know that.'

'I know the world values people by the way they live, by their possessions, by the way they dress... But I have confidence in myself. I will earn enough, I will be able to look after my family. But we have to be together, we have to be husband and wife.' She is silent. After a moment he goes on, 'You've overturned all my plans. The day I saw you, the world changed for me. There was you, only you. I want you, I want us to get married, Aparna Dandekar, I want us to live together, I want to share my life with you. I want you as my wife, do you hear me, Aparna? Why are you so scared of marriage, Aparna? What did that man, your husband, do to you?'

'He showed me what marriage makes of men and women. I swore then I would never marry again.'

'Don't do this Bhishma *pratignya* thing. You know what that resulted in. The Mahabharata war happened because of Bhishma's vow never to marry.'

'Hari, I can't argue with you.'

'All right, tell me then how you want it? We go on as before?'

'No, we live together. In one home. But without marriage.'

'Why?'

'Marriage makes a tight knot, marriage means expectations, demands. We'll quarrel about money, you won't take my money, we'll quarrel about small things, like, if I am not able to come for your programmes. No, I don't want to go through all that again. I've lived alone for too long, Hari, I am not sure I can live my life according to somebody else's ideas.'

'That's not the way it will be with us. We'll do things the way you want, but you have to do this one thing I want – marry me. A small wedding. No one except Anandibai, Madhuritai and for me Krishna and Abhay.'

'A few lines on a piece of paper, a few mantras chanted – why should it matter so much?'

'Because society is organized that way. Oh, let's not argue as if we're debating marriage. Is it good? Is it bad? It's not so difficult a thing, is it? Most of the world gets married. Why can't we? And what will I do if one day you say I don't want to live with you any more and walk out on me?'

'It means the marriage would not have worked, anyway. And we would have to go through all the hassle of a divorce. Never again, no, never again.'

'You've got this idea of living together from America. You got it from living in that country.'

'What!'

'Where else? It won't work in our country, Aparna. Oh, it's okay for film stars and for the very rich, but not for us ordinary people. People will talk.'

'People who know us – your friends, Krishna, Taimavshi, Madhu – they will understand. The rest don't matter.'

'The world is large, Aparna. Everyone won't be kind.'

'Hari, your music world was full of people who broke the social rules.'

'But I'm not like that, I'm a conventional man. I want you, I want to marry you, I want us to have children.' He pulls her close, she can feel his desire, his desperation. Suddenly he pulls away from her and says, 'No, not that, not that.'

They are silent for a moment. Then he asks, 'Why are you so negative about marriage, Aparna? Just because your marriage didn't work, just because your parents' marriage didn't work? But think of all those that work.' Once again he waits for an answer, and when there is none, he goes on himself, 'Don't do this to me, Aparna, please don't do this to me. You taught me about love. My heart, my life is knotted into your life, your heart. To be without you is like living without a part of myself, without a limb. Don't do this to me, Aparna. I want you, I want us to have children, to bring up our children, to…

'Hari, stop, please stop.'

He is silent for a moment and says in a calmer tone, 'I am afraid Apu, I am afraid that if you send me away I might not be able to find my way back to you again. I am afraid I might forget the way.'

Yet again he waits for an answer. Yet again, there is none. 'All right then, I will go. Let's stay apart for some time. But the door is open, Aparna, whenever you want to come to me, the door is open. But it's up to you now. I won't come to you – not again.'

It has been so unexpected, so sudden, she is left in a state of shock. She can't believe she let him go. He'll come back, she tells herself, he said it himself, the door is open, he said. Yes, he'll come back. But what if he doesn't? Why don't I do what the whole world does, why can't I get married to Hari and live with him as his wife? At night, her mind keeps churning up contradictory, confused thoughts. She thinks of her mother, so scrupulous a person, honest to a fault. And Baba, careless of trifles, uncaring of details. Sulu made excuses for him each time he stepped out of line. Your baba, she would say, when will he learn? But she thought even of his faults with a kind of fondness; they were part of his writing self, the offshoots of his creativity. Ultimately he crossed the line and did the unforgivable and for Sulu it was all over.

Now, after all these years, Aparna remembers that the end had begun even before Gaja's affair. It began with that letter dropped stealthily into their letter box, a letter addressed to

Aparna, with scribbled obscene phrases and even more obscene pictures. Sulu had gone crazy then, she was frantic to send Aparna out of Chandrapur. We'll send her to Mumbai, we'll send her to live with Tai, she can do her 12th in Mumbai, she had said.

'Don't, Sulu,' Gaja had pleaded, 'don't do that. The child will leave home when she enters medical college anyway, and then she'll go abroad, get married, have her work, and she'll never live with us. Let's have her with us for two more years.'

He tried to run down the letter, he made it out to be the work of 'stupid boys who don't know how to control themselves. They won't do anything, they're cowards. And do you think I can't protect my own daughter? Just let anyone lay a finger on her and I'll…Sulu, don't send her away.'

But Gaja lost, Sulu won and Aparna left home. Gaja came often to see her. 'Bala,' he would say sadly, 'home is not home without you.'

When Aparna went back for the vacations, it was not the same home to her either. Before she left it had been bad, with constant arguments and angry voices which she tried to keep out by pressing her palms over her ears. Now there was silence and it was worse than the angry words. And then Gaja did the unforgivable and lusted after another woman (he had used the word himself when speaking of it to Aparna in the last few days that they spent together) and it was all over.

Hari is right, it can't happen to everyone. But things can change in other ways. Right now our bodies understand each other so perfectly, much better than our minds can; there is no fumbling, no clumsiness. But the bond between two bodies is such a fragile one. I'm a doctor, I know what drives men and women into sex. I also know how whimsical that urge is, how easily it can die, as happened to Baba. The madness passes, he said. Yes, the madness passes, the passion is spent and what remains? We are two such different people, what is there strong enough to hold us together? She remembers how he speaks of his grandparents, how he touches his ear in reverence when he speaks of his ajoba, his guru. Whereas she speaks of her father with such irreverence. And there are much bigger problems. She remembers how, when she spoke to him of Sada, to whom his wife Anju's death was caused, not by terrorists, but by the Muslims, Hari had seemed to agree with Sada. He said, 'Tell me any other religion that kills people only because they don't belong to your faith?' Yes, she had laughed then, the way Sulu had spoken indulgently about Gaja's faults. She had asked him, 'How can you speak that way when you are so friendly with Salimbhai, I've seen how beautifully you come together when he plays the tabla for you.' And there's the huge abyss of sex between them: he thinks it's sinful, whereas she glories in it, she has no problems of guilt like he has. Guilt towards whom?

As the days pass, hope gives way to despair. She thinks of how unforgiving he can be, how he has erased his father and stepmother from his life. Will I too be ruthlessly cut out, become an unspoken factor in his life, a taboo subject? Luckily there's routine, there's the discipline of work and the demands of patients to keep her going. But Hari had filled her life, her entire day. The sudden emptiness is hard to cope with. At times, grief seems to swamp her like a tidal wave. Then she wants to pick up the phone and talk to Hari, to tell him, we'll do it the way you want, even a big fat wedding with band, baaja and baraat. We'll have it all, the *saptapadi*, the *lajja homa*, even, yes, the *kanyadaan*. All done the way your ajoba would have done it. And we'll also have someone sing the mangalashtaka your ajji wrote. But afterwards? She can't get the word Hari used, 'cheap', out of her mind. How can love between us be cheap? And does it become suddenly wholesome and fragrant with marriage? What about our feelings for each other? She thinks of what he said: 'I want children'. What about me? I destroyed my own child. He thinks he knows me, but there is so much he does not know. Perhaps – no, not perhaps, surely there is much about him I don't know as well.

We need to talk. Things have not ended between us. We must talk. But she does not ring him. Nor does he ring her. She looks at her mobile so often, so compulsively, that finally she puts it off. And then, thinking of the other calls she may be missing, she switches it on again.

Krishna rings her up. He wants to talk to her, he says. She is reluctant, but when he insists, she asks him to come to the hospital, giving him an empty window of time in her day. To her surprise, when he comes she sees a different Krishna, serious, contrite, humble. He apologizes for his remark. I had no idea I was treading on such slippery ground, he says, I never thought that I would cause so much trouble.

'That's okay, Krishna, it would have happened some day. Who told you?'

'Dada, of course. He was so upset…'

As he talks, she sees in him a young boy admiring his older brother, looking up to him. She realizes that, in spite of his worldliness, there's something in him that responds to the beauty and passion he senses in his brother's life. Her animosity against Krishna disappears. We're on the same side, she thinks, we both love Hari, we both want him to be happy. She speaks in a less guarded, more friendly tone. Krishna has come to invite her to his engagement. 'It's on the 20th of next month. Please come.'

'No, Krishna, better not.'

'You're sure?'

'Yes.'

'But if things are okay between Dada and you, will you come?'

'I don't know, Krishna.'

'Don't take what he said very seriously. You know he is very busy. Abhay has got some kind of a contact in the States, he is hoping to arrange a tour for Dada.'

'Is he?'

Before leaving, he says, suddenly, as if he's nerved himself to say it, 'What Dada wants is such a simple thing, it's so normal. Why can't you give it to him, Aparna?'

'This is between him and me, Krishna.'

'I know. I only thought...' His voice trails away and then he is gone.

The thought of her not knowing about his plan of going to the States brings home to her the fact of her exclusion from his life; for the first time, the extent of her loss hits her. I have to talk to someone, she thinks. But Madhu has gone abroad with Abbas. And Taimavshi is disturbed because of Sada's threat to resign from his job, disturbed by Anil's not coming home for the vacation. She can't trouble her now with her problems.

Jyoti comes to her as if in answer to her cry for help. Aparna opens the door and finds her at the door, looking and sounding as if she's breathless. The doctor in her takes alarm.

'Jyoti, are you okay?' Jyoti nods. 'But you're panting, you seem breathless.'

'I'm okay. Just took the stairs too fast, I was so eager to see you. Haven't seen you for quite a while. Are you okay? And Panditji? I haven't seen him either. What's the matter, doc?' Jyoti, who has settled herself in a chair, gets up, comes to Aparna and holds her in her arms. 'My dear doc, my dear dear doc, what is it? Cry, cry your fill, my dear stoical controlled, inhibited restrained doc, cry, it'll do you good. What...?' Jyoti realizes that the muffled sound she's hearing from Aparna is laughter. She lets her go. 'What is this? Hysterics?'

'No, it's your telling me to cry. I never could do anything I was told to do. My tears suddenly dried up. And all those words you used...' The laughter turns to tears again.

'That was to control myself. I've found out that if you use plenty of words, emotions dry up. I was on the point of bursting into tears myself. It's hard to see a stoical person like you break down.'

'I'm all right. I haven't cried like this since Baba died.'

'You were close?'

'Very. And then I turned my back on him. He died a lonely and defeated man.'

'I am sorry. Better now?' Aparna nods. 'So am I. So we're both fine. Now tell me what it is. Panditji? A lover's spat? Tell me if it will help you.'

It's surprisingly easy to speak to Jyoti. When Aparna comes to the end, Jyoti asks, 'Is that all? I can't believe this, I just can't believe it. How can you let him go? If he wants marriage, marry him, what's the problem?'

'It's not just this fact of our marrying or not marrying, Jyoti. It's that he could turn his back on me because of this one fact. That he thinks sex is wrong. He makes me feel like an over-sexed woman, a nymphomaniac. This little seed of difference could create a fissure, split us apart, I've seen it happen.'

'Yes, but what about you? This is stupid, doc. You want a perfect marriage and you're afraid it won't happen. You're a perfectionist, you're crying even before the milk has boiled over. Come on, doc, nothing in the world can be perfect. What's perfect? Look at my body, riddled with flawed cells. Cells gone berserk. We are born flawed, we must accept that. And you can't sacrifice your today for a future you think may be bad.'

'If we break up, I won't survive, I won't.'

'Nonsense, you will survive. We survive more than we can ever imagine. Think of the Jews in the concentration camps. And of people who work for a pittance, slogging all day in the hot sun.'

'Enough. I get the idea. I should stop whining.'

'I'm serious, doc. You think my husband was the hero I'd imagined him to be? The hero I wanted him to be? And I? He thought he'd got a nice little wife he could mould and shape. Boy, did he get a surprise! But we stayed together…' She trails off into silence.

'He thinks sex is sinful,' Aparna says. 'Before marriage,' she adds. Jyoti laughs and the sting, some of it, goes out of the thought. 'I don't. No, I don't.'

'No comment,' Jyoti says.

'I had sworn I would not get married after my first fiasco. I thought I would first live with the person…'

'How long?'

'A year maybe?'

'A year, a few months, a few years, what difference does it make? You might as well take the plunge straight off. Did you tell Hari your plan?'

'I did. He said I must have learnt this in America. He called it an American idea.'

Jyoti laughs. 'Like pizzas and burgers, huh? Never mind. Listen, doc, don't do this, don't be like this.'

'He is ashamed of his desire for me, Jyoti. It's so humiliating. He used the word cheap. What about our feelings for each other? I don't understand him, truly I don't.'

'That's so so…but that's how he is, doc. You can't change people. You think you can, but it's never possible. Anyway, this whole idea of understanding each other seems highly exaggerated to me. It can never happen to any two people, least of all to a man and a woman. Men and women think differently. You have to accept that. I went through this, believe me, I had a lot of trouble accepting the fact that understanding will never come. There are always dark corners of our minds no one can look into.'

'And you still tell me to marry Hari?'

'Don't you want to, doc?'

'I want to be with him, I want to live with him, to live my life with him.'

'That's the same as marriage. Go ahead and ring him up, see how he'll come running. I shouldn't have to tell you this, you see it yourself every day – but life is short. It seems long, but it passes like this.' She snaps her fingers. 'I have become so conscious of my own mortality. Life is not a circle, it's a line. It seems endless when we're living it, but suddenly it ceases at a point and there's nothing. Whatever time you have, doc, live it with the man you love.' She gets up. 'Look at me talking like a swamiji or a guru. I have to go.' She goes to the door and stops abruptly, as if she has just remembered something. 'I quite forgot. I came to tell you something and…'

'What?'

'About Ahalya. It'll keep. I won't speak of it now. I'll send an email as usual. When is Madhuri returning?'

'A fortnight, I think.'

'I'll send her a copy too, as usual.'

She goes away, leaving Aparna to her thoughts. Ring him up and tell him you'll marry him. And then? What will have changed?

That evening Aparna wonders what she had done with herself before Hari entered to her life. She finds herself looking at her mobile all the time and finally puts it away. Then she decides to work and opens her laptop. There's a mail from Jyoti: 'Just a small bit of translation this time, I haven't had time, but I thought you should read this. It's about your father. I wanted to show you this.'

She opens the attachment and reads:

When I began writing this, I thought I was writing it for myself, to clear my own mind, to see my own life from this distance of time. I had no thought of anyone else reading it, I didn't want anyone to read it. I thought I would destroy it, tear it up, put it in the fire. But it's become like a child, I can't bear the thought of destroying it. And yet, how can I keep it? I don't want Durga to read it, she's so soft and loving. I know she will be hurt by the things that happened to me, she will suffer for me. Kashi was stronger, she had the strength of the selfish. But Durga… I wish I could keep it for that little fellow, my grandson. The day Durga had a son was one of the happiest days of my life. I enjoy him as I was never able to enjoy my own children. Yes, I should keep it for him to read. Maybe he will read it some day. He will not suffer for me as Durga will, he will not be shocked as Durga might be, he will not judge me because there is a generation between us. Yes, this is for my grandson. He is my future, I will go on living in him. I don't know what kind of man he will grow up to be. I had dreamt that my son would be like his father. But when my daughters were born, I had no hopes except that they would be with me, that they would never be taken away from me. Kashi was taken from me, but Durga is my saviour, she is my reason for living. And this little boy, Gaja – let him grow up to be a good man, let him lead a good life…

For the first time Aparna thinks of the woman Ahalya as having a connection with her. I never thought that this woman, her story, had anything to do with me. I had heard of Durga, my father's mother, I know she died soon after my parents got married. I know that Baba's father worked in the railways, but Baba never spoke of either of them. Now suddenly a woman comes out of these pages and I see her as Ahalya, my father's grandmother, Durga's mother. I will live in my grandson, she says. Perhaps she lives in me as well. She says that what she wrote was for him, for my father. Gajanan Vidyadhar Dandekar. Gavi, the playwright. Did he read it? Yes, he did, Jyoti says his comments are strewn through the pages. But he never spoke of it to me, or to anyone. (Except to Madhu, but it's only her surmise that this is the novel he was going to write.) When Jyoti sent the translated bits to me, I did not even look at what she had done. Now I will. I'll go back into all the mails she sent – thank god I've saved them – and read about this woman Ahalya, my father's grandmother. I will continue to live in him, she says. She lives in me as well, Gajanan's daughter.

Aparna thinks of how her father, both her parents, made sacrifices so that she could fulfil her ambition of becoming a doctor. Each time a play of his was performed and Gaja got the royalty amount, he would say, here's some more money for Apu's education fund. He never clipped my wings, he let me do what I wanted to do. That was my father. Ahalya would have been proud of him.

I won't survive, Aparna had said to Jyoti. But she does. There is a gnawing pain, a constant ache inside her, a terrible sense of deprivation, even at times anger, which flares up suddenly. But, ultimately, it is routine that helps; routine and work blunt the sharp edges of misery. She had learnt this once, she learns it now all over again. I had planned to live my life alone, anyway. And it's better that this happened now, before the roots went too deep. Later it would have been much more painful to pull the roots out.

In spite of all this sensible rationalization, she has a constant sense of Hari still being with her. She feels him by her side when she is walking on the pavement, she feels his arms protectively behind her, preventing her from being jostled by the crowd, she thinks she hears the doorbell ring and opens it, convinced he is outside, she has a troubling illusion that the phone is ringing and then finds it silent, she sees his face everywhere she goes, she hears his voice, she thinks the man sitting a few seats ahead of her in the bus is Hari, that the man who has suddenly got up when she walks into the waiting room is Hari. And she thinks, it's not over, somewhere it is waiting for us, the time of our getting back together. And then, almost immediately she reprimands herself, she warns herself not to hope, not open herself to fresh sorrow when it does not happen.

Taimavshi's call, inviting her to lunch on Sunday, is welcome. Madhu is returning on Saturday, she will join them too.

'Madhu will visit you? She's coming home?'

'Yes, she says she will. I think she's right, I have no right to keep my daughter away from her own home.'

'And Sada?'

Aparna can almost see Taimavshi's shrug. She knows she has been greatly troubled by the flare-up between Sada and Anil. She told Aparna that she could put up with anything herself, but when Sada couldn't see what he is doing to his own son…

'Anil didn't tell me what happened,' she says to Aparna and Madhu later. 'He only said to me – what's this "I'm a Hindu" stuff Baba has got into? Anil says he's getting into rather strange company. I don't like those men, he said, I don't want my father to be with them. They're haters. My mother was killed by terrorists, not by all Muslims. What's wrong with Baba?'

They are silent, thinking of the boy who has lost his mother, is afraid of losing his father.

'I'm tired, Apu, tired of struggling, of trying to hold people together. It's becoming harder and harder to cope.'

'Enough is enough, Aai. You stay out of it now, I'll deal with Sada. I'm going to invite Anil to come and stay with me, you come too, and then we'll see what Sada has to say. We've been tiptoeing round Sada's behaviour for too long. It's time you lived the way you want, Aai, time we stopped trying to placate him. In fact, that's why I decided I would come home. How can he come between you and your daughter?'

'Sada does not know how to forget. Sulu was the same, she could neither forgive nor forget. I remember Dandekar saying to me once – wisdom and compassion, these are the two things that make living possible. Wisdom is not ours to command, but compassion is something we can find in ourselves if we look hard enough. He was right. But, why are we talking of these things? You two girls are here together after a long time.'

Taimavshi, half fearful, half glad that Madhu has flouted the rules and come to her mother's house, has made an occasion of it. She has cooked a special meal, everything that Madhuri likes.

'What have you got for us,' Madhu asks.

'Wait and see. And don't come in until I call you.'

As soon as she goes in, Madhu asks Aparna, 'Apu, have you got down to reading Jyoti's translation?'

'I read the little bit she sent me the other day. Why?'

'In one of the excerpts, Ahalya speaks of people mixing up religion and culture, she says culture is a way of thinking and living, of being better people. And I thought, my god, here's this woman who lived over a hundred years ago, she found out something we're still not able to grasp. I'm thinking of Sada's *us* and *them*. Ahalya says…'

'Who's Ahalya?' Taimavshi asks as she comes in.

Aparna and Madhu look at each other. It strikes them that she doesn't know, they haven't spoken to her about the notebook, about Ahalya's story. When Madhu tentatively tells her about it, Taimavshi bursts out, 'I can't believe this. No, I can. When you're old, people think you don't need to be told anything. Your poor shrinking brain can't take it.'

'Aai,' Madhu protests laughingly. 'You know it's not like that. I forgot.' And when she realizes her mother is truly offended, she admits she was wrong, she passes the buck to Aparna, saying, 'Apu, you could have told her.'

'You know I left everything to you and Jyoti.'

'Never mind, Apu, it's all right. When you're old, you get used to being ignored. It seems you no longer matter.'

Aparna and Madhu look at each other guiltily, they are aghast at Tavmavshi's reaction. She never was one to indulge in self-pity. This thing of Sada and Anil has hurt her more than I imagined, Madhu thinks.

'Aai, listen to me, listen to me first, then you can scold me as much as you want.'

When Taimavshi calms down – she is never one to nurse her anger – Madhu asks her whether she remembers Ahalya.

'Dandekar's grandmother? No, I never heard of her, never heard him speak of her. I met Durga, she lived for a very short while after Sulu's marriage. A silent woman. In fact Dandekar was the only person in that house who spoke – how he loved to talk, that man. That was how he charmed Sulu.'

'Othello. Anyway, let me send you a printout of Jyoti's translation. No, why do you need that? As soon as Jyoti finishes, we'll get the notebook back and you can read the original. Aai, do you know Ahalya knew Tilak?'

'Bal Gangadhar Tilak?'

'The same. Ahalya and her husband had a run-in with him over the Age of Consent bill.'

They talk of this during lunch and Aparna is glad that it keeps them away from the topic of Hari. But later the question comes. 'How is Shree Hari?' Madhu asks her.

'He's fine.'

'Anything wrong?'

'Nothing.'

'You can't fool me, Apu. There is something wrong.'

Aparna is silent for a few moments, then decides she can't keep it from these two women who are so much a part of her life. The moment she ends, Taimavshi flashes out, as Jyoti had done. 'But this is madness. What do you mean you can't marry!' Then she adds sadly, 'What have your parents done to you, Apu! How much they loved you, what dreams they dreamt for you!'

There are tears in Taimavshi's eyes. Aparna wipes them gently with Taimavshi's own sari, saying, 'Don't, Taimavshi.'

'I've been thinking of Dandekar a lot these days. One of the things he said to me was, *Sulu is the ground on which I stand, she is the earth which supports me. But if that other woman calls me, I will immediately go to her, wherever she is, even to the ends of the earth*. And I thought – he knows, he can think, but he cannot control his emotions. He should have, but he couldn't. He said it was Nature's plan gone terribly wrong. I thought he was stupid, but now I think, perhaps that was how he was made. Don't burden yourself with his failure, with Sulu's and his failure. Each relationship is different, each marriage is different.'

'See, Aai, why we need you? Who else would give us such nuggets of wisdom?'

Madhu is obviously changing the subject, her eyes tell Aparna they will talk of Hari later. (Surprisingly, when they do talk of it, Madhu is on Aparna's side. 'Don't do what you don't want to do, Apu, don't be pressurized into a decision against your wishes. But remember you have to pay the price for that.') Right now, Aparna gives her no chance to talk, slipping away while Madhu deals with some tax problem of Taimavshi's. Going home, she thinks of how all of them think she should marry Hari, they think her fears are groundless. Why can't I feel that way?

She goes to her letter box under the stairs and finds a packet along with some junk mail, a packet addressed to her in Hari's handwriting. No stamp, which means he delivered it by hand. Her heart gives a leap – he was here. And the next moment – why wasn't I here? The she sees a similar packet in Jyoti's box and her mood changes. I'm not singled out, he didn't come here to meet me, he came to leave these for both Jyoti and me. There is a note in the packet which she reads when she gets home. 'This is my first properly recorded CD. I wanted you to have it.'

Yes, me and Jyoti too. Nevertheless she goes home and puts on the CD and listens to it. It contains the abhang he had sung so long ago at a programme and then whispered in her ears: 'Sweet is your form, sweet is your name…'

She meets Jyoti the next day. 'Did you read what I'd sent?'

'What?'

'Ahalya's story?'

'Oh, that. Yes I did.'

Jyoti gives her a questioning look, then says, 'I wanted to finish it before Dada and Jai come, but I'm not sure I can. By the way, did I tell you they're coming?'

Aparna shakes her head.

'Yes, they are. And Mel too. We're having a family holiday. I wanted to ask you whether it's okay for me to go with them.'

'Yes, why not?'

'Actually, it's not a very happy thing. Mel is getting married, Dada's very cut up about it. In fact, Jai is more okay with it than he is.'

She does not speak of the CD. Why did Hari give it to Jyoti? Is it to show me that for him, she and I are the same? That I'm not special? I hope she has taken it, I hope it isn't still lying there. What if someone else takes it? What if it gets lost…

She laughs at herself for her solicitude for an inanimate object. Though her mood does not lighten, the resentment towards Jyoti doesn't last long. Aparna thinks she has never seen a family like Jyoti's, so eager to embrace her into its folds. She is not allowed to stay away, or to distance herself. Deepak comes to visit her. Of course, his talk at first is all about Jyoti. He has read journals and books on cancer, on breast cancer, on TNBC, he has gone on the internet and got more recent information. He talks of angiogenesis and PARP inhibitors, of new drugs and drug trials and asks Aparna whether these drugs are available. 'We could take her abroad, you know,' he says, 'if you can't get the new drugs here.'

She does not want to tell him that there's nothing better than what they have done for Jyoti; let him be hopeful, she thinks. And he is hopeful, because he has read that once Jyoti gets through what he calls the 'danger period', she has a good chance of a long-term survival. 'You can't imagine what it means to me. She's had such a tough life, I want her to see good days, I want her to have a good life. She was a little wild when she was a girl, but now she's so courageous.'

He begins praising Aparna for all that she has done for Jyoti and Aparna is embarrassed. 'What have I done? Just followed the usual protocol of treatment.'

'But you were with her, she says you held her hand all the way.'

He then tells Aparna he wants Jyoti to go and stay with him for a few months. 'Mira says they'll manage and I'm sure they will. Mira's a competent young woman; there's Saguna and there's you…' He speaks of Mel's marriage. 'Jo thinks I resent it, but I don't. Not for my sake. I'm only worried about Jai, he's so much closer to her than to me. Mel says her marriage will make no difference, but how can it not? Loyalties change completely with marriage. Oh, I know Jai will always be first in her life, but marriage makes such claims, such demands. Mel used to say that the heart is not a fort, it's larger than any of us can imagine. All that you need to do to let down the drawbridge. There's room for a great many people. I don't know, I'm not so sure. I'm different, I guess. I've allowed only a few people into mine.'

'Didn't you ever think of remarriage?'

'Who? Me? I guess I'm meant to be lonesome. More and more I find myself reluctant to meet strangers. But who knows, I may suddenly get married one day. We can always surprise ourselves. Mel being free kept me in hope that we could get back together one day. Now…'

'Anyone in mind?'

'If I was a few years younger, or if you, Aparna, were a few years older…'

'Is this a proposal?'

'God, no! Jo will kill me, she's so protective of you. She wants a handsome young man for you, not a balding middle-aged boring man. I think, Aparna, I've lost that thing that makes you wake up in the morning eager to meet the day. Each day is just another day I have to go through. My work seems more and more boring. I guess too much was expected of me when I was young. To my mother I was a genius, I'd get the Nobel Prize one day, never mind in which subject. And my father expected me to take over the family business and make it big. Instead, here I am, a teacher in a small college in a small town in the States. I sometime think I went into academic life only because my father disapproved of it.'

Mel arrives the next day and the house is full of a babble of sounds. The door is open all day and footwear piles up in a corner outside the door. In the evening, when Aparna moves to her balcony as usual with her cup of tea, Jai sees her from their little sit-out and calls out to her, 'Come and join us.'

'Yes, come and have a glass of wine with us.'

Aparna says, 'No, not now,' and goes in, so as not to intrude on them. But Mel comes up to her in a while. 'I thought I'd come and sit with you for a few minutes. It's exhausting watching Deep pretending to be happy for me. He can't stop speaking about how glad he is, what a wonderful guy Mike is…God!'

She tells Aparna she's marrying a colleague of hers. 'We've been teaching in the same school for years, we know each other well. I knew he had a thing for me, but I refused him because of Jai. Now I think Jai can cope, in fact he told me himself to go ahead. I think Jo's illness has shaken all of us up. We're suddenly aware that we can't take time for granted.'

She goes on to tell Aparna that Jai made two conditions: one, that he should not have to consider Madge, Mike's daughter by his first wife, a sister. I have Mira and Tejas, thank you very much, he said. 'And, second, that he will be coming to stay with Jo for a year or two and that I should not associate this with my getting married. I had decided on it long before you said yes to Mike, he said. Easy conditions to agree to.'

Aparna tells Mel that she admires the courage of people who, having had one bad marriage, get into another. Such optimism, she says.

'Optimism? I don't know. Actually my marriage to Deep was more daunting. Different races, different cultures, different religions. In fact, I'd thought of converting to Hinduism when I married Deep. He didn't want me to. But I was fascinated by Hinduism, by the disparity between the philosophy and the practice. I thought that Hinduism and Judaism were very alike, both ancient religions, tenaciously clinging on in spite of the world having changed so much. I'm a Jew, you know. It was never important, but suddenly I find myself interested in it. Mike is a Jew as well, makes some things simpler.'

'And Jai?'

'Deep and I agreed to leave him alone, to allow him to choose for himself when he was older. Strangely, or perhaps not so strangely considering where we live, he seems to be veering towards Christianity. Actually they're all the same, all religions, I mean. Except Islam.' She is silent for a moment, then goes on, 'You know, Aparna, I came across a quote of Arthur Miller's the other day…the American dramatist, you know.'

'I know. My father was a dramatist, he read his plays. He was Marilyn Monroe's husband, wasn't he?'

'Exactly. God, what an identity for the man to have! Anyway, he speaks of what he calls the Jewish viewpoint: that there is tragedy in the world, but the world must go on. That's not just the Jews, is it? It's the basic foundation of all our thinking and living, it's the faith by which all of us live, isn't it, that life must go on, that we will survive in spite of everything.?

The doorbell rings. It's Jai calling Mel to come down – 'Dinner time,' he shouts and then goes down with a loud clatter of steps.

'Well, I must go.' Suddenly, as if she needs to say it, she tells

Aparna, 'It's strange, but my decision to marry brought home to me that there's nothing, nobody more important than Jai in my life. I remember how, when I fell in love with Deep, the world was all him. Now I know that Jai matters above all else.'

After she is gone, Aparna wonders yet again at the courage of human beings. If Deepak and she could not get on, in spite of their love for each other, in spite of their great love for their son, how can she be so optimistic about her marriage to another man? Why can't I have the same courage? Am I a coward? And it's not even as though we belong to two different cultures – though often I feel we do. I feel it each time he touches the feet of older people, each time he touches his ears when he speaks of his gurus, each time he says the shloka before having a meal. My father had erased religion from his life, he often said it had never been part of his life, so it never was part of mine. Two different cultures, yes.

She thinks of her own idea of living with Hari – not tied in the tight bond of marriage, but without it. Tied together only by love. Being friends, companions, lovers. Being together when they want to, being apart when they don't. And then coming back together with ease and joy. She had thought that Hari would compromise, that he would say, okay let's live together, not for a year, only for six months. Or three months. She thinks of his life, of the constant tours, the riaz, the tension before the programmes, the preparation, the constant presence of his team, his friends… I will have to learn to live with all of it, she thinks. Will I? What if I don't?

She remembers her own wedding, how, when it was over and someone opened a champagne bottle, her heart suddenly fell at the loud pop and she had a panic attack, a 'get me out of here' moment. But Hari wants it done properly. He want us to declare to the world that we are husband and wife, he wants us to share everything, he wants us to have children. And I have not told him about the child, the child I got rid of the way I got rid of everything that was part of my marriage. I can't speak to him about the man I slept with even before my divorce, slept with him not for love, not even for lust, or for my bodily need, but out of desperation and loneliness. What will he do if I tell him about it? And if I have to conceal things from him, what kind of relationship will it be?

AHALYA'S STORY

Ever since I started writing, I have begun to understand why they didn't allow women or people of lower castes to write. Once you start writing, you begin to think, you ask questions of yourself. Writing is like a churning of the mind, a Samudra Manthan. And so much comes up, like butter when women churn cream: questions, ideas, opinions, knowledge. I wonder whether this was the real *amrut* the gods and demons were after. For, once these things come to you, you are not the same. You feel a kind of strength in yourself, which comes from knowing, even from trying to know. After this, how can you be a good slave?

I have been thinking of the clash between 'him' and Balasaheb. *(Tr. note: Tilak again. I wonder when they started adding the 'saheb' to the titles or names – Balasaheb, Annasaheb, Bhausaheb, Dadasaheb and so on)* 'He' admired Balasaheb. Balasaheb was a brilliant man. He used his brilliance for society, for the country, not for himself. And what courage he had. 'He' read every word of both Balasaheb's papers, *Maratha* and *Kesari.* And yet there were two occasions when he openly disagreed with Balasaheb. The first time was about the Age of Consent Bill, though, even before that there had been the Rakhmabai case, when a woman who did not want to live with her husband was forced to go back to him because, as her husband, he had every right to her. For some of the very orthodox people, it was like the end of the world for a woman to say she did not want to live with her husband. 'He' was against those who would not allow women to have any choice in the matter. It is hard to think how such a marriage can be a good one, 'he' said, but 'he' was one of a very small number. Balasaheb thought that those who supported the wife were going against the sanctity of our customs. After that came the Age of Consent Bill, when once again 'he' was against Balasaheb. And then came the plague. It came upon us like the end of the world. And now it is almost forgotten. If I say 'the plague', not many young people will know what I am talking about. Nothing lasts. Life goes on.

It started in Bombay. We heard stories of people dying, nobody seemed to know why. And then the dreadful word 'plague' was uttered and people began to flee. The plague came to Pune soon enough. In Mumbai, the government was being very strict – people were not allowed to leave the city, sick people were put together in camps, houses were emptied and cleaned. In Pune, we had an Englishman called Rand who was in charge of controlling the plague. He was a military man and he did his job as if he was fighting a war, not against the disease, but against the people of Pune. Balasaheb was like a lion. He roared with anger against the way things were done, soldiers entering people's homes, throwing out their goods, even their gods, while searching for sick patients. 'He' agreed with Balasaheb, 'he' thought what was being done was wrong. But 'he' did not think that Balasaheb's anger against the British should blind him to the fact that something had to be done to control the plague. 'He' wrote that we could have volunteers, our own people, who would do what was necessary, 'he' wrote about how in hospitals there could be no caste separation; everyone was a patient. He wrote about what the scientists were doing. 'He' was a great admirer of the scientists, specially of one man whose name I could not pronounce then and cannot write now and who is supposed to have found out the germ that caused plague. *(Tr. note: I guess she means Haffkine)* 'He' wrote of the scientists' tireless struggle to find the germ, of their attempts to find something that would work against it (I think they called it vaccine), he wrote of the courage of the man who tested it on himself. 'He' said that vaccination was the only way to control a disease so terrible and which spread so fast and it was stupid to be frightened of it. 'He' begged Balasaheb to advise people to get vaccinated.

To me, 'he' said that if only men like Balasaheb, who loved their country so much, would encourage people not to distrust everything because it came from the English, it would be a greater deed than talking about Swaraj. If only Balasaheb, 'he' said, had advised people to trust science, not customs – and with his great power over the people, perhaps he could have done it – it would have been better for the country than just making everyone hate the English. A man like Balasaheb could have done so much good. Science, 'he' often said, had no country; it belonged to the whole world. And if the English were behaving stupidly, it was because they were frightened, frightened because the plague made no distinction between white people and Indians. For the first time, they could not separate themselves from the 'natives', as they called us.

'He' became the most hated man in Pune, in all of Maharashtra. 'He' was a traitor, a bootlicker of the English, a hater of his own religion and culture. But 'he' kept us, his family, alive. We were among the first to leave our wada and live on the banks of the river, where many people soon came to live in tents. 'He' went every morning into the city to help in the hospitals. My heart was in my mouth until 'he' came back in the evening. I wanted to go with 'him', but 'he' said I had a child, the child needed me, and so my life was precious. (Oh God, if we had seen the future then!) So 'he' went out every day and I stayed behind. My prayers were answered, 'he' was safe and the plague slowly moved away from the city. We were lucky, we had only three deaths, two servants who had gone back to their village and one old aunt who died so quickly we scarcely knew she had the plague.

When it was over, 'he' would not allow us to go back home until 'he' had repaired and cleaned our home. All the rat holes were blocked, the house was painted with lime, the kitchen and the puja room purified and the gods reinstalled. There was a small puja on the day we returned; but it was quiet and serious. We had seen death from too close to celebrate. But we were happy, we were safe, we were all together. The danger was over, it was behind us, we thought. We little knew it was still ahead of us, patiently biding its time, waiting to strike the one man who had kept us alive. But it happened and my life became a cemetery of dead hopes.

Astrologers often speak of good times and bad times. I don't know how true it is, but I know that for us the bad time began with the killing of Rand by two men, the Chaphekar brothers. They were hanged, but Balasaheb too was arrested for driving people to violence with his articles and speeches. He was sent to prison and released after one and a half years. He came out a hero. Everyone looked at him as a great patriot, a great man. And the same men, who rushed to honour Balasaheb, attacked 'him' as a traitor. They made 'his' life miserable, they said 'he' was an enemy of 'his' own country, 'his' own religion.

For the first time, I saw 'him' grieving, for the first time 'he' seemed to lose faith in what 'he' so strongly believed in, that the country would progress through education and science. I had never seen 'him' so disheartened as 'he' was then. It was at this time that 'he' went to a newspaper office with an article and, when they refused to publish it, 'he' walked back home all the way, in spite of heavy rain; it was as if he did not want to take care of himself any more. The next day he had high fever. We thought 'he' would recover in a few days, but 'he' didn't. At times he was delirious, I heard 'him' muttering 'Kahich kela nahi.' It was like a knife in my heart to hear 'him' say that he thought he had achieved nothing. After a few days, Bhausaheb asked Miss Simpson to get the English doctor. When the doctor left, I was told I could not go into 'his' room. 'He' had TB, a very bad kind called galloping TB. It was like a forest fire. Before we could understand that 'he' was seriously ill, 'he' was gone.

This is hard to write. It happened so many years ago, but my body goes cold even to think of it. The same black fear comes back to smother me. All women are afraid of this happening; I had seen from my childhood how women treasured their kumkum. I remember an atya of 'his' who had lost her husband and had come back home. Each morning, we woke up to the sound of her crying, not a hushed sobbing but loud shrill cries. It seemed to be more fear than grief. The cries cut through all the women in the house, we clutched our mangalsutras and said god's name, we muttered, *let it not happen to me, let me go before my husband.*

But 'he' died. At that moment, I wanted to die, I even thought of committing sati. I don't know why I didn't follow the thought, but I am glad I did not, because it would have gone against all that 'he' believed in, all that 'he' had worked for. It would have made 'him' a laughing stock. But grief can drive you mad. And worse than grief was the nothingness. I learnt for the first time the meaning of the word *shunya.* Nothing. That was the world I entered, the world of nothingness. Even the fear I saw in other women's eyes, the fear of having to give up everything and live the life of a widow, did not touch me. I hardened myself, I prepared myself for what was to come. What could be worse than losing 'him'? 'He' was my life. Without 'him', did it matter how I lived – whether I wore good saris, jewels and flowers in my hair, or whether I wore an ugly red sari, had my head shaven and lived without any pleasures? What happened was even worse. Bhausaheb left me in a home for widows and abandoned women and went away. And I knew I could never go back home (home?). I would never see my son again.

Then the painter entered my life. I met him before we married, I liked his gentleness. I agreed to marry him on one condition – I would not take his name, I would not let any man give me a name again, only to take it away from me. I chose my mother's name, Narmada, and after that I was Narmadabai to the world. For a long time we lived like strangers. He did not disturb me, he never insisted on claiming his rights as a husband, he never said anything to make me uncomfortable. He lived the way he had done before he married me. When I realized that he wanted children, realized how much he wanted children of his own, I knew I could not deprive him of what he most wanted, only because I had been told, because I had believed that a woman could have only one husband, that to have a physical connection with any other man was a sin. What did I have to do with religion, with customs? I had given these up long back, the day I knew I lost my son.

In spite of this, it was not easy for me to make up my mind to become the painter's wife in the real sense. Yet I went to him myself, I knew he would not come to me, he was so respectful, he would never touch me. So I went myself. He was unbelieving at first, he asked me whether I was sure. I told him in the only way a woman can, by taking his hand and placing it on my heart. Except for the first few moments of awkwardness, it was all right. After that we were more comfortable with each other. This thing between men and women, when it happens and when it gives both pleasure, it can be put in its place, it is no longer important. It was never the same as it was with 'him', but I taught my mind not to remember, not to compare. When I found myself pregnant and Durga was born, the painter's happiness and my own joy, healed, to some extent, the wound I had inside me. I knew then that what I had done was not a sin, it was not even wrong, it was the right thing. They were my two saviours, Kashi and Durga, they brought me back to life, they made me realize I could still laugh and enjoy life; with them I knew I had repaid what I owed the painter. He loved his two daughters, how he loved them. We lost Kashi, that was a great blow, but she had given me much happiness. As if Kashi knew she had only a short time to live, she was greedy for happiness, for things – a few coloured ribbons and pins, some glass bangles that her father brought her from Mumbai could fill her with joy. She was also greedy for love. As soon as her father came home, she would claim him, she would sit on his lap and say 'My baba,' looking at Durga, as if daring her to displace her. But Durga never would do such a thing. She was more understanding from the beginning, more responsible. My two girls gave me new life, new hope. They say Ganga, when she married King Shantanu, made him vow that he would never question her, whatever she did. He agreed, like a man will when he loves a woman greatly. And so he was forced to remain silent when she killed their babies, seven of them, as soon as they were born. We are told that these were souls who had been condemned to come back to earth, that Ganga was liberating them from life by killing them immediately after birth. I think my two girls were, on the other hand, waiting for life, they were waiting to be born, to come to this earth. I had to bring them to life. And I could do that only by becoming the painter's wife. I have no regrets. A sin to have two men in your life? I find it amusing now. It's such a small thing compared to all the sins that human beings commit. In fact, it is not a sin at all. What 'he' learnt, what 'he' believed in, through 'his' thinking and his ideas, I learnt through living. Through experience.

I have never hated anyone as much as I hated Bhausaheb when he left me and went away, when I realized he had deprived me of my son. I was so angry, it was as if there was a fire burning inside me. How could he deprive me of my son? *'I have kept my promise to my son'*. That was between you and your son. What about me? Did I have to pay the price of keeping that promise. I should have had a say in the matter. Did I have no choice? Why didn't he ask me? Why didn't he give me the choice, ask me whether I wanted to live without my son to avoid the painful lot of a widow's life? I know what I would have chosen. What was the hardship of a widow's life compared to being with my son, of watching him grow, of being part of his life? And now? Suppose we meet, my son and I, I used to think, what will we say to each other? I no longer think of it. We could pass each other on the street and I would not know him, nor would he know me. We would be two strangers. They must have told him I was dead, he must have grown up knowing he had neither a father nor a mother. I used to wonder, to anguish – who brought him up? Did he cry a lot when he found that I was not with him? Who comforted him, who fed him, who slept with him? Bhausaheb could do none of these things, so who did it for him? Did he grow up without a woman's love and warmth?

Time passed and he grew distant. He was a man, I did not have to worry about him. But I always made something sweet on his birthday, Kartik Purnima day, a day that ends in a night of gentle, beautiful moonlight. After a time, though, I stopped worrying, I thought of how he would be alone all his life; not only no parents, but no brothers and no sisters. After Kashi and Durga were born, I thought – now you have two sisters. I thought of telling them, you have a brother. I thought of how Mukunda and I had been, brother and sister, and thought they could be like that. But ultimately I never said anything, not even to the painter who knew my story. And when he died, it became my story alone. When Durga went to Pune to study further, when I sent her to the hostel, I thought for a moment of telling her that she had a brother who lived in the same city. But I did not.

Now that I am coming to the end of my life, I think I see it all having happened for the best. My anger against Bhausaheb is burnt out, not even the embers are left. I feel more charitable towards him; he did what seemed best to him. For him it was important to keep his promise to his son, for which I had to be sent away from home, from the family. I could not have lived in that home without becoming a shaven widow. Unless I was shaven, I would be a source of problems, I would pollute everything. I would have had no place there, belonging neither to the world of normal women, nor to the world of shaven widows. I think he too had some regrets for what he did, for what he had to do, because some time after he left me, a letter came for me. Indutai opened it and gave it to me. It was a letter from Miss Simpson to me, written soon after she learnt of 'his' death. Bhausaheb must have sent it on to me, who else knew where I was? My great comfort is that I have been of greater use than I would have been, living in 'his' home as a dependent. I taught children, I showed girls that there was much they could do, that they did not have to become helpless and totally dependent. Besides, I am sure my son grew up to be a good man. I am sure he was looked after well, that Bhausaheb gave him everything. I no longer have any hopes of seeing him. But if I could have seen him once, just once, if I could have told him I was his mother who had been forced to give him up…

Dreams. Wild dreams. I have accepted the reality of my life and it is enough for me. Miss Simpson's letter is still with me, it is the only thing left to me of my past life. I have to destroy it along with this notebook before I leave my home. *(Tr. note: Did she? If not, where is the letter?)*

Madhuri, doc, it looks like I am coming to the end of Ahalya's story. At one time I thought I would never be able to complete it, in fact, I was almost sure I wouldn't. Now I find myself reluctant to part from Ahalya. She has been with me for so long, for many long months I have had her company, entered her life, sorrowed with her (wept at times), rejoiced with her. What a remarkable woman she was. When I began, I was thinking more about myself. I wanted, oh so badly, to do something that would take me out of myself, out of my diseased body and frightened, confused mind, out of self-pity and anger. Reading Ahalya's story has shown me that I am a small part of a larger world. I and my concerns have not gone away, but they have become part of a bigger story. Obviously, my life and my world are still most important to me, but I got to know these remarkable people, Ahalya, her 'he' and the painter and the loving little girl, Durga. And I feel that as long as the world has such humans, life will continue to be meaningful. I am glad to have been part of this caravan of life, if only for a time. (But all of us join the caravan only for a while, our years are but minute fractions of microseconds when you look at the entire journey)

I have also been thinking, Madhuri and doc, what a wonderful storyteller this woman was. I am humbled when I think of her living in a village most of her life, setting out to write about her life, so as to 'understand what it was all about', to 'make sense of it'. And learning so much, in the process of writing, about writing itself. (In today's world she could have run a Creative Writing Workshop for people who think that writing can be taught.) I can see that she was beginning to understand what writing is. When you are writing, she says somewhere, you have to let go of everything false. Writing, even if it is done in the corner of a small room, is like standing in the marketplace and shouting, she says. I am ashamed that I gave up so easily. I wanted to be a great writer, like some of the writers I had read, I set high standards for myself and thought I could get there overnight. And when I realized I couldn't and that my writing was amateurish, I gave up, not knowing that, by doing so, I gave up all hope of learning about writing. But it's too late now. I did not have the courage she had. If I had taken my courage in my hands and sent what I had written to a publisher, even a 'no' would have helped me, it would have made me try again. But it's too late now. I only hope, though I am not sure, that I have been able to capture the simplicity and honesty of Ahalya's writing in this translation.

Doc, I don't know whether you are reading this, or will read it. I know Madhuri does and her responses and comments are very encouraging. But you, doc, are the strong silent type. When I began, I found your silence frustrating. You don't know how important a reader's responses are to a writer. In fact, a bad response is better than none, because without someone reading what you have written, the writing does not exist. But more than that, I was irritated with you. (Yes, I am afraid I am going to be critical.) I thought, isn't this woman interested in her own past? Isn't she even curious? Now I have begun to realize that most of us are ignorant of our past. What do we know of our families, apart from our parents? And even our parents, how well do we know them? I have begun thinking of how little I know of my own family. I know something of my mother's family because they were so much a part of our life. (There's a family picture, doc, in your house, look for it, look at it. It's so posed, it could be funny today when people are determined to be casual, but it's not funny at all, it's a lovely picture. My grandparents are sitting on chairs, two of their daughters on either side of them. Two others stand at the back, with the two sons like book ends on either side. My mother is sitting at her parents' feet, on a stool I think, her skirt carefully spread around her. Have a look.) My mother's father was a physician, he studied abroad, he did his MRCP (right, doc?) and he became a much respected and well-known physician in Pune. He was a silent man who concentrated on his work and left the running of the home and family to his wife, a woman of great energy. A 'jolly' woman, her children used to say. She had seven children. All the children she conceived were born alive and lived to adulthood, a great achievement in those days. She delivered babies so easily, her children joked that no midwife, nurse or doctor ever got to her in time. My mother, Prabha, was the youngest and was called (what else?) Baby, even after she had children of her own. Her two brothers called her 'ditto ditto' at times, or 'tip top' because of the way she matched her clothes – sari, blouse, petticoat – to perfection. She was always smart and well dressed and wanted to be (this was a total surprise to me when I heard it for the first time after her death) an airhostess. Instead, she was married off at nineteen, because her mother was ill by then and was in a hurry to get her two youngest daughters married in her presence. My aunts and uncles told me that Prabha was lively and spoilt and ready to defy authority when she was young. There is a family story about her which I must have heard from each one of her siblings. Prabha's devotion to her father was a legend in the family. Her two brothers had once heard their father belch and then mutter, 'Forgive me, that was rude'. It became a joke, the two boys belching, repeating their father's words and then bursting into hoots of laughter. Prabha heard them once and this mite, much younger than them, hurled herself at her brothers in a fury. I never saw this Prabha. Her marriage to my father crushed all the spirit in her.

I don't know much about my father's family (and don't want to know much, either) except that he had only one brother with whom he had fought a fierce Mahabharata kind of war (over money and property, of course) and they never saw each other's faces after that. He was a monster, a tyrant, who wanted to dictate the way his wife and children should live. Dada slipped away and I made myself such a hooligan, he decided to leave me alone. So there was only Prabha and he controlled her life totally, he decided what she would do, eat, wear, etc. Fortunately, he couldn't control her thoughts or her emotions and he could not stop her from loving Dada; Dada was the love of her life. By the time I came along, she'd given up. Perhaps. I heard later that they lost a son, born between me and Dada. I don't know how he died, but I am sure that I, a girl, must have been a poor replacement, a great disappointment. So I was totally in the hands of Tarabai, Saguna's mother. Prabha and I came together after my father's death. In fact, she was the one who looked after my kids and gave me courage and support after Aakash died.

I am realizing only now that my mother's family, the Kirtanes, were a most unusual family. Imagine, one of the daughters went abroad to Germany to study chemistry, married, lived and died there. Another became a surgeon – in those days! And Bharati, the third aunt, went to England, came back and became a teacher of English. Even more, or maybe equally unusual, was that they loved being together. I remember the jokes, the laughter, the card games, some of them the silly games they must have played as children, and yes, the drinking. All of them drank whiskey, even my aunts. Except Prabha and Kamala, the two youngest, who were, god knows why, far more conventional. Anyway, doc, Madhuri, this is not about me and my family, all that's a by-the-way. This is about Ahalya, Gavi Dandekar's grandmother, my dear doc's great-grandmother. I now know where Gavi's writing genes came from. There's also that artistic painter grandfather of Gavi's. I wish we could trace some of his paintings. I have a friend who curates exhibitions, I must tell him about the painter. That he has wholly sunk into obscurity may not be because he was not good enough. So many factors help artists to live after their death, sometimes even merit cannot help. Look at the missing women!

When Aparna comes to the end, she sits staring at the screen, thinking, not of Ahalya, but of Jyoti. Of Jyoti working at the translation, absorbed in it, bringing to life a woman who lived and wrote nearly a hundred years ago. She thinks of how Jyoti has gone through a see-saw during the time she was writing this and of how well she seems to be now. But even when a patient seems to be doing well, Aparna holds her breath, there is always a tremor of fear in her. She is relieved when the patient moves out of her orbit and she no longer has to think about her/him; it is a relief not to know the end, not to have to watch the unravelling of all that she has done. This is not possible with Jyoti, because Jyoti is no longer just a patient, their relationship has moved way beyond that. I am with her now, Aparna thinks, I am marching in step with her and I have to be with her on whatever road her cancer takes her on to.

And she has given me back my family. When Baba died, I put away the past, I did not want to even think of it. But now I see my Baba not only as my father, I see him as a lively little boy who gave Ahalya much joy. He was her future. I no longer see him as the suffering, bitter man he became in his last years. Jyoti, in getting back Ahalya, has reclaimed the Baba of my childhood and given him back to me.

Aparna finds Jyoti and Deepak outside their door, obviously waiting for someone. 'Miru,' Jyoti says tersely.

'We're going to visit the Great White Chief,' Deepak adds.

'He means Laxmanmama,' Jyoti explains.

'He says come, so go we must, even if Jo is tired.'

'Tired?' Aparna's voice carries concern.

'Just the delayed flight.'

'We thought we'd stay home tonight. Mel and Jai have left, we thought we'd ask you to join us. I've got a lovely wine, by the way. But no, the Boss says come and we go.'

'Dada, that's not fair. He's lonely, he likes to meet people.'

'I know, but…'

'You have a grievance against the Kirtanes.'

'They called our mother Baby.'

'Out of affection.'

'But Baby…' He makes a disgusted sound.

Mira comes out just then and says, 'Come on, guys. Tejas says he's not coming. Lucky bloke.'

'If nobody wants to go, let's just stay home.'

Jyoti sounds so irritated, Deepak and Mira stare at her and say simultaneously, 'Sorry.'

'Let's go, so we can be back early and you can get a good night's sleep. That'll do your headache much good, Jo.'

The next day Aparna does not meet them, but late at night she hears the sounds of a car door banging, calls of 'bye' and 'ring up' and she knows that Deepak is leaving. She meets Jyoti later that day.

'How are you? Headache better?'

'Much. Dada took it from me. After saying he didn't want to go and after being so critical of Laxmanmama, he didn't want to come back early. Laxmanmama and he seemed to go on and on with their whiskies. Not surprisingly, Dada had a headache. He's a wine man, not really a hardcore whiskey drinker like Laxmanmama.'

The house seems quiet, but Jyoti says she enjoys the quiet after two weeks of constant company. Aparna is going out of town, she tells Jyoti she'll be away for a week or more. She feels relieved to be out of Bombay, she doesn't have to imagine that Hari will ring up, that Hari will come. The silence is more bearable when she is not at home. Perhaps he has gone to the US, she thinks. But Krishna rings her up one day and tells her that the American tour will happen only later in the year. So he's here, but he's staying away. She feels weak with the need to see him, to meet him. His beautiful voice, his soft mouth, his sweet breath, the way he says 'Apu Rani' – am I condemned only to remember these, to dream of them, never to get them any more? She thinks for the first time of Madhu's very hesitant suggestion that she see someone about her fear of marriage.

'Someone? You mean a psychiatrist, I suppose?'

'Anyone who can help, Apu. You're a doctor, you should know it's not wrong to get help.'

'No, thanks. I'm perfectly fine.'

But is she? She does not want to ask herself that question, she does not want to be with anyone whose face asks her the question, 'What's wrong with you?' After her return, reminded by Dr Bhagat that the date of the conference is hurtling towards them, she throws herself into the meetings and plans with enthusiasm. She is glad that work keeps her from thinking of Hari. She does not see Jyoti either. And then Mira comes to her and tells her Jyoti has a fever. 'She has had it for the last two weeks, but she wouldn't let me tell you. And she has a cough.'

Aparna's heart misses a beat. She keeps her composure, though, has a look at Jyoti and prescribes some antibiotics, in addition to the paracetamol. 'Only a virus,' Jyoti says and Aparna says, 'Yes, must be only a virus.'

'So there's no need for any investigations.'

'Well, we'll see. If you respond to the antibiotics, we don't have to worry.'

She doesn't respond. Aparna changes the antibiotic and the fever comes down after a few days. Aparna gives a huge sigh of relief. But Jyoti's cough lingers. And she has lost weight even in this short time, she has no appetite. Aparna is worried. She had hoped for some more time, a few years more. Not so soon, please, not so soon, she prays. 'I think you'd better see Dr Bhagat,' she tells Jyoti finally. 'I'll fix an appointment.'

There is a call from Jyoti's Laxmanmama. 'I believe Bhagat has asked Jyoti to go through all the tests?'

'Yes, sir.'

'Has a chest X-ray been done?' he asks.

'Yes, sir.'

'And?' he prompts Aparna, a little impatiently.

'It's what we feared.'

'Is Bhagat thinking of surgery?'

'No, sir, there are too many lesions.'

'So it's systemic treatment again?'

'I'm afraid so.'

It's his turn to be silent. Finally he says, 'I'll talk to Bhagat. And keep in touch, Dr Dandekar.'

'Yes, sir.'

Jyoti comes to Aparna the day after her visit to Dr Bhagat. Aparna has been expecting her, yet for a moment she is confused, she does not know how she is going to cope with this.

'I'd have come to you, why did you come up?' Aparna asks, putting off the moment when she will have to tell Jyoti the truth. But Jyoti does not ask her any questions, she goes straight into what she has come to say. 'I've come to ask you to keep your promise.'

'What promise?'

'No more investigations, no more treatment. I will not, I will absolutely not go through that all over again.'

'*You* asked for a promise from me. I never gave it to you. Remember?'

'Well, I'm asking you again. You know and I know what the end of this will be. Don't put me through all that again, doc, let me live whatever time is left to me in peace.'

'You can't put me in this position, Jyoti.'

'I've made a living will. Saying I should not be given any treatment when I don't want it.'

'Don't tell me about it. I'm a doctor, not a lawyer.'

Help, Aparna's whole being calls out, *help*, I can't argue with a dying person, I just can't.

'Did Laxmanmama talk to you? What did he say?'

'That it's wrong to reject what medical science can offer you. Why are they struggling so much to find ways of helping patients if patients refuse what they can be given?'

'All you doctors think in the same way. You're just postponing the inevitable.'

'I can tell you of a patient who had a metastasis. She went through the chemo; it's three years now and she's still fine.'

'Don't give me case reports. Or statistics.'

'No, I'll tell you about my mother. She did everything that I asked of her, she went through everything I told her to do –

without a word of complaint. She knew I wanted her to live, she knew I would do anything to give her just one more day of life. She did it for my sake. You have to think of Mira and Tejas, Jyoti, they have a right to be part of your decision.'

Finally, Jyoti gives in. On one condition, she says. 'When I say enough – and I promise I won't say enough easily – you have to stop.'

'Done.'

And so the battle begins all over again. Freny tells her that it is a fearsome sight, the cells are multiplying at such a terrifying speed. Aparna pushes the thought of those fast multiplying cells out of her mind. She knows they have to be careful, Jyoti can't stand the treatment as well as she did last time. They are being very conservative, a single dose therapy, a smaller dose, hoping for minimal side effects. But it's worse this time. There's less hope, less physical strength, less will to fight.

The news spreads, there are constant visitors for Jyoti. 'Each one asks me, how are you? All I can say is that I'm very very tired, I'm exhausted, totally exhausted,' Jyoti tells Aparna.

One day there is a call from Hari. It takes Aparna a moment to realize it's Hari, not because she does not recognize his voice – can she ever forget it? – but because she can't believe he's calling her. Her heart surges in hope. It's Hari, Hari has come back to me, he wants me in his life once again, he... She almost cries out in joy, but before she can say anything, Hari asks, 'I hear Jyotitai is not well?'

Jyoti? He rang me to ask about Jyoti? Not a word for me, not even my name? And her heart, which had soared high, plummets and settles, heavy as lead, within her.

'Yes,' she says dully.

'Is it a meta – metata...'

'Metastasis – yes.'

'Where?'

'In the lungs.'

'Can I see her?'

'Yes, you can. But ring her up, I mean talk to Mira first. She'll tell you whether it's okay for you to visit.'

He rings off. She sits still, staring at the phone, her thoughts beating inside her head like the flapping of a large bird's wings. What have I done, Hari, what have we done to ourselves? A memory comes back, of Hari saying to her, 'I know the word meta…whatever it is, is a bad word. When you say it, your face goes all serious. And I know remission is a good word. When you say it, your face looks bright.'

Hari, come back to me, we can have such a good life together. But the way he spoke, his voice… No, he was not angry, he was not hostile, he was just…disinterested. He spoke as if to an acquaintance. The madness passes – Baba said that. Is it over for him? Has the madness passed? Why, then, has it not left me as yet? How long will I go on hurting so much?

A few days later, Jyoti tells Aparna that Hari did visit her. She does not say anything more and Aparna does not ask. Jyoti is not coping well with the chemo, she seems at the end of her tether. After three sessions they stop the chemo. Jyoti says she can't stand it any longer.

'Give it a chance, Jyoti. We'll postpone the next session if you like.'

'No more talk of survival, I see.'

'But it's there, it's always there, that hope. And who are we, Jyoti, to question the whimsical nature of life? That's why we never give up.'

'Doc, doc, I love you for trying so hard, I love the way you fight for your patients.'

'So listen to me. One more session, let's go on for one more.'

After the fourth session, however, she refuses to go on. And surprisingly, Mira supports her. 'Enough,' she says. 'Tejas also agrees with me.'

Unexpectedly, Jyoti has some good days after this. Hope asserts itself against all that Aparna's medical sense tells her; she know that this is the most wilful of all diseases, it goes its own way, the cells following their own path of growth and destruction. This is the time when many patients turn to other things, they clutch desperately at whatever they think might help them to live – root, herbs, leaves, holy water, ash, homeopathic pills. But Jyoti does none of these things. Having given up hope of any help from her doctors, she seems to have resigned herself to whatever may come. For a few days after they stop the chemo, she seems better, calmer, she is more communicative.

'Doc, do you remember once you asked me how was it that I, an educated woman who is aware of these things, didn't feel my tumour?'

Aparna does not remember, but she nods and Jyoti continues. She has to pause often to catch her breath, whatever little she has. Aparna knows what her lungs are like, she knows what a struggle it is for her to talk. But she does not stop her. She knows Jyoti has to say some things, she has to unburden herself.

'I didn't tell you then, but I can now. It was because I had given up touching myself. I knew that was dangerous. After Aakash died, a few years later, I found myself so desperate with desire, I – I let myself get into a relationship with an old friend. It was only for slaking my bodily desires, nothing more, but it soon changed and I wanted a man in my life, doc, I wanted a man to live with. We thought we would think of marriage at some time. Maybe it would never have happened. Unfortunately, Tejas found us one day and...' She is silent for a while, then goes on, 'He stopped talking to me after that, for a long time he refused even to look at me. It was only when I was diagnosed with TNBC that he changed a little. So that's one good thing the crab has done for me. And Mira too. Neither Tejas nor I told her what happened to make him so hostile to me, yet she turned against me as well. We were at loggerheads all day. Nothing I did was right, nothing I said was good. I preferred Tejas's silence to her constant bickering. And then I became a cancer patient and she has been so…' She stops, tears well out of her eyes. 'I've become so disgustingly emotional, look at me…'

One day she asks Aparna, 'Doc, will you come with me on a special visit?'

'Where?'

'When Dada and I visited Laxmanmama, he told us something very interesting. I was speaking to him of Ahalya's story and of how little we know of our own pasts and he said that he'd only just discovered that his father had endowed a maternity ward – I think they called it a laying-in ward – in his mother's name, in his old college. It's also your college, isn't it? Let's go, doc, and look for it.'

'Sure. As soon as you're better.'

But the good days are coming to an end. The cough returns, the fever remains constant – throw away that stupid thermometer, Mira cries out once, driven to despair. Dr LK scrupulously rings up Aparna every alternate day, she dutifully reports to him. When she says that she thinks the liver is now involved, he is silent for a long time, then says, 'My poor Baby.' She wonders whether he's confused, whether he's talking of Jyoti's mother. There are daily calls from Deepak, who seems desperate to come, but has to wait until his courses are complete. 'I wish I could give up this job,' he says. Almost each time he asks, 'How long do you think she'll last?'

Aparna is surprised by Mira's stoicism, by her tireless nursing. They soon need to have a night nurse, which seems to make Jyoti feel better. There are always one or two people of the family with her, but the atmosphere is normal, not a hushed deathbed one. Aparna visits her every morning and evening. One evening she finds Jyoti arranging her pills on her bedside table. She places them in a row and says, 'All this and it's no use.'

'We never know.'

'You never give up, do you?' she asks with a faint smile.

Another day she suddenly clutches at Aparna's hand and says, 'Don't go, doc, don't go.'

Aparna sits by her until she falls asleep and thinks, this is the punishment for getting close to a patient. Slowly, however, Jyoti becomes less and less aware of Aparna's presence. The invitations asking Aparna to sit with her, to talk to her, stop. No more 'Doc, come and have tea with me', 'Doc, have a meal with us'. Breathing is becoming harder for her, they remove fluid from the pleura, but it's a losing battle. More and more she stays in bed. Saguna tells Aparna that she sleeps most of the time, is confused about things. And then one day Aparna, when she is in the hospital, gets a call from Mira. 'Aparnamavshi, Ma is… Ma is…'

'Give the phone to the nurse.'

'Tai is not responding, doctor.'

'Pulse?'

'*Aahe*.'

'I'll be there.'

It has been threatening to rain since morning. Now it's so dark it's almost like midnight, there's something fearful about it. Aparna thinks she has never seen such a dense mass of thick black clouds before. There is a feeling of panic, people are uneasy, everyone thinking of getting home before it starts pouring. Aparna rushes through what she is doing and tells the duty doctor, 'I'll be back in an hour.' Luckily, she finds a rickshaw. 'Where do you want to go?' he asks her. When he hears it's nearby, he says, 'Get in quickly. I haven't seen a sky like this, ever. And I've lived in Mumbai nearly thirty years.' The moment Aparna enters the building, the rain comes down in torrents. The sound of the rain is like a clap of thunder, it comes down like a solid, dense wall beyond which you can see nothing. Aparna goes into Jyoti's bedroom. Mira is by her side, Tejas sitting on the floor at her feet. Jyoti is in a coma. 'Quickly,' she tells Mira, 'call anyone you want, right away, before the roads are flooded.' She has to raise her voice to be heard above the sound of the rain. Now there is a tremendous clap of thunder, a streak of lightning. Mira flinches, unconsciously moves closer to Aparna. 'And ring Deepak, he may want to come.'

'Don't go, Aparnamavshi, stay with us.'

'I'm here, I'm not going anywhere.'

Saguna gets her a cup of tea. There is nothing to be done for Jyoti, who lies cold and silent. She has moved away from all of them, even from her children, over whom she had agonized so much. Mira is on the phone, Aparna can hear her. Her voice is tremulous, but she doesn't break down. Tejas continues to sit at his mother's feet, his face muffled in his arms. In a while Aparna rings up the hospital, she tells them she can't come back. She is told that all the streets are flooded, traffic has come to an almost complete standstill. 'It's a cloudburst,' she is told, 'and it's high tide.'

She hears whispers, a muffled sob, and wonders who it is, for neither Mira nor Tejas is crying. Above all, there is the continuous sound of the rain, it's like the roar of the monsoon sea. She goes home to leave her handbag, to use the bathroom. But when she gets there, she can't remember what she has gone there for. Finally she changes into an old outfit and picks up her stethoscope. When she goes down, one of the cousins has arrived, but Mira clings to Aparna the moment she sees her. 'You stay here, Aparnamavshi, you don't go,' she says. There is a call from Deepak. 'I'm at the airport, I'll take whatever flight I can get, I'll be there as soon as I can. Is she…?'

Aparna knows what he's asking, but she has no reply. Yes, Jyoti is still alive, but it's only her body. Everything is shutting down inside, soon the machine will stop, we don't know how soon. She remembers her own journey from Paris when she'd heard about her father being in hospital, remember her fear that she would find him dead when she got there, her grief that she would never be able to tell him how sorry she was at the way she had behaved towards him. But he was alive and yet, she never told him her regrets. She stayed with him for a fortnight, perhaps that was like saying 'sorry'; she told him she would come back and take him to her home when she returned, perhaps that was like saying 'sorry'. Perhaps these things showed him what she was thinking and feeling. She looks at Tejas with a new insight and wonders whether he too will go through the agony of never having told his mother that he is sorry.

There are a few more people in the house now. She can see they have walked through the flooded streets, for all of them are drenched, their clothes soggy. Dr LK's son, Manohar, is there and Aparna is thankful she can hand over her charge to him and sit silently like the rest, dreading the moment when Jyoti would stop breathing. But Manohar waves her back to her chair, he says, 'No, doctor, you stay.'

Why are they all asking me to stay? What can I do? But it's right that I should hold her hand. I've held it all this way until now and I have to go to the end with her. It's like a still picture, all of them sitting round the dying woman, as unmoving and silent as her. Mira, eyes fixed on her mother's face, as if her steady gaze can keep her mother alive, Tejas, his face hidden in his arms. No child should have to go through this, Aparna thinks, no child should see… Suddenly Mira calls out loudly, 'Ma, Ma…' Jyoti's body shudders as if she is convulsing, a strange sound emerges from her throat, and then it is over. Aparna takes her hand, checks the pulse, the heartbeat, she looks at her watch, notes the time and turns to Mira. There is total silence in the room as if they all stopped breathing when Jyoti did. Miraculously, the sounds of the rain seem to be more subdued now.

'Mira,' Aparna says and gently loosens Mira's hand from Jyoti's. The others move in closer. I have no place here, she thinks and with a whispered word to Manohar, she goes out of the house. There are people in the foyer, on the stairs, all of them drenched to the skin. A man sitting on the stairs, his hands between his knees, moves to give her room and she sees it is Hari. His jeans and T shirt are wet and clinging to him, but he seems unaware of it. He seems as composed, as if there was no Jyoti dying inside, no rain and floods on the street. He looks up at her, a direct, inscrutable look. 'It's over?' he asks her.

'Yes,' she says and goes past him. Then she stops. He is still sitting there, looking unutterably lonely, and she realizes there's nowhere he can go until the streets become passable. She calls out his name. He looks up. 'Come home, you can wait here,' she says. He says nothing, but he rises and when she gets to the door, he is with her. She gives him a towel and says, 'You can have a bath.'

She goes to her own bedroom and thinks of changing, but cannot bring herself to get up. She hasn't shed a tear for Jyoti so far. She did her duty, closed her eyes, noted the time of death and left her to those who loved her much more – her children, her family. Now there is nothing for her to do, now she can mourn her. And the tears come.

'Aparna,' Hari calls out her name. When she does not respond, he comes into the room and sees her sobbing, her body racked by convulsive sobs. She begins to shiver and he takes a blanket from the bed and wraps it round her, he puts his arms round her to hold the blanket in place.

'It's the shock,' she tells him when she can speak.

'I know.'

He gets her a glass of hot milk, waits by her side until she drinks it. He says, 'Try to sleep now,' makes her lie down and covers her with the blanket. He gets up to go, but the sound of her sobbing stops him. He comes back to her and she holds out her arms to him like a child. He hesitates and then lies down by her, holding her shivering body in his arms.

The next morning, when she wakes, he is gone. She has a

bath, dresses and goes to the hospital. For the first time, she sees what the rain has done to the city though it is some days before she learns the extent of the havoc, of cars stalled overnight, of people who walked miles to get home, walking in the middle of the street on the road dividers, so as to not fall into the drains by the side. She hears of the chains people created, holding hands and moving together for greater safety, she hears of the kindness of people who came down to the stalled cars and gave the marooned people water, tea, something to eat. She hears the horrific stories of people found dead in their cars, dead of carbon-monoxide poisoning. But all this is later. Right now she is thinking only of Jyoti, of getting her death certificate, so that the family can take her on her last journey.

Manohar is waiting for her anxiously at Jyoti's home. 'I'd gone to your place. We need the…'

'Here it is,' she says and gives him the paper.

She goes in and sees that the house is full, the foyer full of footwear. Jyoti has been prepared, she is now lying on the ground, on her last bed, Mira still by her side, Tejas still at her feet. There is a subdued whispering in the hall outside and whispers run through the room. It is time to take her away. Mira gets up, goes to one of the cousins and speaks to him. He listens, nods and goes out. All the activity stops. Somebody reads a prayer, someone else reads a shloka from the Gita. And then Hari's voice comes to her. She expects one of his favourite abhangs. Instead, he recites in his beautiful voice and crystal-clear enunciation the ancient prayer asking for truth, for light, for immortality…

Asato ma sad gamaya
Tamaso ma jyotir gamaya
Mrityorma amritam gamaya
Om shantih shantih shantih.

Early next morning, Aparna hears the sound of a car door opening and closing, she hears Deepak's voice calling out to Mira and Tejas. She knows she should go and meet him, but she avoids him; in fact, she avoids the family altogether. She feels they need to be left to themselves to mourn. Deepak comes to her two days later. She has been working on the conference plans, and it is late when she comes home. Deepak says he has been wanting to see her, 'But you know...'

'Yes, I know.'

'We went to submerge the ashes yesterday. It seems like an end, but it's not, is it?'

He seems to have done with his mourning, though she guesses that grief is still waiting for him. He also seems remarkably composed for a man who has been living with the fear of such a thing happening for quite some time. He tries to thank her for all that she has done for Jyoti.

'No need to thank me,' she says. 'She was a patient, she was a stranger, but she became a friend.'

Then he talks of Mira and Tejas. 'I can't think of anything but them.' The family is meeting after the thirteenth day, he says. 'Actually we were not sure we wanted to have the thirteenth day ritual, it's hard on the kids. But Laxmanmama says it helps, he says it has a purpose. We're having it at his home. We'll make our plans after that.'

Aparna thinks of how life claims the living, taking them away from the dead. She remembers how, after her father's death, she had to deal with the problem of the house, of what to do with it. She wonders now whether the family will expect her to vacate the flat.

She comes home one day to find Mira in her home. The girl rises awkwardly when Aparna enters and looks at her, startled by her presence.

'I'm sorry, Aparnamavshi, I came when you were out. I had the key so… But I'll go away.'

'No, don't. You're welcome here, come whenever you want.'

'I wanted to get away from home, from everyone. Everyone is hovering over us so much, it makes me want to scream.'

'I'm going to have a bath and then have a cup of tea. Will you have it with me?'

'No,' the girl says, then after a pause, 'thank you. Or maybe I will. Shall I make it?'

'Don't. You sit and be quiet by yourself, as you were when I entered.'

Mira tells her the family was with them the entire afternoon. 'They keep asking Tejas and me, what do you want to do? What do we want? We want to go on as before. You can't stay here by yourselves, they say. But we're not children, are we? I'm eighteen and Tejas is fifteen. They want us to have someone with us. They're talking of an old aunt who's living alone in Andheri, she can live with us and give us company, they say. We don't need anyone, we've lost our mother and that's that.'

Aparna lets her vent her grievance, she does not interrupt or make any suggestions. Finally, the tea drunk, Mira gets up to go. Before going she asks, 'Aparnamavshi, I can't get Panditji on the phone – I'm sorry, that's Ma's name for him, I should call him Shree Hari. I've been trying to get him, but I can't.' Aparna's heart misses a beat. 'Do you know if he's in town? Are you in touch with him?'

'No, Mira. Why?'

'I want to thank him for coming that night. For what he did the next morning.'

Aparna hears for the first time that it was Mira who had rung him and told him about Jyoti's condition. That she'd done it because Jyoti had told her to. 'When he came to see Ma earlier, she told him she would like him to be with us at…at the end. So I rang up and he came right away. God knows how he got here, he must have walked miles, but he came. And he was back the next morning and chanted that beautiful shloka. I still get goosebumps when I remember it, specially when he said Ma's name. For the first time, I realized Jyoti means light.'

She begins to sob then and Aparna holds her, saying nothing, letting her cry. Her own eyes are wet. When Mira has gone, she thinks, so it was Jyoti who wanted him. And he came. I can think of only one reason why Jyoti wanted him, but it's no use. I have not heard from him since then; it's over. And yet she remembers the way he looked up at her when she passed him on the stairs, as if he had come to be with her… No, let me stop fooling myself. Like Mira and Tejas, I must make my own plans now.

But her plans are no longer her own, as she finds out when Deepak talks to her before he leaves. He tells her about the thirteenth day. 'It began by being a quiet meeting,' he says. 'The aunts brought out their memories of Jo and somehow, instead of being sentimental, everyone was remembering what a difficult child Jo was. And laughing. It ended in tears, of course.'

Then he tells her that they discussed the children's plans. 'Both Miru and Tejas want to go on living here on their own. They are adamant. They have Saguna, they say, they don't need anyone else. And Jai will be coming here for a year to intern with a newspaper. He's fascinated by Indian newspapers and how much they matter to people. He'd planned this earlier. I'll be coming off and on, of course, and hopefully, Mel will at times. But I've really come here to ask you a favour.'

They want me to go, to vacate the flat, she thinks. But it's otherwise. They want Aparna to be here 'for at least two years more. The family's around, they'll be here when needed, but if you're here, on the spot, so to say, we will all of us feel much better. I know we have no right to ask you to do anything for us, but Miru is very keen on having you here and if you have no other plans…'

She has been thinking of moving away, of getting away from a place so full of memories of Jyoti. And of Hari. She has been discreetly approached by a hospital coming up on the outskirts of Pune, she's been thinking of it, thinking of being the Chief. But suddenly, to her own surprise, she finds herself saying, 'Yes, I'll stay. I can stay for two years. Yes, definitely for two years.'

He seems hugely relieved. He tells her he will be leaving soon, that the kids will be moving out as well for a while, because they're getting the house cleaned and painted, some changes are being made. 'Miru wants to occupy her mother's room. We thought we should paint it, and then Miru said, why not the whole house?'

'I'll keep in touch,' he says when leaving. 'May I ring you up sometimes? Not just for the children, but to talk to you?'

'Sure. No problem.'

She has a feeling he wants to say something more, but he doesn't.

And then suddenly it is quiet. Mira and Tejas go to stay with one of the aunts. Aparna offers her home and kitchen to Saguna, who is left behind, and she has dinner waiting for Aparna every evening.

'You're spoiling me, Saguna. What will I do when the children come back?'

'You have dinner with us even then, Tai. At least if you're around, the children will eat at proper times, they'll eat a proper meal. Jyotitai had a job making them sit down and eat properly.'

On a day, when she finds she is able to get off early, Aparna is suddenly reluctant to go back home, to the emptiness. She is wondering what to do, when she remembers Jyoti asking her, 'Shall we go and look for the ward in my ajji's name in your old college, doc?'

We never did it. Jyoti herself knew it was impossible. It was something she knew would never happen, but the thought of it waiting for her must have made her feel good. Let me go and look for that ward, she thinks. And tell Jyoti, wherever she is, that I've done it.

Aparna hasn't visited her college in years, not since she had gone to get some certificates before going abroad. As she enters the gates, she remember how excited and eager she had been, the first day, when she went to pay her fees and join college. The only snag had been that Baba was with her. Both her parents had come to Bombay to be part of the great occasion of Aparna joining a medical college. But Aparna had resisted the idea of them accompanying her to college on the first day. 'As if I'm a baby,' she had said. 'Everyone will laugh.'

Sulu had agreed to stay back, but Baba had been obstinate. 'Can't I have the pleasure of seeing my own daughter become a medical student?' he had asked Sulu belligerently when she had suggested he stay back as well. In the end, it was a good thing for Aparna that he had been with her. For, while they were waiting in the endlessly long queue to pay the fees, a man had come out of the office through the swing door at the side and suddenly stopped when he saw them.

'Dandekar sir? What are you doing here?'

He was an old student, a great admirer, and in no time he had whisked them into his room – he was the Administrative Officer – and done whatever was necessary. He had given them a cup of tea, reassured Gaja about Aparna. She would enjoy the college and the hostel, he said. He repeatedly told her, 'Anything you want, any problem you have, come to me.' And while her father had beamed, happy at the thought of Aparna having someone who would keep an eye on her, Aparna had cringed, she wanted nothing more than to get out of that room and explore the place on her own.

She finds the college totally changed. The old gracious stone building is dwarfed by an ugly modern multi-storied glass-fronted building; there is almost no empty space left, it's all filled up with new buildings. But the patients are the same, moving from place to place with their attendants, papers in hand, a bewildered, confused look on their faces. The nurses are the same, walking in twos or threes, like schoolchildren being taken out for an excursion. The students are the same, the new ones proud of their coats and stethoscopes, the seniors rushing about with an 'I've-no-time' air about them. She remembers her friends; she is in touch with very few of them. She knows where some are, but most of them have been lost in the whirlpool of life, lost to her forever. And yet there had been a time when they were close, when they were together for nearly twenty-four hours a day.

She decides to go to the canteen first and eat something before starting her search. Nostalgia has driven here there, but when she gets her order of bhajias (her favourite food in her student days) and tea, the smell of onions and hot, rancid oil nauseates her. She pushes away the food and tea, pays her bill and goes out.

It's not easy finding someone who can help her to locate the ward. She goes to the Gynaec and OB building, but the wards, teeming as usual with mothers and babies, are nameless. She's not surprised no one knows about the ward. I was here for nearly seven years and I never heard of it, she thinks, how will anyone know, now, so many years later? Eventually, however, she does meet someone who knows about it. She is asking a woman who looks like she belongs to the hospital about the ward, and the woman, shaking her head, has moved on, when an old man, who has been listening, comes to her. Like most working men of his age, he's skinny, his legs like the legs of the matchstick men she used to draw when she was a child.

'You want the place where women delivered babies? The old building?'

'Yes. Do you know where it is?'

'I was born in that building. My mother often showed me the building and said, my troubles began here, in this building. She was only joking, I was a good son…'

'Where is it?'

'You want me to come with you?'

'No, just tell me, I know this place. I studied here.'

'Oh, you are a doctorinbai? Why didn't you tell me earlier? Go behind this building, then to the left, you know, the way to the side gate, from where they take the dead bodies. Do you know that?' She nods. 'It's there. There's a big arch at the entrance.'

She goes where she was directed and sees a building, one of the older ones, still intact but, obviously, now used as a store or a godown. Untended, cobwebs everywhere, the beautiful balustrades with a thick layer of dust on them. There is an arched entrance, as she has been told, and above that is a board. She has to retreat a few steps to be able to read. She looks up and reads what is written on the board. The Ahalyabai Vithalrao Kirtane Lying-in Ward.

Ahalyabai? Ahalybai Kirtane?

This is the second time she is visiting Dr Laxman Kirtane's house. The first time was when Hari sang for his 80th birthday. She remembers how Hari had looked up when she came, the joy on his face… She sternly dismisses her memories and waits for Dr LK in the room she has been led into by a boy. It looks like the doctor's study, there are books everywhere, but the table is dusty, as if it is no longer in use. He comes in, looking frail but nattily dressed. She wonders whether he dresses like this every evening, doing it as a discipline for himself, or whether this is a kind of courtesy towards her. She notices he is wearing cuff links, gold ones. Gaja had a pair, Sulu's gift to him, but it is long since she saw anyone wearing cuff links.

Dr LK speaks mostly about Jyoti's mother, Prabha, at first and Aparna wonders, once again, whether he's confusing Jyoti with her mother. 'She was the youngest among us and she went first,' he says. And then corrects himself, 'No, Tai was the first to go.' For the first time she learns that Jyoti's father killed himself. 'He shot himself. He lost his money and the company, mismanagement, really, and then he took the easy way out. Thankfully, their house was in Baby's name, we could save it. Which is how she and Deepak could buy the flat, the one you are living in, at the same time that Jyoti's husband bought one for his family.'

She is thankful he says nothing about her having looked after Jyoti. Of course, he's a doctor, he knows she did what she was supposed to. He does thank her, though, for agreeing to stay on for two years more. He tells her the entire family is comforted by the thought.

'It suits me, sir. It's very near the hospital, I don't have to commute.'

'I heard you were approached by the Medteam group?'

How did he get to know? 'Yes, sir, but I am not sure I want to work in a hospital like that. To me it seems a place only millionaires can afford.'

'Disease and suffering are disease and suffering, Dr Dandekar. You can't make a distinction between the rich and the poor.'

'Sir, you and I know there is a lot of difference in the way they are treated.'

'I know. I was merely being contrary. When you have no work to do, if you're idle like I am, you get into arguments to pass the time.'

She now realizes he's not confused, not at all. His mind is alert and sharp, he knows what he's saying. He speaks of how, in his days, it was very important for all ambitious doctors to get an attachment to a public teaching hospital. 'It was the poor who educated us really, it was from them that we learnt about diseases.' He glides smoothly and effortlessly into a Sanskrit verse. '*Sarvepi sukhinah santu, Sarve santu niramaya. Niramaya* means good health,' he explains, at the look of inquiry on her face. 'We understood that prayer when we saw poor patients, we understood why happiness and health are what humans need most. It was a great learning experience for us as students and then as teachers. Our patients trusted us completely. That was a good feeling.'

A woman comes in with a tray, a cup of tea and a plate of chaklis on it, which she leaves on a small table in front of Aparna.

'Eat the chaklis first. Manda is a superb chakli maker, the best in this part of the country, I think.'

'Alone, sir? What about you?'

'I don't eat or drink anything after six in the evening. Apart from some fruits at seven and my whiskey at eight. It puts me to sleep like a baby.'

When the cup and plate have been removed, he asks her, 'Well, what is it? Obviously you have something to say to me.'

'Sir, Jyoti told me that the last time she was here, with Deepak, you spoke of your father having constructed a maternity ward in his mother's name. In your hospital.'

'Yes, I found the reference in a volume the college brought out during their centenary year. I had no idea of it myself. It's your college as well, Jyoti told me?'

'Yes, sir. Jyoti wanted us to go and look for the ward. Of course, we didn't do it, we couldn't. I went on my own yesterday.'

'Yes?' He knows there is more to come; now he is curious, eager for her to go on.

'Your father's mother, your grandmother, that is, was Ahalyabai?'

'Yes. Actually, none of us knew her. My father was only two when she died. We don't even know of what and how. You know how women's deaths go unrecorded. Their lives as well. My father's father, Vithalrao, had died just a little before her, he died of TB. So we can only guess that she died of TB, too. My father was, therefore, an orphan. His grandfather brought him up.'

'And his name was…?'

'Why are you asking me these questions?'

'I am sorry, sir, I have my reasons.'

'My grandfather's name was Vishnupant, but everyone called him Bhausaheb.'

Aparna takes a deep breath. He looks sharply at her. 'I have some books of my grandfather's here.'

'Can I see one?'

'Certainly. Go to the last cupboard. There's a pile on the second shelf, no, not that shelf, the next one. That's right. Bring me the book on top.'

It's a copy of Darwin's *The Origin of Species*. She opens it to the fly leaf and finds the inscription: *To my friend Vithalrao from Jean Simmons*. And on the next page, the name, written in a different hand: Vithalrao Vishnupant Kirtane.

Now she has no more doubts. She has thought long and hard about whether she should speak to this man, about what purpose it will serve. If Jyoti was here, I would have left it to Jyoti. But she is not here and therefore I have to tell this man, her uncle, the head of the family. And so she tells him about the notebook they found among her father's books and papers. She tells him of Jyoti's reaction to the book, of her translation, and how the story came to her and Madhuri through Jyoti's translation.

He listens without interrupting her and when she comes to the end, he says, 'So your father Gavi Dandekar's mother Durga was Ahalya's daughter?'

'Yes.'

'By a second husband?'

'Yes, sir.'

'And I am to believe this story?'

'It's up to you, sir.'

'I am sorry, Dr Dandekar, I shouldn't have said that. But it's hard for me to believe it. We were told Ahalya died.'

'No, sir, she did not die. She was sent away.'

There is a long silence. He sits with his right hand holding up his head, as if it is too heavy for him to hold up without that support. Suddenly there is a burst of voices from somewhere inside the house, voices that sound unnaturally loud in the surrounding silence. The voices die down and then he begins to speak, as if he is talking to himself.

'My parents had seven children. I remember my eldest sister, Tai, a very bold girl, once asking my mother when she was pregnant – I think it was with Prabha. Or maybe Kamala. She said, Baba is a doctor, doesn't he know you shouldn't be having so many children? Doesn't he know it's not good for you? And my mother said, he wants a full house. I remember he never let us go away, not even during our holidays, he wanted us at home. He enjoyed our play, our arguments, he encouraged us to bring our friends home. I think he wanted to fill the silence and the emptiness of his early life with the voices and laughter of children. In spite of all the noise and crowd in the house, he often had a lost look on his face; I've seen that look on the faces of children who've lost their mothers.'

He pauses before going on, 'He was an only child at first, there was only him and his grandfather. I believe Bhausaheb sent away the rest of the family to the village. Men could be dictators in those days. When my father passed out of school, Bhausaheb, after sending our father to England to study medicine, went to live in his village. We learnt these things from my mother. My father spoke very little, he would never dream of telling us about himself.'

He falls silent for a while, then says, 'His grandfather got him married before he sent him abroad – he was seventeen then and my mother was twelve – imagine that! But I think he did it for a reason, for when my father came back, though Bhausaheb was not alive, my mother's family was there for him. Our maternal grandparents were very much part of our life.'

He falls silent again. Aparna is silent too. She does not want to interrupt his thoughts.

'I'm ashamed, I'm so ashamed,' he bursts out. 'I was – I still am – so proud of my family. Our parents were very liberal, my sisters were educated the same way my brother and I were. Tai joined Gandhiji's movement, she married a fellow Gandhian; my parents never objected. One sister, Bharati, never married; she too was allowed to live the way she wanted to. But Ahalya, to send her away, to deprive her of her son, to deprive him of his mother, to say she was dead – I find it hard to imagine such cruelty.'

'Perhaps he had no choice. Ahalya speaks of Bhausaheb's promise to his son. Perhaps the son had made his father promise his wife would not be made a shaven widow.'

'We know nothing of our grandfather, Ahalya's husband. We heard that he wanted to be a doctor, but couldn't.'

'Yes, his father wouldn't allow it. And therefore, perhaps, Bhausaheb made his grandson a doctor. Jyoti, when she came to the end of her translation, spoke of Ahalya's story as a love story. Ahalya's love for her husband shines through her book.'

'That's a wonderful thing to hear. The one ray of light. We heard our grandfather was an unusual man, that he believed in science, that he was against old customs.'

'Yes, you have to read the book to see that.'

'And your father Gavi's grandfather? Ahalya's second husband, that is?'

'He was a painter. Ahalya calls him painter. She speaks highly of him, but your grandfather was the love of her life. And losing her son her greatest tragedy.'

'Can I read the book?'

'The original Marathi or the English translation?'

'Both.'

'Yes, sir, I'll get them for you. The books are in Jyoti's house. As soon as Mira returns, I'll get them from her.'

He is still thinking of something. 'So Ahalya married twice?'

'Yes.'

'And the man she married the second time, the painter, was Durga's father?'

'Yes, sir. There was another daughter, Kashi, who died.'

'And you are Durga's granddaughter?'

Yes, sir.'

He seems to be in continuing need of confirmation of what he has been told.

'*Hum aapke kaun hain.*' He surprises her by quoting the title of a wildly popular movie of some years back, but it is a serious query. 'Or is it *Hum aapke hain kaun*?'

She laughs. 'I don't know. I'm not good, either at films or relationships. Neither of my parents had much of a family.'

'Oh, I can work it out myself. It's just the – how differently you see a person when you hear that there is a connection. It's amazing. I find it hard to think that we were connected to Gavi Dandekar. I knew of him, of course. But I never saw any of his plays. Now I wish I had. And anyway, the question still remains – what do these connections mean? It's going to take me long to get used to the idea of the cruelty done to that poor woman.'

'It was so long ago, sir. Why do you take it so hard?'

'The sins of the fathers. Look at the way we Brahmins are hated. I sometimes think, rightly so. Apart from what they did to their own women, look at the way they treated others. My younger son, Manoj, he left the country because he said he could not bear the injustice being done to Brahmins. He was furious about the reservation in professional colleges. What about the injustice of thousands of years? I asked him. And yet he was right, why should he suffer because of something his ancestors did centuries back?'

He seems to be brooding for a while. Then he asks, 'Does anyone know about this? Apart from you and your…?'

'My cousin Madhuri. No, sir, no one does.'

'Please don't speak of it to anyone.'

She smiles. 'Sir, it's so long ago, nobody will be interested, nobody will mind.'

'I mind,' he suddenly flashes at her, showing her the temper that lay under the civilized surface. Then he says, 'I'm sorry, Dr Dandekar.'

'It's all right, sir. You have every right to be disturbed.'

She had thought he would be surprised but pleased, that he would find the whole thing a marvellous coincidence. But he is disturbed, and not much interested in the coincidence aspect of it. She wonders what Vithalrao, man of science, would have made of the coincidence. Would he have admitted that coincidences and miracles are a part of life? That there are times when life vaults over reason? For this old gentleman, it has been a shock. Is it the injustice done to Ahalya that has disturbed him, or his father having been deprived of both parents? She knows, he has admitted it, that his pride in his family has suffered. I wish Jyoti were here, I wish we'd known this when she was alive. She would have…she would have… She stops, thinking, there I go again, playing the game of what the dead would have liked, what they would have wanted, shaping them to my own desires. It no longer matters what Jyoti would have thought and done. The dead play their role and go, it is for us to do what we want to do.

Before going, she gives him the letter she has found, the letter from Miss Simmons that Ahalya had mentioned. I found it among Baba's books, she tells him. He reads it quietly, handling the paper, yellowed, creased, almost falling apart, with reverence.

Dear friend Ahalya,

I cannot come to see you, I know it will not be allowed. Therefore I am writing to you, though I have no words to express my grief at what has happened. It is hard to believe. He was so brilliant, so full of ideas, a man who wanted to do so much for his country. I grieve even more for you. I know what your life will be like now. A life of hardship and denial. Even worse, you will be cut off from all thinking and intellectual pursuits. I wish I could help you. If there is anything I can do, tell me and I will try my best. Be assured that this friend will always have you in her prayers. I pray that your life will continue to have meaning and that you will use your strength to keep yourself alive, to bring up your son the way his father would have done, to do the work you would like to do and which Vithalrao wanted you to do.

In love and friendship,

Jean Simmons

He reads it and gives it back to Aparna.

'No, sir, you keep it.'

He stares at the letter for a moment, then says to Aparna, 'Give me that book.'

She hands him Darwin's book. He places the letter carefully among the pages and holds it out to Aparna. 'You take it. You are Ahalya's heir, I'd like you to have it.'

'So are you her heir, sir.'

'No, my great-grandfather cut us off from her, we cannot claim her now. Take it, Aparna.'

'I will treasure this.'

'I know you will. You know, I read Darwin many years back, when I was unwell and had to stay home. And I wondered at the modesty of the man. There he was, trying, it seems, to find the origin of life, and he presents it like any scientist would any other study.'

He sees she is standing up, the book in her hand, and realizes she is ready to leave. 'Come again, Aparna,' he says.

'Yes, I will.'

He's a lonely man, Jyoti had said. It's true. And he's called her Aparna finally, not Dr Dandekar, as if he has accepted the connection.

Her house is dark and empty when she goes back. Saguna has gone out. Aparna finds it hard to settle down to anything. She wants to talk to someone, to Madhuri. (For who else is there to talk to, now that the old gentleman has pronounced a ban on speaking to anyone?) She could ring her up, but she decides this is best done in person. She rings her up and says, 'Madhu, are you home? Can I come?'

'Now?'

'Yes, right now.'

'Anything wrong?'

'I want to talk. Stop asking questions, just tell me if I can come.'

'Of course. And you are a godsend. Abbas has gone to one of those events, they're giving him some sort of an award. He didn't want to go, but Aman made him. So here I am, alone at home, staring at a bottle of wine, wondering whether to open it, or whether it's a sign of becoming an alcoholic to drink by myself. So, come.'

Madhuri is waiting for her with the bottle open and two

glasses. 'Here's to…what? I hope you're giving me some good news.'

'Not good, but amazing news. Listen.'

And she tells her about her discovery of who Ahalya was, of her conversation with Dr LK, she tells her of his reaction. Madhu listens in total silence and speaks only when Aparna pauses. 'I can't believe this, I just can't.'

'Oh, there's no doubt at all. I saw a book inscribed '*to my friend Vithal by Jean Simmons*'.

'Jyoti's family? Jyoti's…? What was Ahalya of Jyoti's?'

Aparna smiles, remembering the old man's *Hum aapke kaun hai?*

'Jyoti was Ahalya's, yes, her great-granddaughter. Like I am.'

'Oh my god, it's amazing. What a story. I must tell Abbas, we can…'

'No Madhu, I've promised this won't go to anyone else. Don't even think of making a movie or a documentary of it.'

They argue about it. 'You know Abbas has been looking for a subject for a long time, he's getting frustrated,' Madhu pleads. But Aparna is firm, she convinces Madhu she has given Dr LK her word.

'Oh well,' Madhuri reluctantly concedes, 'we'll leave it alone. But don't you see, this story is crying out to be told? It's so relevant, the conflict between science and religion is coming back. The woman had predicted it, she was so prescient…'

'What woman?'

'Ahalyabai. Imagine, Apu, I can say the word prescient correctly after all that wine. So I'm fine.' She pats herself on her back. 'And Apu, what if Gajakaka had known the whole story and written a play about it? What a hit the play would have been.'

'His own life was melodrama enough,' Aparna says bitterly. And adds, 'No, I won't be harsh on him, I shouldn't be. I won't shed tears for him either. Remember, Aparna, he said to me, no tears for me.'

‘And you shed enough tears to drown Chandrapur. Apu, Apu, how little we know what is waiting for us.’

‘But I’m being punished for what I did to him, Madhu. I lost my Hari.’ Aparna is sobbing now. ‘I was so sure of my hold on him, I never thought I would lose him.’

‘Ring him up, you stupid girl.’

‘No, I can’t.’

‘Then don’t tell me your sob story. I’ll listen to you only when you talk to him. Come on, let’s eat now, I think we need some food after the drinking and the sobbing over lost lovers. I hope you’re staying the night?’

‘Of course.’

Aparna falls asleep the moment she gets into bed. Wine does this to her. She wakes up in the early hours of the morning, knowing she won’t be able to sleep again. It’s not just sleeplessness, she is feeling uneasy, sick. Finally she gets out of bed, goes to the bathroom and is properly sick. It’s the wine, she thinks. I shouldn’t drink more than two glasses. It happened in the college canteen as well…

Suddenly a blinding dazzling light illuminates her mind and she thinks, it’s not the wine. Or is it? She swiftly makes her calculations from the night of Jyoti’s death and thinks, it’s possible. But I can’t be sure. I’ll wait, she thinks.

She goes to work the next day, the thought running in her mind all the while: was it the wine or…? She remembers how, after she decided to end her marriage, she had wanted to get rid of everything associated with it, with the man she had married. She had discarded everything she had, including her ring and her mangalsutra, which she sent back to him. She had been a ruthless executioner, dealing with the life she carried inside her, the result of their loveless time together in Paris, with the same cold-bloodedness with which she had got rid of all the other things. Will I have to go through that again?

In a few days, she is sure. I can do what I did last time, she thinks, that is the best solution. She knows exactly how the foetus looks, she knows its size. She remembers the foetuses in the college museum, preserved in formalin in jars and how they looked, as if they had nothing to do with the human race. Yet, she had had to steel herself to be able to take her decision, she had encased her heart in ice so that she would not feel. It does not matter whose child it is, it makes no difference to the woman bearing the child – this was something she had learnt then. But this is Hari's. Can I become an executioner once again?

He came to be with me that night, she thinks, remembering how he sat with her while she sobbed her heart out for Jyoti. But a child? She remembers the painting in their hall in Chandrapur, a painting of Vishwamitra, the old fraud (oh these rishis!), standing erect and haughty, one arm covering his eyes from the sight of his baby, the other arm, rigid, gesturing to Menaka to go away, telling her, most probably, to go to hell. And Menaka, holding out the baby to Vishwamitra, her face pleading, her posture that of a supplicant. Would Hari do a Vishwamitra to her, would he say to her, 'Go away, woman'? No, he wouldn't. And she won't plead with him either. The baby will be hers. Hers? There's a moment of panic. What do I know of babies? And if Hari thinks sex before marriage is wrong, what will he say to unwed motherhood? To a baby born outside marriage? Poor baby. No, I can't tell Hari, I won't give him a chance to make me feel that once again, I loved a man who didn't deserve my love. But it's his child, he should have the choice. She remembers Ahalya's words: 'Why didn't they give me a choice? Why didn't they let me choose?' She thinks of the night of Jyoti's death. She had thought it was grief that had brought Hari and her together, but the sperm and the ovum recognize neither grief, nor love, nor hate. When they want to come together to create, they do so. And so it has happened to me. Baba, she says, addressing him as if he is standing before her, Gajanan Vidyadhar Dandekar, Gavi, your grandmother wrote that she would live through you. Now I will give you your future and it doesn't matter that you are not here to know it. That you will live in your grandchild is joy enough for me.

She wakes up in the morning and comes out to the balcony, her mug of tea in her hands, and sits in her usual chair. She is a little light-headed after an almost sleepless night, but filled with an ineffable lightness of being. She hears voices. Tejas and Mira. They must have returned last evening. She has seen the house being scrubbed and cleaned, Mira has been in and out, putting things in order. And now they are back. In a moment, they emerge from the building and run across the road, their young bodies lithe and graceful. When they reach the bus stop on the opposite pavement, Tejas says something to Mira and runs back in. Aparna sees the tension in Mira's body as she leans forward and looks in the direction from where the bus is to come. She is almost dancing in her impatience when she sees Tejas and waves to him urgently, as if she is saying, Come on, come on.

Aparna thinks: if they look up, if they see me, if they smile, if they wave, I will talk to Hari. Tejas runs across the road, joins Mira just as the bus comes round the corner. And then they both look up and see her, they smile, they wave…

ACKNOWLEDGEMENTS

Novelists often require a great amount of information on a vast variety of subjects and have to depend on either research or talking to people. I was very fortunate in my 'informants', Dr Rekha Kumar and Bharathi Prathap, who were marvellously quick to grasp what I needed, listened to my queries with patience and generously gave me exactly the information I required in their respective fields of medicine and music. I can truly say that without them this novel could not have been written. A huge grateful thank you to both of them, with the usual acknowledgement that any lapses or mistakes are entirely my fault. And, thanks to the doctors in my family, as well, for allowing me to pick their brains.

Scan QR code to access the
Penguin Random House India website